Praise for *Last Bus to Wisdom*

Named a Best Book of the Year by *The Seattle Times*, *San Francisco Chronicle*, and *Kirkus Reviews*

"One of Doig's best novels . . . Enchanting . . . It's warming to think that in his final months [he] shared the writing hours with one of his greatest characters: a version of his younger self wound up and set spinning on the long zigzag adventure called life in the American West."

—*The New York Times Book Review*

"With his final novel, Doig aptly crowns a luminous literary legacy. . . . Forever the master of colorful characters and landscapes reflecting the vastness and vulnerability of the human heart, [he] has left us with a rollicking road trip filled with both."

—*The Seattle Times*

"[A] rambunctious adventure packed with color, vitality and characters worth rooting for . . . A masterful fusion of picaresque exploits and ripping yarns."

—*San Francisco Chronicle*

"Moving, vivid, and funny . . . Doig's adolescent narrator recalls his literary cousins, Scout Finch, Augie March, Huck Finn, [and] Claudia MacTeer, as his openhearted curiosity provides readers a sense of unmediated engagement with an expanding world. . . . *Last Bus to Wisdom* takes us back sixty-five years to an era when the West was a little more rugged and the ethos of wide, open spaces allowed for mythical endings."

—*Chicago Tribune*

"[D]elightful . . . a fitting and fine last work from a writer we'll miss for his endearing stories, his engaging characters, and his enduring humanity."

—Minneapolis *Star Tribune*

"[A] fun summer read, and a way to pay tribute to Doig's wonderful combination of memory and imagination that gives us one more vision of the unique history of the American West."

—*Christian Science Monitor*

"Contains . . . [Doig's] trademark wonderful writing about the Western landscape, and plenty of gentle humor. . . . Doig will be missed by his many faithful readers, and for them, this last offering will be welcome and bittersweet."

—*The Oregonian*

"Over the course of a thirty-six-year literary career, Doig . . . painted as detailed and complete a picture of the American West as any writer of the last century . . . [and] remained, at heart, an old-fashioned storyteller. . . . *Last Bus to Wisdom* is an unpredictable and boisterous road novel . . . [that] offers a fresh take on several familiar Doig themes: nontraditional families, deep connection to the land, the West as a hardscrabble world of work and the profoundly (and often humorously) interwoven nature of everyday individual lives and political and social history."

—*Paste*

"*Last Bus to Wisdom* is a treasure; one suspects that the beloved Ivan Doig—a red-haired boy who lived with his grandmother and grew up to tell stories—chuckled as he plotted to leave his readers a part of himself."

—*Shelf Awareness* (starred review)

"A delightful sprawl of a novel . . . big-hearted, joyfully meandering work by a master."

—*BookPage*

"Chock-full of rollicking humor, blissfully good storytelling and characters so alive on the page they live on in the reader's mind, Doig's last book is a paean to this country as it existed half a century ago. . . . [*Last Bus* is] so purely involving and so much fun to read, it's easy to label as an American classic, as is Ivan Doig the most engaging storytelling the West has ever known."

—KUER-FM, *Books & Beats*

"A book worthy of its author's enduring legacy in Montana and the rest of the English-reading world."

—*Bozeman Daily Chronicle*

"*Last Bus to Wisdom* . . . does what all [Doig's] best books have done: given us indelible characters of the American West—timeless, beautifully flawed, interesting people who never give up trying to find happiness in life."

—Omnivoracious.com

"A marvelous picaresque showing off the late Doig's ready empathy for all kinds of people and his perennial gift for spinning a great yarn. He will be missed."

—*Kirkus Reviews* (starred review)

"An utterly charming, goodhearted romp . . . This posthumous publication will be greeted enthusiastically as a fitting tribute to a memorable body of work."

—*Booklist* (starred review)

"Heartwarming [and] memorable."

—*Publishers Weekly*

"Doig's superb storytelling does not disappoint. The dialog is snappy, funny, and true to the charming characters. With the author's passing in April, this is the last journey into familiar Doig territory we've come to admire."

—*Library Journal*

LAST BUS
TO
WISDOM

ALSO BY IVAN DOIG

FICTION

The Sea Runners

English Creek

Dancing at the Rascal Fair

Ride with Me, Mariah Montana

Bucking the Sun

Mountain Time

Prairie Nocturne

The Whistling Season

The Eleventh Man

Work Song

The Bartender's Tale

Sweet Thunder

NONFICTION

This House of Sky

Winter Brothers

Heart Earth

RIVERHEAD BOOKS
NEW YORK

RIVERHEAD BOOKS
An imprint of Penguin Random House LLC
375 Hudson Street
New York, New York 10014

The Library of Congress has catalogued the Riverhead hardcover edition as follows:

Doig, Ivan.
Last bus to wisdom : a novel / Ivan Doig.
p. cm.
ISBN 9781594632020
1. Boys—Fiction. 2. Uncles—Fiction. 3. Travelers—Fiction. I. Title.
PS3554.O415L37 2015 2015014721
813'.54—dc23

First Riverhead hardcover edition: August 2015
First Riverhead trade paperback edition: August 2016
Riverhead trade paperback ISBN: 9781101982563

Printed in the United States of America
11 13 15 17 19 20 18 16 14 12

BOOK DESIGN BY AMANDA DEWEY

To Tony Angell

For friendship as enduring as stone

What is that feeling when you're driving away from people
and they recede on the plain till you see their specks dispersing?—
it's the too-huge world vaulting us, and it's good-by.
But we lean forward to the next crazy venture beneath the skies.

—JACK KEROUAC,
On the Road

THE DOG BUS

June 16–17, 1951

1.

THE TOWN OF GROS VENTRE was so far from anywhere that you had to take a bus to catch the bus. At that time, remote locales like ours were served by a homegrown enterprise with more name than vehicles, the Rocky Mountain Stage Line and Postal Courier, in the form of a lengthened Chevrolet sedan that held ten passengers besides the driver and the mailbag, and when I nervously went to climb in for the first time ever, the Chevy bus was already loaded with a ladies' club heading home from an outing to Glacier National Park. The only seat left was in the back next to the mailbag, sandwiched between it and a hefty gray-haired woman clutching her purse to herself as though stage robbers were still on the loose in the middle of the twentieth century.

The swarm of apprehensions nibbling at me had not included this. Sure enough, no sooner did we pull out for the Greyhound station in Great Falls than my substantial seatmate leaned my way enough to press me into the mailbag and asked in that tone of voice a kid so much dreads, "And where are you off to, all by your lonesome?"

How things have changed in the world. I see the young people of today traveling the planet with their individual backpacks and weightless independence. Back then, on the epic journey that determined my life and drastically turned the course of others, I lived out of my grandmother's wicker suitcase and carried a responsibility bigger than I was. Many, many miles bigger, as it turned out. But that lay ahead, and meanwhile I heard myself pipe up with an answer neither she nor I was ready for: "Pleasantville."

When she cocked her head way to one side and said she couldn't think where that was, I hazarded, "It's around New York."

To this day, I wonder what made me say any of that. Maybe the colorful wall map displaying Greyhound routes COAST TO COAST—THE FLEET WAY, back there in the hotel lobby that doubled as the Gros Ventre bus depot, stuck in my mind. Maybe my imagination answered for me, like being called on in school utterly unready and a whisper of help arrives out of nowhere, right or not. Maybe the truth scared me too much.

Whatever got into me, one thing all too quickly led to another as the woman clucked in concern and expressed, "That's a long way to go all by yourself. I'd be such a bundle of nerves." Sizing me up in a way I would come to recognize, as if I were either a very brave boy or a very ignorant one, she persisted: "What takes you so awful far?"

"Oh, my daddy works there."

"Isn't that interesting. And what does he do in, where's it, Pleasantville?"

It's funny about imagination, how it can add to your peril even while it momentarily comes to your rescue. I had to scramble to furnish, "Yeah, well, see, he's a digester."

"You don't say! Wait till I tell the girls about this!" Her alarming exclamation had the other ladies, busy gabbing about mountain goats and summertime snowbanks and other memorable attractions of Glacier National Park, glancing over their shoulders at us. I shrank farther into the mailbag, but my fellow passenger dipped her voice to a confidential level.

"Tries out food to see if it agrees with the tummy, does he," she endorsed enthusiastically, patting her own. "I'm glad to hear it," she rushed on. "So much of what a person has to buy comes in cans these days, I've always thought they should have somebody somewhere testing those things on the digestion—that awful succotash about does me in—before they let any of it in the stores. Good for him." Bobbing her head in vigorous approval, she gave the impression she wouldn't mind that job herself, and she certainly had the capacity for it.

"Uh, actually"—maybe I should have, but I couldn't let go of my own imaginative version of the digestive process—"it's books he does that to. At the *Reader's Digest* place."

THERE WAS a story behind this, naturally.

I lived with my grandmother, who was the cook at the Double W, the big cattle ranch near Gros Ventre owned by the wealthy Williamson family. One of the few sources of entertainment anywhere on the ranch happened to be the shelf of sun-faded *Reader's Digest* Condensed Books kept by Meredice Williamson in the otherwise unused parlor of the many-roomed house, and in her vague nice way she permitted me to take them to the cook shack to read, as long as Gram approved.

Gram had more than enough on her mind without policing my reading, and lately I had worked my way through the shipboard chapters of *Mister Roberts*, not so condensed that I couldn't figure out what those World War Two sailors were peeking at through binoculars trained on the bathroom onshore where nurses took showers. Probably during that reading binge my eye caught on the fine print PLEASANTVILLE NY in the front of the book as the source of digested literature, and it did not take any too much inspiration, for me at least, to conjure a father back there peacefully taking apart books page by page and putting them back together in shortened form that somehow enriched them like condensed milk.

. . .

"WHY, I have those kind of books!" my fellow passenger vouched, squeezing her purse in this fresh enthusiasm. "I read *The Egg and I* practically in one sitting!"

"He's real famous back there at the digest place," I kept on. "They give him the ones nobody else can do. What's the big fat book, *Go like the Wind*—"

"*Gone with the Wind*, you mean?" She was properly impressed any digester would tackle something like that. "It's as long as the Bible!"

"That's the one. See, he got it down to about like yay." I backed that up with my thumb and finger no more than an inch apart.

"What an improvement," she bought the notion with a gratified nod.

That settled matters down, thanks to a wartime story cooked down to the basics of bare-naked nurses and a helping of my imagination. The spacious woman took over the talking pretty much nonstop and I eased away from the U.S. mail a bit in relief and provided *Uh-huh* or *Huh-uh* as needed while the small bus cruised at that measured speed buses always seem to travel at, even in Montana's widest of wide-open spaces. There we sat, close as churchgoers, while she chatted away the miles in her somber best dress that must have seen service at funerals and weddings, and me in stiff new blue jeans bought for the trip. Back then, you dressed up to go places.

And willing or not, I was now a long-distance traveler through time as well as earthbound scenery. When I wasn't occupied providing two-syllable responses to my seatmate, this first leg of the journey was something like a tour of my existence since I was old enough to remember. Leaving behind Gros Ventre and its green covering of cottonwoods, Highway 89 wound past the southmost rangeland of the Two Medicine country, with Double W cattle pastured even here wherever there were not sheepherders' white wagons and the gray sprinkles of ewes and lambs on the foothills in the distance.

Above it all, the familiar sawtooth outline of the Rocky Mountains notched the horizon on into Canada. There where the South Fork of English Creek emerged from a canyon, during the Rainbow Reservoir construction job my folks and I had crammed into a humpbacked trailer house built for barely two. I had to sleep on the bench seat in back of the table, almost nose to nose with my parents squeezed into their bunk. But the thrill of being right there as bulldozer operators such as my father—the honest-to-goodness one, I mean—rode their big yellow machines like cowboys while building the dam that bottled the creek into the newest lake on earth never wore off.

Next on the route of remembering, however, butted up against a rocky butte right at the county line as if stuck as far out of sight as possible, a nightmare of a place reappeared, the grim rambling lodging house and weather-beaten outbuildings of the county poorfarm—we pronounced it that way, one word, as if to get rid of it fast. Once upon a time my father had graded the gravel road into the place and dozed out ditches and so on while my mother and I spent creepy days looking out a cabin window at the shabby inmates, that lowest, saddest category of people, wards of the county, pottering listlessly at work that wasn't real work, merely tasks to make them do something.

Seeing again that terrifying institution where the unluckiest ended up gave me the shivers, but I found I could not take my eyes off the poorfarm and what it stood for. In most ways I was just a dippy kid, but some things get to a person at any age, and I fully felt the whipsaw emotions of looking at the best of life one minute, and this quick, the worst of it.

Mercifully the highway soon curved and we passed Freezout Lake with its islands of snowy pelicans, within sight of the one-room Tetonia school where I went part of one year, marked mainly by the Christmas play in which I was the Third Wise Man, costumed in my mother's pinned-up bathrobe. A little farther on, where the bus route turned its back on the Rockies to cross the Greenfield Canal of the huge irrigation project, I was transported once more to a summer of jigging for trout at canal headgates.

What a haze of thoughts came over me like that as memory went back and forth, dipping and accelerating like a speedometer keeping up with a hilly road. Passing by familiar sights with everything known ahead, maybe too much of a youngster to put the right words to the sensation but old enough to feel it in every part, I can only say I was meeting myself coming and going, my shifting life until then intersecting with the onrushing days ahead.

That near-stranger who was me, with his heart in his throat, I look back on with wonder now that I am as gray-haired as my talky companion on the Chevy bus was. The boy I see is a stocky grade-schooler, freckled as a spotted hyena, big for his age but with a lot of room to grow in other ways. Knowing him to be singled out by fate to live a tale he will never forget, I wish that things could have been different enough then to let him set off as if on a grand adventure, turned loose in the world at an age when most kids couldn't unknot themselves from the apron strings of home. He has never been out of Montana, barely even out of the Two Medicine country, and now the nation stretches ahead of him, as unknown and open to the imagination as Pleasantville. And he knows from Condensed Books that unexpected things, good about as often as bad, happen to people all the time, which ought to be at least interesting, right? On top of it all, if worse comes to worst, tucked in those new blue jeans is a round-trip ticket home.

But that was the catch. Home to what, from what?

I MUST HAVE BEEN better than I thought at hiding my double-edged fear, because the chatterbox at my side seemed not to notice anything troubling me until I shifted restlessly in my seat because the object in my pants pocket had slipped down to where I was half sitting on it and was jabbing me something fierce. "Aren't you comfortable? Heavens to Betsy, why didn't you say so? Here, I'll make room." With a grunt she wallowed away from me a couple of inches.

"Huh-uh, it's not that," I had to confess as she watched my contortions with concern, because I still needed to squirm around and reach deep into my pants to do something about the matter. Knowing I dare not show it to her, I palmed the thing and managed to slip it into my jacket pocket sight unseen while I alibied, "My, ah, good luck charm sort of got caught crosswise. A rabbit's foot on a key chain," I thought up, hoping that would ward her off.

"Oh, those," she made a face. "They sell the awful things so many places these days I'm surprised the bunnies have any tootsies left." With that, to my relief, she went back to dishing out topic after topic in her chirpy voice.

"Donal," she eventually got around to pondering my name as if it were one of the mysteries of the ages. "Without the *d* on the end? That's a new one on me."

"It's Scotch, is why," I came to life and informed her quick as a flash. "My daddy said—says—the Camerons, see, that's us, were wearing kilts when the English still were running around buck-naked."

From the way her eyebrows went up, that seemed to impress her. Emboldened, I confided: "You know what else, though? I have an Indian name, too."

Her eyebrows stayed lofted as, for once, I leaned in her direction, and half whispered, as if it were just our secret: "Red Chief."

She tittered. "Now you're spoofing."

People can be one surprise after another. Here she hadn't let out a peep of doubt about anything I'd reeled off so far, but now when I told her something absolutely truthful, she clucked her tongue against the roof of her mouth the funny way that means *That's a good one.*

"No, huh-uh, honest!" I protested. "It's because of my hair, see?"

My floppy pompadour, almost always in need of a haircut, was about as red as anything from the Crayola box. And if that didn't earn me a tribal alias, I didn't know what did. Maybe, as Gram would tell me when I got carried away with something, this was redheaded thinking. It seemed only logical to me, though. If Donal was tagged on me when I came into the world bald as a baby can be, didn't it make sense to have a spare that described how I turned out? Indians did it all the time, I was convinced. In the case of our family, it would only have complicated things for my listener to explain to her that my alternate name had come from my father's habit of ruffling my hair, from the time I was little, and saying, "You've got quite a head on you, Red Chief."

My seatmate had heard enough, it seemed, as now she leaned toward me and simpered, "Bless your buttons, I have a grandson about your age, a live wire like you. He's just thirteen." Eleven going on twelve as I was, I mutely let "about" handle that, keeping a smile pasted on as best I could while she went on at tireless length about members of her family and what I supposed passed for normal life in the America of 1951.

That fixed smile was really growing tired by the time we pulled into the Great Falls bus depot and everyone piled out. As the club ladies tendered their good-byes to one another, in one last gush my backseat companion wished me a safe trip and reminded me to be sure to tell my father how much she enjoyed digested books.

I blankly promised I would, my heart hammering as I grabbed my suitcase and headed on to the next bus ride which, while way short of coast to coast, was going to carry me far beyond where even my imagination could reach.

2.

"WHY DUMB OLD WISCONSIN, THOUGH?" I'd tried not to sound like I was whining, at the beginning of this. "Can't I just stay here while you're operated on?"

"You know better than that." Gram went down on her knees with a sharp intake of breath to dig out the wicker suitcase from under her bed. "They need the cook shack for whatever gut-robber Wendell Williamson hires next."

"Yeah, but—" In a panic I looked around the familiar tight quarters, lodgings for Double W cooks since time immemorial, not much more than a cabin-size room and a few sticks of furniture, yet it had providently housed the pair of us the past two years, and if we were being kicked out, temporarily or not, I couldn't help clinging to whatever I could. "I can stay on the ranch, I mean. Be in the bunkhouse with the haying crew, why not. I bet nobody would care and I wouldn't take up hardly any room and—"

"For one thing, Donny, you're not old enough for that." Trying not to be cross with me but awful close to it, she squinted my direction through the bifocals that made her look like her eyes hurt along with the rest of her. "For another, Wendell may be short on brains, but he's still not about to let you gallivant around the ranch on your own. So don't talk just to hear your head rattle, we need to get a move on or you'll miss the mail bus." After more or less dusting off the suitcase, which was the best that could be done with wicker, she flopped the thing open on my bed. I didn't care that it came from the old country with my grandfather's father or somebody, to me it was just outdated and rickety and I'd look like some ridiculous comic strip character—PeeWee, the dim-witted little hobo in *Just Trampin'* readily came to mind—carrying it around. Ignoring my fallen face, Gram directed, "Hurry up now. Go pick out your shirts. Three will have to do you, to start with."

I stalled. "I don't know what to take. What's the dumb weather like back there?"

"About like anyplace else," she said less than patiently. "Summer in the summer, winter in the winter. Get busy."

Grudgingly I went over to the curtained-off nook that substituted for our closet. "Fuck and phooey," I said under my breath as I sorted through shirts. I was at that stage—part of growing up, as I saw it—where cusswords were an attraction, and I'd picked up this expression from one of the cowhands being sent out in the rain to ride herd on stray cattle all day. It applied equally well to a dumb bus trip to Wisconsin, as far as I was concerned.

"What was that?" Gram queried from across the room.

"Fine and dandy," I mumbled, as if I'd been talking to the shirts, and grabbed a couple I usually wore to school and my dressy western one. "Put that on to wear on the bus," Gram directed from where she was aggregating my underwear and socks out of the small dresser we shared, "and these," surprising me with the new blue jeans still in store folds. "People will think you're a bronc rider."

Oh sure, a regular Rags Rasmussen, champion of the world at straddling saddle broncs, that'd be me, riding the bus like a hobo with a broken-down suitcase. Knowing enough not to say that out loud, I stuck to: "I bet they haven't even got rodeos in *Wiss*-con-sun."

"Don't whine." Cheering me up was a lost cause, but she made the effort. "Honest to goodness, you'll look swayve and debonure when you get on the bus." I took that as a joke in more ways than one, suave and debonair the furthest from how I could possibly feel, packaged up to be shipped like something out of a mail-order catalog. She gave me a wink, not natural to her, and that didn't help, either.

Folding things smartly like the veteran of many moves that she was, she had the suitcase nearly packed while I changed into the stiff pants and the purple shirt with sky-blue yoke trimming and pearl snap buttons, which ordinarily would have lifted my mood. Back and forth between gauging packing space and my long face, Gram hesitated. "You can take the moccasins if you want to."

"I guess so." Truth told, I didn't care what else went in the hideous suitcase as long as those did. The pair of decorated Blackfoot moccasins rested between our beds at night, so whichever one of us had to brave the cold linoleum to go to the toilet could slip them on. Each adorned with a prancing fancy-dancer figure made up of teeny beads like drops of snow and sky, they were beauties, and that couldn't be said for any other of our meager stuff. Gram somehow had acquired them while she was night cook at the truck stop in Browning, the rough-and-tough reservation town, before she and I were thrown together. By rights, she deserved them. My conscience made a feeble try. "Maybe you'll need them in the—where you're going?"

"Never you mind. They'll have regular slippers there, like as not," she fibbed, I could tell. "And after"—staying turned away from me, she busied herself more than necessary tucking the moccasins into the suitcase—"the nuns will see to things, I'm sure."

After. After she had some of her insides taken out. After I had been sent halfway across the country, to a place in Wisconsin I had never even heard of. My voice breaking, I mustered a last protest. "I don't want to go and leave you."

"Don't be a handful, please," she said, something I heard from her quite often. She took off her glasses, one skinny earpiece at a time, to wipe her eyes. "I'd rather take a beating than have to send you off like this, but it can't be helped." She blinked as if that would make the glistening go away, and my own eyes stung from watching. "These things happen, that's how life is. I can hear your granddad now. 'We just have to hunch up and take it.'" Gram kept in touch with people who were no longer living. These were not ghosts to her, nor for that matter to me, simply interrupted existences. My grandfather had died long before I was born, but I heard the wise words of Pete Blegen many times as though he were standing close beside her.

Straightening herself now as if the thought of him had put new backbone in her, she managed a trembling smile. "Nell's bells, boy, don't worry so."

I didn't give in. "Maybe I could just go to the hospital with you and the nuns would let me live with them and—"

"That's not how something like this is done," she said tiredly. "Don't you understand at all? Kitty and Dutch are the only relatives we have left, like it or not. You have to go and stay with them for the summer while I get better," she put it to me one last time in just so many words. "You'll do fine by yourself. You're on your own a lot of the time around here anyway."

She maybe was persuading herself, but not me. "Donny," she begged, reading my face, "it is all I can think to do."

"But I don't know Aunt Kitty and him," I rushed on. "I've never even seen a picture. And what if they don't recognize me at the bus station back there and we miss each other and I get lost and—"

Gram cut me off with a look. As redheaded as a kid could be, a wicker suitcase in hand, I was not especially likely to escape notice, was I. No mercy from her on the rest of it, either. "I seem to remember," she said flatly, "telling you not five minutes ago that I wrote down their address and phone number and tucked it in your memory book, just in case. Quit trying to borrow trouble, boy."

"Yeah, well, I still don't know them," I muttered. "Why couldn't they come in a car and get me, and see you and help you go to the hospital and things like that?"

This caused her to pause. "Kitty and I didn't always make music together, from girls on," she finally came up with, hardly the most enlightening of explanations. "The Great Kate, you'd think her full name was back then, the stuck-up little dickens." She sighed, sad and exasperated in the same breath. "She always did have her own ways, and I had mine, and that was that. So we haven't much kept in touch. I didn't see any sense in trying, until now." Gram drew what seemed to be another hard breath. "Because when that sister of mine gets a certain notion in her head she can't be budged. I suppose that's how she's got to where she is in life. And your Uncle Dutch is"—a longer pause—"something else, from what I hear."

Whatever that was supposed to mean, she lost no time changing the subject, saying my big trip was a chance that did not come often in life, really, to get out in the world and see new sights and scenes and meet people and have experiences and all that. "You could call it a vacation, in a way," she tried hopefully.

"It's vacation *here*," I pouted, meaning school was out and I had the run of the ranch and could do pretty much what I wanted without being shipped off to complete strangers back east in Wisconsin.

"Oh, Donny," she groaned, and let loose with, "I swear to Creation, I don't know up from down anymore"—one of her standard sayings when things became too much for her. Outbursts of that sort scared the daylights out of me at first, but I had learned such squalls passed as quickly as they came. Certain complaints gathered on a person with age, it seemed. This woman who meant everything to me carried the burden of years and deprivation along with all else life had thrust on her, including me. As much as I adored her and tried to fit under her wing without causing too much trouble, my grandmother was from another universe of time, another century, actually. My six grades of schooling already were twice what she ever received in the sticks of North Dakota, if North Dakota even had sticks. She read recipe books with her finger, her lips silently moving, and had to call on me to help out with unfamiliar words such as *pomegranate*. Not that she lacked a real vocabulary of her own, for besides sayings that fit various moods and occasions, she possessed a number of expressions that edged right up to cussing, without quite qualifying. The way she'd meet something dubious with "That's a load of bulloney" always sounded to me suspiciously close.

At least she didn't resort to any of that now, instead telling me to temper my attitude in what for her were measured terms. "It's not the end of the world," a look straight at me came with the words. "School starts right after Labor Day, you know that, and this is only till then. Kitty"—she loyally amended that—"your Aunt Kitty will make sure you're back in time, and I'll be up and around by then, and we'll get on with life good as new, you wait and see."

BUT I DIDN'T NEED TO wait to see, plain and simple, that if what was happening to us wasn't the end of our world, it was a close enough imitation. Just the sight of Gram, the way her apron bagged on her never very strong build, caused a catch in my throat. There was not much of her to spare to surgery, by any measure. And while I did not fully understand the "female trouble" discovered in her by some doctor at the Columbus Hospital in Great Falls, I grasped that the summerlong convalescence in the pavilion ward run by the nuns made her—us—a charity case. Maybe we weren't poorer than lint, like the worst-off people, but apparently not far from it. If that, plus losing our only shelter on earth—the cook shack, for what it was—did not add up to the edge of disaster, even without my banishment to a town in Wisconsin I wasn't even sure how to spell, I didn't know what did. This awful day, the second worst of my life, both of us were becoming medical casualties. Gram was the one with the drastic condition, but I was sick at heart. For I knew if this operation of hers did not come out right, we were goners, one way or the other. If something went wrong, if at the very least she could no longer work, it would be the poorfarm for her. And what I knew with terrible certainty would happen to me then was keeping me awake nights.

Argument over as far as she was concerned, Gram gave a last pat to my packed clothes. "That's that, the suitcase is ready and I hope to high heaven you are."

By now I didn't want to look at her and couldn't look away. My mother's face was legible in her drawn one at times like this, women without any extra to them to start with and hard luck wearing them down even more. It was showing every sign of being a family characteristic, if I didn't dodge it.

Call it luck or not, but right then I had an inspiration. An impulse on top of an inspiration, more like. "Can I run up to the boss house for a minute? With my autograph book?"

"Not unless you want Sparrowhead's," she dismissed that out of hand. "And you know how he is. Sometimes I think that man has a wire down." Then she added, as if I had forgotten, "He's the only one there, with Meredice away."

"Yeah, well, that's sort of what I had in mind," I fumbled out. "It's just, you know, I have everybody else's."

Gram's pursed expression questioned my good sense, judgment, and maybe other qualities, but she only said, "Child, you get some of the strangest notions."

Biting her tongue against saying more on that score, she checked the clock. "All right, I suppose if you have to. But make it snappy, pretty please. You need to catch your ride to town with the vet as soon as he's done in the cow shed."

MY MIND BUZZED as I crossed the grassless packed earth of the yard, so called, that separated the cook shack, bunkhouse, barn, sheds, corrals, and the rest of the sprawl of the Double W from the extravagant structure in "ranchin' mansion" style that was the stronghold of the Williamsons. Rather, of the Williamson men who had ruled the huge ranch for three generations, while the Williamson wives of equal duration had as little as possible to do with the white-painted pile of house poking up out of the prairie.

"I don't blame Meredice for scooting off to California every chance she gets," Gram sympathized wholly with the current lady of the house. "It's like living in a hide warehouse in there." That may have been so, but the ranch headquarters, the so-called boss house with its dark wooded rooms and manly leather-covered furniture and bearhide rugs and horned or antlered heads of critters on the walls—most spectacularly, that of the bull elk shot by Teddy Roosevelt on one of his visits to the ranch before being president took up his time—held a sneaking allure for me. Cowhide furniture and trophy heads can do that to you when you've lived the bare-bones style Gram and I were stuck with.

I entered by the kitchen door without knocking, as the kitchen and the adjoining windowed porch where the ranch crew ate at a twenty-foot-long table were Gram's domain, where I hung around to lick the bowls when she was baking and even did small chores for her like taking out the ashes and filling the woodbox. Pausing in the familiar surroundings to gather myself, I gazed around for possibly the last time at the cookstove of the old kind that cooks called a hellbox and the creaky cupboards and the rest of the tired kitchenware Gram had made do with, three times a day, three hundred sixty-five days a year, as the latest in the succession of Double W cooks fending with a shortage of modern conveniences and a surplus of Wendell Williamson, classic tightfisted employer. I swallowed hard. What I was about to do was a gamble, but I was a hundred percent sure it would work. Well, fifty percent at least, the rest maybe the kind of hope only someone at that age can have. "Hunch up and take it" might be good enough advice if you were willing to go through life like a jackrabbit in a hailstorm, but I was determined to try for better than that.

Getting ready, I smoothed open the autograph book. A memory book was another name for it, because collecting autographs really was an excuse to have people dab in some lasting bit of wisdom, humor, or simply something supremely silly along with their signature.

WHAT WOULD I HAVE DONE, in that difficult period of life, without the inch-thick, cream-colored album with the fancily lettered inscription YE WHO LEND YOUR NAME TO THESE PAGES SHALL LIVE ON UNDIMMED THROUGH THE AGES embossed on the cover in gold or at least gilt? Autograph books were one of those manias that sweep through a student population, and at our South Fork one-room school it started when Amber Busby, as spoiled as she was curly-haired and dark-eyed, showed up with a fancy leatherette one she'd been given for her birthday and began cornering all of us to write in it. Immediately everybody, from the littlest kids just able to print their names to the seventh- and eighth-grade galoots edging up on the fact of a world half filled with girls, had to have an autograph book; it's a miracle how something ceases to be sissy stuff when everyone does it. Like other schoolyard manias, this one wore itself out in a week or two, but I kept at it, away from school as well as in. Gram, always desperate to keep me occupied—over time I had worn out enthusiasms on jigsaw puzzles, pen pals, board games, and things since forgotten—wholeheartedly encouraged this particular diversion, not that I needed extra motivation. The variety of sentiments people came up with to be remembered by appealed to the grab-bag nature of my mind, and by now I had a good start on filling the pages. I knew there was a long way to go, though, because I wanted to set a record. I loved the *Ripley's Believe It or Not!* panel in the Sunday funnies of the Great Falls *Tribune* that the Williamsons passed along to us when they thought of it, with its incredible facts that a North Dakota man ate forty-one pancakes in one sitting and that the Siamese twins Cheng and Peng shared a total of six wives in their lifetime and so on. I could just see myself in a full-color drawing: Donal Cameron—my name correctly spelled and everything—the Montana boy who collected more autographs and their attached memories than any other known human being. What that total was, of course, remained to be determined, but I was working at it. And this next autograph request counted double, in a sense.

Flipping past the scrawled sentiments of my classmates and the other schoolkids—*When you see a skunk in a tree / Pull his tail and think of me* was pretty typical—I picked out a nice fresh page, holding the place with my thumb, and set off for the office down the wood-paneled hall.

Only to slow to a halt as ever at the display table in the hallway nook. The show-off table, Gram called it, there to impress visitors with items discovered on the ranch from pockets of the past. I never passed without looking the fascinating assortment over. A powder horn and bullet pouch from the days of the fur trappers. A long-shanked jinglebob spur a cowboy lost on a trail drive from Texas. A big bone of some beast no longer seen on earth. All stuff like that until the array of Indian things, spearpoints and hide scrapers and flint skinning knives and other remnants of buffalo hunts long before Double W cattle grazed the same land. And resting there prime amid those, the object I longed for, the dark black arrowhead that was my find.

I was heartbroken when Gram made me turn it in. I'd been hunting magpies in the willows when I spotted the glassy sparkle in the gravel bottom of the creek crossing. When I reached in the water and picked it up, the glistening triangular shard of rock was sharper and more pointed than other arrowheads that sometimes surfaced after winter frosts or a big rain. Much more beautiful, too, solid black and slick as glass—which actually it was, I later learned, a hardened volcanic lava called obsidian from somewhere far away—when I stroked it in the palm of my hand. My excitement at gaining such a treasure lasted until I burst into the cookhouse and showed it to Gram, and was given the bad news.

"Donny, I'd rather pull my tongue out than tell you this, but you can't keep it."

"W-why not? That's not fair!" Dismay sent my voice high. "I'm the one who found it, and if I hadn't, it'd still be there in the creek and the haying crew might break it when they pull the stacker across, and so I saved its life, sort of, and I don't see why I can't—"

"You can talk that way until you're blue, but I just don't like your having something that rightfully might be theirs," she laid down the law as she saw it. "Sparrowhead makes the riders turn in anything like this they come across, you know that." I absolutely could not see why the Williamsons were entitled to something that had fallen to the ground probably before the ranch even existed, but Gram's mind was made up. "Go on up to the house and give it to him."

"Good eye, Buckshot" was all the thanks I got from Wendell Williamson when I did so. "Lucky to find one of these. It's pre-Columbian." He liked to say things like that to show he had been to college, although Gram claimed it only went to prove he was an educated fool besides a natural-born one. Anyway, when I looked up the meaning of the phrase in the Webster's dictionary Meredice Williamson kept in the bookcase with the Condensed Books, I was awed. Older than Columbus! That made the black arrowhead even more magical for me. Just think, it had lain there all those hundreds of years, until, as the man himself said, I was lucky enough to be the one to find it. Equally unlucky, it had to be admitted, to be forced to part company with it. Well, that would not have to happen for good if my gamble of calling on the boss of the Double W paid off in that way, too.

. . .

With hope and trepidation, I now approached the office. The door was open, but I knew to knock anyway.

When he saw it was me, Wendell Williamson sat back in his swivel chair, which Gram claimed was the only thing on the ranch he knew how to operate. "What can I do you for, Buckshot?"

This was new territory for me, as I had only ever peeked in when he was not there. The office smelled of tobacco and old hides like the mountain lion skin and head draped over a cabinet in one corner, enough to set a visitor back a little, but I advanced as though life depended on it. "Hi," I said, my voice higher than intended.

The man behind the desk, no taller nor heftier than average, had a kind of puffy appearance, from his fleshy hands to a pillow-like girth to an excessive face, his hairline in deep retreat up to a cluster of curly gray in the vicinity of his ears. Gram called him Sparrow-head behind his back because of what she believed was the quality of birdbrain under that jag of hair. Or sometimes her remarks about her employer were more along the line that he was the sort of person who'd drown kittens to keep himself busy. Regardless of what she thought of him, or he of her, they had maintained a prickly standoff, the boss of the ranch reluctant to fire the tart-tongued cook because of her skill at feeding a crew on the cheap, and the often-disgusted mealmaker who ruled the kitchen putting up with his stingy ways on account of me.

Gram's bad turn of health was about to bring all that to a crash-ing end, if I couldn't do something about it. Wendell—I didn't dare think of him as Sparrowhead just then—was examining me as if he hadn't seen me every day of the past couple of years. "I hear you're getting a trip to Minnesota."

"Wisconsin."

"Nuhhuh." This strangulated utterance was a habit of his. Gram said it made him sound like he was constipated in the tonsils. "It amounts to about the same, back there." I suppose trying to be civil, he drawled, "Come to say 'Aw river,' have you?"

The joke about "au revoir," if that was what it was, went over my head. "Uh, not exactly," I stammered in spite of myself. "It's about something else." He waited expressionlessly for me to get it out. Heaven only knew what rash requests had been heard in this office down through the years by one poker-faced Double W boss or the next. None quite like mine, though. "What it is, I want to get your autograph."

He gave me a beady look, as if suspicious I was making fun of him. I quickly displayed the autograph book. "Mered—Mrs. Williamson—already put in her name and a sort of ditty for me."

That changed his look, not necessarily for the better. "She did you the honor, did she. You must have caught her when she wasn't packing up for Beverly Hills again." He reluctantly put out a paw-like hand, saying he guessed he'd better keep up with her any way he could. Taking the album from me, he splayed it on the desk with the practiced motion of someone who had written out hundreds of paychecks, a good many of them to cooks he'd fired. I waited anxiously until he handed back what he wrote.

> ***In the game of life, don't lose your marbles.***
> ***Wendell Williamson***
> ***Double W ranch***
> ***in the great state of Montana***

"Gee, thanks," I managed. "That's real good advice."

He grunted and fiddled busily with some papers on his desk, which was supposed to be a signal for me to leave. When I did not, he frowned. "Something else on your mind?"

I had rehearsed this, my honest reason for braving the ranch boss in his lair, over and over in my head, and even so it stumbled out.

"I, uh, sort of hoped I could get a haying job. Instead of, you know. Wisconsin."

Wendell could not hide his surprise. "Nuhhuh. Doing what?"

I thought it was as obvious as the nose on his face. "Driving the stacker team."

This I could see clear as anything, myself paired with the tamest workhorses on the place, everyone's favorites, Prince and Blackie, just like times on the hay sled last winter when whoever was pitching hay to the cows let me handle the reins. The hayfield job was not much harder than that, simply walking the team of horses back and forth, pulling a cable that catapulted a hayfork load onto the stack. Kids my age, *girls* even, drove the stacker team on a lot of ranches. And once haying season got underway and gave me the chance to show my stuff at driving the easy pair of horses, it all followed: Even the birdbrain behind the desk would figure out that in me he had such a natural teamster he'd want to keep me around as a hayhand every summer, which would save Gram's spot as cook after her recuperation, and the cook shack would be ours again. To my way of thinking, how could a plan be more of a cinch than that?

I waited expectantly for the boss of the Double W to say something like "Oh man, great idea! Why didn't I think of that myself?"

Instead he sniffed in a dry way and uttered, "We're gonna use the Power Wagon on that."

No-o-o! something inside me cried. The Power Wagon for *that*? The thing was a huge beast of a vehicle, half giant jeep and half truck. Talk about a sparrowheaded idea; only a couple of horsepower, which was to say two horses, were required to hoist hay onto a stack, and he was going to employ the equivalent of an army tank? I stood there, mouth open but no words adequate. There went my dream of being stacker driver, in a cloud of exhaust. I was always being told I was big for my age, but I couldn't even have reached the clutch of the dumb Power Wagon.

"Cutting back on workhorses, don't you see," Wendell was saying, back to fiddling with the papers on the desk. "Time to send the nags to the glue factory."

That did that in. If charity was supposed to begin at home, somehow the spirit missed the Double W by a country mile. Apprentice cusser that I was, I secretly used up my swearing vocabulary on Wendell Williamson in my defeated retreat down the hallway. I can't account for what happened next except that I was so mad I could hardly see straight. Without even thinking, as I passed the show-off table and its wonders for the last time, I angrily snatched the black arrowhead and thrust it as deep in my jeans pocket as it would go.

Gram watched in concern as I came back into the cook shack like a whipped pup. "Donny, are you crying? What happened? Didn't the fool write in your book for you?"

"Got something in my eye," I alibied. Luckily the veterinarian's pickup pulled up outside and honked. In a last flurry, Gram gave me a big hug and a kiss on the cheek. "Off you go," her voice broke. "Be a good boy on the dog bus, won't you."

3.

AND HERE I WAS, stepping up into what I thought of as the real bus, with GREYHOUND—THE FLEET WAY TO TRAVEL in red letters on its side and, to prove it, the silver streamlined dog of the breed emblematically running flat-out as if it couldn't wait to get there. Maybe not, but I had two days and a night ahead of me before climbing off at the depot in farthest Wisconsin, and that felt to me like the interminable start of the eternity of summer ahead.

At the top of the steps I stopped short, not sure where to sit. The seats in long rows were easily four times as many as in the Rocky Mountain Stage Line sedan, the roomy high-backed sets on each side of the aisle making my ride from Gros Ventre squashed between the mailbag and the bulky woman seem like three in a bed with room for two, as Gram would have said. This was a vehicle for a crowd, and it already was more than half full. Way toward the back as though it was their given place sat some soldiers, two together on one side of the aisle and their much more sizable companion, who needed the space, in the set of seats across from them. Slumped in front of them was a bleary, rumpled guy in ranch clothes, by every sign a sheepherder on a spree, who appeared to have been too busy drinking to shave for a week or so. Across from him, like a good example placed to even him out, rested a nun in that black headgear outlined in white, her round glasses firm on her set face. Then toward the middle were scattered leathery older couples who I could tell were going home to farms or ranches or little towns along the way, and some vacationers dressed to the teeth in a way you sure don't see these days, coats and ties on the men and color-coordinated outfits for the women. One and all, the already-seated passengers were strangers to me, some a lot stranger than others from the looks of them, which didn't help in making up my mind. Much more traveled than I ever hoped to be, Gram had forewarned, "The dog bus gets all kinds, so you just have to plow right in and stake out a place for yourself." Yeah, but where?

Now I noticed the dark-haired woman nearest me, with her name sewn in red on her crisp blouse in waitress fashion, although I couldn't quite read it. Wearing big ugly black-rimmed glasses that made her look like a raccoon, she took short quick drags on a cigarette while reading a movie magazine folded over. She was sitting alone, but her coat was piled in the seat beside her, not exactly a friendly signal. Robbed of that spot—I'd have bet my bottom dollar that she knew how to be good company, snappy when talking was called for but otherwise minding her own business; some people simply have that look—I kept scanning the seats available among the other passengers, but froze when it came to choosing. It was a bad time to turn bashful, but I decided to take potluck and ducked into an empty set of seats a row behind the nonstop smoker.

No sooner had I done so than I changed my mind. About potluck, I mean. What was I going to do if the bus filled up and whoever sat next to me was anything like the nonstop talker about the digestive system? Or if the drunk sheepherder toward the back, recognizing me as fresh off the ranch—my shirt said something like that—came staggering up the aisle to keep me company? Or the nun decided to sneak up and get going on me about God? I didn't know squat about religion, and this was not the time to take that on. It panicked me to think about trying to keep up with conversations like those all the way to the next stop, Havre, or who knew, endless hours beyond that.

I bolted back out of the bus, drawing a glance between rapid-fire puffs as I passed the seated woman.

Luckily I was in time. The lanky driver in the blue Greyhound uniform and crush hat like a pilot's was just then shutting the baggage compartment in the belly of the bus. "Sir? Mister?" I pleaded. "Can I get my suitcase?"

He gave me one of those *Now what?* looks, the same as when he'd punched my ticket and realized I was traveling by myself at my age.

Straightening up, he asked with a frown, "Not parting company with us, are you? There's no refund once you're checked onto the bus, sonny."

"Huh-uh, no," I denied, "nothing like that," although jumping back on the Chevy bus for its return trip to Gros Ventre was mighty tempting. "I need to get something out, is all." He hesitated, eyeing the profusion of suitcases in the compartment. "Something I need helluva bad."

"That serious, is it." He seemed more amused than compelled by my newfound swearing skill. "Then I guess I better pitch in. But make it quick. I can do my tire check while you're at that. Remind me, which bag is yours?" When I pointed, he gave me another one of those looks. "Don't see that kind much anymore."

Kneeling on the concrete while the traffic of the busy Great Falls depot went on around me, I unlatched Gram's old suitcase and dug out the autograph book, stuffing it in the pocket of my corduroy jacket. While I had the suitcase open, I reluctantly tucked the black arrowhead in under the moccasins; I hated not to be carrying it as a lucky piece, but I didn't want to risk being jabbed in my sitting part all the way to Wisconsin, either.

Missions accomplished, I returned the suitcase to the baggage compartment as best I could. Headed to climb back on the bus, I nearly bumped into the driver coming around the front. I still was on his mind, apparently. "Say, I saw you come straight off the Rocky bus—did you get your Green Stamps?"

I plainly had no idea what he was talking about. "They're a special deal this summer, long-distance passengers get them for their miles. You're going quite a ways across the country, aren't you?" I sure was, off the end of the known world. "Then, heck, go in and show your ticket to the agent." He jerked a thumb toward the terminal. "Hustle your fanny, we're leaving before long."

My fanny and I did hustle inside, where I peered in every direction through the depot crowd before spotting the ticket counter. Miraculously no one was there ahead of me, and I barged up to the agent, a pinchfaced woman with a sort of yellowish complexion, as if she hadn't been away from the counter for years, and rattled off to her while waving my ticket, "I'm supposed to get Green Stamps, the driver said so."

"Those." She sniffed, and from under the counter dug out sheets of stamps, about the size you would put on a letter but imprinted with a shield bearing the fancy initials *S&H*, and sure enough, sort of pea green. Next she checked my ticket against a chart. "Sixteen hundred and one miles," she reported, looking me over as though wondering whether I was up to such a journey. Nonetheless she began counting out, telling me I was entitled to fifty stamps, a full sheet, for every hundred miles I was ticketed for. As the sheets piled up, I started to worry.

"Uhm, I forgot to ask. How much do they cost?"

"What the little boy shot at and missed," she answered impassively, still dealing out green sheets.

Really? Nothing? Skeptically I made sure. "The dog bus just gives them away?"

"Believe it or not," she muttered, little knowing that was the most convincing reply she could have given me.

Pausing, she squared the sheets into a neat stack. "That's sixteen," she announced, studying the chart again with a pinched frown. The one extra mile evidently constituted a problem for her. "What the hey," she said, and tossed on another green sheet.

"Wh-what do I do with them?" I had to ask as I gathered the stack of stamps off the counter. Handing me what she called a collector book, which was right up my alley, she explained that I was supposed to stick a sheet onto each page and when enough pages were filled, I could trade in the collection for merchandise at any store that hung out an S&H sign. "You've always wanted a lawn chair, I bet," she said expressionlessly.

"Uh, sure." Shoving the Green Stamp haul into my opposite jacket pocket from the autograph book, I turned to dash to the bus. Behind me I heard her recite, "God bless you real good, sonny."

ALREADY THIS WAS some trip, I thought to myself as I dodged through the depot crowd, enriched with a pocketful of trading stamps and a blessing, not really sure I was glad of the latter if that implied I might need it. In any case, I scurried out and vaulted back into the impressive silver-sided Greyhound. The same seat was available and I dropped into it as if I owned it.

There. I felt more ready. Now if I was trapped with someone who wanted to talk my ear off about canned succotash or similar topics, I could head them off by asking for their autograph and get them interested in my collection. It was at least a plan.

As the loudspeaker announced the last call for the eastbound bus, which was us, I waited tensely for whatever last-minute passenger would come panting aboard and, as surely as a bad apple falls tardily from a tree, plop into the seat next to mine. And sure enough, the sound of someone setting foot on the steps reared me half out of my seat to see. But it was only the driver, who shook his head to himself as I sank back down and he started a passenger count with me, then slid in behind the steering wheel. The next thing I knew, we were pulling out of Great Falls and lurching onto the highway.

ONCE UNDERWAY, the bus lived up to that tirelessly loping emblem on its side. In short order, the country along the highway turned to grainfield, miles of green winter wheat striped with the summer fallow of strip farming and tufted here and there with low trees planted around farm buildings as windbreaks. I stayed glued to the window, which for a while showed the blue-gray mountains I had been used to all my life, jagged tops white with snow left over from winter. All too soon, the familiar western peaks vanished behind a rise and did not come back. Apparently everything this side of the Rockies was dwarfed in comparison and only any good for plowing, not a cow or horse anywhere in sight. I could just imagine Wisconsin, the whole place a cornfield or something.

Watching the miles go by, with no company but my indistinct reflection, loneliness caught up with me. It had been held off by the woman talking a blue streak at me on the ride from Gros Ventre and then the confusion of getting settled on the Greyhound, but now if I could have seen myself, hunched in that seat amid the rows of passengers confined within themselves by the cocoon of travel, surely I matched the picture of despair conjured by one of those sayings of Gram's, lonely as an orphan on a chamber pot.

Eleven going on twelve is a changeable age that way. One minute you are coltish and sappy, and the next you're throwing a fit because you're tired or hungry or something else upsetting is going on inside you. Right then my mood churned up a storm. Things had been tossed turvy, and although I was the one cast out alone onto a transcontinental bus, home was running away from me, and had been ever since some doctor's dire words to Gram. For if I lost the last of my family to the poorfarm or worse, with that went everything connected to the notion of home as I had known it, and I would be bound for that other terrifying institution, the orphanage.

Full of instinct and intrigue as a schoolyard is, kids grasp to a terrifying extent what losing the world you have known means. Too many times had I heard the whisper race through recess, jackrabbit telegraph, that so-and-so was "going to the other side of the mountains." Packed up and dumped in the state-run orphanage over at Butte, that meant, across the Continental Divide where the sun went down and so did kids' lives. Designation as an orphan truly did sound to me fatal in a way, the end of a childhood in which my parents, in their shortened lifetimes, literally moved earth, and would have done the same with heaven had it been within immediate reach, to keep me always with them no matter how unhandy the circumstances.

So, right then it did not seem at all imaginary that life was turning against me, Gram and me both, to an awful extent. I resented the human plumbing or whatever it was in her case that produced this situation. If that nun back there playing with her beads or whatever wanted to do something useful, why didn't she pray up a better system of women's insides so a boy wouldn't worry himself sick about losing his grandmother, all he had, to some kind of operation?

And getting booted out of the cook shack and off the ranch like we were nobody—if that wasn't enough cause for resentment, I didn't know what qualified. I could have driven that stacker team in haying time just fine, and if Wendell Williamson didn't think so, he needed his sparrow head examined.

The list didn't stop there. These shirttail relatives I was going to be stuck with for an endless summer—why hadn't this Kitty and Dutch pair, the Brinkers by name, ever visited us, so I'd at least know what they looked like? Even if they were dried-up old coots who probably kept their teeth in a glass at night, as I figured they must be, it would have helped if I could picture them at all.

I COULD HAVE gone on and on like that, nose against the window and feeling sorry for myself, but that gets old, too. Stirring myself so plowed fields would not bore me out of my skull, to be doing anything I took out the autograph book. It opened to *In the game of life, don't lose your marbles.* Right. If you were lucky enough to own any marbles to start with. Moodily I moved on from the Double W brand of advice, flipping to the front of the book. Naturally, Gram's was the very first inscription. Wouldn't a person think, in a nice autograph book that she'd spent real money for, she would have carefully written something like *To my one and only grandson . . .* ? Instead, in her scrawl that barely did for grocery lists:

> *My love for you shall flow*
> *Like water down a tater row.*
>
> *Your Gram,*
> *Dorie Blegen*

I was finding out that people came up with surprising things like that almost automatically when presented with the autograph book. It was as if they couldn't resist putting down on the page—their page, everyone got his own, I made sure—something of themselves, corny though it might be, and happily signing their name to it. Wistfully thumbing through the inscriptions, I lost myself for a while in the rhymes and remarks of my school friends and teachers and the ranch hands and visitors like the veterinarian and, when I hit it lucky, a big shot like Senator Ridpath when he spoke in the Gros Ventre park on the Fourth of July. That was my prize one so far; the senator was surely famous, if for nothing more than having been in office almost forever. What a pretty piece of writing his was as I looked at it with admiration again, every letter of the alphabet perfectly formed, and the lines about the pen being mightier than the sword composed there as balanced as a poem.

The senator's elegant citation was even more fitting than he could have known, because along with the autograph book, Gram had given me my very own ballpoint pen—not the plain old type then that was an ink stick with a cap on the end, but a fancy new retractable kind called a Kwik-Klik. It wrote in a purplish hue that seemed to me the absolute best color for an autograph collection, and I made sure to have people use it when composing their ditties rather than just any old writing instrument. Of course, there were exceptions—Wendell Williamson was represented in that deathly black Quink fountain pen stuff—but page to page, the creamy paper showed off the same pleasing ink, like a real book.

And then and there, the way a big idea sometimes will grow from a germ of habit, it dawned on me that a dog bus full of passengers, as captive as I was, presented a chance to fill a good many more of those pages with purplish inscriptions.

Sitting up as if I'd had a poke in the ribs, I snuck a look toward the back of the bus for likely candidates. The soldiers were talking up a storm, joking and laughing. The tourists yakked on across the aisles. A number of passengers were napping. The only ones not occupied, so to speak, were the nun and the sheepherder.

Mustering my courage, I stacked my jacket to save my seat and started down the aisle, swaying when the bus did. Saying "Excuse me" a dozen times, I made my way past pair after pair of aisle-sitting conversationalists. As if reading my mind, the sheepherder dragged himself upright and lopsidedly grinned at me as if he were thirsty for company. But just as I reached his vicinity, the bus rocked around a curve and I lurched into the empty seat behind him, like a pinball into a slot.

The big soldier who had been sitting by himself raised a bushy eyebrow at my abrupt arrival beside him. "Hi," I piped up as I recovered, the top of my head barely reaching the shoulder patch of his uniform.

"What's doing, buddy?" he wondered.

My voice high, I hurriedly told him, displaying the autograph book. His eyebrow stayed parked way up there, but he sort of smiled and broke into my explanation.

"Loud and clear, troop. If there's a section in there for Uncle Sam's groundpounders, you've got them up the yanger here." Holding out a hand that swallowed mine, he introduced himself. "Turk Turco." The soldiers across the aisle sent me two-fingered salutes and chipped in their names, Gordon in the near seat and Mickey by the window.

"Mine's Donny," I said to keep things simple. "Where you guys going?"

The one called Gordon snickered. "Sending us east to go west, that's the army for you. We catch the train at Havre. Then it's Fort Lewis, good old Fort Screw Us, out by Seattle. And after that it's"—he drew out the next word like it was sticky—"Ko-re-a."

"Where we'll get our asses shot off," Mickey said glumly.

Turk sharply leaned over, just about obliterating me. "Lay off that, will you, numb nuts. You're scaring the kid. Not to mention me."

The thought that the Korean War, which like any American youngster of 1951 I'd grasped only from *G.I. Joe* comic books and radio reports, could claim the lives of people I'd met face-to-face, had never occurred to me. It struck with lightning force now. Glancing guiltily around at the three soldiers in their pressed khakis, I almost wished I had lit in with the mussy sheepherder, who could be heard carrying on a muttered conversation with himself in front of us.

"I'm just saying," Mickey stayed insistent. "Think about it, there's Chinese up the wazoo over there"—I was fairly sure that amounted to the same as up the yanger and could not be good—"must be a million of the bastards, then there's us."

"And the whole sonofabitching rest of the army," Turk pointed out. "C'mon, troop, this is no time to come down with a case of nervous in the service."

Mickey was not to be swayed. "I wish to Christ they were shipping us to some base in Germany where we wouldn't get our asses shot off, is all."

That startled me. The Chinese were an enemy I had not quite caught up with, but Germans still were the bad guys from the last war, as far as I was concerned. Fiends all the way up to Hitler, and down to the enemy soldiers my family had a personal reason to hate forever.

"Yeah, right, Mick." Gordon rolled his eyes about Germany for me. "Over there where you could put on your jockstrap spats and wow the fräuleins."

"Go take a flying fuck at a rolling donut, Gordo."

I was starting to realize what a long way I had to go to be accomplished in cussing.

Snickering again, Gordon maintained that if anybody's ass was going to get shot off, it could not possibly be his. "Mine's gonna be the size of a prune, from the pucker factor." All three soldiers roared at that, and while I didn't entirely get it, I joined in as best I could.

When the laughter died down, I figured maybe I ought to contribute something. "My daddy was in the war," I announced brightly. "The last one. He was on one of those boat kind of things at Omaha Beach."

"A landing craft?" Turk whistled through his teeth, looking at me a different way. "Out the far end!" he exclaimed, which took me a moment to savvy as soldier talk for outstanding and then some. "D-Day was hairy. Came back in one piece, did he? Listen up, Mick."

I didn't have the heart to tell them the truth about that. "He always, uh, says he's in pretty good shape for the shape he's in."

Gordon leaned across the aisle. "So what's your old man do?"

"He's a"—it's amazing what a habit something like this gets to be—"crop duster."

"No crap?" Gordon sounded envious. "Grainfield flyboy, is he. Then how come you have to travel by dog? Why doesn't he just give you a lift in his airplane?"

"It's too far. See, I'm going to visit my rich aunt and uncle. They live back east. In Decatur, Illinois."

"Never heard of the place. What's there?"

"The Cat plant." That drew three blank looks. "Where they make bulldozers and graders and stuff like that." I was developing a feel for the perimeter of story that could be got away with. A detail or two expanded the bounds to a surprising extent, it seemed like.

So, there it went, again. Out of my mouth something unexpected, not strictly true but harmlessly made up. Storying, maybe it could be called. For I still say it was not so much that I was turning into an inveterate liar around strangers, I simply was overflowing with invention. The best way I can explain it is that I was turned loose from myself. Turned loose, not by choice, from the expected behavior of being "a good kid," which I was always a little restless about anyway. "You're being a storier," Gram would warn whenever I got carried away spinning a tale about one thing or another. Now, with no check on my enthusiasm when it started playing tricks upstairs in me—the long bus trip seemed to invite daydreaming, mine merely done out loud—I was surprising myself with the creations I could come up with. I mean, what is imagination but mental mischief of a kind, and why can't a youngster, particularly one out on his own, protectively occupy himself with invention of that sort before maturity works him over? One thing for sure, the soldiers on their way to their own mind-stretching version of life ahead did not doubt my manufactured one in the least.

Shoulders shaking with laughter, Mickey forcefully nudged Gordon. "If it was the cat house, you'd know all about it, huh, Gordo?"

Gordon turning the air blue in response, Turk nudged me for the autograph book. "Somebody's got to go first." I instructed him in the mystery of the Kwik-Klik, and with it in hand, he balanced the book on his knee and wrote for a good long time. When he was through, I passed things across to Gordon, who looked over Turk's entry with a mocking expression but didn't say anything before writing his own.

Mickey balked when the autograph collection reached him. "I don't know about this happy horseshit of writing in here. What am I supposed to say?"

"Pretend it's your coloring book," Gordon wisecracked. But Turk took right in on the reluctant penman. "Get with the program, troop. If the kid's good enough to give a damn about us, the least we can do is put some ink on the page for him."

Without looking up, Mickey did so, and after laboring through, passed the autograph book and pen across to me. Gratefully thanking the three of them up, down, and sideways, I retreated to my own seat to catch my breath.

GIDDY WITH SUCCESS, I read the soldiers' inscriptions over and over, the pages as distinct from each other as handwriting could possibly be.

Life is like a deck of cards.
When you are in love it's ♥s.
Before you are married it's ♦s.
After you are married it's ♣s.

When you are dead it's ♠s.
May your long suits be hearts and diamonds.
Alvin "Turk" Turco, Pfc.

TIME FLIES LIKE AN ARROW,
WHY I'VE NEVER UNDERSTOOD.
FRUIT FLIES LIKE A BANANA,
NOW THAT SOUNDS PRETTY GOOD.
Gordon Jones
General Nuisance, U.S. Army

Mickey O'Fallon is my name
America is my nation
Butte, Montana, is my home
Korea is my destination.

Like the Turk one had said, *Out the far end!* Three fresh pages of inscriptions, just like that. Now, though, I faced a dilemma. Stretch my luck and go back for Kwik-Klik tidbits from other passengers, or quit while I was ahead? The bus was belting along through nondescript country with nothing much to show for itself except a brushy creek and flat buttes, so Havre or any place else was not in the picture for a while yet, and I had time if I wanted to brave the gauntlet of strangers again. But if I wasn't mistaken, the nun had looked about ready to pounce as I hustled past to stop me from keeping company with the swearing soldiers. Was it worth it to risk falling into her clutches, or for that matter, end up with some talky tourist bunch like the ladies' club on the Chevy bus?

While I was hung up trying to decide, blue puffs rose steadily as ever from the passenger in front of me as if she were putting up smoke signals.

Making up my mind, I leaned way forward to the crack between the seats. I could just see the side of the woman's face as she smoked away, eyes down on her movie magazine.

"Uh, can I bother you?" I spoke into the narrow gap. "Talk to you about something, I mean? It'll only take a jiffy. Honest."

Somewhere between curious and skeptical, she took a peek at me through the crack. "A jiff, huh? In that case, I guess come on up and let's hear it."

Scooping her coat off the seat and stuffing it down beside her purse as I slid in next to her, she gave me a swift looking-over. Up close, she was eye-catching in spite of the raccoon glasses, I was somewhat surprised to see, with big dark eyes that went with her glossy black hair, and quite a mouth, full-lipped with cherry-red lipstick generously applied. From the sassy tilt of her head as she sized me up, I could imagine her giving as good as she got if someone smarted off to her, which was not going to be me if I could help it.

Before I could utter a word, she dove right in. "What's on your mind, buttercup? You're quite a jumping bean, you know. First time on a bus?"

Uncomfortably I owned up to "Almost."

"Takes some getting used to, especially in the sit bones," she said with a breezy laugh. Just then a flashy Cadillac of the kind called a greenback special—Wendell Williamson had one like it, of course—passed us like the wind. "What has big ears and chases cars?" she playfully sent my way, not really asking. "A Greyhound full of elephants."

I giggled so hard I hiccuped. So much for being businesslike with the autograph book. My partner in bus endurance, as she seemed to be, didn't bat an eye at my embarrassing laughing fit. Still treating me as if I were an old customer, she tapped me on the knee with the movie magazine. "Don't wear yourself out worrying, hon, this crate will get you there. Always has me anyway. Betsa bootsies, there's always a bus to somewhere."

With all that said, she plucked up her cigarette from amid the lipstick-stained butts in the armrest ashtray and took a drag that swelled her chest. Trying not to look too long at that part of her, my eyes nonetheless had to linger to figure out the spelling of the name stitched there in pink thread. *Leticia*, which stood out to me in more ways than one. Determinedly lifting my gaze to meet her quizzical expression, I rattled out my pursuit of autographs to remember my trip by, producing the creamy album in evidence.

"So that's what's got you hopping," she laughed, but nicely. Taking that as encouragement, I fanned open the pages to her. "See, people write all kinds of stuff. Here's my favorite, just about. It's from Miss Ciardi, best teacher I ever had." Together we took in the deathless composition:

A flea and a fly in a flue
Were caught, what could they do?
"Let us flee," said the fly.
"Let us fly," said the flea.
So they flew through a flaw in the flue.

"Tough competition," she laughed again. The cigarette met its fate with the other mashed-out ones as she surprised me with a drawn-out sigh. "Sure, I'll dab something in for you, why not. Your tough luck it's me instead of her, huh?" She flourished the movie magazine, open to a picture of Elizabeth Taylor with a cloud of hair half over one sultry eye and nothing on above her breastbone.

"Aw, anybody can be named Elizabeth," I spouted, feeling brave as I extended the open autograph book and special ballpoint to her. "But Leticia, whew, that's something else."

Solving the pen with no trouble at all, she gave me a sassy grin.

"Had your eye on the tittytatting, have you," she teased. "Letting the customers get to know you right up front on the uniform helps the tips like you wouldn't believe."

"I think it's a really great idea," I got caught up in a rush of enthusiasm. "I wish everybody did that. Had their name sewn on them, I mean. See, mine is Donal without a *d* on the end, and hardly anybody ever gets it right at first, but if it was on my shirt, they couldn't mess it up like they always do."

Listening with one ear while she started to write, she pointed out a drawback to having yourself announced on your breast. "Like when some smart-ass leans in for a good look and asks, 'What's the other one's name?'"

It took me a moment to catch on, then several to stop blushing. Thankfully, she still had her head down in diligence over the autograph page. She had whipped off her glasses and stuck them in her purse—she looked a lot younger and better with them off—and I couldn't contain my curiosity.

"How come you wear your glasses to read but not to write?"

"Don't need 'em for either one," she said offhandedly. "They're just windowpane."

"So why do you wear them ever?"

Another one of those grins. "Like it probably says in the Bible somewhere: Guys don't make passes at gals who wear glasses." She saw I wasn't quite following that. "Honey, I just want to ride from here to there without every man who wears pants making a try at me. The silly specs and the ciggies pretty much do the trick—you don't see those GIs sniffing around, do you."

"They've got something else on their minds," I confided as if wise beyond my years. "They're afraid they're going to get their asses shot off in Korea."

Frowning ever so slightly, she made a shooing motion in front of her face. "Flies around the mouth," she warned me off that kind of language. She glanced over her shoulder toward the soldiers, shaking her head. "Poor babies." Going back to her writing, she finished with a vigorous dotting of *i*'s and crossing of *t*'s, and handed book and pen back to me. "Here you go, pal. Signed, sealed, and delivered."

I saw she had done a really nice job. The handwriting was large and even and clear, doubtless from writing meal orders.

> ***Life is a zigzag journey, they say,***
> ***Not much straight and easy on the way.***
> ***But the wrinkles in the map, explorers know,***
> ***Smooth out like magic at the end of where we go.***

"That's pretty deep for me," I admitted, so far from the end of my unwanted journey that I could not foresee anything remotely like magic smoothing the way. More like a rocky road ahead, among people as foreign to me as a jungle tribe. Still, I did not want to hurt her feelings and resorted to "You really know how to write."

"Learned that ditty in school, along with the one about burning your candle at both ends. Funny how certain things stick with you," she mused as I was reluctantly about to thank her and excuse myself. But then I stiffened, staring into the autograph book. "What's the matter, kiddo?" she asked offhandedly, her next cigarette on the way to her lips. "Did I spell something wrong?"

What had stopped me cold was her rhyming signature. *Letty Minetti*.

"The truck stop at Browning," I blurted, "did you work there?"

In the act of lighting up, she went stock-still with the cigarette between the fingers of one hand and the Zippo in the other. "Okay, Dick Tracy, I give." She turned and studied me narrowly now. "How come you're such an expert on me?"

"Oh, I wouldn't say that, expert, I mean," my sentences stumbled in retreat. "More like interested, is all. See, my grandmother used to cook there, and she couldn't help talking about those times. She thought you were the greatest at being a waitress, 'out front' as she called it."

Letty, as she was to me now, sucked in her cheeks as if tasting the next sentence before she said it. "So you're him."

Him? What him? I looked at her in confusion.

"Don't take me wrong," she said quickly. "All I meant, Dorie told me what was up when she had to quit the truck stop. To take on raising you, at that cow outfit."

Blank with surprise, I stared back at the waitress who suddenly was the expert on me.

Letty nibbled her lip, disturbing the lipstick a bit, then uttered the rest. "When she left to be with you, she had me put flowers on the crosses every month."

WHITE AS BONES, the roadside trio of short metal crosses stood in memoriam on the long slope up from the Two Medicine River. One for my father, one for my mother, and although I could not see why he deserved the same, one for the drunk driver whose pickup drifted across the centerline and hit theirs head-on. Only once had I seen the crosses, on a school trip to the Blackfoot museum in Browning not long after the funeral, and I had to swallow sobs the rest of the trip. I almost wished the American Legion post would quit marking highway deaths like that—for some of us, too much of a reminder—but my father had been a favorite at Legion halls, someone who came out of the D-Day landing badly wounded but untouched in his personality, ready with a laugh and a story anytime he and my mother blew in for a drink and a nice supper and some dancing. The flowers, which I remembered were yellow, must have been Gram's own ongoing remembrance, by courtesy—a great deal more than that—of Letty Minetti.

A jolt went through me like touching the hot wire of something electric. Connected by accident, she and I were no longer simply strangers on a bus. This woman with the generous mouth knew all about me, or at least enough, and I was catching up with her circumstances. Wherever she was headed with her name on her uniform, it was not to work the counter at the Browning truck stop, a hundred miles in the other direction. "You do that anymore?" I rushed out the words, then hedged. "The flowers, I mean?"

Letty shook her head and lit the interrupted cigarette. "Couldn't, sorry. Been in the Falls a year or so," she expelled along with a stream of smoke, "busting my tail in the dining room at the Buster. You know it?"

Surprisingly, I did. The Sodbuster Hotel was a fancy place where the Williamsons stayed during the Great Falls rodeo, so Wendell could oversee—or according to Gram, mess with—the handling of the Double W's string of bucking horses. My new confidante let out her breath, nothing to do with smoking this time. "It didn't work out. I'll tell you something. The more dressed up people are, the harder they are to wait on," laughing as she said it, but not the amused kind. "I missed the Browning gang. The rez boys tip good when they have a few drinks in them, you'd be surprised. And truckers leave their change on the counter. It adds up."

What wasn't adding up was her presence on this bus with the rest of us nomads, so I outright asked. "What are you doing on here, in this direction?"

She flicked me a look, but answered readily enough. "Taking a job in Havre. New town, fresh start. That's the way it goes."

That didn't sound good. People were always saying about Havre, off by itself and with not much going for it but the railroad that ran through, *You can have 'er.*

Something of that reputation must have been on Letty's mind, too. "Hey, you know any French?"

"'Aw river,' maybe."

"Nah, more than that. See, the place where I'll be working is called, capital *T*, The Le Havre Supper Club." She nibbled her lip. "Something doesn't seem quite right about that, don't you think? Anyway, that's why I'm wearing my work shirt," meaning the uniform top with the prominent stitching, "in case I have to go on shift right away. Some morons"—she pronounced it *mo-rons*, with the same note in her voice as when Gram would say "Sparrowhead"—"put you to slinging coffee almost before your keister is through the doorway, would you believe."

I made a sympathetic noise, but my attention wasn't in it. By now I had a crush on her. Oh, man, my thinking ran, wouldn't it be great if she and Gram could get a job together at the Top Spot cafe back in Gros Ventre, if Havre didn't pan out for her and if Gram was as good as new after her operation and if I made it through whatever waited in Wisconsin, and we could all share a real house together, not a cook shack, right there in town? When you are as young as I was then, a world of any kind begins at the outskirts of your imagination, and you populate it with those who have proven themselves to you. The unknowns are always lying in wait, though. Trying not to, I kept glancing at Letty's hand and the wedding ring that showed itself with every drag on her cigarette.

She caught me at it. "You don't miss much, do you." She flexed that finger away from the others. "My husband's still in Browning. Tends bar there, chases women on the side. We made a great pair."

She shrugged as if the next didn't matter, although even I knew it was the kind of thing that always does. "We split. He was jealous. There was this one trucker, Harv, I got a little involved with. Harv's some piece of work," she grinned a way that said more than she was saying. "The strong silent type straight out of the movies, you know? Doesn't say much, but when he does, it's right on the money." The grin humorously tucked in on itself. "Even looks a little like Gregory

Peck if you close one eye a little." Then her face clouded. "Trouble is, he's sort of hard to keep up with because he's on the road so much, trucking here and there. But when he's around"—her voice dropped to a confidential level—"sparks fly."

"Holy wow," I said, as if I knew anything about such matters. "He sounds like a real boyfriend."

"Real as they come." She blew a smoke ring as I drifted along on the romantic mood. "We're more or less engaged, or will be when that husband of mine gets it through his thick head to agree to a divorce." Dabbing the ash off her cigarette, she mused, "Haven't seen Harv lately, though. Hated to do it, but I had to leave word for him at the Buster that I'd moved on to The Le Havre." Then her grin sneaked back infectiously. "Absence makes the heart grow fonder, truer words were never. Harv's good at catching up on things."

"I bet he is," I endorsed him sight unseen, talented as he sounded in areas a little beyond me.

"Anyway, what's done is done," she said briskly. "You ought to have that in your book." She mashed out the latest cigarette. "Hey, enough of the story of my life. How's Dorie these days? Why isn't she with you?"

"She's got to have an operation." I poured out everything, the cook shack and charity nuns and Wisconsin and all, my listener taking it in without saying anything.

When I finally ran down, Letty bit her lip again. "Jeez, that's rough on both of you. Tough deal all around." The bus changed speed as the driver shifted gears on a hill, bobbing us against our seatbacks, and when that stopped, Letty still rocked back and forth a little. "You know what? You need something else to think about."

Reaching in her purse, she took out a compact and redid her lipstick, which surprised me because she'd already been wearing quite a gob. Working her lips together to even it out the way women do, when she was satisfied she snapped the compact shut and asked:

"Ever been kissed?"

"Well, sure," I stammered. "Lots."

"Besides nighty-night?"

"Uh, not really, I guess."

"Scooch down a little like you're showing me something real interesting in the book there, and turn this way, and we'll do something about that." She craned around to make sure no one was watching, and I really hoped the nun wasn't.

Dazed, I did as she said. And she did what she said, bringing her warm lips to mine in a kiss I felt to the tips of my ears. She tasted like tobacco and lipstick, but a lot more than that, too, although I was too young to put a name to such things.

We broke apart, her first. "There you go, kiddo, that's for luck." Grinning broadly, she opened the compact again to show me myself plastered with the red imprint of her lips, as if I needed any evidence, before tenderly wiping away the lipstick with her hanky. "First of many smackeroos in your career," she said huskily. "You'll get good at it. Betsa bootsies you will. Now you better scoot back to your own seat, sugar, we're just about there." That was true of her and the pink tittytatting that pointed the way. I still was trying to catch up with the dizzying twists and turns of the day.

4.

"**HAVRE**, the Paris of the prairie," the lanky driver called out in a mechanical way. "You may disembark if you so wish and stretch your legs. The Greyhound bus depot, proud to serve you, has full conveniences."

To me that meant the one that flushes, and with Gram's number-one instruction for riding the dog bus in comparative comfort urgently in mind—*Every stop, you make sure you get in there and go before the bus does*—I was the first one off and into the station, fantastic Letty first giving me a good-bye pat on the cheek and wishing me all the luck in the world.

I could have used some by the time I emerged from the men's restroom and tried to navigate the waiting room crowded with families of Indians and workgangs of white guys in bib overalls and a mix of other people, the mass of humanity causing me to duck and dodge and peer in search of something to eat. My meal money, a five-dollar bill Gram had tucked into my jeans, was burning a hole in my pocket. Besides that, on the principle that you never want to be separated from your money while traveling among strangers, I had a stash under my shirt, three ten-dollar bills that she had folded snugly and pinned behind the breast pocket with a large safety pin, assuring me a pickpocket would need scissors for hands to reach it. These days, it is hardly conceivable that three perforated ten-spots and a fiver felt to me like all the cash in the world, but at the time a cup of coffee cost only a dime, as did that stimulant for the younger set like me, comic books, and a movie could be seen for a quarter, and a pair of blue jeans would set you back two bucks and a half at most.

Be that as it may, besides providing me with a little to spend during the Wisconsin stay—"mad money," Gram's words for it probably fitting my tendencies all too accurately—the shirt stash was meant to outfit me with school clothes back there to come home with as well. School clothes were a big deal then, no real family wanting to look stingy about it. So, scraping that much cash together to send me off with was no easy thing—it amounted to half of Gram's last monthly paycheck from the tight fist of Sparrowhead—and that's why I had firm instructions from her to stretch the pocket fiver through the trip by confining lunches to a sandwich. No milkshakes, no pieces of pie, no bottles of pop, in other words no getting rambunctious with the tantalizing five-spot.

Which sounded okay in theory, but less so in a thronged bus depot when I was hungry as a wolf. Wouldn't you know that the lunch counter, offering greasy hamburgers if a person did not want runny egg salad sandwiches wrapped in wax paper, was jam-packed by the time I could get there and service was slow as ring-around-the-rosy. Havre really needed Letty.

Desperately looking around as my stomach growled, I spied the newsstand that sold magazines and cigarettes and other sundries. Gram had not thought to say anything about candy bars.

I hurried over, one eye on the clock. No one else was buying anything, but the gum-chewing woman clerk had to tend to freight parcels as well as the candy counter, and it took a very long couple of minutes to get her to wait on me. "A Mounds bar, please"—dark chocolate with coconut inside, you can't beat that—I said as rapidly as I could. Then I remembered that suppertime would not be until

North Dakota, as distant to me as the cheese side of the moon. "Make it three."

THE GREYHOUND had its motor running when I dashed out of the terminal, peeling a Mounds as I ran. The door was open, but the driver was resting a hand on the handle that operated it. "Cutting it pretty close, sonny," he said, giving me the stinkeye as I panted up the steps, the door sucking shut behind me.

To my amazement, the bus had filled up entirely, except where I had saved my window spot with my cord jacket. And if I could believe my eyes, there next to it sat a big-bellied Indian with black braids that came down over his shoulders.

Oh man, here was my chance! A seatmate I could talk to about all kinds of Indian things! The Fort Belknap Reservation was somewhere in this part of Montana, I knew, and he and the Indian families taking up about half the bus must be headed home there. My head buzzed with the sensation of double luck. Here delivered right to me was not only someone really great for the autograph book, but who could palaver—that's what Indians did, didn't they?—with me about the black arrowhead if I went about it right. What a break!

"Hi!" I chirped as I joined him.

"Howdy," he said in a thrilling deep voice that reverberated up out of that royal belly—maybe he was a chief, too!—as he moved his legs enough for me to squeeze by to my window seat.

The bus lurched into immediate motion, as if my fanny hitting the cushion was the signal to go, and I settled into eating my candy bar and sneaking looks sideways at my traveling companion. He was dressed not all that different from me, in blue jeans and a western shirt with snap buttons. All resemblance ended there, though. His buckskin face could have posed for the one on nickels, and then there were those braids. I envied him his straw cowboy hat, beat-up and curled almost over on itself at the brim and darkly sweat-stained from what I would have bet was life on one of the small ranches scattered around on the reservation, riding Appaloosa horses and hunting antelope and dancing at powwows and a million other things that beat anything I had been through at the Double W.

Mind your manners no matter what, so people won't think you were born in a barn, I could all but hear Gram reciting in my ear, and so I politely turned away to the window to wait until we were out of town and freewheeling toward the reservation before striking up a conversation about him being an Indian and my second name or nickname or whatever it was being Red Chief. That ought to get the palaver going. Then when obsidian arrowheads became the topic, should I tell him, just sort of casually, that I had one in my suitcase? For all I knew, possessing such a rarity maybe made a person special in the tribe. Possibly I was already a sort of honorary chieftain and didn't know it, from whatever sacred quality—to me, that meant pretty much the same as magic—a glistening dark treasure like that carried.

Yet there was another consideration, wasn't there. While I was surer than sure that Wendell Williamson did not deserve an arrowhead older than Columbus, what about the Indians from that time on? What if my braided seatmate were to tell me the black arrowhead was a lucky piece that they worshipped, and there was a whole long story about how tough life had been for Indians ever since it was lost? I'd feel bad about having it. I decided I'd better play it safe at first and start with his autograph.

Finally the bus labored out of the last of Havre and we were rolling ahead on the open prairie. Expectantly I turned toward my braided seat partner for conversation to be initiated, by me if not him.

The straw cowboy hat was pulled down over his eyes. Oh no! Phooey and the other word, too! He was sound asleep.

I was stymied. Talk about manners and Gram's commandment.

I couldn't very well poke a total stranger in the ribs and tell him, "Hey, wake up, I want to palaver with you." That was born-in-a-barn behavior, for sure. However, if I accidentally on purpose disturbed his slumber, that was a different matter, right?

Retrieving another Mounds from a coat pocket, I noisily unwrapped it, crumpling the wrapper as loudly as possible while I munched away. No result on the sleeper.

I coughed huskily. He still didn't stir. Not even working myself into a fake coughing fit penetrated his snooze.

I squirmed in my seat, jiggled the armrest between us, made such a wriggling nuisance that I bothered myself. Sleeping Bull, as I now thought of him, never noticed. The man could have dozed through a cavalry charge.

Well, okay, Red Chief, you'd better figure this out some, I told myself. After all, the prize sleeper was not the only autograph book candidate and possible conversation partner on the packed dog bus, by far. If I wanted Indians, a small tribe of them was scattered up and down the aisle, entire families with little kids in their go-to-town clothes and cowboy-hatted lone men sitting poker-faced but awake, all of them as buckskin-colored as the one parked next to me. Then at the back of the bus, a white-bibbed workgang, off to some oil field where a gusher had been struck according to their talk, was having a good time, several of them playing cards on a coat spread across a couple of laps, others looking on and making smart remarks. From snatches I could hear, there wasn't any doubt I could pick up the finer points of cussing and discussing from them just as I'd done with my buddies the soldiers, last seen shouldering their duffel bags to head in the direction of Korea, poor guys. A new gold mine of names and all that came with them was right there up the aisle waiting, if I could only reach it.

I gauged my seatmate, who seemed to have expanded in his sleep. Getting by him posed a challenge, but I figured if I stretched myself just about to splitting, I could lift a leg over him into the aisle and the other leg necessarily would follow.

Here goes nothing from nowhere, another of Gram's old standards, got me perilously up and with one leg spraddled over his round midriff, as if mounting a horse from the wrong side, when the fact struck me. *Moron, there aren't any empty seats.* I'd have to stay standing as I went along the aisle. Already I saw in the rearview mirror that the driver had his eye on me.

Defeated, I dropped back in my seat, silently cussing to the limits of my ability. To console myself, I ate my last Mounds. Maybe my luck would change at the next stop, I told myself. Surely the bus would let some passengers off in Chinook. In the meantime, punch-drunk on candy, I must have caught the sleeping sickness from my hibernating seatmate, as my eyelids grew heavy and the rhythm of the bus wheels on the flat open road lulled me off into a nap—only until something happened, I drowsily promised myself.

"TWENTY-MINUTE STOP, FOLKS."

The driver's droning announcement that we could disembark if we so wished and take advantage of the conveniences of the Greyhound terminal jerked me out of a nightmare. It was one of those bad dreams where you try to hide but never get anywhere, in this case in some big awful building where Wendell Williamson was after me, but every time I ran down a long hallway or up a staircase, he would barge out of a room and demand, *"Where's that arrowhead? Hand it over or I'll tell your folks."* Groggily I looked up and down the aisle of the bus, trying to come to grips with my surroundings. Then looked again, blinking, to see whether I still was in a dream, not a good one.

The Indians had vanished. Likewise the oil field crew. The passenger load was down to a precious few, myself and one of those tourist couples out to see the world on the cheap and a man in a gabardine suit of the kind county extension agents and livestock buyers wore. All the rest of the seats, including the one next to me, were empty.

I couldn't get my bearings. The bus already had slowed to town speed, but this was no drop stop as Chinook or Fort Belknap would be. I whirled to see out the window to the street. A Stockman Bar, a Mint Bar, a Rexall Drug, a Buttrey's grocery, those could be anywhere. Then I spotted a storefront window with the old-fashioned lettering GLASGOW TOGGERY—MEN'S WEAR AND MORE. Glasgow! I had slept away a sizable portion of Montana. The Indians, including my seatmate, must have got off long since, the oil roughnecks likewise. I felt ridiculously cheated, yet with no one to blame but myself. Staying awake on a once-in-a-lifetime journey should not be that hard a job, I could about hear Gram chiming in.

Kicking myself about all the unfulfilled pages of the autograph book and the lost chance to palaver about the black arrowhead, I scrambled off for the restroom the moment the bus door whished open, vowing to get the Kwik-Klik into action from here on, no matter what it took.

WHEN PASSENGERS FILED on again, things looked more promising, several fresh faces, although no obvious Indians. I was nothing if not determined, singling out seats I could pop in and out of as the autograph book and I made the rounds. Itching to start, I waited impatiently for the driver to finish some paperwork he was doing on his lap. All at once, I saw him look up in surprise, spring the bus door open, and address someone outside.

"Afternoon, Sheriff. Prize customer?"

"A steady one, for damn sure," an irritated voice replied. "Returning him to the stony lonesome at Wolf Point again. He's their prisoner. Supposed to be anyhow, if the escape artist didn't keep showing up here. I'll catch the local back after I dump him."

Sheriff. Prisoner. The stony lonesome, which meant jail. I sat up sharply.

Sure enough, up into the bus stepped a rangy man with strong features and dark expressive eyebrows and a set mouth as if he were on a mission. He looked like he could carry a six-gun natural as anything, and know the right way to use it.

He, though, unfortunately was not the sheriff, according to the handcuffs on his wrists. Right behind him came a sawed-off guy not much more than half his size, wearing the biggest kind of crow-black Stetson and a star badge. "Here, Romeo," the runty one directed. "Across from the kid will do."

Oh man! Not only had my luck changed, the rush of it flattened me back against my seat as the pair of them settled in and the bus started into motion, the prisoner by the window and the sheriff on the aisle. The butt of a revolver protruded out of a well-worn holster on his hip like a place to hang his hat.

Noticing me gaping, the sheriff cackled a little. "Getting an eyeful of law enforcement, bucko?"

"Yeah! How come you take him by bus?"

The lawman grimaced as if he'd been asking himself that very question. "My deputy's out on a domestic dispute call, and the jail's full of rangutang drunks from Saturday night. Not the way I want, doing this by Hound." He looked around the bus with distaste. "But it'd be just like the master criminal here to bail out of the patrol car if I drove him. Tried that last time, didn't you."

"We weren't going that fast."

The sheriff laughed nastily. "Not gonna be bailing out of the bus, are you."

"To tell the truth, I don't see how."

"Damn right you don't. You're on a one-way ticket back to behind bars and that's that."

"You needn't be quite so tickled about it. I'm not exactly public enemy number one."

"Oh, hurting your feelings, am I. Ain't that just too damn bad." The sheriff glanced up at the composed figure nearly a head taller than him and complained, "I've got a whole hell of a lot of better things to do than pack you back to Wolf Point, you know. Do you have to be such a pain in the britches? First you get in a fight with some fool bartender because you think you've been shortchanged and tear up the bar." So much for my imagining this was an escaped murderer, being delivered to the cold scales of justice. "Then you keep breaking out of that half-assed excuse for a jail they have over there and showing up back here in my jurisdiction." With his face squinched like one of those apple dolls that have dried up, the sheriff groused, "Can't you for christ sakes light out in some other direction for a change? Go get yourself a haying job somewhere? Stacking hay is about your speed, Harv."

"I explained that, Carl," the prisoner said patiently. "My girlfriend Letty waits tables in Great Falls. How else am I supposed to get to see her?"

"I KNOW HER! Leticia, I mean, it was right there in pink!"

My bray startled both men, their heads whipping around to scrutinize me. "She was here on the bus, see," I gave out the news as fast as I could talk, "so I met her and we talked for a long way and she was really nice to me, boy, she's a piece of work." I reported further to the surprised prisoner, "She told me all about you, sort of. The trucker part."

"Oh, swell," the sheriff said sardonically. "Now she's running around the countryside, too. What is it about you two, claustrophobia?"

The prisoner ignored the sarcasm, leaning forward to see around the sheriff. "Why was she on the bus, my friend? Start at the beginning."

It seemed a good time to keep the beginning close to the end. "She got sick and tired of uppity customers at the Buster hotel, so she's gonna try Havre."

"Havre." The men looked at each other as if that were the bottom of the barrel.

Harv recovered enough to maintain, "Letty'd have her reasons."

"Eh, her," the sheriff scoffed. "The cause of all this. Isn't that so, loverboy?"

"Only because you arrested me when I was on my way to go see her in Great Falls, before Havre came up," the prisoner said, patient as paint. "I was hitchhiking just fine until I had to stop for a bite to eat."

"For crying out loud," his captor groused. "I leave the office for lunch at the Highliner Cafe like usual, and there you come waltzing up the street, big as life. What was I supposed to do?"

"You could have looked *down* the street."

"Oh, sure, wink and let a jailbreaker run around loose, even if it's you." The sheriff shook his head in disgust. A mean little smile crept in after that expression. "Anyway, this Letty sounds like she isn't waiting for you, Harv old kid."

"We'll fetch up together, sooner or later," the big quiet man in cuffs vowed calmly, and jailbreaker notwithstanding, I found myself pulling for that to be true.

The sheriff sighed in exasperation. "You're being a fool for love, worst kind. Honest to God, Harv, if brains was talcum powder, you couldn't work up a sneeze."

Aware that my fascination with all this showed no sign of letting up, the sheriff tipped his hat back a fraction with his finger as if to have a clearer look at me. I had already noticed in life that shrimpy guys didn't like the idea of being shrimpy guys, and so they acted big. The sheriff still wasn't much bigger than I was when he fluffed himself up to ask suspiciously, "What about you, punkin, what's a little shaver like you doing on here by yourself? Where's your folks?"

"Me? I'm, uhm, I'm going to visit our relatives," which I hoped was just enough truth to close the topic.

His eye level the same as mine, this tough kernel of a man simply stared across the aisle at me. "Traveling on the cushions, huh? Pretty good for a kid your age. Where you from?"

"Gros Ventre," I said distinctly, as people from over east, which was most of the rest of Montana, sometimes didn't know it was pronounced *Grove On*.

"That's some ways from here. I didn't hear you say how come your folks turn you loose to—" The bus suddenly humming in a different gear, it dropped down in a dip and showed no sign of coming out, the road following the Missouri River now. The broad river flowing in long lazy curves with thickets of diamond willows and cottonwood trees lining the banks impressed me, but the sight seemed to turn the sheriff's stomach. Beside him, though, his handcuffed seat partner smiled like a crack in stone.

"There 'tis, Carl. What's left of the river, hmm?"

"Shut up, Harv, I don't need to hear about it." Sounding fit to be tied, the sheriff shot a look over to where I still was taking in everything wide-eyed, and growled, "We're just past Fort Peck Dam, the outlaw is talking about." His mouth twisted. "Franklin Delano Roosevelt didn't think the Missouri River worked good enough by itself, so he stuck in a king hell bastard of a dam," a new piece of cussing for me to tuck away.

"Biggest dirt dam in Creation." The sheriff was becoming really worked up now. "Biggest gyp of the American taxpayer there ever was, if you ask me." He scrunched up worse yet, squinting at the river as if the grievance still rubbing him raw was the water's fault.

"Every knothead looking for a nickel came and signed on for a job, and next thing I knew, I'm the law enforcement having to deal with a dozen Fort Peck shantytowns with bars and whorehouses that didn't shut down day or night."

"I know." I nodded sagely. "I'm from there."

That was a mistake. His apple-doll face turning sour, the sheriff spoke as if he had caught me red-handed. "You wouldn't be pulling my leg, would you?"

SO MUCH FOR the value of the unvarnished truth.

For it was absolute fact that I was born in one of those damsite shantytowns the sheriff despised. By then, 1939, the Fort Peck Dam work was winding down but there still was employment for skilled heavy equipment operators like my father, Bud Cameron, catskinner. Young and full of beans, he was one of those ambitious farmboys raring to switch from horses to horsepower, and he must have been something to see sitting up tall on the back of a bumblebee-yellow Caterpillar bulldozer, manipulating the scraper blade down to the last chosen inch of earth, on some raw slope of the immense dam.

I may as well tell the rest of the Cameron family story, what there is of it. My mother, teenage girl with soft eyes and fashionably bobbed dark hair according to the Brownie box camera photos from the time, was waitressing there at the damsite in an around-the-clock cafe where Gram was day cook. I imagine Gram met it with resignation when, much as her younger self Dorothea Smythe had met roustabout Pete Blegen in the cook tent of a Glacier Park road-work construction camp twenty years earlier, her daughter Peggy fell for the cocky young catskinner across the counter. Fell right into at least one of his capable arms, I can guarantee, because this live wire who became my father always had a necker knob, the gizmo that clamped onto the steering wheel for handy one-fisted driving, on every car he ever owned, from Model A to final Ford pickup.

Marriage came quick, and so did I. I had my footings poured, to use the Fort Peck term, in a thrown-together shacktown called Palookaville. Later, whenever we were living at some construction site or in another crude housing, my parents would think back to that time of a drafty tar paper shack between us and weather of sixty below, and say, "Well, it beats Palookaville anyway." Once the Fort Peck work shut down for good, we began a life of roving the watersheds along the Rockies. My father was six feet of restlessness and after the Depression there were irrigation and reservoir projects booming in practically every valley under the mountains, where a man who knew his stuff when it came to operating heavy equipment could readily find work. For her part, my mother learned bookkeeping, and jointly employable Bud and Peg Cameron moved from one construction camp to the next, with me in tow.

The war interrupted this pattern. In 1943 my father went in—enlisted or drafted, I have never known; it is one of the mysteries of him—and at Omaha Beach on D-Day he was badly shot up in the legs. He spent months in a hospital in England where surgeons put in rods and spliced portions of tendon from elsewhere in him into his knees and on down. Eventually he came home to my mother and me, at least to Fort Harrison hospital in Helena, where he advanced from casts to crutches to learning to walk again. Perhaps it says most about my father that he went right back to being a catskinner, even though you operate a bulldozer as much with your legs, working the brake pedals, as with your hands. Whatever it cost him in pain and endurance, Bud Cameron never veered from that chosen line of work, and in a way his stubborn climb from a cripple's life summed up our family situation, because we were always getting on our feet. Money was tight when earthmoving jobs shut down for the winter, and Montana winters are long. Hopping to whatever water project was first to hire skinners when the ground thawed, with me attending whatever one-room school happened to be anywhere around, my folks had hopes of moving up from wages to contracting projects on their own. They had managed to take out a loan on a Caterpillar D-10 dozer and were on their way to the Cat dealer in Great Falls to sign the final papers, when the drunk driver veered across the centerline on the Two Medicine hill.

If the big-hatted lawman poking his nose into my life asked about any of that, I was ready to tell him.

THE SHERIFF SNIFFED as if smelling something he didn't like after I protested that I really had been born at Fort Peck, honest.

"That's as maybe," he allowed, leaning toward me as if to get a better look. "Tell me something, laddie boy." His tone turned into something I did not like to hear. "You don't happen to be running away from home, do you?"

"No! The other way around! I mean, Gram and me got kicked out of the cookhouse and so we don't have anywhere, and she's sending me off to these people like I told you for someplace to go, honest!"

Characters in the funnies sometimes act out a situation to the fullest and whenever the *Just Trampin'* hobo PeeWee and his buddies encountered a sheriff like this, they squawked, "Yeeps! It's the constabulary!" and their hair stood on end. I can't prove the top of my head was a red pompadour reaching for the sky, but it felt that way as I faced the scowling little lawman across the aisle. I was as dumbfounded as I was scared. Could a person be arrested for riding a Greyhound bus? And if so, would my suitcase be searched? How could I explain the obviously precious black arrowhead to a sheriff already full of suspicion? *It's really mine, see, because I found it, but my grandmother made me hand it over to Sparrowhead and so I got it back when he wouldn't let me stay on the ranch and—* That sounded fishy even to me, let alone a skeptical law enforcement officer. Then and there, with that star badge full in my face, the consequences of my impulsive grab at the Double W went through me like a fever spasm.

Afflicted as I was by something I'd done without thinking, now I had to strain my brain for how to head off the inquisitive sheriff. The prisoner sent me a knowing look of sympathy that didn't help. Somehow I needed to dodge incrimination—the first step to getting back to Gros Ventre and turned over to the authorities, I was sure—by proving I actually was going to visit relatives like I'd said. "Here, see?" Frantically I dug out the autograph book from my jacket pocket and produced the slip of paper Gram had written the Wisconsin address on.

Still spooked to my eyeballs, I held my breath as the sheriff studied Gram's spidery handwriting.

"Hell if I know what people are thinking anymore, the things they do these days," he muttered as he kept squinting at the scrawl. Finally the evidence seemed to convince him, if reluctantly. Handing back the scrap of paper, he rasped, "It's still bad business, I say, turning a kid young as you loose in the world."

The prisoner Harv rumbled a laugh. "How old do you always say you were, when you set out on your own? Barely out of short pants, right?"

"Nobody asked you, Harvey," the sheriff snapped. His attention diverted from me, he folded his arms on his chest and shook his head at the lovelorn suitor in his custody and the dammed river that had saddled him with wide-open boomtowns, the things a lawman had to put up with.

Although I was still shaky from the close call, my impulse was to get back to an even footing as a legitimate Greyhound passenger if I possibly could. Screwing up my courage, I took a gamble. "Uh, sir?" I tried to keep the squeak out of my voice. "I've never had anything to do with a sheriff before, so how about signing my autograph book for me, please, will you, huh?"

That seemed to amuse him to no end. "Kind of a feisty squirt, hnn?" he cackled. "I can believe you was hatched at Fort Peck." In the next blink, though, habit or something set in and he made a face and pushed away the opened album I was trying to give him. "I don't have time for foolishness."

Harv came to my rescue. "Aw, come on, Carl. Don't you remember at all what it was like to be a kid?"

The sheriff shot him a look, but for once didn't snap "Shut up." Shifting uncomfortably, he muttered, "Oh hell, give the thing here." He took the album as if it might bite him, fumbled with the pen until I showed him how to click it, then bent his head and wrote.

Like they say at Fort Peck, keep your pecker dry
Carl Kinnick, Sheriff,
Hill County, Montana

"Gee, that's a good one," I managed to more or less thank him. "Can I get his, too?"

The sheriff laughed meanly. "What do you say to that, Harv? I bet you're not used to writing your John Hancock except to bounce checks." Entertained, he passed the autograph book to the handcuffed prisoner.

With great concentration, the arrested man went to work at writing. It took him a long time, even considering the contorted way he had to hold the pen and book. "What in hell-all are you writing, the Bible?" the sheriff derided.

Finally the prisoner thrust his manacled hands across to give me the finished product, only to have it intercepted, the sheriff growling, "Not so fast. Let me see that."

Reading it with a pinched look, the sheriff at first couldn't seem to believe his eyes, saying to himself, "Huh. Huh." Finishing, he burst out: "Harv, you're hopeless! That's schoolhouse mush if I ever saw any."

Unperturbed, Harv stated, "Letty is worth every word of it."

Sourly the sheriff passed the opened album for me to take in the painstakingly shaped words.

Holy wow, I thought to myself, that pretty well described Letty, except for the pink stitching.

The sheriff was still expressing disgust with his prisoner. "Where'd you pick up that list of schoolkid stuff, loverboy?"

"Belowdecks on a troop carrier headed for the Guam invasion," Harv countered, with a level gaze at his captor.

Somewhere amid their back-and-forth and my thrilled admiration of his construction on the page, I finally fully took in the signature beneath.

Harvey Kinnick, serving time in this life.

I blurted, "Y-you've got the same last name?"

"We're brothers," the prisoner specified. "Aren't we, Carl."

The sheriff folded his arms on his chest in practically a pout. "*Step*-brothers."

5.

THE PAIR of them got off at Wolf Point, a town so scrimpy it was no surprise that it could not hold Harv the jailbreaker. "Don't do anything I wouldn't do, button," the sheriff left me with. I thought to myself, as I have ever since, that left a large margin for error, given the behavior of certain adults.

Wolf Point seemed to be the cutoff between what is generally thought of as Montana and the notion of North Dakota, farms sprinkled across a big square of land. By now passengers had dwindled drastically—there wasn't much of anywhere to pick someone up until the supper stop at Williston, a couple of hours away—and I managed to gather only the autographs and inscriptions of a Rural Electrification troubleshooter and two elderly Dakota couples retired from wheat farming and moved to town, so much alike right down to the crow's-feet wrinkles of their prairie squints that they could have been twins married to twins. Maybe inspiration flattens out along with the countryside, because they all tended to come up with sentiments along the lines of *Remember me early, remember me late, remember me at the Golden Gate.* But every page filled went toward my goal of a world-famous collection.

At the Williston depot, for once the driver beat me in getting off, handing over the paperwork to the next driver at the bottom of the bus steps. As I scooted for the restroom, I overheard him say to the new man, "Carrying a stray," and the response, "I'll keep an eye on him."

That exchange made my guts tighten. Was that what I was, a stray? Like a motherless calf? That was not the kind of fame I wanted, and unfair besides. I had Gram yet, and like it or not, the unknown great-aunt and -uncle ahead in Wisconsin. It was only between here and there that I was unclaimed, I tried telling myself.

But I was further unsettled when the lunchroom's supper offerings did not include chicken-fried steak or anything remotely like it, only stuff such as macaroni and cheese or meatloaf that wasn't any kind of a treat, anytime. In direct violation of Gram's orders, feeling guilty but fed, I had a chocolate milkshake and a piece of cherry pie, à la mode. Maybe Minnesota, on tomorrow's stretch of the trip, would feed better.

The bus added a dozen or so passengers in Williston, but I was too played out by the full day to go up and down the aisle with the autograph book. Instead, I settled in for the night, which took a long time coming in horizontal North Dakota. First thing, making sure no one was watching, I took out my wallet and put it down the front of my pants, another of Gram's strict orders. It felt funny there in my shorts, but nobody was going to get it while I slept. Then I remembered the Green Stamps, of inestimable or at least unknown worth, and stuck those down there to safety, too.

Bundling my jacket for a pillow, I made myself as close to comfortable as I could and thought back on the day while waiting for sleep to come. Oh man, was Gram ever right that the dog bus gets all kinds. The soldiers going to meet their fate in Korea. The nun and the sheepherder, both of whom I had miraculously escaped. That hibernating Indian. Heavenly Letty. The cantankerous little sheriff and his gallant prisoner. And that didn't even count the digestive woman back at the start of the trip. They all filled in the dizzying span of my thoughts like a private version of *Believe It or Not!* And wherever life took them from here on, most of them had left a bit of their existence in my memory book. A condensed chapter of themselves, maybe, to put it in Pleasantville terms. I had much to digest, in more ways than one, as I lay back in the seat.

WITH THE SUN glinting in the panel window my jacket pillow was crammed against, I woke up confused about where I was. Blinking and squinting, I wrestled myself upright until it all began to become familiar, the ranks of seats around me, some with heads showing and some not, the road hum of the bus tires, the countryside—greener than it had been the day before—flying past at a steady clip.

"Uh, sir?" I called to the latest driver, still foggy. "Where are we?"

"Minnie Soda," he responded in a mock accent. "Meal stop coming up in Bemidji."

What language was that? Actually, my stomach didn't care. It was ready for one of Gram's prescriptions that I could obey to the letter—stuff myself with a big breakfast.

HE MUST HAVE singled me out there by myself at a side table as I wolfed down bacon and eggs and hotcakes. The man in the ill-fitting suit, who has haunted me to this day.

As misfortune would have it, my classy western shirt caught a dribble of maple syrup from a forkful of hotcake, and stayed sticky no matter how I wiped at it. Not wanting to draw flies for the rest of the trip, I checked around the depot for the bus driver and spotted him in conversation with the ticket agent. Finishing off my breakfast as fast as I could, I scurried over to ask if I could please have my suitcase long enough to change shirts. That drew me a look, evidently my reputation among bus drivers as a stray not helping any, but he took pity on me and out we went to the luggage compartment. "Better hurry, freckles, I have to keep to the schedule," he warned as I hustled to the restroom with the suitcase.

In there, a lathered guy was shaving over a sink and a couple of others were washing up, and there was what I thought was only the usual traffic to the toilet stalls, so I didn't feel too much out of place opening the wicker suitcase on the washbasin counter and stripping off my snap-button shirt and whipping on a plain one. Tucking the syruped shirt away in the suitcase, I did the same with the batch of Green Stamps, a nuisance to carry around. Then I had to dash for the bus, but the driver was waiting patiently by the luggage compartment, and I wasn't even the last passenger. Behind me was the man, who must have been in a toilet stall while I was busy at my suitcase.

I deposited myself in my same seat, feeling restored and ready for whatever the day brought. I thought.

"Hello there, cowboy. Mind some company?" The man, whom I had not really been aware of until right then, paused beside the aisle seat next to me, looking around as if I were the prize among the assortment of passengers.

"I guess not." For a moment I was surprised, but then realized he must have noticed my bronc rider shirt, as Gram called it, before I changed. He appeared to be good enough company himself, smiling as if we shared a joke about something, even though he did remind me a little of Wendell Williamson in the way he more than filled his clothes. Wearing a violet tie and pigeon-gray suit—I figured he must have put on weight since buying it and I sympathized, always outgrowing clothes myself—he evidently was fresh from the barbershop, with a haircut that all but shined. Easing into the seat next to mine, he settled back casually as the bus pulled out and did not say anything until we left Bemidji behind and were freewheeling toward Minneapolis, some hours away. But then it started.

Crossing his arms on his chest with a tired exhalation, he tipped his head my direction. "Man alive, I'll be glad to get home. How about you?"

"Me, too," I answered generally, for I would be glad beyond measure to have Wisconsin over and done with, and the return part of my round-trip ticket delivering me back to Gram and whatever home turned out to be, if that could only happen.

"Life on the road. Not for sissies." He shook his head, with that smile as if we both got the joke. "You're starting pretty young, to be a traveler."

"Twelve going on thirteen," I stretched things a little, and for once my voice didn't break.

He maybe showed a tic of doubt at that, but didn't question it. Himself, he was going gray, matching the tight-fitting suit. He had a broad, good-natured face, like those cartoons of the man in the moon, although, as Gram would have said, he must have kept it in the pantry; his complexion was sort of doughy, as if he needed to be outdoors more. "I'm all admiration," he said with that confiding shake of his head. "Me, I'm on the go all the time for a living, and anybody who can do it for pleasure gets my vote."

I must have given him a funny look, although I tried not to. The only thing about my trip that had anything to do with pleasure was phony Pleasantville, so I steered the conversation back to him. "What do you do to keep the sheriff away?"

"Eh?" He glanced at me as if I'd jabbed him in the ribs.

"See, that's what my father always says when he wants to know what a person does for a living."

"Sure, sure," he laughed. Gazing around as if to make sure no one heard but me, even though I couldn't see anyone paying any attention to us—the driver in particular had no time to eye us in the rearview mirror, Minnesota crawling with traffic in comparison with North

Dakota—he lowered his voice as if letting me in on a secret. "I sell headbolt heaters, the Minnesota key chain. Bet you don't know what those are."

I thrust out my hand so quickly to take the bet he batted his eyes in surprise. "You take a bolt out of the engine block and stick the headbolt thinger in there and plug it in all night and you can start your car when it's colder than a brass monkey's balls," I couldn't help showing off and getting in some cussing practice.

"You're something else, aren't you." He tugged at his tie as he appraised me. "Where've you been anyway, donkey school?"

Mystified, I furrowed a look at him.

"You know, where they teach you to be a wiseass?" He nudged me, smiling like a good fellow to show he was just kidding.

"Oh man, that's a good one," I exclaimed, wishing I had it in the autograph book. If only the sleeping Indian had been this talkative! Taken with the back-and-forth, I said in the spirit of things, "I skipped wiseass school, see, for a dude ranch. Out west."

"That so?" Still with a sort of a grin, he prodded: "Saddled up Old Paint, did you, to go with that cowboy shirt I saw?"

The idea seemed to entertain him, so I expanded it for him. "Sure thing. I won it in the roping contest. That and the jackpot." I was having so much fun, I threw that in as if it were prize money in a regular rodeo; Gram had been teasing about people thinking I was a bronc rider, but twirling a lasso didn't seem beyond me. I built it up a touch more: "The other dudes couldn't build a loop worth diddly-squat, so yeah, I hit the jackpot." I couldn't help grinning at the slick double meaning. Carried away even further, I confided, "And there was another prize, too, even better."

"You don't say. The grand prize to boot?" he said in a kidding voice, although I could tell he was impressed.

To keep him that way, it was on the tip of my tongue to airily say the prize was nothing less than an arrowhead blacker than anything and older than Columbus. But something made me hold that in, for the time being. Instead I resorted to:

"You pretty close to guessed it. Beaded moccasins."

"Indian booties?" That had him eyeing me as if to make sure I was on the level. "How are those any big deal?"

"They were made a long time ago for the best Blackfoot fancy-dancer there ever was, that's how." I didn't need to fumble for a name. "Red Chief, he was called." My enthusiasm built with every detail that flashed to mind. "See, when there was this big powwow about to happen with Indians coming from everywhere, the tribe gathered all its beads on a blanket, and the best moccasin maker chose the prettiest ones and spent day and night sewing the design." Expert of a kind that I was from donning the soft leather slippers for so many middle-of-the-night calls of nature, I lovingly described their blue and white prancing figures that seemed to lighten a person's step, like wearing kid gloves on the feet.

"They're real beauties," I assured my blinking listener, "and when the guy, Red Chief I mean, put them on for the fancy-dancing contest against all the other tribes, he won everything. And so, after that the moccasins were called 'big medicine'—that's Indian for 'magic,' see—and nobody else in the tribe could even touch them but that one fancy-dancer.

"When he got old and died, though"—my tone hushed just enough to draw my audience of one in closer—"the tribe was going to sell them to a museum back east, but the dude ranch owner heard about it and traded a bunch of horses to the Blackfeet for them." For all I knew, this part approached the truth. Admittedly in very roundabout fashion, but the fact was that my grandmother, the sharp-trading fry cook there in the reservation town of Browning, had bargained someone out of the impressive moccasins somehow.

I had to really reach for the next portion, but I got there. "When the dude rancher tried them on, they had shrunk up real bad and didn't fit him, so he made them the grand prize for the roping contest. They're just right for me," I finished modestly.

My seatmate's jaw kept dropping until I reached the end, then as if coming to, he studied my feet. "I'm surprised you don't have them on, show them off some."

"Uh-uh, they're way too valuable," I fielded that, "I have to keep them tucked away in my suitcase. I'll only wear them at home, around the house."

"A fortune on your tootsies, huh? I tell you, some guys have all the luck."

Good-natured about it, though, he drew back as if to make room for his admiration of me, topping it off with "Look at you, just getting started in life and you've got it knocked," and I went still as death.

HOW CAN A WORD, a saying, do that? Make your skin prickle, as memory comes to the surface?

Innocent as it sounded, the utterance from this complete stranger echoed in me until my ears rang. Gram was more used to this sort of thing, the sound of someone speaking from past the grave. Past a white cross on the side of Highway 89, in this instance. How many times had I heard it, waiting with my mother in a kitchen table card game of pitch or a round of dominoes or some such while my father scouted for work, for the next construction camp that needed a hot-shot catskinner, and in he would come at last, smiling like the spring sun as he reported, "They're hiring at Tiber Dam," or the Greenfield irrigation project it might be, or the reservoirs capturing creeks out of the Rockies, Rainbow and Pishkun and those. Each time his voice making the words wink that certain way: "We've got it knocked." Wherever it came from—World War Two? the Depression?—for me the expression indeed meant something solid we were about to tap into, wages for my folks after a lean winter and a firmer place to live than wherever we had fetched up when the ground froze hard enough to resist a bulldozer blade. It entered me deeper than mere words generally go, as Gram's sayings did with her, to the point where I perfectly well knew, even though I wasn't there, that starting out on that trip to take possession of the bulldozer that would set them—us—up in life for once and for all, Bud Cameron and his wife Peg declared in one voice or the other that they had it knocked. Until they didn't.

BRISKLY MY TEMPORARY companion prodded me out of the spell, tugging at his suit cuffs as he asked, "Where's home that you're gonna parade around in those fancy moccasins?"

"Chicago." The rest came to me from somewhere, natural as drawing breath. "My father's a policeman there."

"You don't say," he said again, with a couple of blinks as if he had something in his eye. "A harness bull, is he?"

"Huh?"

"You know, a cop on the beat?"

"Huh-uh. Detective. He solves murders."

He studied me as if really sizing me up now. "That what you're going to be? A flatfoot?" He winked to signal we both knew the lingo, didn't we.

"Nope. A rodeo announcer. 'Now coming out of chute four, Rags Rasmussen, saddle bronc champeen of the world, on a steed called Bombs Away,'" I gave him a rapid-fire sample. My parents never missed a Gros Ventre rodeo, and given all the hours I had sat through bareback and saddle bronc riding, the announcer's microphone spiel was virtually second nature to me.

"Whew." My seatmate gave that little shake of his head again as if I were really something. "Whatever it is, you seem to know the ropes."

If I knew any, it was that it was time to quit fooling around. He wasn't as good at making up things as I was, whatever that was about. Maybe he was embarrassed about being a headbolt heater salesman and not able to afford to dress better than he did. In any case, I didn't have time for bulloney from him, I needed to get going with the autograph book. In several seats not far behind us was a group of women all wearing hats with various floral designs, and from what I was able to overhear of their chatter they were a garden club who called themselves the Gardenias, and were out for fun, which seemed to consist of staying at a lakeside lodge with a flower garden. I didn't want to miss out on the bunch of them, so I produced the album to deal with my seatmate first and then scoot down the aisle to those hats bursting with blossoms.

He registered surprise at seeing the book open to an inviting page, and the Kwik-Klik seemed to throw him, too. "Tell you what, maybe later." He wiggled his hand as if it needed warming up.

"Okay, then. Let me past, please."

"Hey, don't rush off," he protested, showing no sign of moving. "How often do I get to visit with a jackpot roper?" he said with a palsy-walsy smile.

"Yeah, but—" I explained what a golden chance the bus was for building up my collection and the only way to do it was, well, to get out there in the aisle and do it. I made ready to squeeze by him, but he still hadn't budged and he was as much of a blockade to try to climb over as the plump Indian.

I don't know what would have happened if the bus hadn't started slowing way down, for a reason that caught me by surprise. And one that made him change his mind in an instant about keeping me for company.

"What do you know, here's my stop." He craned to look ahead through the windshield. "Lost track of the time."

I dropped back in my seat, stretching my neck to see, too. We were pulling in to what looked like an old mercantile store with a gas pump out front and a faded sign under the Mobil flying red horse, LAKE ITASCA GARAGE—FUEL, FOOD, AND FISH BAIT. Half the building appeared to be the post office and a little grocery shop. The rest of the crossroads settlement was three white-painted churches, a bar calling itself a tavern, a small cafe, and a scattering of houses. It looked to me like a neatened-up Palookaville. And the driver was announcing this was only a drop stop, as soon as the passengers getting off had their luggage we'd be on our way.

Although we were nearest the door, my companion in conversation was super polite in waiting for the garden club to file off first, before winking me a good-bye along with "Say hi to Chi," which it took me a moment to translate as Chicago, and then launching himself to the bus door as if he had to get busy.

In his wake, I gazed out the window at the sparse buildings, idly thinking Minnesotans must be a whole lot more foresighted than Montanans, who waited to rush out and buy headbolt heaters when the first real snow came, around Thanksgiving. I felt sorry for the man in the suit, disappointing company though he'd turned into there toward the end, for having to slog around all summer dealing with places like this rundown garage, which looked all but dead. And besides the size of suitcase that would take, he must have to lug round a—what was it called?—sample case, although I hadn't noticed any when my own suitcase was put back in the belly of the bus at Bemidji.

All at once the awful fact hit me. I grabbed my shirt pocket to make sure. When I changed out of the pearl-button shirt, I hadn't thought to unpin the folded ten-dollar bills in back of its pocket and secure them in the fresh shirt I was wearing. Except for loose change in my pants to use for meals, all my money now resided in my suitcase. Gram would have skinned me alive if she knew I'd let myself get separated from my stash.

Feeling like a complete moron, I charged out the door of the bus.

The Gardenias were in a clump while the driver sorted out their bags as they pointed in the compartment. I had to skirt around them to where I knew mine was, and was startled to see the broad back of a familiar suit. The man had ducked behind the driver and was grabbing for the only wicker piece of luggage.

"He's after my suitcase!" I shrieked. A cry that carried with it moccasins, arrowhead, money, clothing, my entire trip, everything I foolishly was about to lose.

At my hollering like that, the flowery hats scattered far and wide, but the driver bravely spun right around and clamped the sneak's wrist before he could bolt. Wresting my suitcase from the thief, he roughly backed him against the side of the bus.

"Yardbird on the wing, are you," the driver sized him up with distaste while pinning him there below the racing silver greyhound. "Suit from the warden and all. How'd you like the accommodations in the pen?"

The penitentiary! Really? I goggled at the ex-convict, or maybe not-so-ex. Trying to display some shred of dignity, he maintained in a hurt voice, "Paid my debt to society. I'm a free man."

"Swell," the driver retorted, "so you go right back to swiping things like a kid's suitcase."

"Just a misunderstanding, is all," the captured culprit whined. "I thought the youngster was getting off here, and I was going to help him with his luggage."

"Sure you were." The driver turned his head toward me as the Gardenia group clucked in the background. "What do you say, champ, you want to press charges? Attempted robbery?"

How I wished for that half-pint sheriff in the big hat right then. This Lake Itasca place, not much more than a wide spot in the road, didn't look like it had any such. I could tell that the driver was antsy about the delay it would take to deal with the criminal, and come right down to it, I did not want my trip, complicated enough as it was, to be hung up that way, either.

"Naw, let him go," I said, sick of it all. When the driver turned the thieving so-and-so loose—my swearing vocabulary wasn't up to the description he deserved—he swaggered off in the direction of the cafe, adjusting his suit, careful not to look back. The garden club ladies fussed over me, but I only looked at the bus driver with a long sigh. "Can I get something out of my suitcase again?"

6.

"PAINT IT RED" was my father's backhand way of saying "Forget it," and I did my best to follow that advice after the close call with the jailbird. But it was the sort of thing you can't blot out in your mind by saying so. Even after I hurriedly fixed the money matter by retrieving the stash from the shirt in the suitcase and pinning it under the pocket of the one I was wearing, there was no covering over the fact that I had nearly lost just about everything I owned—the precious autograph book excepted, thank goodness—by my bragging. *That'll teach you, Red Chief,* I mentally kicked myself, and for the rest of that morning on the ride down to Minneapolis I kept to my seat and watched the other passengers out of the corner of my eye lest I be invaded by some other wrongdoer.

Luckily that did not happen, the bus inhabitants minding their manners and leaving me alone—maybe I was painted red to them—and around noon my attention was taken up by the way the Greyhound little by little was navigating streets where the buildings grew taller and taller. We were now in the big half of the Twin Cities, according to the driver's good-natured announcement, and whatever the other place was like, everything about Minneapolis was more than sizable as I perched on the edge of my seat peering out at it all. The first metropolis—it puffed itself up to that by stealing half the word, didn't it—of my life.

Wide as my eyes were at the sights and scenes, it was hard to take it all in. Even the department store windows showing off the latest fashions seemed to dwarf those in, say, Great Falls. Likewise, the sidewalks were filled with throngs that would not have fit on the streets back in Montana. People, people everywhere, as traffic increasingly swarmed around us, the tops of cars turtling along below the bus windows barely faster than the walking multitudes.

As the Greyhound crept from stoplight to stoplight, I couldn't help gawking at so many passersby in suits and snappy hats and good dresses on an ordinary day, each face another world of mystery to me. Where were they going, what drew them out dressed to the gills like promenaders in an Easter parade? Where did they live, in the concrete buildings that seemed to go halfway to the sky or in pleasant homes hidden away somewhere? I wished this was Wisconsin so I could start to have answers to such things, all the while knowing I was many miles yet from any kind of enlightenment.

When we at last pulled in to the block-long driveway of the terminal, with numerous buses parked neatly side by side as if the silver dogs were lined up to start a race, the driver called out that routine I knew by heart now, lunch stop, conveniences, and so on. Minneapolis, however, was his changeover spot, so he got off ahead of the rest of us, but the relief driver was not there yet, and when I reached the bottom of the steps, the departing driver gave me a little salute and said with a serious smile, "Take care of yourself, son."

Son. My chest was out, I'm sure, as I charged through the double doors of the bus station. I knew the driver had only said it because we were inadvertent buddies after dealing with the larcenous man in the suit, but no one had called me that for the past two years.

In high spirits, I gazed around the teeming depot to scout matters out. The slick-looking blue building, when we'd pulled up to it, took up most of the block, with a rounded entrance on the corner where three fleet greyhounds the same as on the bus seemed to be in an everlasting chase after one another around the top of the building. But more impressive to me was an actual restaurant, just like you'd find on a street, tucked inside the majestic terminal, with a full menu posted. It hooked me at first sight; all due apology to Gram and her decree of a sandwich for lunch, my stomach was only interested in a real meal. Hadn't I been through a lot since Bemidji, coping with the danger of being robbed blind? That kind of narrow escape was bound to cause an appetite, right? Besides, I still was carrying loose change wanting to be spent.

Anyway, feeling highly swayve and debonure out on my own in grown-up territory, I found a table where I could see the big clock over the ticket counter—most of an hour yet until the bus was to leave, but I wasn't taking any chances—and was served Swiss steak by a pleasant waitress, although I didn't know what she was called because it wasn't written on her breast. To me in my grand mood, only one name in pink stitching deserved such prominence anyway.

LETICIA. Moonily I daydreamed again, imagining that when I was done with that summer of living out of a wicker suitcase, Gram would meet me at the Greyhound station in Great Falls, healed up and feisty as ever, telling me, guess what, she had the old job as fry cook at the top spot in Gros Ventre. And guess what again, Letty was waitress on the same shift. Havre didn't work out, I was not surprised to hear. And sure enough, there Letty was from then on, red-lipsticked and sassy as she dealt out the meals Gram made appear in the kitchen's ready window, sneaking a cigarette whenever the counter wasn't busy, and boldly taking up where she left off with Harv the trucker. With his jailbreaking past and mean sheriff brother behind him, and regular as the days of the week in courting Letty—who wouldn't be, linked up with the world's best kisser?—he was my great companion as well. To top off this dreamlike turn of life, I took all my meals there at the cafe, with Gram dishing up chicken-fried steak whenever I wished and Letty giving me a wink and asking, "Getting enough to eat, sonny boy?"

"I SAID, are you getting enough to eat, sonny boy?"

I came to with a start, the Minneapolis waitress puncturing that vision as she started to clear away my empty plate. "Fine, yeah, I'm full as can be," I mumbled my manners as real life set in again, the public-address system announcing departures and arrivals the same as ever.

Rousing myself with still plenty of time until I needed to be back at the bus, I left a dime tip as I had seen the person at the next table do, and roamed out into the busy waiting area, where I was naturally drawn to the news and candy stand.

The stand was piled on all sides with newspapers and magazines, a dozen times more than the Gros Ventre drugstore had to offer, and after buying a Mounds that I justified as dessert I circled around, investigating who was famous just then. On cover after cover was someone smiling big, although not President Truman, who seemed to be having trouble with a Wisconsin senator named McCarthy, according to *Time* and *Newsweek*. Of the others pictured, though, biggest of all in every way was the well-known face of the impressively hefty singer Kate Smith on the oversize cover of *Life*, which identified her as AMERICA'S FAVORITE SONGSTRESS—BLESSED WITH A VOICE LIKE NO OTHER. If a voice like no other meant singing "God Bless America" over and over until it stuck in the head of everyone in the country, she sure had that, all right. Giving her the admiring look of someone who, as Gram would have said, couldn't carry a tune in a bucket, I passed on to a whole section of the newsstand populated by movie stars—Elizabeth Taylor again, and Ava Gardner and Gary Cooper and Robert Taylor and a good many I had never heard of, but they were clearly famous. How I envied every gleaming one of them.

. . .

PERHAPS IT GOES without saying that my fame fever was a product of imagination, but there was greatly more to it than that. Call me a dreamer red in the head back then, but becoming famous looked to me like a way out of a life haunted by county poorfarm and orphanage the other side of the mountains. A change of luck sort of like winning a real jackpot, in other words. Wouldn't we all take some of that, at eleven going on twelve or any other age? The missing detail, that I had no fixed notion of what I might best be famous at—the talent matter—other than a world-record autograph collection, maybe even constituted an advantage, giving me more chances, as I saw it.

I became more engrossed in the faces of fame than I knew. When I remembered to check the clock, I looked twice, the second time in shock. The hour was up, the bus would be leaving in less than a minute.

I ran as hard as a frantic human being can with a depot full of travelers in the way as I raced for the departure gate.

But too late. By the time I scrambled through the maze of passengers lined up out in the loading bays for other buses, I could see mine rumbling onto the street and pulling away.

I stopped dead, which right then I might as well have been. There I was, in a strange city, with only the clothes on my back, while my every other possession—including the slip of paper with Aunt Kitty and Uncle Dutch's address and phone number tucked into the autograph book in my coat pocket left on my seat—sped away in a cloud of exhaust. Helpless is pretty close to hopeless, and right then I felt both. For the second time that rugged day, eleven years old seemed much too young to be facing the world all by myself.

Too overcome even to cuss, I was only dimly aware of the thickset man, who'd been dropping bundles of newspapers off at the stand while I still was deep in the magazines, now wheeling an empty hand truck out to his van, whistling carelessly as he came. "'Scuse, please, comin' through," he made to get past me on the walkway, but halted when he had a look at my face. "Whasamatter? You sick? Gonna throw up, better get over to the gutter."

"I missed my bus," I babbled, "it left without me and my suitcase is on it and my jacket and autograph book and moccasins and—"

"Them puppy bus dickheads," he said with disgust. "At's about like them. Which way you goin'?"

"W-W-Wisconsin."

He waved me toward the green van with TWIN CITIES NEWS AGENCY on its side as he trundled the hand truck over and heaved it in with a clatter. "Hop in, kiddo."

"Are you gonna take me there? To Wisconsin?"

"Naw, can't quite do that." He gestured so urgently I jumped in the open-sided van. "C'mon, we'll catch 'em in Saint Paul."

"Is it very far?"

He gave me a look as if I was mentally lacking. "They don't call these the Twin Cities for nothin'." Crouched over the steering wheel and shifting gears fast and furious, he goosed the van out into the street traffic, blaring the horn at anything in our way. I hung on to one of the newspaper bin dividers behind him as we went clipping past the big buildings and fancy stores at daredevil speed.

"Don't that beat all," my Samaritan kept up a one-sided conversation as he willy-nilly changed lanes and ran stoplights on the blink between green and red. "Pullin' out without even lookin' around for you any. What kind of bus drivin' is that?" He shook his head at the state of Greyhound affairs. "Dickheads," he repeated.

I held my breath as we swerved around a yellow taxicab and zoomed through an intersection with a few warning honks of the horn. When I could speak, I felt compelled to stick up for the earlier bus driver who had saved my skin at Lake Itasca. "They aren't all like that, honest."

"Hah. You don't know the half of it."

Before I could ask about the half I was missing, I was distracted by the high bridge we were atop without warning, over a river that seemed to go on and on. Which is basically what the Mississippi does. As the van rumbled across the seemingly endless bridge and the chasm below, I kept my death grip on the divider and leaned down to speak into my escort's ear. "So how come you think they're all"—I tried out the new word—"dickheads?"

"They ain't union." He pointed to an encased certificate up by the visor. By squinting, I at least could read the large type, INTERNATIONAL BROTHERHOOD OF TEAMSTERS.

At last, something I knew about! "Horses!" I burst out as a hayfield teamster, if only anyone would let me. "You drive those, too?"

He cast me a grin over his shoulder. "In the old days, every Teamster did, you bet your pucker string they did."

"Me, too! I mean, I know how to harness up and drive a team and everything. See, I wouldn't be here at all if Sparrowhead back at the ranch in Montana had let me drive the stacker team like I know I can and—"

"Life's tough, ain't it?" He held up a hand as if letting the air rush through his fingers. "Feel better? We're in Saint Paul."

"Really?" It looked the same as Minneapolis to me, the Identical Twin Cities evidently. The van kept up its rapid clip, the rush of wind through the open side making my eyes water. I had to hope my fellow teamster could see all right, as we were cutting in and out of lanes of traffic by the barest of space between us and other vehicles. "Smooth move!" I let out like one race driver complimenting another when he skimmed us around a double-parked delivery truck by inches and blazed on through a changing traffic light. "Nothin' to it," he claimed, flooring the gas pedal in a race to beat the next light. "You just gotta keep on the go.

"Lemme think now," I heard him calculate as we wove our way

through downtown traffic, the street checkered with shadows thrown by the high buildings. "When we reach the station, you be ready to jump off and tell that doggy driver you belong on the bus, 'kay?"

"S-s-sure," I said uncertainly. I didn't have time to worry about how I would do at that, because ahead in blinking neon was a towering sign that read from top to bottom, GREYHOUND.

"Goddamn-it-to-hell-anyway," the teamster addressed the unwavering red light that held us up at the cross street. On the other side, so near and yet so far, the St. Paul terminal, which was fancied up with plaster-like decorations of fruit and flowers, appeared to be older and smaller than the Minneapolis one and must not have dealt in as many passengers, because fewer buses with the racing dog on the side were backed into the loading area in the open-arched driveway. I had eyes only for one, with MILWAUKEE in the roller sign above the windshield, and I spotted it immediately, its door cruelly folding closed as if shutting me out.

"There it is! It's leaving again!"

"That's what he thinks, the dickhead." The newspaper van revved and so did the teamster, bouncing slightly in his seat, as the stoplight took agonizingly long to change.

The instant it did, we shot across the street and along the arches of the terminal driveway, directly toward the warning sign at the far end, reading in red letters of descending order EXIT WRONG WAY DO NOT ENTER.

"Hang on!" shouted the teamster, and whipped the van around the curb into the exitway, jamming us to a halt, nose to nose with the bus.

By reflex, the wide-eyed driver of the bus had hit the brakes, and even more so the horn. "Here you go, kiddo. Have a nice trip," said my Good Samaritan daredevil at the wheel, giving the Greyhound driver the finger. In the blare resounding in the arched driveway, I could barely be heard thanking the van-driving teamster as I leaped out and he gave me a little bye-bye wave.

Peering down at me through the broad windshield, his eyebrows dark as thunderclouds, the bus driver at last let up on the deafening horn as I edged through the slit of space between the facing vehicles and popped out at the bus door. With faces watching curiously in every window above the ever-running streamlined dog, I wildly pantomimed that I needed in, until the driver, keeping his hand dubiously on the door lever, cracked things open enough that I could make myself heard.

"You left me! In Minnesota, I mean Minneapolis. My jacket was holding my seat like always, see, but I stayed in the bus station a minute too long and when I ran to where the bus was, it wasn't there and—"

"That's yours?" Looking more upset than ever, the driver fished my jacket from behind his seat. "You should have kept better track of it, junior. I didn't see it in time or I'd have turned it in back there before we started."

As I gulped at one more near miss, he pointed a further accusing finger at me. "And technically, if a passenger misses the bus, it's his own tough luck." I was so afraid of exactly that, I couldn't form words. "It says right in the regulations," he kept on reading me the dog bus version of the riot act, "it is the passenger's responsibility to—"

Just then a sharp blast of horn from the van made him jerk his head around, glowering back and forth from me to the motionless teamster, unbudging as a bulldog.

In exasperation, he yanked the bus door open. "Okay, okay, step on and show me your ticket."

7.

TO MY INTENSE RELIEF, I found the autograph book safe and sound in the jacket and simply huddled in my seat with an arm wrapped around them both as if they might get away again, until the bus finally trundled out of the last of St. Paul and its troublesome twin and the tires were making the highway humming sound. Naturally the other passengers had gawked for all they were worth as I scrambled aboard and ducked into the first vacant set of seats—where I was sitting before was occupied by a mother with a fussy baby, I saw with a pang—so I wouldn't be pestered by a seatmate about the whole experience. From the tone of remarks that followed my adventurous arrival, I could tell that my fellow riders were divided between thinking I was lucky beyond belief in catching up with the bus the way I had or a menace to society for missing it in the first place. I wasn't going to argue with either point of view. And until dog bus life settled down a great deal more, I would stay quiet and still and have nothing to do with anybody.

I reckoned without the elderly couple across the aisle from me.

"Tsk," first I heard the woman. "It just makes me want to take and shake him. Imagine doing what he did."

"Dang right. Must have been a star pupil in fool school, is all I can think," her husband pitched in.

From the corner of my eye, I apprehensively studied the couple, way up there in years, clucking their tongues about me now. Both of them were short and sparely built, like a matched pair that had shrunk over time. Actually the woman reminded me of Gram, even to the skinny wire eyeglasses emerging from the cloud of gray hair bunched in no particular identifiable hairdo. She had on what looked like a churchgoing dress, the darkest blue there is with touches of white trim and what resembled a really valuable carved ivory rose brooch, which she wore with about the same authority as the Glasgow sheriff did his badge. Her husband also was dressed in Sunday best, a baggy brown suit and wide green tie with watermelon stripes. Bald and small-headed and with his skinny glasses perched on the knobby end that old noses sometimes form into, he didn't look like much, a druggist or something. But when he leaned forward to scrutinize me further through the tops of his glasses, I glimpsed the hat line where his forehead turned from suntanned to pearly pale. Ranchers and farmers had that mark of lifelong weathering, and I didn't know any others who did. This added another hayload to my mortification. People who ought to have recognized me for what I was, if I only had been wearing my rodeo shirt instead of slopping syrup on it, were against me. My best hope was that the *tsk tsk*ing pair of old busybodies was getting off at the next stop, and it couldn't come too soon.

"I tell you, a soul can't simply sit by after seeing that without saying something," the woman was definitely saying, in that hen-yard voice. "It runs contrary to common decency."

"You're right as rain," her husband vigorously bobbed endorsement to that. "Speak your piece, it's entirely called for in this dang kind of a situation."

With that, here she came across the aisle as if catapulted out of her seat, landing right next to me while I cringed back to the window.

"We want to let you know"—she leaned right in so close on me I could smell Sen-Sen on her breath—"we think it was downright awful of the fool up there in the driver's seat to go off and leave you like that."

I sat up like a gopher popping out of its hole. "Really? You do?"

"Bet your britches we do," the man chipped in, sliding over into her seat on the aisle and sticking his head turtle-like across toward us. "It was uncalled for, that dang kind of behavior when it's up to him to be on the lookout for his passengers, is what I say."

I barely resisted contributing "Well, yeah, he's a dickhead," but condemnation of the guilty party humped over the steering wheel seemed to be going along just fine with *dang*s. All of a sudden, the dog bus was the top of my world again, given these unexpected backers. Fortunately, the three of us were far enough from the driver that he couldn't make out what we were saying about him, although he was watching us plenty in the rearview mirror, looking sore that the commotion back and forth across the aisle plainly involved me one more time.

IN THE BURST of introductions, they made themselves known to me as Mae and Joe Schneider, and I recited by heart Donal without a *d* and how it dated back to Scotland and Cameron kilts and buck-naked Englishmen, which seemed to interest them to no end. They in turn lost no time filling me in on the Schneider clan, as they called it, three boys with children of their own, one son who ran what they referred to as "the ride" at the place they were going to, Wisconsin Dells, and another they had just visited who was a doctor in Yellowstone Park, treating people who fell into scalding pools or were mauled by bears. *Wow,* I thought, *talk about being famous, he must be the talk of the park every time he patched up some dumb tourist like that.* A third son, it turned out, ran the family farm in Illinois—somewhere called Downstate, which from my fuzzy geography I guessed had nothing to do with Chicago—while, as Mrs. Schneider said, she and Joe "trotted around having the time of our lives."

Trotting around by dog bus for the fun of it was a new notion to me, and as I listened to one and then the other peppily telling of their travels, I longed for the cushion of family that was theirs, in contrast to Gram and me on our own with only the distant relatives—literally—that I was being packed off to like a fruitcake at Christmas.

Something of this must have shown through in me, because Mr. Schneider interrupted himself to ask, wrinkled with concern, "Now, where is it you're going, Donal?"

"Manitowoc."

The Schneiders glanced at each other as if their hearing had failed.

I repeated the tricky word. "My grandmother says it means 'Where ghosts live' in Indian." That didn't seem to help.

"Don't know it atall. You, Mae?"

"Not a bit. Where in heaven's sake is it, somewhere far? Back east?"

The other somewheres of my trip—Pleasantville, Decatur, Chicago—the map dots of my imagination, my protection against the unknown that awaited me in one last bus depot where I was to give myself over to strangers, glimmered for a wistful moment and passed into simple memory. These two honest old faces could not be storied to, nor did I want to, hard truth the destination I had to face now.

"No, no, it's in Wisconsin, honest, see." Producing the autograph book from my jacket pocket, I showed them the precious piece of paper with the Manitowoc address and phone number. And more than that, I told them the whole story, Gram's scary operation and my parents killed by the drunk driver and the summer ahead of me in the hands of relatives who might as well be ghosts for all I knew about them, and the dog bus proving out Gram's prediction that it gets all kinds, like the huffy little sheriff who thought I was a runaway and the slick convict who almost made off with my suitcase—it spilled out of me in a flood, although I did hold back being soundly kissed by a vagabond waitress with *Leticia* stitched on her breast.

"Whew," Mr. Schneider whistled when I finally ran down, "you're a trouper for not letting anything throw you," and Mrs. Schneider added a flurry of *tsk*s, but the good kind that marveled at all I had been through. They put their heads together and figured out where Manitowoc must be from my ticket that showed I'd have to change buses in Milwaukee and ride for only a couple hours beyond that, which indicated that the place must be on Lake Michigan. That made them fret somewhat less. As Mr. Schneider put it, the town didn't sound like it was off at the rear end of nowhere.

Time flew in their company, comfortable as they were with a boy from having raised three of their own, and I felt next thing to adopted as our chatter continued across the miles. I could just see their prosperous farm, with a few horses still on the place for old times' sake, and no Power Wagon or Sparrowhead to ruin a summer. The saving grace of an uncorked imagination such as mine was that it always carried me away, as Gram all too well knew, waking dreams that I could more than halfway believe in if life would only correct itself in the direction of good luck instead of bad for her and me. I knew with everything in me Joe Schneider would have given me a chance to harness up a team of workhorses and prove myself in the fine fields of Illinois instead of running me off like an underage hobo, and Mae Schneider would never be a tightwad about kitchen matters. In my trance during the valuable time with this sage old couple—wizened must have had something to do with wisdom, mustn't it?—I could hardly bear not to ask if they needed a teamster and a cook.

But then Mrs. Schneider looked out at some Palookaville the bus was passing through and exclaimed, "Can you believe it, we're almost to the Dells," and that bubble popped. I came to with a start, realizing I hadn't had them write in the autograph book, and they chorused that they'd fix that in a hurry.

"A memory book," Mrs. Schneider said wistfully as I handed her the album and pen. "Why, I haven't seen one of these since our children had theirs." I watched over her shoulder, a growing lump in my throat, as she penned in a neat hand:

When twilight drops a curtain
and pins it with a star,
Remember that you have a friend
Though she may wander far.

He took a lot more time with his, a mischievous twinkle in his eye as he wrote and wrote. When his wife told him for heaven's sakes hurry up, he shushed her with "Never you mind, this is man talk between me and Donal," using my name with exquisite courtesy. When he passed the book back to me, along with a knowing grin, I saw he had composed:

Here's to the girlfriends,
you'll have them in numbers,
you'll have them in plenty,
1, 2, 3, 4, 5, 6, 7, 8, 9, 10,
11, 12, 13, 14, 15, 16, 17, 18, 19, 20.

The Wisconsin Dells stop was so brief I didn't get off, merely pressed my nose against the window as the Schneiders waved to me and were met by their family. Whatever dells were, I goggled at what appeared to be a lake turned into an amusement park, with a fleet of landing craft like my father's at Omaha Beach, except these advertised on their sides WISCONSIN DUCKS—FUN! ADVENTURE! ON LAND AND WATER! That was not even the most thrilling thing, though, as rising over the water like a railroad that had decided to jump the lake was a swooping roller-coaster track—sure as anything, the "ride" operated by the Schneiders' son. Oh, how I ached to stay there, just once in my life be a member of that world of pleasure. For as the bus pulled out, I knew in my heart of hearts nothing like that awaited me in some hard-to-spell town with not a thing going for it except the Indian explanation that it was where ghosts lived. Dead, in other words.

8.

MILWAUKEE. The last hazardous stop I had to get through appeared to me endlessly gray and runny, drizzle streaking the bus window, as though the church steeples every block or two poked leaks in the clouds. Either a very religious place or one in serious need of saving from its sins, this big city looked old and set in its ways, streets of stores alike from neighborhood to neighborhood even when the spelling on the windows was different kinds of foreign.

Humped up trying to see out to the blurred brick buildings set tight against one another, I was as bleary as the weather. Ever since Wisconsin Dells, I kept going over my all too adventurous day, the close calls with the badly dressed master criminal and the wild ride to catch up with the bus in St. Paul—luck on my side but only barely until the Schneiders came along to stick up for me when I most needed it—my imagination darting back and forth to what could have happened instead of what did. *Life is a zigzag journey,* Letty's inscription predicted, and how astute that was turning out to be.

Yet, already those experiences, bad and good, seemed farther past than they were. In some way that I could not quite wrap my mind around, distance messed up time, the miles accumulating since I climbed on the dog bus in Great Falls putting me unfathomably farther away from my life up till then than simply the count of hours could show. I had to think for a bit to realize that by now it was Sunday, and that Gram had gone into the hospital for her do-or-die operation. That thought swelled my imagination almost to bursting, my head crowded with doctors and nurses and nuns clustered around one familiar frail form, talking their hospital talk in tones as hushed as any in the gloomy Milwaukee churches the Greyhound was nosing past.

Determined as I was not to cry, my eyes were as blurry as the watery bus window by the time the driver called out the announcement about the depot's conveniences and so forth.

Jumpy at having to change buses at what was bound to be another overwhelmingly busy terminal, I scrambled out directly behind the driver and seized my suitcase as soon as he heaved it out of the baggage compartment. I headed straight down the long bank of swinging doors with arrivals and departures posted beside them, not veering an inch toward the waiting room newsstand and its lure of Mounds bars.

Way down at the end of the doorways, past ST. LOUIS and KANSAS CITY and even BEMIDJI, I finally spotted a sign like a string of letters in alphabet soup.

SHEBOYGAN MANITOWOC WAUSAU EAU CLAIRE

The bus was sitting there empty, no driver in sight. I checked the posted departure time and saw that I had plenty of leeway to go use the nearby convenience, so as a precaution in I went, hugging my suitcase to me. It was there, washing my hands afterward, that the red lettering on the machine on the wall registered on me.

MAXIMUM PROTECTION

That drew my interest. Keeping a death grip on my suitcase, I went over to see what was being dispensed that qualified as so surefire against jeopardy of whatever kind. In smaller print but still in blazing red letters above the coin slot was the explanation, more or less.

TUFFY PROPHYLACTICS

THE STRONGEST CONDOM COMING AND GOING

Well, that indicated to me, in an inexact schoolyard way, the vicinity of what these were for. But only that? The further wording touting how stout and reliable a Tuffy was included the word *sheath*. That in turn brought to mind one of the poems Miss Ciardi had made us memorize by the dozens in the sixth grade. *Noble Cyrano sheathed his knife / And spared the foul assassin's life.* I had something sharp to sheath, too, did I ever.

After all, people carried good luck charms for a reason—because they brought luck—which I had not been able to do with the practically knife-edged arrowhead stashed in the suitcase. If I could just somehow have it in my pocket without getting jabbed like crazy every time I sat down, maybe it would work more like a lucky piece was supposed to. In short, protection was what I needed, and here it was, promised for twenty-five cents.

Risking one of my few remaining coins, I turned the knob on the machine. Into the trough at the bottom dropped a round packet disappointingly small.

And when I unwrapped it, the so-called sheath seemed all too thin. Huh. I thought by reputation these things were made of rubber. Instead, the material was sort of like fishskin, and while stretchy, didn't strike me as terribly strong. When I dug the arrowhead out of the suitcase and compared lengths, though, the condom thinger looked just about right.

For all I knew, maybe more than one at a time was needed in this matter of protection, like putting on extra socks in zero weather. I had a last couple of quarters left and inserted them one after the other into the Tuffy dispenser, drawing quite a look from a guy at the nearest urinal. Then over in a corner at the sink counter, working carefully, carefully, with a little toilet paper padding to help out, I managed to tug the triple layer of condoms over the arrowhead. Definitely sheathed, it fit in my pocket as not much bigger than an ordinary charm like a rabbit's foot, and finally felt like a lucky piece should, ready and waiting.

BACK OUT in the boarding area, the driver showed up at the still-empty bus at the same time I did. Burly and black-mustached and still settling his company crush hat on his head, he looked me over enough that I was afraid he'd heard about me, the entire Greyhound fleet alerted about the stray whom trouble followed like a black cat's shadow. But he only remarked, "Early bird, aren't you," and stuck the antiquated suitcase safely in the baggage compartment. I went up the steps right at his heels, and for quite some time we were the only ones on the bus, me securing a window seat partway down the aisle but away from the bumpy ride over the back tires, and him behind the steering wheel dealing with paperwork.

At last a few others dribbled aboard, but to my puzzlement, not as many as at any point of the trip since passengers dwindled away into the void of North Dakota. Was Manitowoc such a ghost town no one wanted to go there? Soon enough I'd know, wouldn't I. If the Greyhound ever got itself in gear, which I was starting to doubt.

I was about to ask the driver if he was ever going to start us rolling, when I heard him say to himself, "Hoo boy, here they are," and he climbed off in a hurry to punch tickets and handle baggage. I turned to the window to see what was happening, and gasped.

A disorderly line of kids, snaking from side to side like one of those Chinese dragons in a parade, was pouring out of the depot, each with a suitcase in hand. There was an absolute mob of them, and worse than that, entirely boys, and even worse yet, the worst I could imagine, they all were about my age and there were more than enough redheads among them to confuse anyone. I knew it! Redheaded thinking it surely was, but this clearly was a disaster in the making. Just like I had tried to tell Gram, there was no conceivable way Aunt Kitty and Uncle Dutch could pick me out, confronted with red mopheads everywhere they looked.

The whole pack of them stormed onto the bus laughing and shoving and talking at the top of their voices as I sat dismally watching the pandemonium. A couple of fretful adults were in charge, or trying to be, but they were no match for the stampede. The kids swarmed as they pleased through the aisles, claiming seats and instantly trading. The bus filled up, and the next thing I knew, three boys descended on where I was sitting, one of them flopping down next to me and the others straight across the aisle.

As sharp-featured as if he'd been whittled, my new seatmate had a natural nose for poking into other people's business, eyeing me with none too friendly curiosity. "What'ja do, get on the bus early?"

"Sort of. Yesterday."

"Yeah? Where ya from, then?"

I told him, his snoopy pair of chums listening in. If the new bus riders were impressed by my distant point of departure, they had a funny way of showing it. "Monta-a-a-na," they bleated like sheep. "Know any cowboys? Like Hopalong Assidy?" They snickered roundly at the idea.

What to do? Lay it on them about the past two years of hanging around the bunkhouse with the Double W riders every chance I got, sometimes even being permitted when I caught Gram and Sparrowhead both in the right mood to saddle up and help move cows and calves to a new pasture, riding right next to cowboys not of the phony movie ten-gallon-hat-on-a-half-pint-head Hopalong Cassidy variety but as genuine as they come, as shown by their imaginative cussing?

These kids, not a freckle from the outdoors on their milk-white faces, did not seem like a promising audience for any of that. For once, I figured I'd better tone matters down.

"Well, sure, I couldn't help but know plenty of them, could I," I said offhandedly. "My grandmother's the cook on the biggest ranch in Montana, see, and the whole crew, cowboys and all, eats together at a table as long as this bus." That did stretch the matter a little, but not unreasonably so, I thought.

"Huh. Sounds like basement supper at church," my seatmate mouthed off. "Jeez, you must have wore a hole in your butt, on here that long," one of the others came up with.

"Uh-huh, it's cracked a little, too," I shot back, making them laugh in spite of themselves, and matters relaxed somewhat.

The way kids will do, we gingerly got around to names. The one sitting next to me was Kurt, with a *K*, he informed me, as though that made him something special and not just a victim of poor spelling. The duo across the aisle weren't named much better, Gus and Mannie. They looked like brothers but didn't act like it, Gus nervous as a pullet and Mannie the kind who would stare you in the eye while he took your lunch. Kurt was the leader, I could tell. Leaders always sat by themselves, or in this case by the seatfiller I happened to be. I wished I had drawn the set of boys directly behind us, who were quietly reading comic books.

Still trying to figure out this many punks my age being transported somewhere in one clump, I couldn't help but ask. "Is this a school trip?"

"Where'ja get that?" Kurt looked at me like I was crazy. "School's out. We're goin' to camp."

"Sleep outside like that?" Why on earth would anyone with a home and a bed, as these milksops surely had, camp for the night on the cold ground? "What for?"

"Outside, nothin'," the big talker who spelled his name with a *K* turned up his nose at that. "We're goin' to Camp Winnebago. It has cabins and everythin'."

Hope flickered in me for the first time since this horde speckled with redheads showed up. If they were not all to pour off at the Manitowoc depot in a sea of confusion, maybe the aunt and uncle who had never seen me would have a chance of finding me after all. Cautiously I asked, "H-how do you get there? To Camp Winnegabo, I mean."

"How do you think?" Kurt sneered. He crossed his eyes at me like one moron talking to another, while Gus and Mannie rolled theirs. "What goes down the road like sixty but always turns around to chase its tail?"

"Bus." I exhaled the answer, relieved at the thought that the driver would dump this bunch off at some mosquito patch that called itself a camp—before or after Manitowoc, I didn't care which.

"Give that man a dicky bird." With that, Kurt pinched the back of my wrist black-and-blue.

"OW! Hey, quit!" Trying to shake the sting out of my hand, I at least had the consolation that Kurt was groaning as he rubbed his ribs and complained, "Oof, you gave me a real whack," which, in all justice, my elbow automatically had done when he pinched the bejesus out of me. Somehow it seemed to make him think better of me.

"So, Don"—I had prudently trimmed mine to that in the exchange of names, seeing as theirs were as short as bullets—"where you goin', anyhow?" he asked almost civilly.

But when I told him, he snickered, while across the aisle Gus, or was it Mannie, jeered, "Ooh, old Manitowocee, couldn't make it to Milwaukee."

Swallowing hard, I changed the subject. "What do you do when you get to dumb camp?"

"All kinds of stuff!" They were only too glad to tick off activities to me. "Swimmin'! Makin' things with leather! Tug-o'-war! Archery!"

It was Gus, the fidgety pullet one, who interrupted the litany with "Don't forget singin'," causing Mannie next to him to hoot out, "The campfire ditty!" and before you could say *Do re mi*, all three of them were laughing like loons and raucously chorusing:

> *Great green gobs of greasy, grimy gopher guts,*
> *Mutilated monkey meat.*
> *Dirty little birdie feet.*
> *Great green gobs of greasy, grimy gopher guts,*
> *And me without my spoon.*

That was impressive, I had to grant, as did the harried grown-up who came rushing down the aisle and told them to quit showing off. As one, they snickered at his retreating back. The candy company should have put the three of them on the Snickers bar, like the Smith Brothers on cough drop boxes.

I didn't have much time for that kind of thinking, however, as they turned their attention back to me, the Mannie one looking particularly hungry for a crack at me.

"So," I blurted the first thing that came to mind, "you guys shoot bows and arrows, like Indians. That's pretty good."

"You bet your butt it is." Unable to resist showing off, Kurt drew back archer-style with an imaginary *twang*, the other two loyally clucking their tongues to provide the *thwock* of arrow hitting target.

Oh, the temptation that brought on. To see the look on their faces when I coolly announced that when it came to things like arrows, I just happened to have a lucky arrowhead older than Columbus right there in my possession. The only hitch was, if they clamored to see it I'd have to show it in its wrapping of Tuffies, and I sensed that was not such a good idea. I hated to miss the chance to be superior about the archery matter, but maybe I had something better up my sleeve.

"How about guns?"

My question silenced them for a full several seconds.

Mannie was the first to recover and break out a sneer. "What, cap pistols? Little-kid games ain't for us."

"That's not what I mean," I responded, innocent as the devil filing his fingernails, as a Gram saying best put it. "Remington single-shot .22s. Like I use, at the ranch."

"Yeah?" Kurt sat up and a little away from me. "Use on what?"

"Magpies."

"Yeah? What's those?"

"Birds. Big black-and-white ones that would just as soon peck your eyes out as look at you." He flinched back as I spread my hands in a sudden gesture. "With tails about yay long. Don't you have those here?"

"Naw, I don't think so." He looked across uncertainly at Gus and Mannie, who were shaking their heads in slack-jawed ignorance of one of the most common birds in Creation. Talk about having a wire down; if any of these three had a brain that worked, it would be lonesome.

"Then how do you make any money?" I pressed my advantage, Kurt still leaning away as if his ass might get shot off from my direction. "See, there's a bounty on magpies, on account of they eat the eyeballs right out of calves and lambs and things, and"—I had a moment of inspiration—"they really do gobble gopher guts." At that, my audience was agog, if slightly green around the gills.

"So what you do," I continued in expert style, "after you shoot them, you cut off their legs with your jackknife and turn those in for the bounty. Fifty cents, just like that." I snapped my fingers like a shot, if a person imagined a little. "They're pretty easy to shoot, I got seventeen so far this year," I concluded, as if dead magpies were notches on my gun belt.

By now I was being looked at as if I was either a gunslinging hero of the eleven-year-old set or the biggest liar on the face of the earth. But it was totally true that Wendell Williamson, tightwad that he was, ponied up for dirty little birdy feet, magpies being the hated nuisance they were on ranches, after Gram vouched that my father had taught me how to shoot the .22 and she swore I was responsible enough to hunt along the creek willows without endangering the cattle.

My listeners stirred uncertainly. Gus's lips were moving as he worked out fifty cents times seventeen, while Mannie gauged me more warily than before. It was up to Kurt to rally the campers.

"Yeah, well, bows and arrows can kill stuff, too. Like, uh, frogs. We're goin' frog huntin' the first night at camp, ain't we, guys."

"We'll murder the buggers!" and "Frog legs for breakfast!" from across the aisle backed that up as if hunting hopping amphibians in the dark, Indian-style, was a tried-and-true camp activity, which I seriously doubted.

Now even the would-be holy terrors of the frog world fell still as an announcement boomed out from the driver that we were not stopping in Sheboygan as scheduled, because no one was ticketed to there and no more passengers could be taken on. Actually, I suspected he was in a hurry to get rid of the mess of campers. No doubt to put minds at rest, so to speak, about a restroom, he added, "Manitowoc in fifteen short minutes."

Really? The comprehension began to sink in that I was nearly there at last. Fifteen minutes truly did sound like no time after all my hours on the bus, the never-to-be-forgotten encounters I'd had, close calls especially. In an odd way, I started to miss all that, the bits and pieces of my immense journey coming to mind while my latest companions thought it was a big deal to go up the road a skip and a jump to the same dumb camp year after year. But the mind does funny things, and half listening to their razzing back and forth about which of them was most likely to shoot himself in the foot with an arrow, I had a sudden itch toward the autograph book. After all, here was my last chance on the dog bus for who knew how long, and three candidates right here handy. So what if they behaved like nose pickers, when they knew stuff like that campers' song. Goofiness had its place in the pages of life, too.

Impulsively I pulled out the album, its cream-colored cover somewhat smudged from so much handling but overall less the worse for the trip than I was, and showed it off to Kurt.

"Yeah?" his answer to almost everything. He fanned through the pages like a speed-reader. "So you want us all to put somethin' in it."

I said I sure did, which brought about quite a reaction across the aisle. Gus giggled in Mannie's face. "Gonna write *My name is Manfred Vedder, I'm an old bed wetter*, ain'tcha?"

"Sure, dipshit, just like you're gonna sign yours *Augustus Dussel, that's me, I barely have brains enough to pee*," Mannie jeered back.

Nervously I pasted on a grin at their name-calling contest. Whatever their parents had been thinking in saddling them with those wacky christenings, these brats would be a different kind of material for the autograph book, for sure. And I couldn't help but wonder what Kurt the leading loudmouth was going to come up with when he committed ink to paper.

Meanwhile he still was toying his way through the pages, and to get things going, I was about to hand him the Kwik-Klik and explain how it worked, when he clapped the book shut and held it out to show Gus and Mannie. "Gotta better idea. We'll take it to camp and everybody there can write in it for ya. The counselors, even." All three of them snickered at that, you can bet. "Don't blow your wig," Kurt said, as if I shouldn't have a care in the world, "we'll send it back to you in Monta-a-a-na when it's full."

"Hey, no! I need to keep it, I just want you guys to write in it."

"We'll get around to it," he breezed by that. "Letcha know how the frog huntin' goes."

Getting really worried, I made a grab for the book. With a laugh, he tossed it across the aisle to Gus, who whooped and shoveled it to Mannie as if this were a game of keep-away.

In desperation, I shoved the heel of my hand into Kurt's surprised face and kicked my way past him—he didn't amount to much of a barrier compared to the braided Indian or the man in the bad-fitting suit—and launched myself onto the giggling pair across the aisle, calling them dickheads and sonsofbitches and whatever other swear-words came to my tongue. It was two against one, but they were underneath and I was all over them with flailing limbs. In the scuffle, I elbowed Gus hard enough to take the giggle out of him. Mannie was chanting "Uh uh uh, don't be grabby!" when I got on top of him enough to knee him in a bad place and snatch the album back.

By now the grown-ups who supposedly were in charge of this band of thieves had floundered onto the scene and were pulling me off a howling Mannie, while the bus driver bellowed, "Everybody siddown!"

Still cussing to the best of my ability, I was grappled by one of the adults into the seat across the aisle, Kurt having retreated to the window as far as he could get from me.

"We wasn't gonna keep it, honest," he whined, the liar, as I furiously checked things over. The autograph book miraculously had survived without damage, but my shirt was wrecked all to hell, a pocket dangling almost off—fortunately not the one with the money pinned to it—and a number of buttons were missing, and I could feel a draft from rips under the arms and long tears down the back as if I'd been fighting clawed animals, which I pretty nearly was.

About then I spat something out. A piece of tooth. My tongue found the chipped spot. One of the sharp teeth next to my bottom front ones. Sharper now. Baring my choppers at him, I gave Kurt another murderous look, and he whimpered, the fearless frog hunter.

While I was trying to take inventory, catch my breath, nurse my tooth, and pull my ruined shirt together enough for decency, the bus abruptly slowed and steered off to one side. I reared up, blinking, looking around for Manitowoc. But no, we were braking to a halt on a roadside pullover, the parking lot for a picnic area, and the driver had something else in mind. Climbing out from behind the steering wheel with grim determination, his mustache bristling, he stalked down the aisle to the four of us dead-still in various states of apprehension.

"You." He pointed a finger at me and then jerked a thumb toward the front of the bus. "Up there, where I can keep an eye on you."

My ears burning, I followed him to the seat nearest the steps, swapping with some unlucky camper about to have Kurt inflicted on him. I guess by the same token, the kid in the window seat next to my new spot shrank away from me like he'd been put in a cage with a wild beast.

ACTUALLY, I discovered much, much too late, I'd been banished to the best seat on the bus. Why didn't I think of this at, say, Havre? Up there with nothing in front but the dashboard and the doorwell, I could see everything the driver could, every particle of road and scenery, clear as if the bus-wide windshield were a magnifying glass. Except for the chipped tooth my tongue kept running over, all of a sudden I felt like a new person. For the next some minutes I sat entranced as the world opened ahead of me, no longer sliding past a side window. And so it was that I had the best possible view of my destination from the outskirts on in.

BY THEN I HAD seen sixteen hundred miles' worth of towns, from Palookavilles to the Twin Cities busy as double beehives to gray soppy Milwaukee spiked with churches. At this first sight of Manitowoc, though, I did not know what to think. The houses looked old, many of them small and with gray siding, on streets with some flower gardens fringing the lawns but none of the overtowering cottonwood groves of Gros Ventre or Great Falls. Nothing about the tight-packed neighborhoods appeared even remotely familiar except Chevys and Fords dotting the streets, and those were strangely pulled in sideways—parallel parking had not converted Montana. Plenty of church steeples here, too, like arrow tips in the hide of the sky. As for the people out and about, they were not as dressed up as in Minneapolis, yet the women looked like they had on nylons, which not even Meredice Williamson wore on an everyday basis at the ranch, and the men sported hats that would scarcely keep the sun off at all, not a Stetson among them.

My eyes stayed busy as could be, my mind trying to keep up with all the different sights and scenes—Gram had been right about that, I had to admit—as the bus approached the more active downtown section, with long lines of mystifying storefronts. We passed a business calling itself a SCHNAPPS SCHOP, which looked like a bar, and the bars I could recognize all had a glowing blue neon sign in the window proclaiming SCHLITZ, THE BEER THAT MADE MILWAUKEE FAMOUS, which was news to me—it hadn't done so in Montana—while what looked like restaurants commonly had the word SCHNITZEL painted on the plate glass, and an apparent department store had SCHUETTE'S, a very strange-sounding product if it wasn't a name, spelled in large letters above its show windows. I was no whiz at other languages, but I had the awful growing suspicion that if ghosts walked in Manitowoc, they had better speak German to find their way around this weird town.

Like a thunderclap following that realization, the bus rumbled across a drawbridge over a murky river, with half-killed weeds clinging to its banks, and on past huge shed-like buildings with signs saying they were enterprises unknown to me, such as boiler works and coal yards. Fortunately I caught a reassuring glimpse of a sparkling gray-blue lake that spilled over the horizon, and the best thing that had yet come into sight, a tremendously long red-painted ship in the harbor with ORE EMPRESS in big white letters on its bow.

Then the bus was lurching into the driveway of the depot, and the next thing I knew, the driver killed the engine, swung around in his seat with relief written on his face, and announced:

"Manitowoc, the pearl of Lake Michigan. Everybody off."

I was thunderstruck, but not for long.

"HEY, NO, EVERYBODY SIT TIGHT! YOU'RE NOT THERE YET!"

My outcry halted the driver and probably everyone else on the bus. "You're taking them to Camp Winniegoboo!" I instructed the open-mouthed man at the wheel. "They told me so!"

He recovered enough to sputter, "What're you yapping about? A camp bus picks them up here." I went numb. "They're off my hands," he briskly brushed those together, disposing of me at the same time. "Besides, what do you care? You're ticketed to here like everybody else, aren't you? End of the line, bub. Come on."

I nodded dumbly, and followed him off the bus into the unloading area. There still was a chance, if I could grab my suitcase and hustle into the waiting room ahead of the throng of campers. But of course at Milwaukee mine had been the first one stowed in the baggage compartment, and as infallibly as Murphy's Law that anything that can go wrong is bound to go wrong, every camping kid received his bag and filtered into the depot before the wicker suitcase was reached. Directly ahead, as I slogged in dead last, Kurt and his gang looked back and gave me various kinds of the stink eye, but stayed a safe distance away.

INSIDE THE DEPOT, it was just as I feared. The waiting room was jammed with the camp kids madly swirling around until their bus arrived, everything in total confusion, redheads bobbing everywhere in the milling herd, and I knew, absolutely positively knew, picking me out was impossible. Tucking in my shredded shirttail as best I could and trying to cover torn seams with my elbows, I stood there, desperately looking around, but while there were all kinds of grown-ups mixed in with the crowd, for the life of me I couldn't see anyone I imagined to be an Aunt Kitty or an uncle named Dutch.

When my greeters didn't show up and didn't show up, I decided there was only one thing to do. Resort to the slip of paper with their phone number. Not that I knew squat about using the instrument evidently hidden in the forbidding closet-size booth with GREAT LAKES PAY PHONE on it, all the way across the terminal. Pay phone? Like a jukebox, was that, where you stuck coins in and a bunch of machinery was set in motion in the guts of the apparatus, or what? Everywhere I had lived, the construction camps, the ranch, telephones were a simple party line where you merely picked up the receiver and dinged two longs and two shorts or whatever the signal was for whoever you were calling. This was not the best time to have to figure out strange new equipment, especially if you were as close to having the heebie-jeebies as I was.

Then I slapped my pants pocket, remembering. I'd spent the last of my loose change buying Tuffies for the arrowhead. To get coins to call with, I would need to break a ten-dollar bill from the stash under my remaining shirt pocket, which meant undressing even further right here in the most public place there was, where anyone like the convict in the suit and tie could be watching. I didn't dare retreat to the men's room to do it out of sight—that was a guaranteed way to miss Aunt Kitty and Uncle Dutch should they show up looking for me. This was becoming like one of those nightmares in which the predicament gets deeper and deeper until you think you never will wake up back to sanity.

Trying to fight down the jitters, I cast another wild gaze around the teeming waiting room, hoping for salvation in the form of anyone who might resemble Gram enough to be her sister. No such luck, not even close. People of every shape and form and way of dress, but none showed me any recognition and of course I couldn't to them. I must have been looked past hundreds of times, as if I were too ragged for anyone to want to pack home. I was stuck.

There was no help for it, I was going to have to throw myself on the mercy of GREAT LAKES PAY PHONE. Setting down my suitcase to try to get things in order, especially myself, I first of all reached out the autograph book from my jacket pocket and flipped through the pages to find the slip of paper with the phone number. Then again. My fingers began to shake.

The piece of paper was gone. It must have fallen out when the campers, the grabby bastards, were tossing the album around.

Distress hit like an instant paralysis, as a terrible omission caught up with me. Worse, what might be called the commission of an omission. I hadn't bothered to so much as glance at the phone number or street address even when showing those to the Schneiders. Now I stood rooted there, feeling worse off even than I was when stranded in Minneapolis—unmet, my clothing half torn off, as good as lost in a weird city, with night coming on and not even the dog bus as a haven anymore. Rough introduction into being a total orphan, it felt like.

I was dissolving into utter surrender, tears next, when I heard the melodious voice behind me.

"So here you are, sweetie pie. We wondered."

I whirled around to the woman and man who evidently had appeared from nowhere. "How do you know I'm me?" I blurted.

The woman trilled a laugh. "Silly, you look just like Dorie, two peas from the same pod." Gram and me? Since when?

In the meantime the man was giving me a bucktoothed expression of greeting, like a horse grinning. "Looks run in the family, hah?" he said in a voice as guttural as hers was musical. "Hallo." He shook hands, mine swallowed in his. "I am Herman." Not Dutch? Gram had said he was something else, but not that he was something you couldn't put a name to for sure. Seeing my confusion, he grinned all the more. "You are thinking of how I used to be called, I betcha. Herman fits me more now."

Blinking my way out of one surprise after another, I simply stood planted there, gawking at the two of them, one tall and slope-shouldered, the other nearly as broad as the fat lady in a carnival. Long-faced and with that horsy grin and glasses that made his eyes look larger than human, with an odd glint to them, he was quite a sight in his own right, but it was her I was stupefied by. I could only think Gram hadn't spelled her out to me to save the surprise. Oh, man! *She* was in our family, what there was of it? This was like a wish come true, life all of a sudden springing the better kind of trick for a change.

I still almost couldn't believe it, but the more I looked at this unexpected personage, the more excited I became. I would have known her anywhere, an unmistakable figure in more ways than one, big around as a jukebox, jolly double chins, wide-set doll eyes, hairdo as plump as the rest of her, the complete picture. The exact same face I had seen big as life—well, *Life*, really, the picture magazine that showed what was what in the world every week—just that same day at the Minneapolis newsstand, and the melodious voice, familiar as if it were coming out of the radio that very moment. My Aunt Kitty was clearly none other than what the magazine cover described with absolute authority as America's favorite songstress, and unless a person was a complete moron and deaf to boot, recognizable as the treasured vocalist of every song worth singing, Kate Smith.

At last, I had it knocked.

WHERE MANITOU WALKS

June 17–30, 1951

9.

IT MADE PERFECT sense to me. Although the mention went in one ear and out the other at the time, hadn't Gram herself spoken of her little dickens of a sister—although that description was quite a few sizes too small anymore—as "the great Kate," in saying the two of them just could not make music together from girlhood on? Well, who could, with a singer whose voice carried her to the very top? Back then, I could not have defined palpitations, but did I ever have them, so excited was I to possess this famous woman for an aunt. Great-aunt, but close enough. I gazed raptly up at her, top-heavy as she was with that mighty chest but as cool and composed there in the hubbub of the bus station as if posing for her picture in a magazine. And wasn't she smart to condense *Smythe*, her and Gram's maiden name that looked to me like one of those trick words in a spelling contest, to good old *Smith* to sing under? *Believe It or Not!* disclosed this kind of thing all the time, you could hardly read the Sunday funnies without learning that Patti Page before she reached the hit parade with songs like "Tennessee Waltz" was plain Clara Ann Fowler, a name switcheroo if there ever was one. Besides, as Red Chief myself, I was naturally in favor of sprucing up what you called yourself in any way possible.

So the great Kate Smith, dressed in a peach-colored outfit that made her look like a million dollars, monumental in every way as she peered down at me with a perfectly plucked eyebrow arched, represented rescue, relief, reward, a miraculous upward turn in my circumstances. And I needed whatever I could get, ragged and snaggle-toothed as my appearance was. Her expression turned to puckered concern as she tallied my missing buttons, dangling pocket, and the rest of my shirt more or less torn to shreds. "Heavens, child, you look like you've been in a dogfight."

Well, yeah, that pretty close to described scuffling with the pack of campers, and there was a story that went with that, but this did not seem like the time for it. I looked down as if apologizing to my shirt. "It got caught on something, is all."

"We'll have to get you changed"—she noted the heavy traffic into the men's restroom, and frowned—"later." A new note of worry crept in at my general disarray and the wicker suitcase, which itself was looking the worse for wear, if that was possible. "You did bring something presentable, I hope?"

"Sure thing," I defended my and Gram's packing, "I have a clean shirt left. My rodeo one sort of needs washing, though."

"Road-ee-oh," came a guttural expression of interest from her silent partner, up to this point. "Not ro-day-oh, hah?"

Paying no attention to that, she seemed to make up her mind to smile at me, the extra chin and the famous chubby dimples involved. She had the bluest eyes, which mine swam in guilelessly. "If you're ready, honeybunch," she was saying in that voice so melodious I was surprised she could pass herself off in public as Aunt Kitty at all, "we may as well go."

I nodded eagerly. Herman—somehow I had trouble applying Uncle to him, without Dutch to go with it—insisted on taking my suitcase.

Out we went, he and I trailing her as she plowed through the depot crowd, drawing second looks every step of the way. At the curb, I was glad to see, an idling bus that was not even a Greyhound was filling with the kids going to camp, the poor saps. If there was any justice, Kurt, Gus, and Mannie were in there watching and eating their weasel hearts out at my royal welcome.

Herman hustled ahead to the car, not the limousine I was looking forward to but a big old roomy four-door DeSoto, I supposed because someone the size of Kate Smith required a lot of room.

I fully expected her, and if I was lucky, me, to establish in the backseat, the way rich people did. But while Herman was putting my suitcase in the trunk, she drew herself up by the front passenger door and stood there as if impatient for it to open itself, until I realized I was supposed to be the one to do it.

When I leaped and did it, she enunciated, "That's a little gentleman," but still didn't budge until I caught on further and scrambled in to the middle of the seat. She followed, the car going down on its springs on that side under her weight, until Herman evened things up somewhat by settling himself behind the steering wheel.

Doing so, he slipped me a sly grin and I heard him say what sounded like "Welcome to Manito Woc," as if the town were two words.

I was about to ask if that was actually how to pronounce it when the Kate Smith voice hit a note of warning. "Brinker, don't fool around. Look at the time—we have to go to the station."

"Yah, Your Highness," he answered as if used to being ordered around, and the DeSoto came to life after he pulled out the throttle a little and the choke farther than that and stepped hard on the starter and did another thing or two.

Meanwhile it was all I could do not to bounce up and down with delight at her pronouncement. The station! The dog bus, that loping mode of transportation full of starts and stops and disruptions and tense connections, somehow had delivered me right in time for her radio show. *Kate Smith Sings*, all anyone needed to know about it.

I glanced at her hopefully. Maybe she even could slip into the program some hint that I had arrived, and Gram would hear it in her hospital room and know I had come through my harrowing journey safe and sound, mostly. I didn't want to ask that yet, shy about bothering someone getting ready to perform for a national audience. I would not have been surprised if she exercised her vocal cords right there in the car, but the only sign she gave of impending performance was humming to herself while she tapped a hand on the round rise of one thigh as steadily as a telegraph operator in a shoot-'em-up western.

I figured she was entitled to a few jitters. What had that first seatmate of mine, the stout woman on the Chevy bus, said? *I'd be such a bundle of nerves.* And that was merely about my supposed journey to Pleasantville, nothing like facing a radio microphone and a live audience and singing for the thousandth time "God Bless America" the way everyone coast-to-coast was waiting to hear again. If I was a trouper like Joe Schneider had said, the famous entertainer sitting right here at my elbow was the biggest example imaginable. It must run in the family.

"How is Montana?"

Herman's question out of nowhere jostled me out of that line of thought, and somewhat nervously—maybe it was catching—I responded, "In pretty good shape for the shape it's in, I guess."

"Yah, I betcha. Like Old Shatterhand would say, up on its hind legs and still going, hah?"

His laugh came from the bottom of his throat, like his words. His lingo threw me a little at first, but I knew I'd get used to it, accustomed as I was to hired hands in the bunkhouse or the barracks at a construction camp who were called Swede or Ole or Finnigan if from Finland, and spoke "that broken stuff," as it was called. Squarehead was the catch-all term for such types. Herman's accent and name I guessed must have come straight from Holland with its tale of Hans Brinker and the silver skates and all that, and it only added to the surprise of my sensational arrival. His choppy voice now reached a wistful register as he declared, "Out in cowboy land, you are in luck."

"Pretty please"—from the other direction came a prompt response with not the usual sweet intonation on that phrase—"don't be filling the boy's mind with nonsense."

"No, it's fine," I spoke up, trying to sit tall enough to be a factor between them. "I'm around those all the time, see. On the ranch. Cowboys, I mean. I'd be there in the bunkhouse with them right now if Sparrowhead—Wendell Williamson, I mean—had let me be stacker driver on the haying crew like I asked to."

It took them each a few moments to put that together, and I'm not sure he ever did get there. She, though, said as if thinking the matter over, "But instead you're very much here, dumpling."

"Yeah!" Only minutes before, I would have had to fake this kind of answer, but landing in the spacious lap of Kate Smith, in a manner of speaking, I had no trouble whatsoever being enthusiastic. "This is so much better than there, it knocks my socks off."

Just then the DeSoto pulled off the street, Herman steering with his hands wide apart like the captain at a ship's wheel, and I craned for the first sight of the radio station. But he had only stopped for gas, and went inside to use what he called the man's room while the attendant filled the tank and checked the oil and wiped the windshield, whistling all the while as if he had caught the musical spirit from the great Kate beside me. Staring off into the night, she continued to hum to that fitful pitty-pat rhythm on her mound of thigh.

With only the two of us in the car, I couldn't help feeling this was my chance. It was all I could do not to yank the autograph book out of my coat pocket and ask her to write in it, right then and there, in the greenish-yellow glow of the gas station's pump lights. And of course I would want her to sign it *Kate Smith*, not something like *Your devoted Aunt Kitty*, to elevate the autograph collection toward true *Believe It or Not!* territory. I bet she knew all kinds of other celebrities who would write their famous names in it for me, too. Talk about a jackpot! Herman had said a mouthful, about my being in luck. The sacred black arrowhead could not have been doing its job better. I cleared my throat to make my request. "Can I ask you for a real big favor?"

She jumped a little at the sound of my voice, nerves again, understandably. Glancing down at me, she composed herself and said, not entirely clearly to me, "That depends on how big is real big, doesn't it."

The autograph book was burning a hole in my pocket, but something about her answer stayed my hand. Quick like a bunny, I switched to:

"Can I call you Aunt Kate? Instead of Kitty, I mean."

"Why, of course you can, adorable." She nodded into her second chin in relief. "It's my given name, after all. That sister of mine started the 'Kitty' thing when we were girls, and heaven knows why, it stuck."

I squirmed at anything said against Gram, but maybe that was the way sisters were.

Herman returned and went through the dashboard maneuvers and what else it took to start the DeSoto. "Home to the range," he sang out, earning a sharp look from Aunt Kate.

As we pulled out of the gas station, I felt dumb as they come. Obviously I had the wrong night about the radio show. Now that I thought about it, back at the Greyhound terminal Aunt Kate most certainly would have said something like "We have a surprise for you tonight, dear," if I was going to be part of the audience for *Kate Smith Sings*, wouldn't she. Sheepish, I fell back to the early bus habit of "Uh-huh" and "Huh-uh" as Herman tried to make conversation on the drive to their house.

IT WAS DARK by the time the DeSoto rocked into a bumpy driveway. The house, painted that navy gravy-gray shade like in pictures of battleships and with a peaked roof and lit sort of ghostly by the nearest streetlight, appeared big as a ranchin' mansion to me after the cook shack, although looking back, I realize that only meant it had an upstairs as well as a downstairs.

As we went in, Aunt Kate instructed Herman to leave my suitcase at the foot of the stairs, to be dealt with after dinner. Since it was pitch-black out, I deduced that must mean supper, another Wisconsin mystery like schnitzel and schnapps and going to camp with a bunch of boy hoodlums.

"You can change your shirt in our bedroom," she told me, definitely more than a hint. "Just drop that and your other one in the laundry chute, I'll do them with our washing in the morning." Herman showed me the chute in the hallway. These people knew how to live—when their clothes got dirty, they mailed them to the basement.

I stepped into the indicated bedroom, and too timid to put the light on, swapped shirts as fast as I could. Straining to take in the exact place where Kate Smith slept, even in the dimness I was convinced I could see a telltale sag in the near side of the double bed.

Hurrying so as not to miss anything in this remarkable household, I dispatched my needy shirts into the laundry chute and followed promising sounds into the kitchen. Fussing with cooking pots, Aunt Kate was humming again when I presented myself, fully buttoned and untorn. "Now then. We're having a Manitowoc specialty." She beamed at me to emphasize the treat as she put on an apron twice the size of any of Gram's. "Sauerkraut and franks. I know you like those. Boys do, don't they."

Not this boy, because Gram viewed frankfurters—wienies by another name, right?—with dire suspicion whenever she was forced to boil up a batch to feed the crew toward the end of a month's kitchen budget, convinced that the things were made from leavings lying around the butcher shop. "Tube steak," she'd mutter as she plopped wienies by the handful into the pot. "You might as well be eating sweepings from the slaughterhouse." Not the best thing to build an appetite for frankfurters. But my stomach and my hunger had no time to debate that, as I was shooed out of the kitchen and told I was free to look around the house while dinner was being fixed.

I edged into the living room and onto a pea-green rug so deep I left footprints wherever I stepped. It was like walking on a mattress. Intimidated, I crept across the room, studying the unfamiliar surroundings. A big, long leathery davenport, also green but closer to that fakey shade of lime Kool-Aid, sat prominently in front of a bay window, where the sill was crammed with potted plants of kinds I couldn't recognize. On an end table next to the arm of the davenport rested a phone, pink as bubblegum, of another type I had no experience of, with a cradled receiver and a circular dial full of numbers and letters. Whatever else this strange territory of the summer proved to be like, it definitely did not seem to be party-line country.

Across the room from all this, on either side of a fancy cabinet radio but some distance apart, bulked his and hers recliner chairs, the kind with a lever on the side that tips a person back as if to get a shave from a barber. Over what was more than likely Herman's hung the picture of dogs sitting around a table playing poker that you see so many places, while over hers was a framed sampler with a skyline of a town—largely steeples—and a ship on the lake with a spiral of thread for smoke, and underneath those, a verse in red and blue yarn, MANITOWOC—WHERE MAN HAS BUT TO WALK, TO HEAR HIS BLEST SOUL TALK.

Yeah, well, okay, I supposed that went with the reputation of ghosts walking around town, but now what had me more interested was a cubbyhole room off the far end of the living room.

The door was partway open and I glimpsed what appeared to be a daybed under a plain gray cover. Lured by hope, when I poked my head in and saw piles of cloth of different colors atop a table and spilling onto a chair, I knew at once this must be the sewing room, even before I spotted the shiny electric Singer machine by the window. Who would have thought Kate Smith sewed her own clothes? But everyone needs a hobby, I reminded myself, or maybe in her dress-size situation, doing it herself was a necessity. Any fat girl at school got teased about her clothes being made by Omar the Tentmaker, and while I felt guilty about that uncharitable thought, there was the big-as-life fact that Aunt Kate was a much larger woman than clothing stores usually encountered.

Of greater significance to me was that daybed, just my size, really—I'd slept on any number of cots like that, jouncing through life with my parents—and I'd have bet anything this nice snug room was where I was going to be put up for the summer, special guest in a special place of the house.

THROUGH TAKING in these new surroundings, something else needed taking care of, and I had to retreat to the kitchen to ask.

"Aunt Kate? I need to use the convenience."

Parked at the stove where the pot of supper—dinner, rather—was on, she gave me a funny look.

"Uhm, restroom, I mean. Toilet. Bathroom." I finally hit on the word appropriate in a setting that wasn't a Greyhound depot.

"It's through there." She pointed to the end of the hall. "Remember to wash your hands, won't you."

I most certainly did remember, and more than that, I took the opportunity to examine my chipped tooth in the mirror over the sink. Baring my teeth in a kind of maniac smile, I saw that the damaged one stood out menacingly from the others. A snag, in fact, the chip having left it as pointed as a fang.

Studying my reflection, I decided I sort of liked the snaggletooth sticking up that way. It made me look tough, like I'd been through some hard going in life.

My admiration of this new feature was interrupted when all of a sudden I heard singing.

I went still as stone to make sure. Yes! Distinct as anything, from the direction of the kitchen. A solo, to keep the famous Kate Smith voicebox tuned up, I bet. And not just a song, but *the* song! Oh man, this was almost like going to the radio show!

> *God bless America,*
> *Land that I love.*
> *Stand beside her*
> *And guide her*
> *Through the night with a light from above.*

I tell you, that singing went right under my skin and raised goose bumps. The one-of-a-kind beautiful voice, the words every schoolchild—every parent, even—knew by heart. And here I was, the lucky audience to this performance by the most famous singer in America, maybe in the world. This settled it. I absolutely had to ask for the treasured autograph as soon as the song was over. It was bound to please the performer in the kitchen as well as me. Out of the bathroom in a flash, I sped to where my jacket was piled atop my suitcase, grabbed out the album, and darted back to the kitchen.

Herman had reappeared, sitting at the table, paging through a book and not even particularly listening, he evidently was so used to the glorious sound. Rocking ever so slightly side to side to the rhythm, Aunt Kate stood at the stove with her back turned to us, as if it were nothing to be pouring out the best-known song since "Happy Birthday" while cooking kraut and weinies. I stood entranced there at the other end of the kitchen, listening to her sing just for me. Then as the most soaring part rolled around again, the beautiful voice reaching its height—

To the prairies,
To the oceans white with foam,
God bless America,
My home sweet home.

—she turned around, her mouth full of the half-cooked wienie she was munching.

For a moment I was only confused. But then when I saw her take another bite, eyes half-closed in pleasure, the inside of me felt like it fell to the floor. Meanwhile the song played on a bit more, until there came a burst of applause in the living room and a man's silky voice doing a commercial for La Palina cigars.

When I recovered the ability to speak, I stammered, "You're—you're not Kate Smith? On the radio?"

She swallowed the last of the wienie, fast. "Good grief, *that*," she groaned, frowning all the way down to her double chins.

"I telled you, too many sweets," said Herman, licking his finger to keep on turning pages.

Ignoring him, she scrutinized me. "Where in the world did you get that notion?" she asked suspiciously, although I didn't yet know about what. "Didn't Dorie tell you anything about us?" I shook my head. "Heaven help us," she let out this time, shutting her eyes as if that would make this—and maybe me—go away.

Herman spoke up. "The boy made a notcheral mistake. It could happen to Einstein."

"Another country heard from," she snapped at him. Worry written large on her—there was plenty of space for it—she studied me again but not for long, her mind made up. Whirling to the stove, she set the pot off the burner and turned back to me, with a deep, deep breath that expanded her even more into Kate Smith dimension, in my opinion. "Sweetiekins, come." She marched into the living room, killed the radio, planted herself on the davenport on an entire cushion, and patted the one beside her. I went and sat.

She looking down and me looking up, we gazed at each other in something like mutual incomprehension. I squirmed a little, and not just from the clammy touch of the davenport through the seat of my pants. Dismayed as I was, she too appeared to be thrown by the situation, until with a nod of resolve she sucked in her cheeks, as much as they would go, and compressed her lips to address the matter of me.

"Now then, lambie pie, there's nothing to be ashamed of," her tone became quite hushed, "but has your grandmother or anyone, a teacher maybe, ever said to you there might be a little bit something"—she searched for the word—"different about you?" Another breath from her very depths. "Just for example, do you get along all right in school?"

"Sure," I replied defensively, thinking she had figured out the shirt-shredding battle royal with the campers. "I'm friends with kids in more schools than you can shake a stick at, back home."

"No, no." Her bosom heaved as she gathered for another try at me. "What I mean is, have you ever been set back in school? Failed a grade, or maybe even just had teensy-weensy trouble"—she pincered her thumb and first finger close together to make sure I understood how little it would be my fault—"catching on to things in class?"

I understood, all right, shocked speechless. She figured I had a wire down. Aghast at being classified as some kind of what Letty termed a mo-ron, I sucked air like a fish out of water, until my voice came back.

"Me? No! I get straight A's! In deportment, even!" I babbled further, "I heard Miss Ciardi, that's my teacher, say to Gram I'm bright enough to read by at night."

My frantic blurts eliciting the throaty response "I see," although she didn't seem to, Aunt Kate tapped her hand on her thigh the jittery way she'd done in the car when I assumed singing to all of America was upmost on her mind.

Before she could say anything more, Herman stuck up for me from the kitchen doorway.

"Notcheral, like I telled you." His guttural assertion made us both jump a little. "Donny is not first to find the resemblance, yah? If it bothers you so great to look like the other Kate, why do you dress up so much like you could be her?"

"When I want your opinion, I'll ask for it," she flared, giving him a dirty look. "A person should be able to dress the way she likes. And if Kate Smith happens to resemble me, that is her good luck, isn't it?" A sentiment that made her draw herself up as if double-daring him to contradict it. I breathed slightly easier. If they were going to have a fight, at least that might put me on the sideline temporarily.

Not for long. Aunt Kate shifted a haunch as she turned toward me, a movement that tipped me into uncomfortably close range. "Honey bear," she tried to be nice, the effort showing, "if you're that intelligent, then you have quite the imagination."

"Maybe a little bit more than most," I owned up to.

My modest admission, she rolled over like a bulldozer. "You mustn't let it run away with you," her voice not Kate Smith–nice now. "You know why you're here, because of Dorie's—your grandmother's—operation. We can't have you going around with your head in the clouds while you're with us, we all just need to get through this summer the best we can." Another glare in the direction of the kitchen doorway. "Isn't that so, Brinker?"

Looking almost as caught as I was, Herman protectively hugged the book he was holding. "Donny and I will be straight shooters, bet your boots."

From the look in her eye, she was making ready to reply to that reply when I pulled the album out from behind my back. "All I wanted was your autograph when I thought you were you-know-who." I knew to put as much oomph into the next as I could, even though the same enthusiasm wasn't there. "I still want it, for sure. And Herman's."

"I see," she said, a little less dubiously this time. She certainly helped herself to an eyeful of the memory book as she took it from me, her lips moving surprisingly like Gram's in silently reading that cover inscription, YE WHO LEND YOUR NAME TO THESE PAGES SHALL LIVE ON UNDIMMED THROUGH THE AGES. "So that's what this is about," she said faintly to herself in flipping to one of the entries. I hoped not the Fort Peck sheriff's about keeping your pecker dry.

On pins and needles, I waited for her reaction as she dipped into the pages until she had evidently seen enough. "I need an aspirin." She spoke with her eyes clamped shut, pinching the bridge of her nose. "And then we are going to eat dinner with no more interruptions." That last, I sensed, was spoken as much for Herman's benefit as mine.

"Sweetie"—once more she made the effort to be nice to me, handing back the autograph book before heaving herself off the davenport and marching to the kitchen—"we'll be sure to write in it for you, but it can wait. Now then, come to the table, we'll eat as long as we're able." She summoned the other two of us with an obvious lift of mood, improving with every step toward the dinner pot.

No sooner was the tube steak meal ingested if not digested than Aunt Kate declared in a sweetened mood, "Chickie, you look tuckered out from your trip," which I didn't think I did, but she topped that off with the message impossible to miss, "Your room is ready for you."

The night was still a pup compared to the Greyhound's long gallop through the dark, but if she wanted to settle me in the cozy sewing room with that nice cot, I was ready for that anytime. "It's best for you to have a room all to yourself," she said, leading the way into the hall—*Wow*, I thought, *she's really putting herself out, giving up her sewing room for my sake*—"so we have fixed a place for you, haven't we, Brinker."

He oddly answered, "Yah, you come to Manito Woc and rough it like a cowboy, Donny. Make you feel at home, hah?"

And whiz, just like that, I was bypassing the cubbyhole sewing room and instead trooping upstairs behind Herman, with him insisting on lugging my suitcase—"You are the guest, you get the best"—while in back of us, Aunt Kate strenuously mounted one tread at a time. And as the stairs kept going, quite a climb by any standard, the suspicion began to seep in on me as to where we were headed, even before Herman shouldered open the squeaky door.

TO THIS DAY, that "room," up where the hayloft in a barn would be, is engraved in me. Aunt Kate could call it what she wanted, but I had bounced around enough with my parents in makeshift quarters to recognize this as nothing more than the attic. Bare roofbeams and a sharply sloping underside of the roof and probably mice and spiders, the whole works.

The first thing to strike me in my shock was the frilly bedspread flowered with purple and orange blossoms the size of cabbages, instead of the cozy quilts Gram and I slept under every night of our lives, and pillows, pillows, pillows, the useless small square ones with tassels and gold fringe and sentiments stitched on such as IT TAKES TWO LOVEBIRDS TO COO. To give Aunt Kate the benefit of good intentions, which I was not about to do, I suppose all that was an attempt to camouflage the suspect bed, which I could tell from its ancient iron legs would skreek every time a person turned over. The rest of the furniture amounted to a cheap fiberboard dresser, a rickety straight-backed chair, and a bedstand holding a lamp with a stained shade. The remainder of the space was taken up by a sagging bookcase shelved with the unmistakable yellow spines of many years' worth of *National Geographics*, and stacks of storage boxes labeled *Xmas tree lights & curtain material* and such.

A kind of concentrated Palookaville, in other words. But veteran of makeshift quarters that I was from life with Gram and my folks in construction camp circumstances, I could have put up with my so-called home for the summer but for one thing. "The thing on the wall," I immediately thought of it as, and still do. That dimestore plaster-of-Paris wall plaque no kid old enough to be acquainted with death wants to have to see the last thing before the lights are put out, the pale kneeling boy in pajamas with his hands clasped and eyes closed perhaps forever, praying a prayer guaranteed to sabotage slumber:

Now I lay me down to sleep,
I pray the Lord my soul to keep.
If I should die before I wake
I pray the Lord my soul to take.

There could not have been a worse verse facing down on me with Gram somewhere between living and dying in a faraway hospital.

That spine-chilling ode to death in the night, making it out to be no big deal as long as you got on your knees right before going to bed, unhinged me so badly that if someone had written it in the autograph book, I honestly believe I would have scissored it out.

As things were, I had trouble tearing my eyes away from the praying boy as Aunt Kate swirled around in the confined quarters, instructing me where to put things, while Herman stood well back out of the line of fire.

"There now," she said when I was installed to her satisfaction, "and you know where the bathroom is." Yeah, about a mile downstairs. "Kiss kiss." She patted her cheek in a particular spot. I kissed Gram good night every bedtime, but only reluctantly put my lips to where I was ordered in these circumstances. Gram always returned the kiss, but Aunt Kate wasn't about to. "Nighty-night, sleep tight," and away she went, clumping down the stairs one by one. Kate Smith would not have left me with anything that babyish, I knew with a sinking heart, but at least Herman came through with "Have a good shut-eye" and another of those half-cockeyed man-to-man glances as he followed her into the stairwell.

BUNKHOUSE VOCABULARY FAILED me as I undressed for bed, faced with endless nights ahead stuck up under the rafters like another piece of junk. I could have cried, and maybe should have, but instead, cold dismay welled in me. How did I land in this fix? More to the point, why? Did this whopper of a woman who was my last remaining relative after Gram hate me at first sight? Was I asking for it by showing up looking more like a stray hobo than the little gentleman she wanted me to be? What was I going to do all summer long, be kicked around in this household where the grown-ups bickered like magpies? Try as I might to think my way out of this tough situation, captive to an aunt who not only was not Kate Smith but thought I must be missing a part between my ears, the only advice I could find for myself was that bit whispered from those interrupted existences Gram kept in touch with. Hunch up and take it.

Everything churning in me that way, I lay there like the corpse promised in the thing on the wall if Manitowoc did me in before morning, until finally the exertions of the day caught up with me and I drowsed off.

Only to shoot awake at a tapping on the door and Herman's hoarse whisper:

"Donny? Are you sleeping?"

"I guess not."

"Good. I come in."

Furtively he did so, closing the door without a sound and flipping the light on, grinning at me from ear to ear. "Soldier pachamas, I see," he noted my undershirt when I sat up in bed wondering as a person will in that situation, *Now what?*

"The Kate is in the bath," he explained, as if we had plotted to meet in this secret fashion. With the same odd glint he'd had at the Greyhound station, he scooted the chair up to my bedside, displaying the book he'd been paging through earlier, thumb marking a place toward the middle. "What I wanted to show you, *Deadly Dust*, it is called in English."

This was a case where you could tell a book by its cover, with cowboys riding full-tilt while firing their six-shooters at a band of war-painted Indians chasing them in a cloud of dust. At first glimpse it might have been any of the Max Brand or Luke Short or Zane Grey shoot-'em-ups popular in the Double W bunkhouse, but the name under the title was a new one on me. Recalling my earlier encounter with the kind of person who spelled his perfectly ordinary name with a *K*, I asked skeptically, "Who's this Karl May guy?"

"'My' is how you say it," said Herman. "Great writer. All his books, I have. *Flaming Frontier. The Desperado Trail.* Lots others.

Same characters, different stories." He bobbed his head in approval. "You don't know Winnetou and Old Shatterhand?" He tut-tutted like a schoolteacher. "Big heroes of The West." I could hear his capital letters on those last two words.

Maybe so, but when he opened the book in evidence, in his squarehead language as it was and fancy-lettered like in an old Bible, not a single word was recognizable to me. That didn't matter a hoot to Herman as he proudly showed me the illustration he had hunted down in the middle of the book, translating the wording under it.

"On the bound-less plains of Montana," he read with great care, adjusting his glasses, *"the tepee rings of the Blackfoot, Crow, and Ass-in-i-bone tribes—"*

"I think that's Assiniboine," I suggested.

He thanked me and read on. *"—are the eternal hunting tracks of following the buffaloes, the be-he-moths of the prairie."*

Triumphantly he turned the book so I could not miss the full effect of the picture, which looked awfully familiar, similar to a Charlie Russell painting seen on endless drugstore calendars. It depicted Indian hunters in wolf skins sneaking up on foot to stampede a herd of buffalo over a cliff, the great hairy beasts cascading to the boulders below.

"There you go, hah?" Herman whispered in awe at the spectacle. "Such a place, where you are from."

It took all the restraint I had, but I didn't let on that right over there in my pants was a little something from Montana that might have slain many a buffalo. This Herman was wound up enough as it was; the night might never end if we got off on more or less lucky arrowheads and so on. I stuck to the strictly necessary. "Can I tell you something? It's Mon-TANA, not MONT-ana."

"Funny things, words. How they look and how they say." He

broke off, glancing toward his feet. Letting out an exclamation I couldn't decipher, he reached down and picked up one of my moccasins.

"I stepped on it!" he cried out, as if he had committed a crime. "I hope I didn't break it none."

I could tell by a quick look that the decorative fancy-dancer still had all his limbs and that the rest of the beadwork had survived, too, so I reassured Herman no harm had been done, while scooping the other moccasin out of range of his big feet.

"Fascinating," he said under his breath, pronouncing it *faskinating*, lovingly turning over and over in his hands the deerskin footwear he had tromped on. When he right away had to know what the beaded stick figure cavorting there on the toe and instep was supposed to be, I explained about fancy-dancing contests at big powwows.

Still fondling the moccasin as if he couldn't let go, he asked in wonder, "You got from Indians?"

"As Indian as they come." This time I couldn't resist. Before I could stop myself, I was repeating the tale I'd told the ex-convict about the classy moccasins having been made for a great Blackfoot chief, temperately leaving out the part about my having won them in a roping contest on a dude ranch and instead circling closer to the truth by saying Gram had lucked onto them on the reservation. Herman did not need to know they'd been hocked at a truck stop by a broke Indian.

"How good, you have them. You are some lucky boy." Maybe so, if the rotten sort was counted along with the better kind, I thought darkly to myself there on the skreeky bed.

He ran his fingers over the beadwork and soft leather one more time and carefully put the moccasin side by side with the other one.

"So, now you know about Winnetou and I know about fancy-dancing. Big night!" He grinned in that horsy way and clapped

Deadly Dust shut. Evidently gauging that Aunt Kate's bath was about done, he rose from his chair. "We palaver some more tomorrow, yah?" he whispered from the stairwell as he sneaked back downstairs.

I sank onto the swayback pillow, wide-awake in the darkness of a summer that was showing every sign of being one for *Believe It or Not!*

10.

I WAS AN old hand at waking up in new places, worlds each as different from the last one as strange planets visited by Buck Rogers while he rocketed through the universe in the funny papers. In fact, when my father's series of dam jobs landed us at the Pishkun reservoir site, we were quartered in an abandoned homestead cabin wallpapered with years' worth of the Great Falls *Tribune*'s Sunday funnies. The homesteader must have had insulation on his mind more than humor, randomly pasting the colorful newspaper sheets upside down or not. Little could match the confusion of blinking awake in the early light to the Katzenjammer Kids inches from my nose going about their mischief while standing on their heads. But that first Manitowoc morning, opening my eyes to attic rafters bare as jail bars, the thing on the wall hovering like a leftover bad dream, my neck with a crick in it from the stove-in pillow, I had a lot more to figure out than why Hans and Fritz were topsy-turvy.

Such as how to get on the good side of the Kate, as Herman tellingly designated her. Plainly she was something unto herself, by any measure.

And so, determined to make up for my dumb jump to the wrong conclusion last night—although was it my fault both she and Kate Smith were the size of refrigerators and shared jolly numbers of chins and dimples and all in all looked enough alike to be twins?—I dressed quickly and headed downstairs.

Nice manners don't cost anything, Gram's prompting followed me down the steps. C'mon, Donny, Donal, Red Chief, I pulled myself together, it shouldn't be all that hard to remember to be polite and to speak mainly when spoken to and to not mix up when to look serious and when to smile, and similar rules of the well-behaved. Hadn't I gotten along perfectly fine with tons of strangers on the dog bus? Well, a couple of drivers, the ex-convict, and one fistfight aside.

Surely those didn't count toward the main matter, which was to survive for the time being in a household where Aunt Kate seemed to wear the pants and Herman tended to his knitting in the company of beings with names like Winnetou and Old Shatterhand.

In the light of day it was clear that if I knew what was good for me, I had better fit somewhere in between them, tight as the fit might be, and strolling in at breakfast with a sunny "Good morning!" and the white lie "I slept real good" ought to be the place to start.

Only to be met, before I even was out of the stairwell, by raised voices.

"Will you kindly quit playing with your food? How many times have I told you it's disgusting."

"Same number I telled you, it helps with the digestion."

"Toast does not need help!"

"Hah. Shows what you know. More to it than feed your face like a cow."

Whoa. I backed off to the bathroom, out of range of the blowup in the kitchen, in a hurry. Staying in there a good long while, I ran the faucets full blast and flushed the toilet a couple of times to announce my presence, and finally cracked the door open to test the atmosphere. Not a sound of any kind. Deafening silence, to call it that, was spooky in its own way and maybe not an improvement, but I couldn't stay in the bathroom permanently. Mustering myself, I approached the deadly quiet kitchen.

Herman was nowhere to be seen. Aunt Kate was sitting by herself there, in a peppermint-striped flannel robe and fuzzy pink slippers that would never be mistaken for part of Kate Smith's wardrobe, drinking coffee while reading the newspaper spread open on the table. "There you are, sugarplum." She looked up as if reminding herself of my existence, before I could say anything. That voice made the simplest greeting musical. "Did you sleep all right, poor tired thing?"

Nervously I met that with "Like a petrified log."

There may have been a surprising amount of truth in that, because sunshine was streaming through the window at quite a steep angle. I checked the clock over the stove and was shocked to see it was nearly nine. On the ranch, breakfast was at six prompt, and no small portion of my shock, beyond sleeping in halfway to noon, was that she and Herman started the day so late and casually. Their plates, one littered with dark crusts of toast, still were on the table. I was no whiz about schedules, but I doubted that time zones alone accounted for such a difference.

"Now then," Aunt Kate said with no urgency, licking her finger and turning a page of the newspaper, "what in the realm of possibility can we get you for breakfast, mmm?"

I answered with more manners than good sense. "Oh, just whatever you've got."

Aunt Kate barely had to budge to honor that, reaching to the counter for a cereal box I had not seen in time. Puffed rice, the closest thing to eating air. Swallowing on that fact, if not much else, I found a bowl in the cupboard as she directed and a milk bottle in the refrigerator and spied the sugar bowl and did what I could to turn the puffed stuff into a soup of milk and sugar. A parent would have jumped right on me for that, but she paid no attention.

Evidently the kind of person who did not have much to say in the morning—although that was not what it had sounded like from the stairwell—she kept on drinking coffee and going through the paper, occasionally letting out a high-pitched hum of interest or exasperation at some item, as I spooned down the puffed-up cereal. The scatterings of crust on what must have been Herman's plate seemed like a fuller meal than mine.

Finally I saw no choice but to ask, polite or not. "Suppose I could have a piece of toast, please?"

That drew me a bit of a look, but I was pointed to where the bread was kept and warned about the setting on the toaster. "He likes it incinerated," Aunt Kate made plain as she pushed off to answer the phone ringing in the living room.

"This is she." I learned a new diction while attending to my toast. That voice of hers turned melodious even in talking on the phone, rising and falling with the conversation. "Yes. Yes. You're very kind to call. That's good to know." Wouldn't it be something if people sounded like that all the time, halfway to music? "I see. No, no, you needn't bother, I can tell him." Her tone sharpened. "She did? Oh, all right, if you insist." Industriously buttering my toast, I about dropped the knife when I heard:

"Donny, come to the phone."

LIKE THE FIRST time of handling the reins of a horse or the gearshift of a car, things only grown-ups touched previous to then, I can still feel that oblong plastic pink receiver as I tentatively brought it close to my mouth.

"Hello? This is . . . he."

"I am Sister Carma Jean," the voice sounding exactly like you would imagine a nun's came as crisp as if it were in the room, instead of fifteen hundred miles away at Columbus Hospital. I was dazed, unsure, afraid of what I might hear next.

"Last thing when I was at her bedside, your grandmother wished me to tell you yourself"—echo of *last wish* in that; I clung harder to the receiver—"she has come through the operation as well as can be expected."

I breathed again, some.

"Of course, there are complications with that kind of surgery," the Sister of Charity spoke more softly now, "so her recuperation will take some time." Complications. Those sounded bad, and right away I was scared again. "But we have her here in the pavilion," the voice on the line barely came through to me, "where she is receiving the best of care. You mustn't worry." As if I could just make up my mind not to.

Aunt Kate hovered by the bay window pinching dead leaves off the potted plants while I strained to believe what was being recited by the holy sister in Great Falls. "She says to tell you," the nun could be heard gamely testing out Gram's words, "you are not to be red in the head about things, the summer will be over before you know it."

"Can I—" My throat tight, I had trouble getting the sentence out, but was desperate to. "Can I please talk to her?"

"I'm sorry, but she's resting now." That sounded so protective I didn't know whether it was good or bad. "Is there something you would like for me to tell her?"

I swear, Aunt Kate was putting together everything said, just from hearing my side of the conversation, as snoopy as if she were the third party on the line. Why couldn't she go back in the kitchen, or better yet, off to the bathroom, so I could freely report something like *I'm stuck in an attic, and Aunt Kitty who isn't Kate Smith and Herman who isn't Uncle Dutch turn out to be the kind of people who fight over the complexion of a piece of toast.*

"I guess not," I quavered, squeezing the phone. Then erased that in the next breath. "No, wait, there is, too. Tell her"—I could feel the look from across the room—"the dog bus worked out okay." Mentally adding, *But Manito Woc or however you say it is even a tougher proposition than either you or I ever imagined, Gram. So please get well really, really fast.*

AS SOON AS I clunked the phone into its cradle, Aunt Kate squared around to me from patrolling the potted plants and trilled as if warming up her voice, "Wasn't that good news. Mostly."

"I guess."

That word *complications* rang in my ears, and no doubt hers, as we faced each other's company for an unknown length of time ahead.

"Well, now, we must keep you entertained, mustn't we. I know you like to be busy, so I set up the card table and got out a jigsaw puzzle. Those are always fun, aren't they."

Maybe I was not the absolute shrewdest judge of character, but I had a pretty good hunch that habit of agreeing with herself covered up her desperation at not knowing what to do with a kid. This household didn't have so much as a dog or cat, not even a goldfish. By all evidence so far, Aunt Kate was only used to taking care of herself and the constant war with Herman, as it gave every appearance of being.

Right now she was at her most smiling and dimpled as she led me over to the card table, stuck as far out of the way as possible in the corner of the living room, and the puzzle box front and center on it. MOUNT RUSHMORE—KNOW YOUR PRESIDENTS, and in smaller type, *1,000 Pieces.* Worse yet, it was one I had already done in my jigsaw period, when Gram was trying to keep me occupied. "Yeah, swell," I managed to remark.

Ready to leave me to the mountain of puzzle pieces and my cold toast, Aunt Kate headed for the basement to see if the laundry was finished yet. "Oh, just so you know," she sang out as she started down the cellar stairs, "I put your snap-button shirt in with our washing, but the other was torn so badly I threw it away. It wasn't worth mending."

"Doesn't surprise me," I called back. Catching up to the fact I hadn't bothered to remove my stash from the ruined shirt the night before, what with everything else going on, I inquired for the sake of keeping current, "Where did you put my money?"

The footsteps on the stairs halting, her voice came muffled. "What money is that?"

"It was safety-pinned to the back of the good pocket, Gram did that so a pickpocket couldn't steal it and—"

For someone of her heft, she came up out of those cellar stairs in a terrific burst of speed, turned the hall corner at full tilt, and barreled through the kitchen and out to the garbage can at the top of the driveway, flannel robe billowing behind her, me at her heels. Her backside was too broad for me to see past as she flung open the lid of the can and looked in, and I was afraid to anyway.

"Too late," she moaned, "it's been picked up."

"C-can't we get it back?" Frantically I ran down the driveway, followed by Aunt Kate at a heavy gallop. Pulling up short at the curb, I shot a look one way along the street and she the other, then our heads swung in the opposite directions, staring past each other. No garbage truck. We listened hard. Nothing to be heard except her puffing and blowing.

"Maybe we could go to the dump," I stammered, "and head it off."

"Impossible," she said in a way that could have meant either the dump or me. With that, we trudged back up the driveway, the slap-slap of her fuzzy slippers matching the thuds of my heart.

Outside the kitchen door, she rounded on me furiously. "Why didn't you tell me it was pinned there?"

"I—I didn't know you were going to do the wash so soon," I blurted, which was not the real answer to the real question.

That was coming now, as she drilled her gaze into me and started in. "More than that, why didn't you—"

But before she could rightfully jump all over me for forgetting to rescue the money myself before dropping the shirt in the laundry chute, she stopped and pinched between her eyes in that way that signaled she needed an aspirin. After a moment, eyes still tight shut, she asked as if she could not face any more of this, "How much was it?"

"Th-thirty dollars, all I had," I said, as if it were an absolute fortune, which to me it was. As I've said, no small sum in those days, to someone like her either, according to the excruciating groan she let out.

"See," I tried to explain, "I was supposed to buy my school clothes with it, and whatever comic books I wanted, and go to a show once in a while if you said it was okay, and—" I looked at her angry, flushed face, twice the size of my merely red one, and abjectly tailed off—"wasn't supposed to be a nuisance to you about money."

"That didn't quite work out, did it," she fried my hide some more as she stomped back into the kitchen, still mad as could be. I shrank behind her, keeping a cautious distance. "Now this," she declaimed, "on top of everything else," which seemed to mean me generally. "And I have all these things to do," she further declared, just as if she had not been sitting around drinking coffee and reading the newspaper half the morning.

I babbled another apology to try to make amends, although I wasn't getting anything of the sort from her for failing to go through my pocket before junking my shirt and costing me every cent I possessed, was I?

"Why don't you start on your puzzle," she said darkly, heading for the basement again.

"Maybe later." By now I felt the right to sulk. Even if I had been in the wrong about not retrieving the money from that shirt, I didn't think I was the only one, and I was not going to let myself be sent to the permanent dunce corner, which the card table with Mount Rushmore in a thousand pieces amounted to. It occurred to me that, with this woman as mad at me as a spitting cat, it would really help to have someone on my side, or at least another target to draw her fire. "Where'd Herman go?" I wondered, hoping he might show up any moment to get me off the hook.

No such luck. Gone to "work," where else, she forgot about the basement long enough to circle back and huff, the quotation marks speaking loudest. When I asked what his job was, she sorted me out on that in a hurry.

"Job?" She drew the word out mockingly as she clattered stray breakfast dishes into the sink in passing. "That will be the day. The old pooter"—that bit of Gram's language out of her startled me—"is out in that greenhouse of his again." My mention of him did change matters, though, because at the cellar stairs she whipped around to me, with a different look in her doll eyes.

"You can go help him, dearie, wouldn't that be nice?" she suggested, suspiciously sweet all of a sudden. "Make yourself useful as well as ornamental." Gesturing around as if chores were swarming at her and I was in the way, she exclaimed that life was simply too, too busy. "After I deal with the laundry, I have to get ready." She didn't bother to say for what, and from the set of her chins, I could tell she did not want to hear anything more out of me but footsteps as I hustled my fanny to that greenhouse.

"Maybe I'll go say hi," I mumbled, and trooped out to the backyard, where the odd shed of glass gleamed in the sun. Already at that time of the morning, the Wisconsin air felt heavy to me, as if it could be squeezed out like a sponge, and I plucked at my one wearable shirt of the moment and unbuttoned my sleeves and rolled them back onto my forearms for a bit of ventilation as I crossed the lawn, Herman's big footprints ahead of me fading with the last of the dew.

I had been curious about the mystifying structure when the DeSoto's headlights reflected off it the night before, which now seemed a lifetime ago. Halfway hidden in a corner of the hedge at the rear of the yard, the greenhouse, as I now knew it, seemed like it ought to be transparent but somehow could not actually be seen through, whatever the trick of its construction was.

It did not reveal much more about itself in broad daylight as I approached past a neatly marked-out vegetable patch, the small glass panels that were the walls and roof of the shed frame splotchy as if needing a good washing. Funny way to grow things, the soot smears or whatever they were blocking out full light that way, I thought. Weird old Wisconsin, one more time.

"Knock knock," I called in, not knowing how to do otherwise when everything was breakable.

"Hallo" issued from I didn't know where in the low jungle of plants, until Herman leaned into sight amid the greenery, where he was perched on a low stool while spooning something into a potted tomato as if feeding a baby. "Come, come," he encouraged me in, "meet everybody."

There certainly was a crowd of plants when I ducked in, all right, and according to their names written on markers like Popsicle sticks in the clay pots, several kinds you could not grow in Montana in a hundred years, green peppers and honeydew melons and such. I also spotted, at the other end of edibility, a miniature field of cabbage seedlings, sauerkraut makings.

Properly impressed with his green thumb, I stood back and watched Herman fuss over his crop, pot by leafy pot. Pausing to tap the ash off a smelly cigar that undoubtedly would not have been allowed into the house, he made a face that had nothing to do with the haze of smoke that had me blinking to keep my eyes from watering.

"You have escaped with your scalp, yah? I heard the Kate on the warpath again."

"Yeah, well, she's sort of pee oh'd at me," I owned up to, making plain that the feeling was mutual.

Herman listened with sympathy, as best I could tell behind his heavy glasses and the reeking cigar, while I spilled out the story of the torn shirt and the fatally safety-pinned bills. He tut-tutted over that, saying throwing money in the garbage was not good at all. But he didn't lend me any encouragement as to how I was supposed to get through the summer flat broke.

"The purse is the Kate's department," he said with a resigned puff of smoke. Reflecting further, he expressed effectively: "She is tight as a wad."

I must have looked even more worried, if possible, for he added, as if it would buck up my spirits, "Sometimes she barks worse than she bites. Sometimes."

By way of Gram, that was the kind of statement I had learned to put in the category of free advice and worth just what it cost. At the moment there was nothing I could do about an aunt who either barked or bit, so I took a look around to see what "helping" Herman in the greenhouse might consist of. Except for possibly scrubbing the blotchy windows, nothing suggested itself, inasmuch as he had turned the glass shed into a greatly more cozy place than, say, my rat hole of an attic. Long wooden shelves along either side handily held not only the miniature forest of plants he had started in pots, but garden trowels and snippers and other tools and a colorful array of fertilizer boxes and so on, a coffee thermos, a cigar box, and a stack of books by Karl May, who evidently had more *Deadly Dust* up his sleeve after that Montana buffalo hunt. Stashed in a corner was an old gray duffel of the seabag sort, doubtless holding more treasures the Kate had banned from the house.

Growing interested in spite of myself, I made the offer the lukewarm way—"Uhm, anything I can do?"—a person does just to be polite.

"Yah, keep me company." He dragged out a wooden fruit box from under the shelf for me to sit on. "Tell me about Montana," he pronounced it pretty close to right. "Cowboy life."

THAT GOT ME STARTED, almost as if I was back on the dog bus telling yarns free and easy. I regaled Herman with this, that, and the other about life on the Double W, from riding out with the actual cowboys to check on the cattle, to hunting magpies along the creek, making him exclaim I was a pistoleer, by which I figured he meant gunslinger. Puffing away on his stogie and babying his plants with spoonfuls of fertilizer and careful irrigation from a long-necked watering can—a couple of times I interrupted myself to go and fill it for him from the spigot at the back of the house—Herman listened to all of it as though I were a storyteller right up there with his idol who wrote the pile of books about cowboys and Indians.

In the end, my storying naturally led around to the whole thing, Gram and me being chucked out of the cook shack and her into the charity ward and me onto the dog bus, when I could just as well have been earning wages in the hayfield the entire summer, and while I couldn't quite bring myself to lay out my full fear about the poorfarm looming in her future if medical things did not go right, and orphanage starkly in mine, he grasped enough of the situation to tut-tut gravely again.

"A fix, you are in," he said with a frown that wrinkled much of his face. "The Kate didn't tell me the all."

Somehow I felt better for having poured out that much of the tale, even if it went into squarehead ears, so to speak. At first I was suspicious that Herman resorted to a kind of Indian speakum in talking about anything western, but no, it became clear that was genuinely his lingo from the old country mixed in with the new.

Whatever the travels of his tongue, I was finding this big husky open-faced man to be the one thing about Wisconsin that I felt vaguely comfortable with, despite his evident quirks and odd appearance. In most ways, he was homely as a pickle. That elongated face and the prominent teeth, taken together with the cockeyed gaze magnified by his glasses, gave him the look of someone loopy enough that you might not want to sit right down next to, although of course there I was, plotched beside him like just another potted plant. Together with everything else in the humid greenhouse, he himself seemed to have sprouted, his shoulders topping my head as he stretched from his stool here and there to reach into his menagerie of vegetation, his big knuckles working smoothly as machine parts in crimping a leaf off a tomato plant near its root—"Pinch their bottoms is good for them," he told me with a naughty grin—or tying a lagging bean stalk to a support stick. The dappled light streaming through the glass ceiling and walls brought out the silver in his faded fair hair, which I suspected made him older than Aunt Kate, although there was no real telling. I'd have bet anything gray hair did not stand a chance on her; she would rather, as not much of a joke had it, dye by her own hand.

About then, as I was yammering away with Herman, I noticed a strange smudge of some sort on the back of my hand. Dirt is to be expected in a greenhouse, so I went to brush it off, but when that didn't get rid of it, I peered more closely. Then gasped. A ghostly scrap of face, an eye clear and direct, feminine eyebrow and ladylike cheekbone distinct in outline, had scarily materialized on my skin. Yanking my hand away as if burned, I sent Herman one hell of a look. Whatever this stunt was, I didn't like having it pulled on me.

"Surprises your daylights out, yah?" he said, unperturbed. "They do that." He pointed upward with the cigar between his fingers. "Photo graphic plates," he spoke it as three words.

I tipped my head back and must have gaped, my eyes adjusting even if my brain was lagging. When looked at closely, reversed faces spookily gazed down from every glass pane, eyes and hair empty of color while the rest of the countenance was dark as night. Bygone people, for I could make out old styles of men's collars and women's hairdos—the lady who appeared on my hand again when I hesitantly put it out and held it at the right distance to bring her portrait pose into full miniature was done up in marcel curls, her probably black tresses tumbling ever so neatly down the sides of her head.

Agog, I kept looking back and forth from her image there on me to the shadowy section of glass overhead, still not seeing how this worked. "These—these things were in cameras? How?"

Patiently Herman explained, enlightening me that photographic plates made to fit in large box cameras that stood on tripods were the way pictures used to be developed, before there were film negatives. "Old-timey, but they last good and long," he concluded. That was for sure. The gallery of little windows faithfully saved for posterity milk-complexioned women and bearded men and sometimes entire families down to babies in arms, everyone in their Sunday best, sitting for their portraits way back when and now turned into apparitions keeping company with the pair of us and the vegetable kingdom.

"So, Donny," the master of the house of glass went on with a squint that was all but a wink. "When Schildkraut's Photography Shop went *pthht*," he made the noise that meant kaput, "these are for the dump but I get there first. The Kate thinks I am crazy to do it, but glass is glass, why not make a greenhouse, hah?" He tapped his forehead, his eyebrows lifted toward the plates pintoed dark with people. "I give a little think whether to scrape people off. Nuh-uh, leave them like so. Makes it not too hot in here." He had a point. Without those clever dabs of shade and a pair of hinged windows that let some air through, the greenhouse would have been an oven by the afternoon.

Along with me, Herman gazed up at the ranks of panes of glass with their memories showing. Picking up a box lid large enough to catch more than a single phantom photo from overhead, he now showed me that the smoky blotches turning into recognizable pictures like the one on me were a trick of the brightening sunshine as the day went along, the rays hitting the photographic substance a certain way like a darkroom enlarger.

I more or less grasped that, but still was spooked enough to ask in nearly a whisper:

"Who are they?"

"Manitowocers," he said around the stub of his cigar, or maybe "Manito Walkers," I couldn't be sure which he meant. At the time, I assumed he merely meant those in the old days who had but to gallivant around town to think they were hearing their blest souls talk, according to the cross-stitched sampler hanging in the living room. I was disappointed the figures preserved in glass were as ordinary as that, but maybe that was Manitowoc for you, nothing to do but hoof around being airy.

Just then, the back door of the house banged like a shot, making me nearly jump out of my skin, Herman reacting with a jolt, too, the ash spilling off his cigar. A dressed-up Aunt Kate was advancing on us with quick little steps, high heels tricky on the lawn. Again my heart twinged, that someone who was such a perfect mirror reflection of Kate Smith was not the real thing.

I did not have time for much of that kind of regret, as she minced right up to the doorway of the greenhouse—plainly she was not setting foot in the place—and announced, "I'm off to canasta. You two are on your own if you think you can stand it."

At first I thought she was picking up and leaving for another town with one of those Wisconsin names, which raised my spirits no little bit, until Herman said without a trace of expression, "Cut the deck thin and win," and I realized she was only off to a card game.

Tugging at her lemon-colored outfit, which was as tight on her as fabric would allow, she addressed me on my fruit box as if having sudden second thoughts about dispatching me to the care of Herman and the greenhouse. "I hope he isn't talking your ear off about cowboys and Indians, sweetie. He has them on the brain."

"Oh, no, he's been introducing me to the vegetables, is all."

That drew me a swift look from her, but her attention reverted to Herman. "Don't forget, Brinker, you'll need to fix lunch," she told him as if he'd better put a string around his finger.

"We will eat like kings," he answered, puttering with a tomato plant.

"Just so it isn't like jokers wild," she deadpanned, which I had to admit was pretty good. "Toodle-oo, you two," she left us with. "I'll be back when you see me coming," another echo of Gram that surprised me.

I watched her pick her way to the DeSoto and drive off speedily. Showing less interest in the tomato plant now, Herman peered at me through his specs. "She is off to her hen party. They will yack-yack for hours. Now then," he luxuriously mimicked that word combination of hers that made less sense the more you thought about it, patting around on himself to find his matches and light up another cigar, as if in celebration of the Kate being gone. He gave me a man-to-man grin. "So how do you like Manito Woc?"

There it was again. "How come you say it that way?"

And again the bucktooth grin turned ever so slightly sly. "It is where Manito walks, you don't think?"

I shrugged, although I could feel something about this conversation creeping up on me. "Who's Manito?"

"To be right, it is Manitou," he amended, spelling it. "You don't know Manitou?" I couldn't tell whether he was teasing or for real. "From Indian?"

I was hooked. "Huh-uh. Tell me."

He blew a stream of smoke that curled in the heavy air. "Gitche Manitou is the Great Spirit."

"Gitchy," I echoed but dubiously, wondering if my leg was being pulled.

"Yah, like Gitche Gumee, from the poem?" He looked saddened when I had to tell him I was not up on Hiawatha.

"*By the shore of Gitche Gumee*," he recited, his accent thumping like thunder. Again, I had to shrug. "*By the shining Big-Sea Water*," he persisted. I shook my head, wishing he would try me on something like "*A flea and a fly in a flue . . .*"

Despairing of my lack of literary education, he held up crossed fingers. "Longfellow and Karl May were like so. Poets of Gitche and Winnetou."

"Good for them," I tried faking hearty agreement to clear dead poets out of the growing crowd of specters in the greenhouse, and get to what I saw as the point. "Then where are any Indians in Manitowoc?"

"Gone." He waved a hand as if tossing a good-bye. "That is why it is said the spirits walk, hah?"

SUPPOSEDLY IT TAKES one to know one, right? So, then and there, my own sometimes overly active mind, red in the head or however the condition of seeing things for more than they are can best be described, was forced to acknowledge that this odd bespectacled yah-saying garden putterer and henpecked husband, fully five times older than me, had a king hell bastard of an imagination. Possibly outdoing my own, which I know is saying a lot. Wherever Herman Brinker got it from, he'd held on to the rare quality that usually leaves a person after a certain number of years as a kid, to let what he had read possess him. I saw now why Aunt Kate was forever at him about taking to heart too much the stories of Karl May in what seemed to be, well, squarehead westerns. Not that I wanted to side with her, storyteller of a sort that I sometimes turned into. But from my experience of his mental workings so far, notions Herman had picked up out of books did not appear to be condensed from their imaginative extent any at all, let alone properly digested.

PUT IT WHATEVER WAY, this was getting too thick for me, people dead and gone but still strolling around in my cigar-smoking host's telling of it, as well as shadows on glass flaring to life like lit matches, Manitowocers here, Manitou walkers there—a lot more than potted plants flourished in this greenhouse of his.

I shifted uncomfortably on my fruit box. "Spirits like in ghosts, you mean? Herman, I'm sorry, but I don't think we're supposed to believe in those."

"We can believe in Indians, I betcha." He had me there. I could see him thinking, cocking a look at the dappled shed's glassy figures, and as it turned out, beyond. "So, paleface cow herders, you know much of. How about—?" He patted his hand on his mouth warwhoop style, mocking the Kate's charge that he had cowboys and Indians on the brain.

With an opening like that, how could I resist?

"Well, sure, now that you mention it," that set me off, "I've been around Indians a lot," skipping the detail that the last time, I'd slept through most of a busload of them. Trying to sound really veteran, I tossed off, "I even went to school with Blackfoot kids most of one year at Heart Butte."

"Heart? Like gives us life, yah?"

"Yeah—I mean, yes, same word anyhow."

Herman leaned way toward me, cigar forgotten for the moment. "Heart Bee-yoot. Bee-yoot-iffle name. Tell more."

I didn't bother to say that was the only thing of any beauty at the remote and tough little Blackfoot reservation school where, around Dwayne Left Hand and Vern Rides Proud, I wisely kept my trap shut about my Red Chief nickname and endured being called Brookie for the freckles that reminded them of the speckles on eastern brook trout. That Heart Butte schoolyard with its rough teasing and impromptu fistfights was at least as educational as the schoolroom. But if Herman was gaga about things Indian, here was my perfect chance to confide the Red Chief nickname to him.

He was impressed, more so than he really needed to be, I noted somewhat apprehensively when I was done. "Up there with Winnetou, you are," he exclaimed, slapping his knee. "Young chiefs. No wonder you got the fancy moccasins."

"Yeah, but"—I stole an uneasy glance at the pile of Karl May books—"who's this Winnetou anyway? What tribe he's from, even?" If he was Blackfoot, my Red Chief tag might as well shrink back to Heart Butte invisibility in comparison.

Herman puffed on his cigar, maybe seeking smoke signals, as he gave it a think about how best to answer. Finally he said, "An Apache knight, he was."

I tried to sort that out, never having heard of an Indian clanking around in a suit of armor, and said as much.

Herman laughed. "Not iron clothes, hah. Leather leggings and a hunting shirt, he dressed in, and, best yet"—he nodded approvingly at me—"fancy moccasins." Turning serious again, he went on. "Karl May calls him a knight because he was honorable. His word you could trust. He fought fair. Like a chief supposed to, yah." He nodded at me gravely this time.

"Uhm, Herman, you better know." In all this Indian stuff, I didn't want to end up chewing more than I could bite off. "I haven't had much practice at any of that, see. I mean, with me, you can tell where the Red came from"—I flopped my hair—"but the Chief thinger is just from my dad. Sort of kidding, in a way, is all."

"Maybe not all." He gave me one of his cockeyed glances through the thick glasses. "Maybe he thought the name fit more than"—he kept a straight face, but it still came out sly—"your scalp."

11.

One thing about hanging around with Herman, time went by like a breeze. That noontime, with Aunt Kate gone to canasta, the house was without commotion as Herman assembled lunch, laying out the kind of store bread that came sliced and without taste, but announcing we would have plenty of sandwich meat, which to me meant good old baloney slathered with mayonnaise and had me licking my lips, after the menu in this household so far. I stayed out of the way by reading the funnies in the newspaper until he called me to the table. "Meal fit for an earl."

When I looked blank at that, he winked and said, "Earl of Sandwich, invented guess what."

Some sense of caution caused me to peek under the top slice of bread, revealing a gray slab pocked with gelatin and strange colonies of what might be meat or something else entirely. "Is this"—I couldn't even ask without swallowing hard—"headcheese?"

"Yah. A treat." Herman took a horsebite mouthful. "The Kate won't eat it," he said, chewing. "She calls it disgusting, if you will imagine."

I was entirely with her on that, for I had seen the ingredients of headcheese, each more stomach-turning than the next, come off the hog carcass at butchering time when the animal's head and feet and bloody tongue were chucked in a bucket for further chopping up. But at any mealtime, Gram's voice was never far distant—*If it's put in front of you, it's edible at some level*—and by not looking at the jellied pork rubbish between the sandwich bread, I got it down.

This Wisconsin incarceration evidently requiring digestive juices of various kinds, I stayed at the table stewing on matters, trying to assimilate what all had happened since my arrival into this unnerving household, while Herman pottered at washing up our few dishes. When he was done and hanging up the dish towel in a fussy way not even the Kate could criticize, I ventured: "Can I ask you a sort of personal thing?"

"Shoot, podner," he responded agreeably enough, pointing a finger and cocked thumb at me like a pistol, which I figured must be something he picked up from a Karl May western.

"Right. How come you don't go by the name 'Dutch' anymore?"

He pursed his lips a couple of times as if tasting the inquiry, then came and sat at the table with me before answering, if that's what it was. "Down with the ship, it went."

He appeared to be serious. *Oh man,* I thought to myself, *first the Gitchy something or other, walking around dead, now this. Was this some squarehead joke?*

"Sounds funny, yah?" Herman conceded. "But when the *Badger Voyager* sinked, my name 'Dutch' was no more, after." Again he made the *pthht* sound. He folded his big hands on the table as he looked straight across at me in that uneven gaze of his. "Onshore, 'Herman' got new life."

I still didn't grasp that swap, and said so.

Herman grabbed for the sugar bowl with sudden purpose. "You know about ore boats any, Donny?"

At the shake of my head, he instructed, "This is ore boat. *Badger Voyager*, pretend. Table is Great Lakes. Gee-oh-graphy lesson, hah?"

Plotching a hand here and there across the tabletop, he named off the bodies of water—Superior, Michigan, Huron, Erie, Ontario—while I paid strict attention as if about to be called on in class.

He steered the sugar bowl toward me. "Where you sit is Duluth. Full of iron mines. How it works, *Badger Voyager* comes, loads ore, takes it maybe here, maybe there"—he maneuvered the sugar bowl in winding routes to various ports of call, where he told me the ore was turned into steel, Chicago, Cleveland, all the way to Buffalo.

Very instructive, yes, if you could make yourself interested in that kind of thing. "But what about—"

"'Dutch,' yah. Coming to that."

He peered at the sugar bowl through his strong glasses as if encouraging me to have a close look, too. "He is on the ore boat, see. Me, I mean. Twenty years." Pride shone out of him as he sat back, shoulders near square enough to burst out of his shirt. "A stoker I was."

I puzzled over that. Like stoking a stove? A cook's helper, like I sometimes was in kitchen chores for Gram? He pawed away that supposition, explaining a stoker's job in the boiler room of a ship. "Mountains of coal have I shoveled."

"But you don't do that anymore," I said, thinking of Aunt Kate's mocking response when I'd asked about his job.

"Hah, no. I am onshore, so 'Dutch' is no more. No shipmates to call me that. I change to 'Herman,' who I was before."

This was a whole lot more complicated than my Red Chief nickname coming and going at will, I could see. Still, something had been left out of the story, and my guarded silence must have told him I knew it had. Herman, who looked to me as if he could still stoke coal all day long if he wanted to, read my face with that unsettling cockeyed gaze. "The Kate did not blabber it to you? Something wrong. Her tongue must be tied up."

He sat back again and folded his arms as if putting away the hands that fit a coal shovel. "A settlement I have."

Thinking the word through, I took it apart enough to ask hesitantly, "Wh-what got settled? Like a fight?"

"I show you."

He navigated the sugar bowl back to the Lake Superior territory of the table, then began wobbling it so drastically I thought it would spill.

"Straits of Mackinaw," he pronounced the word that is spelled *Mackinac*. For some moments, he didn't say anything more, a tic working at the corner of his eye as if he had something in it, all the while staring at the imaginary piece of water. At last he said in a strained voice: "Bad place any old time. Bad and then some, when Witch of November comes."

Another one of those? One more Great Spirit of Gitche Gumee or whatever, I didn't need. My skin was starting to crawl again.

All seriousness, he cupped his hands around the sugar bowl as if protecting it. "Witch of November is big storm. Guess what time of year."

He drew a breath as if girding himself for that mean-sounding storm. "When Witch of November comes, you are on the boat, no place to go"—opening his hands to expose the fragile sugar bowl—"and waves big like hills hitting the deck, send you over the side if you don't hang on hard as you can. Drown you like a kitten katten in a bag, it will."

That description did make quite a bit of an impression, I had to admit. But we still weren't anywhere near how the name Dutch went down with the ship and Herman was sitting here big as life. Maybe I was being a sucker, but I said, "Go on."

"Night of thirtieth of November, *Badger Voyager* gets to Straits of Mackinac," his voice growing husky as he maneuvered the sugar bowl. "We feel lucky, no Witch that year, nineteen and forty-seven. Then it starts storming, middle of night—Witch of November saving up all month, hah? Worst I was in, ever. Lost an old friend, the bosun." Teeth clenched, he girded himself again for telling this. "We sailed together maybe hundred times on the Lakes. This time, bad luck is with him. One minute he is giving orders like ever, and the next, the Witch takes him in biggest wave yet and he is gone." Sugar shook from the bowl, he quivered it so hard. "After that, the *Badger Voyager* sinked, like I say. Big waves broke her in half." He lifted his hands and mimicked snapping a branch.

You can bet I was on the edge of my chair for the next part. "Raining and wind blowing like anything when order comes, 'Abandon ship.'" He continued slowly, as if retelling it to himself to make sure he got it right. "I go to climb in the lifeboat, and a pulley swings loose from the davit and hits me, like so."

All too graphically, he clapped a hand over his left eye and I couldn't help recoiling in horror.

"Hits 'Dutch,' yah?" he made sure I was following all the way. Now he removed his glasses, set them aside, and took the spoon out of the sugar bowl. Reaching up to his left eye with his free hand, he held his eyelids apart. My own eyes bugged as he lightly tapped his eyeball with the spoon handle, *plink plinkety-plink-plink plink-plink* distinct as anything.

Immediately enthralled, I let loose with "Holy wow, doesn't that hurt at all?"

Grinning and even winking with that false eye, he shook his head.

"Herman, that's out the far end!" The squint of his good eye questioned me. "That's soldier talk, it means something is really something! Can you do it again?"

He obliged, this time with the recognizable rhythm of *Hap-py birth-day to you.* I couldn't get over the stunt; the carnival sideshow that set up camp in Gros Ventre at rodeo time didn't have tricks nearly as good as playing *shave and a haircut, four bits* and the birthday song and who knows what else on an eyesocket. Still overcome with enthusiasm, I pointed to its eyeball or whatever its substitute ought to be called. "What's it made of?"

"Glass," he said with a half wink this time, donning the eyeglasses again. "Like a greenhouse of the head, hah? Only it grows this, from the ship company." He rubbed his thumb and fingers together, which with a penniless pang I recognized meant money. "Dutch is name buried at sea," he dropped his voice as if at a funeral. "Herman stays on land, no more Witches of November."

THAT WAS HERMAN in the ways most meaningful that first adventurous day, or so I thought. I can't really say a glass eye sold me on spending a stifling summer in Wisconsin, but he did make things more interesting than expected.

Aunt Kate was another matter, a sizable one in every way. After the morning's catastrophe with my money and our general lack of meeting of minds—if she even credited me with one—I didn't know what I was going to be up against when she returned from canasta, but suspected it probably would not be good.

So when Herman went off for a nap—"Shut-eye is good for the digestion"—I figured I had better show some progress on the jigsaw puzzle. Spilling out the pieces that half covered the card table and sorting the ones of different colors with my finger, I had quite a stretch of the sky-blue top edge fitted into place, strategy recalled from having done the damn thing before, working my way down onto George Washington's acre of forehead, when I heard the DeSoto groaning up the driveway and then Aunt Kate's clickety high heels on the kitchen floor, instantly stilled when she reached the plush living room rug.

"Yoo hoo," she called as she swung through on her way to hang up her purse in the sewing room, as if I wasn't just across the room from her.

"Yeah, hi." Figuring it couldn't hurt, could help, I tried a slight initiative that might be construed as politeness. "How was the, uh, card party?"

"A disaster," she moaned, flinging a hand to the vicinity of her heart. "It ruins the whole summer. Of all the bad luck, why, why, why did this have to happen on top of everything else?"

Continuing the drama, she dropped heavily into the recliner beneath the Manitowoc sampler, whipped around to face me where I was stationed at the card table, and cranked the chair back until she was nearly sprawling flat. In the same stricken voice, she addressed the ceiling as much as she did me: "It's enough to make a person wonder what gets into people."

Apprehensively listening, a piece of George Washington in my hand, I contributed, "What happened? Didn't you win?"

Now she lifted her head enough to sight on me through the big V of her bosom. "It's ever so much worse than that," she went on in the same tragic voice. "Years and years now, the four of us have had our get-together to play canasta and treat ourselves to a little snack. *Religiously*," she spiked on for emphasis, "every Monday. It starts the week off on a high note."

To think, Kate Smith might have uttered those exact last couple of words. But this decidedly was not America's favorite songstress, with me as the only audience trying to take in what kind of catastrophe a dumb card game could be.

"And now, can you believe it, Minnie Zettel is going off on a long visit," Aunt Kate mourned. "Why anyone would go gadding off to Saint Louis in the summertime, I do not know. She will melt down until there is nothing left of her but toenails and shoe polish, and it will serve her right."

Her chins quivered in sorrow or anger, I couldn't tell which, but maybe both—they were double chins, after all—as she fumed, "The other girls and I are beside ourselves with her for leaving us in the lurch."

Having been beside herself with me not that many hours ago, she was having quite a day of it, all right. Getting left in the lurch seemed pretty bad, whatever it meant. I made the sound you make in your throat to let someone know they have a sympathetic audience, but maybe I didn't do it sufficiently. Still flat in the recliner, Aunt Kate blew exasperation to the ceiling, wobbled her head as if coming to, and then her sorrowful eyes found me again, regarding me narrowly through that divide of her chest.

"Donal," she startled me by actually using my name, which I think was a first time ever, "do you play cards?"

"Only pitch, a real little bit," I said very, very carefully. All I needed was gambling added to the rest of my reputation with her. "Gram and me at night sometimes when there's nothing on the radio but preachers in Canada."

"Mmm, I thought so." She mustered the strength to nod her head. "When we were girls, Dorie was always one to haul out a deck of cards when nothing else was doing. I must have caught it from her."

That'd be about the only thing she and Gram were alike in, I morosely thought to myself, minding my manners by nodding along in what I took to be her bid for sympathy while I kept at the jigsaw, nine hundred and fifty or so pieces to go, when all at once she swelled up and exhaled in relief.

"Good. Then you can learn canasta and fill in for Minnie."

I don't know if my hair stood straight on end at that or what.

Aunt Kate busily began dismissing my swarm of doubts before I could sputter them out, cranking her chairback higher with every burst of sentence. "There's no way around it, we need a fourth for canasta and that's that."

Upright in the chair by now and facing me dead-on, she manufactured a sort of smile. "You needn't look so alarmed, kitten. I'll teach you the ins and outs of the game. We have an entire week for you to learn, isn't that lucky? It will help take your mind off your imagination, mmm?"

Still speechless, I tried to think how to head her off in more ways than one as she heaved herself out of the recliner and quickstepped over to me. “Now then. It’s too bad, but we need the card table.”

Before I could come out of my stupor, she was crumbling the sky-blue edge and George Washington’s forehead and scooping the pieces along with the rest of the puzzle into its box. “Don’t worry, child, you can start over on it once you’ve learned canasta.”

12.

THE PUZZLE PIECES were barely settled in the box before Aunt Kate was pulling up across the table from me and had the cards flying as she dealt a stream to each of us and to our absent opponents. Herta and Gerda—even their names sounded mean. Helplessly watching her deliver the valentines, as the poker game regulars in the Double W bunkhouse termed it, I felt unsure of myself but all too certain that turning me into a Minnie Zettel for hen parties was going to test the limits of both of us. And this was before I had any inkling that a contest of hearts, diamonds, clubs, and spades could become such a dangerous game.

While she was rifling the cards out, Herman wandered by the living room and took a peek at what was happening, which sent his eyebrows way up and quickened his step until he was safely past and out the back door. No rescue from that direction, so I cussed silently and kept stuffing cards into my overloaded hand.

Finishing dealing with a flourish, Aunt Kate slapped the deck down squarely in the middle of the table and sang out, "Now then, honeybun, the first thing is, you have to catch up a weensy bit by learning a few rules, mmm?"

THAT BEGAN a spell of time when the high point of my days was the sugar on my cereal.

Far from being the adventure I had been so excited about when I was met at the bus station by the living image of Kate Smith, my Wisconsin summer bogged down into the same old things day after day. Afternoons were canasta, canasta, canasta, and mornings veered from boredom when, after getting up hours earlier than anyone else and doctoring some puffed rice with enough spoonfuls of the white stuff, all I could find to do was to hole up in the living room reading an old *National Geographic* brought down from the attic, until the time came to tread carefully around the first of the battles of the Brinker household. Every day, Aunt Kate and Herman had a fight to go with breakfast. Generally it was her to start things off with a bang. "Can't you quit that?" Her first salvo would make me jump, even though it was not aimed at me. "It's childish and a nasty habit, how many times do I have to tell you?"

"Is not," he would pop right back. "Toast is made for such things."

"That is absolutely ridiculous. Why can't you just *eat*?"

"Hah. It goes in my mouth, same as you push it in yours."

"It is not the same! Oh, you're impossible."

The one constant in the repeated quarrels was Aunt Kate holding her ground in the kitchen, while Herman retreated elsewhere, waiting to scrap over toast scraps another breakfast time. Eventually, when it sounded safe, I would abandon the green leather couch and *National Geographic*—even the attractions of people pretty close to naked in "Bali and Points East" can hold a person only so long—and creep across the living room to peek into the kitchen. The remains of the daily toast war, which might still be sitting there at lunch or beyond, I could not figure out. Sometimes on what had to be Herman's plate would be nothing but crusts, other times a pale blob of toast from the middle of a slice. In any case, I would face the inevitable and call out "Good morning" and she'd look around at me as if I'd sprung up out of the floor and ask, "Sleep well, honeykins?" and

I'd lie and reply, "Like a charm," and that was pretty much the level of conversation between us.

I have to hand it to Aunt Kate, she was a marvel in her own way. To say she was set in her habits only scratches the surface. Regular as the ticks and tocks of the kitchen clock, she maintained her late start on the day, parked that way at the breakfast table, dawdling over the newspaper sensations and coffee refills, yawning and humming stray snatches of tunes, until at nine sharp she arose and clicked the radio on and one soap opera after another poured out, the perils of Ma Perkins and Stella Dallas and the others whom she worried along with at every devious plot turn.

Needless to say, monotony was not my best mode. Herman's, either, fortunately. During the soap opera marathon, he hid out in the greenhouse, where I sooner or later would join him so as not to have radio performers' woes piled atop my own.

"What do you know for sure, podner?" he would greet me, as no doubt one cowboy in a Karl May western would drawl to another.

Actually not a bad question, because the one thing I was sure of was what a mystifying place Manitowoc was, from toast fights to smoky portrait sitters inhabiting greenhouse windows to Manitou walking around dead to the strange nature of the neighborhood. I mean, I seemed to be the only kid anywhere. As used as I was to being in grown-up company at the Double W, now I apparently was sentenced to it like solitary confinement, with the street deadly quiet, no cries of Annie-I-over or hide-and-seek or boys playing catch or girls jumping rope, nobody much making an appearance except a gray-haired man or woman here and there shuffling out to pick up the morning paper or position a lawn sprinkler. It made a person wonder, did every youngster in Wisconsin get shipped off to some dumb camp to hunt frogs?

In any case, the sleepy neighborhood was getting to me, so I finally had to put the question to Herman as he fiddled with a cabbage plant. "Aren't there any other kids around here at all?"

"Like you?" I was pretty sure I heard a note of amusement in that, but he soon enough answered me seriously. "Hah uh, kids there are not. The Schroeders on the corner got boys, but they're older than you and don't do nothing but chase girls." Taking the stogie out of his mouth, so as not to spew ashes on the cabbage leaves, he shook his head. "Except them, this is all old folks."

I still had a hard time believing it. "In this whole part of town? How come?"

"Shipyard housing, all this. From when Manitowoc builds submarines in the war. The last one," he said drily, I supposed to mark it off from the one going on in Korea. "People did not go away, after. Now we are long in the tooth," he mused. He gave me a wink with his artificial eye. "Or ghosts."

That was that, one more time. I pulled out a fruit box and settled in while he went on currying the cabbages.

Under the circumstances, with no other choice except Aunt Kate, hanging around with Herman in the greenhouse suited me well enough. Whenever he wasn't pumping me about ranch life or telling me some tale out of Karl May's squarehead version of the West, I was free to sit back and single out some family or man and woman in the photographic plates overhead, catching them on the back of my hand thanks to a sunbeam, and daydream about who they might have been, what their story was, the digest version of their lives. It made the time pass until lunch, when I'd snap out of my trance at Herman's announcement, "The Kate will eat it all if we don't get ourselfs in there."

After lunch, though, inevitably, the nerve-racking sound in the living room changed from soap opera traumas to the slip-slap of the canasta deck being shuffled and the ever so musical trill, “Yoo hoo, bashful,” and all afternoon I’d again be a prisoner of a card game with more rules than a stack of Bibles.

“NO, NO, *NO*!” She put a hand to her brow as if her mind needed support, a familiar gesture by this third or fourth day—I was losing track—of card game torture. “What did I tell you about needing to meld a full canasta before you can go out?”

“I was thinking about something else, excuse me all to pieces. What do I do now?”

“For a start, pay attention, pretty please.”

I suppose I should have, but nothing was really penetrating me except the something else I kept thinking about. My money. The disastrous shirt-in-the-garbage episode that left me broke as a bum. No mad money meant no going to a show, no comic books, not even a Mounds bar the whole summer, for crying out loud. But that wasn’t nearly the worst. It bothered me no end that if I went back to Montana in the fall without the school clothes Gram had expressly told me to stock up on, I would have to go to class looking like something the cat dragged in. People noticed when a kid was too shabby, and it could lead to official snooping that brought on foster care—next thing to being sentenced to the orphanage—on grounds of neglect. Gram would never neglect me on purpose, but if she simply couldn’t work and draw wages after her operation, how was she supposed to keep me looking decent? With all that on my mind, here was a case where I could use some help from across the card table, and I didn’t mean canasta. The one time I had managed to broach the subject of school clothes and so on between her morning loafing at the breakfast table and soap opera time, Aunt Kate flapped her fingers at me and said, “Shoo now. We’ll figure out what to do about that later.” But when?

. . .

BY EVERY SIGN, not while I was stuck with a mittful of canasta cards. Back to brooding, I sucked on my chipped tooth as draw-and-discard drearily continued.

A little of that and Aunt Kate was grimacing in annoyance. "Don't they have dentists in Montana? What happened to that tooth, anyway?"

"Nothing much." I sat up straight as a charge went through me, my imagination taking off in the opposite direction from those modest words. "I got bucked off in the roundup, is all."

"From a *horse*?" She made it sound like she had never heard of such a thing.

"You betcha," I echoed Herman, pouring it on more than I had to, but a person gets carried away. "See, everybody's on horseback for the roundup, even Sparrowhead," I stretched the matter further. "I was riding drag, that's at the rear end of the herd, where what you do is whoop the slowpoke cows and calves along to catch up with the others. Sort of like *HYAH HYAH HYAH*," I gave her a hollering sample that made her jerk back and spill a few cards.

"Things were going good until this one old mossie cow broke off from the bunch"—the story was really rolling in me now—"and away she went with her calf at her heels. I took out after them, spurring Snipper—he's a cutting horse, see—and we about got the herd quitters headed off when Snipper hit an alkali boghole and started bucking out of it so's not to sink up to his, uhm, tail. I'm usually a real good rider"—modesty had to bow out of this part—"but I blew a stirrup and got thrown out of the saddle. I guess I hit the ground hard enough that tooth couldn't take it. I was fine otherwise, though." I couldn't resist grinning at her with the snag fully showing.

"Good grief," my listener finally found her voice. "That's uncivilized! Poor child, you might have been damaged any number of ways!"

"Aw, things like that happen on the ranch a lot."

That put the huff back into Aunt Kate in a hurry. "Whatever has gotten into Dorie?" she lamented, catching me off guard. "That sister of mine is raising you to be a wild cowboy, it sounds like. Tsk," that tail end of the remark the kind of sound that says way more than words.

"Oh, it's not that bad," I tried to backtrack. "Gram sees me with my nose in a book so much she says my freckles are liable to turn into inkspots."

"Does she." As if looking me over for that possibility, she scanned my earnest expression for a good long moment, with what might have been the slightest smile making her jowls twitch.

"All right then, toothums. Let's see if that studious attitude can turn you into a canasta player." Laying her cards facedown, she scooped up those of the phantom Gerda, drew from the deck, hummed a note of discovery, then discarded with a flourish, saying, "My, my, look at that."

A fourspot, what else. I perked up, ready to show her that I knew what was what in this damn game. With a flourish I melded some fours and other combinations to get on the board, and then as she watched with that pinched expression for some reason deepening between her eyes, I flashed the one fourspot I'd held back and a joker to scoop in the pile when the voice across the table rose like a siren.

"No, no, no! Wake up, child. You can't take that without a natural pair."

"Huh? Why not?"

Rolling her eyes, she put a hand to the peanut brickle plate. Finding it empty, she bit off instead: "Because it's a rule. How many times have I gone over those with you? Mmm? Can't you put your mind to the game at all?"

At that, our eyes locked, her blue-eyed stare and my ungiving one right back. If she was exasperated enough to blow her stack, so was I.

"There are too many rules! This canasta stuff goes through me like green shit through a goose!"

I KNOW IT is the mischief of memory that my outburst echoed on and on in the room. But it seemed to. At first Aunt Kate went perfectly still, except for blinking a mile a minute. Then her face turned stonier than any of those on Mount Rushmore. For some seconds, she looked like she couldn't find what to say. But when she did, it blew my hair back.

"You ungrateful snot! Is this the thanks I get? That sort of talk, in my own house when I've, I've taken you in practically off the street? I never heard such—" Words failed her, but not for long. "Did you learn that filth from him?" She flung an arm in the direction of the greenhouse and Herman.

"No!" I was as shrill as she was. "It's what they say in the bunkhouse when something doesn't make a lick of sense."

"Look around you, mister fellow," she blazed away some more. "This is not some uncivilized bunkhouse on some piddling ranch in the middle of nowhere. Dorie must be out of her mind, letting you hang around with a pack of dirty-mouthed bums. If she or somebody doesn't put a stop to that kind of behavior, you'll end up as nothing more than—"

She didn't finish that, simply stared across the table at me, breathing so heavily her jowls jiggled.

"All right." She swallowed hard. Then again, "All righty right. Let's settle down."

If sitting there letting her tongue-lash the hide off me without so much as a whimper wasn't what might be called settled down, I didn't know what was. My tight lips must have told her so, because her tone of voice lessened from ranting to merely warning: "That is enough of those words out of you, understand?"

My face still closed as a fist, I nodded about a quarter of an inch, a response she plainly did not like but took without tearing into me again. "That's that," she said through her teeth, and to my surprise, threw in her hand and began gathering in all the other cards on the table.

"I need to go and have my hair done, so we won't try any more cardsie-wardsie today. Now then"—she shoved the cards together until they built into the fat deck ready for my next day of reckoning—"while I'm out, find something to do that you don't have to swear a blue streak about."

NATURALLY I RESORTED to Herman. He was sitting there, book in hand, in the greenhouse, comfortable as a person can be on a fruit box, smoking a cigar while he read. As soon as I called out "Knock, knock" and sidled in, he saw I was so down in the mouth I might trip over my lower lip. Squinting over his stogie, he asked as if he could guess the answer. "How is the canasta?"

"Not so hot." Leaving out the part about what went through the goose, I vented my frustration about endless crazy rules. "I try to savvy them, really I do, but the cards don't mean what they're supposed to in the dumb game. Aunt Kate is half pee oh'd at me all the time for not doing better, but I don't know how." I ended up dumping everything into the open. "See, she's scared spitless her card party is gonna be a mess on account of me. So am I. But she's got it into her head that she can teach me this canasta stuff by then."

"The Kate. Sometimes her imagination runs off with her," said the man paging through *Winnetou the Apache Knight*.

Herman nursed the cigar with little puffs while he thought. "Cannot be terrible hard," he reasoned out canasta with a logic that had eluded me, "if the Kate and the hens can play it. Betcha we can fix." Telling me, cowboy-style, by way of Karl May, to pull up a stump while he searched for something, he dragged out the duffel bag from the corner of the greenhouse.

Dutiful but still dubious, I sat on a fruit box as ordered and watched him dig around in the duffel until he came up with a deck of cards that had seen better days and a well-thumbed book of Hoyle. "We reconnoiter the rules, hah?" A phrase that surprised me, even though I pretty much knew what it meant. But we needed more than a rulebook, I told him with a shake of my head.

"We're still sunk. Aunt Kate and them play partners, so it takes two decks."

"Puh. Silly game." He swung back to the duffel bag, stopped short, turned and gave me a prolonged look as if making up his mind. Then thrust an arm in again. Scrounging through the bag up to his shoulder, he felt around until he grunted and produced another deck of cards even more hard-used than the first.

"The Kate is not to know," he warned as he handed me the deck and pulled out a box to serve as a table. "Man-to-man, yah? Here, fill up your eyes good."

I was already bug-eyed. The first card, when I turned the deck over for a look, maybe was the queen of hearts all right, but like none I had ever seen—an old-time sepia photograph of a woman grinning wolfishly in a bubble bath, her breasts out in plain sight atop the soapy cloud like the biggest bubbles of all.

With a gulp, I spread more of the cards faceup on the box table, which meant breasts up, legs up, fannies up, pose after pose of naked women or rather as close to naked as possible without showing the whole thinger. Who knew there were fifty-two ways of covering that part up? That didn't even count the joker, a leggy blonde wearing a jester's cap and coyly holding a tambourine over the strategic spot. Mingled with the Manitowocers' shadow pictures from the photographic panes overhead, the frolicsome set seemed to be teasing the portrait sitters into what a good time could be had if they simply took all those clothes off and jumped into bathtubs and swimming pools bare naked.

"French bible," Herman defined the fleshy collection with a shrug, as I still was pop-eyed at it. Scooping the deck in with the tamer one, he shuffled them together thoroughly, the kings and queens and jacks now keeping company with their nude cousins and the ghostly Manitowocers.

He had me read out canasta rules from Hoyle while he dealt hands of fifteen cards each as if four of us were playing, the same as Aunt Kate had just tried, but that was the only similarity, the cards flying from his fingers almost faster than the eye could follow. I felt justified to hear him let out an exasperated "Puh" at the various rules that threw me. After scooping up his hand and studying it and then doing the same with the other two and mine, he instructed me to sort my cards into order, from kings—in the girly deck, even those were naked frolickers around a throne or doing something pretty close to indecent with a crown—on down, left to right, with aces and wild cards and any jokers off the end together for easy keeping track, something Aunt Kate had never bothered to tip me off to. I will say, the bare parts of the French ladies peeking from behind the usual queens and jacks garbed to their eyebrows did cause me to pay a good deal more attention to the display of my cards.

His eyeglasses glinting with divine calculation—or maybe it was a beam of light focused through a photographic pane of glass overhead—Herman lost no time in attacking our phantom opponents. "First thing after everybody melds, freeze the pile, yah? Throw on a wild card or a joker even, so they must have a natural pair to take what is discarded. Get your bluff in, make it hard for the hens to build their hands."

That made more sense than anything Aunt Kate had dinned into me in all the afternoons. I had to part with a wild-card deuce featuring a sly-looking brunette skinny-dipping in a heart-shaped swimming pool, but reluctantly figured it was worth it to place her crosswise on the discard pile to indicate it was frozen.

About then, Herman noticed my hand visiting deep in my pants and tut-tutted with a frown. "Donny, sorry to say, but this is not time for pocket pool."

Turning red as that seven of hearts, I yanked my hand out at the accusation. "No, no, it's not that, honest. What it is, I carry, uh, a lucky charm and it's got to be rubbed for, you know, luck."

He cocked his head in interest at my hasty explanation. I still was flighty about letting anyone see the arrowhead. But something moved me, maybe the spirit of Manitou, and I suppose somewhat ceremoniously I dug out the arrowhead and peeled back its sheaf of Tuffies enough to show him.

He laughed and laughed when I explained the need for protection from the sharp edges. "First time in history ever those are used that way, I betcha." When I handed him the condom pouch with the arrowhead catching enough light through the glass panes to glisten like a black jewel, he fell silent for a minute, holding it in the palm of his hand as if it were precious beyond any saying of it. At last he murmured, "Bee-yoot-iffle," and handed it back to me with great care. "Where did you get such a thing?"

I told him about finding it in the creek, right where some Indian dropped it, way back before Columbus, adding none too modestly, "It's rare."

"Goes with your moccasins, you are halfway to Indian," he puffed up my estimate of myself even further. His long face crinkled in a surprisingly wise smile. "You are right to use it as lucky piece and rub it often. Luck is not to be sniffled at, wherever it comes from."

Stoking up with a fresh cigar, Herman turned back to Hoyle and how to arm me for the hen party, running his finger down the canasta page black with rules. “Hah, here is oppor-tun-ity. Hoyle don’t say you got to put meld down anytime quick.” Reaching over, he grabbed up the cards I had melded and tucked them back in my hand. “Bullwhack the hens. Hide what you will do, yah?”

It took me a few blinks to rid myself of the mental picture that conjured and figure out he meant “bushwhack.” Then to grasp his idea of an ambush, by holding back meld cards so Gerda and Herta wouldn’t have a clue to what was in my hand, until the twin card-playing demons blindly discarded something I had a bunch of and could snatch up the pile and put together melds like crazy.

“Eye-dea is, surprise their pants off,” he formulated, already tracing through the dense print for further stunts I could pull. I giggled. That would put them in the same league as the undressed womanhood peeking various parts of themselves out from card to card. Canasta Herman-style was proving to be worth ever so much more close attention than that of Aunt Kate.

IN OUR SESSION THE NEXT DAY, my amazed partner praised my new powers of concentration and confidence and what she unknowingly termed a better feel for canasta. “That’s more like it,” she declared, celebrating with a chunk of peanut brickle. “Honeybun, I knew you could do it. All it takes is patience, mmm?” If you didn’t count whatever could be squeezed out of a French bible and a lucky arrowhead wearing condoms.

“All righty right,” she munched out the words, “you’ve learned the hard way what a canasta is. Let’s don’t futz with it anymore today.”

My ears must have stood straight out at that. Hearing one of Gram’s almost cusswords come from high-toned Aunt Kate shocked me all the way through.

Nor, it turned out, was that the end of her capacity to surprise. After popping another piece of brickle into her mouth, one for the road, she rose from her chair and beckoned me to follow her. "Come see, honeybunch. A certain seamstress has been working her fingers off," she all but patted herself on the back, "and I have something to show you in the wardrobe department."

Wardrobe. I knew that meant clothing, and lots of it, and instantly I envisioned what must be awaiting in the sewing room.

Oh man! Suddenly, something made sense. The sewing machine zinging away during the soap operas, her shooing me off when I tried to bring up the matter of the missing money—all this time, she'd been busy making shirts and the rest to surprise me with. Those baby-blue stares of hers sizing me up in the best sort of way, when I'd unkindly thought she was in the habit of eyeing me as if I were a stray left on the doorstep. What a relief. I wouldn't have to go back to school in the fall looking like something the cat dragged in, after all.

Giddy with this turn of events, I revamped my attitude about everything since I arrived. No wonder she stuck me away in the attic, in order to have the sewing room produce what I most lacked, a wardrobe! Forgiving her even for canasta, I nearly trod on her heels as she paraded us across the living room, dropping smiles over her shoulder.

"I do hope you like what I've done," she was saying as we entered the snug room full of piles of fabrics, "I put so much work into it." She plowed right into the stack on the daybed.

"Ready?" she trilled, keeping up the suspense. "Usually I have a better idea of the size, so I had to guess a little." Of course she did, unaccustomed to making things for someone eleven going on twelve.

"I bet it'll all fit like a million dollars," I loyally brushed away any doubt.

"You're too much," she tittered. "But let's see."

Proudly she turned around to me with an armful of cloth that radiated colors of the rainbow, and, while I gaped, let what proved to be a single garment unfold and descend. It went and went. Down past her cliff of chest. Unrolling along the breadth of her waist, then dropping past her hamlike knees without stopping, until finally only the tips of her toes showed from beneath the curtain of cloth, striped with purple and yellow and green and orange and shades mingling them all, that she held pressed possessively against her shoulders.

"My party outfit," she said happily. "The girls will get their say, but I wanted you to see it first."

It was a sight to be seen, all right, the whole huge buttonless sheath of dress, if that's what it was. Straight from the needle of Omar the Tentmaker, it looked like.

Still holding the wildly colored outfit up against herself, she confided, "They wear these in Hawaii. I came across a picture of one in a *National Geographic*." Crinkling her nose with the news, she informed me: "It's called a muumuu."

"It's—it's sure something."

Beyond that, words failed me, as the same old situation sank in, no school wardrobe, no mad money, no hope of prying either one out of the clotheshorse preening over her creation. Or was there?

Sweeping the creation over her shoulders to try to get a look at herself from behind in the full-length mirror, she asked, as if my opinion actually counted for something: "What do you think, dearie? Does it look all right from behind?"

The muumuu made her rear end look like the butt of a hippo, but I kept myself to "It's, ah, about like the front. Fits where it touches. Like Gram would say."

"Oh, you. But you're right, it is supposed to fit loosely." Humming full-force as she twirled this way and that in front of the mirror that was barely big enough to accommodate her and the tent of fabric both, she was in her own world. Not for long, if I had anything to do with it.

"Gee, yeah, the moo dress will look awful nice on you," I fibbed wholeheartedly. "And you know what, I sure wish I had any good clothes to go along with it at the card party." I furthered the cause of a spiffy homemade wardrobe by angling my head at the sewing machine. "I wouldn't want to look like something the cat dragged in, when you're so dressed up," I clucked as if we couldn't stand that.

That took the twirls out of her in a hurry. She frowned at the reflection of the two of us in the mirror, seeing my point. My hopes shot up as she chewed on the matter, studying back and forth from the crazily colored muumuu to me dressed dull as dishwater as usual. I cast another longing look around at the waiting sewing machine and stacks of enough material to outfit me twenty times over, but she was not going to be outfoxed that easily.

"I just remembered, sweetums," she exclaimed as if reminding me, too. "You have your wonderful rodeo shirt to wear, don't you." She smiled victoriously. "We'll put on a fashion show for the girls, mmm?"

WITH HEN PARTY day looming beyond and me not one stitch better off than I'd been, Saturday arrived, with the soap opera characters taking the day off to recuperate from their harrowing week—I could sympathize with them—and I was leery that Aunt Kate might have second thoughts about any canasta futzing and sit me down for one last drill all forenoon. Instead she let me know in no uncertain terms that she had things to do to get herself ready for the party and I needed to find some way to occupy myself. "You can do that if you put your mind to it a weensy bit, I'm sure."

I was puzzled. "Can't I be in the greenhouse with Herman like always?"

"Hmpf," she went, pretty much her version of his *Puh*. "Him? Didn't the old poot tell you? He won't be here."

Just then Herman appeared from the direction of their bedroom, surprisingly dressed up, at least to the extent of wearing a blue-green tie with mermaids twined coyly in seaweed floating all over it. "She is right, can you imagine. Time to go take my medicine." He stuck a few small bills she must have doled out to him into his wallet, saying, "It is not much, Your Highness."

She answered that with a dirty look and "It's the usual, it will have to do—there's no such thing as a raise when there's no income, is there."

He shrugged that off, but juggling the car keys, he halted across the kitchen table from her. "Donny can come with, why not?"

Aunt Kate snorted and barely glanced up from the scandals of the Manitowoc *Herald Times Reporter*. "Brinker, he is only eleven years old, that's why not."

"Old enough. We both knowed what was what in life by then, yah?" Not waiting for whatever she had to say to that, probably plenty, he turned to me with a wink of his glass eye. "Up to Donny, it should be. What do you say, podner?"

A trip along to a doctor's office did not sound any too good. On the other hand, it might help the case of cabin fever I was coming down with from my shacky attic room and the allures of Bali and other boundless places shown in the *National Geographic*s.

"Sure, I guess so," I said, as if I didn't care one way or the other, hoping that would keep me on the straight and level with Aunt Kate. According to the parting snort she gave as Herman and I headed out to the DeSoto, it didn't.

IN NO PARTICULAR HURRY, Herman drove in that sea captain fashion, his big knuckly hands wide apart on the steering wheel while he plied me with questions about Montana and the Double W ranch and as many other topics wild, woolly, and western as he and Karl May could come up with. All of it was really on his mind, to the point where he asked how long my folks and Gram and hers had been out west. Oh, practically forever as far as I knew, I told him, Gram's grandfather having been a Wegian—Herman gave me a hard look until I explained that was bunkhouse talk for *Norwegian*—who packed up and came from the old country to homestead, which explained the wicker suitcase. And my father's side of the family, the Campbells, I guessed had similarly been in Montana for as long as Montana had been around.

"Must have been like Canaan for them, maybe," he thought out loud. "Like in Bible—the Promised Land, I betcha."

"How do you know all this stuff?" I had reached the point of popping questions like that, since he never hesitated to bring up things out of nowhere. "The Bible and Longfellow and Karl May and so on?"

"Plenty of time to read on the ore boats," he answered soberly. "*Badger Voyager* and the others gived me my learning, in manner of speaking."

I DIDN'T DOUBT THAT, and let the matter go as I tried for some learning of my own, trying to figure out Manitowoc if I was going to be stuck there for the whole long summer. It appeared to be an even more watery place than I'd thought, the river with the same name as the town taking its time winding here and there—Gitche Manitou really got around on his spirit walks—before finding Lake Michigan. When we reached downtown, street after street of stores occupied brick buildings grimy with age—if this was the pearl of Lake Michigan, it needed some polishing. An exception was the movie theater with a marquee full of colored lightbulbs brightly spelling out the current show—TOMAHAWK—with Van

Heflin and Yvonne De Carlo, which I immediately set my heart on seeing until I remembered I was broke.

As Herman puttered us through the downtown traffic, I passed the time noting more of those stores with the same caliber of names that I'd spotted from the dog bus, as if anyone going into business had to line up way down the alphabet. Schliesleder Tailoring. Schröeter Bakery. The schushy sound of the town sounded awful German to me, and I tried to savvy at least a little of it.

"Hey, Herman? What's schnitzel?"

He worked on that as we pressed on past the main-street buildings toward the more grubby waterfront ones. "What are little cattles in English?"

"Calves? You mean the schnitz stuff is a way of saying calf meat? Veal, that's all it is?"

"Yah. Fixed fancy with stuff on, you got schnitzel. Old German recipe."

"What's schnapps, then?"

"Firewater, Red Chief. Old German drink."

"Boy oh boy, those dumb old Germans really went for some funny stuff, didn't they."

"Story of mankind," he gave a blanket answer to that.

That was not nearly as many definitions as I'd wanted, but another matter quickly had me wondering as the DeSoto pottered across the drawbridge of the weedy river and on past the coal sheds and boiler works. This doctor's office was in an odd part of town and I tried to think what kind of ailment Herman needed to be treated for in a run-down neighborhood. Firmly built right up to the gray summit of his head, he looked healthy enough to me. "Uhm, this medicine of yours, what exactly is it?"

"Neck oil."

Now he had me. I didn't see anything stiff about the way he

swung his head to give me a big bucktoothed smile—not the usual attitude that preceded a visit to the doctor, anyway.

Revelation arrived when he turned the car onto the last waterfront street, a block with the lake actually lapping under buildings held up by pilings, and parked at a ramshackle establishment with a sign over its door in weathered letters, THE SCHOONER. This I did not need to ask about, the Schlitz sign glowing in the window telling me all I needed to know.

Herman escorted me in as if the porthole in the door and the sawdust on the floor were perfectly natural furnishings where you go to take medicine, ha ha. I had been in bars before, what Montana kid hadn't? But this one looked like it had floated up from the bottom of the harbor. Sags of fishnets hung from the entire ceiling like greenish-gray cloudbanks. Above the doorway were wicked-looking crossed harpoons, and the wall opposite the gleaming coppertop bar was decorated with life preservers imprinted with *Northwind* and *Pere Marquette* and *Nanny Goat* and *Chequamegon* and other wonderful ships' names. Into the mix around the rest of the long barroom were walrus tusks carved into intricate scrimshaw, and long-handled grappling hooks that looked sharp as shark's teeth, and those bright yellow slicker coats called sou'westers, as if the wearers had just stepped out to sniff the sea air. To me, the place was perfect from the first instant, and I could tell Herman felt at home simply entering its briny atmosphere.

Still setting up for the day, the man behind the bar was so round in his various parts that in the wraparound apron and white shirt he looked more like a snowman than a bartender, but plainly knew his business when he turned with towel and glass in hand to greet Herman. "Well, well, it's the Dutcher. Must be ten o'clock of a Saturday." Me, he eyed less merrily. "Uh oh, Herm, who's your partner in crime?"

I waited for the guttural response I knew was going to turn my stomach, that I was his wife's sister's grandson, practically worse than no relative at all. Instead, I heard proudly announced, "Ernie, please to meet my grandnephew Donny from a big cowboy ranch in Montana."

There. My full pedigree. Stuff that in your pink telephone, why don't you, Aunt Kate.

I grew an inch or two and swaggered after Herman to a bar stool just like I belonged. As I scooted on, Ernie met me with a belly laugh—he had the full makings for it—while saying he didn't get many cowboys in the Schooner and warning me not to get drunk and tear up the place. Just then the building shook, and I started to bolt for dry land.

"Sit tight, happens all the time." Herman was chuckling now as he caught my arm before I could hit the floor running. Ernie informed me it was only the ferry to Michigan going out and the joint had never floated away yet, although it kept swaying thrillingly as I gawked at the gray steel side of a ship sweeping by the porthole windows facing the harbor and lake. Oh man, I loved this, almost the sense of sailing on the Great Lakes as Herman had so heroically done.

As the slosh of the ferry's wake died down and the building quit quivering, Ernie snapped his towel playfully in Herman's direction. "Ready to take your medicine? Gonna beat you this time."

"Always ready for that, and it will be first miracle ever if you beat me," Herman replied breezily. Laughing up a belly storm, the bartender moved off along the line of beer spigot handles extending half the length of the bar, running a hand along them the way you do a stick in a picket fence. The assortment made me stare, beer tap after beer tap of brands I had never heard of, nor, I would bet, had even the most seasoned drinkers in Montana. Rhinelander. Carling Black Label. Bavarian Club. Stroh's. Schlitz, naturally, but then Blatz, followed by Pabst, for some reason spelled that way instead of Pabzt.

On and on, down to the far end, where Ernie stopped at a handle with a towel draped over it so it couldn't be read. "No peeking, Dutcher," he sang out. "You either, Tex."

"No reason to peek," Herman replied with utter confidence and gazed off into the fishnets and such, the mermaids on his tie looking perfectly at home. I had no problem joining him in losing myself in the nautical trappings, knowing full well a ship did not have a bunkhouse, but this was the most comfortably close to such a thing since the Double W.

Shortly, Ernie came back scooting a shotglass of beer along the bar between thumb and forefinger. "Here you go, just up to the church window like always." I saw he meant by that it was only up to the jigger line, not even a full shotglass. Huh. Herman must be a really careful drinker, I thought.

Sure enough, he took the little glass of beer in a long slow sip, almost like you do drinking creek water out of your hand. Swirled it in his mouth as if thinking it over, then swallowed with satisfaction. "Hah, easy—Olde Rhine Lager."

The bartender slapped the copper top of the bar with his towel in mock fury. "Goddamn it, Herm, how do you do it? I had that brought in all the way from Buffalo to fool you."

"Takes more than Buffalo," Herman said with the simple calm of a winner and still champion, and set the shotglass aside like a trophy while the bartender trooped back to the hitherto mystery tap and drew a genuine glass of the beer, which is to say a schooner. "What about Cowboy Joe here?" he asked as he presented Herman the free beer. "I might as well stand him one, too, while I'm giving away the joint."

"Name your poison, podner," Herman prompted me, as if we were in a saloon with Old Shatterhand, and so I nursed a bottle of Orange Crush while the two men gabbed about old times of the

Great Lakes ore fleet and its sailors, Herman soon buying a beer to even things up a bit in the tasting game and a second Orange Crush for me, adding to the general contentment. I was drifting along with the pair of them to the Straits of Mackinac and Duluth and Thunder Bay and other ports of call, when I heard Ernie utter:

"So how's Tugboat Annie?"

I went so alert my ears probably stood straight out from my head. Somehow you just know a thing like that out of the blue, or in this case, the fishnets. Aunt Kate, he meant.

Herman took a long slug of beer before answering. "Same same. Thinks she is boss of whole everything."

Ernie laughed, jowls shaking like jelly. "She was that way even when she was slinging hash down here on the dock, remember? Order scrambled eggs and they'd just as apt to come fried and she'd say, 'Eat 'em, they came from the same bird that cackles, didn't they?'" He let out a low whistle and propellered his towel somehow sympathetically. "You got yourself a handful in her, Herm."

"Armloads, sometimes," said Herman, not joking at all.

Wait a minute. I was trying to catch up. The Tugboat Annie part I got right away, that rough-and-tough, hefty waterfront character in stories in the *Saturday Evening Post*. But was Aunt Kate ever a *waitress*? Snooty as she was now, with her Kate Smith wardrobe and insistence on good manners and all? It almost was beyond my ability to imagine her, twice the size of shapely Letty, with her name sewn in big sampler letters on the mound of her chest, bawling meat orders from behind a cafe counter to someone like Gram in the kitchen. And strangely enough, in their breakfast battles over slices of toast, Herman never threw that chapter of the past in her face.

EVENTUALLY WE DEPARTED the Schooner, Ernie vowing he would stump Herman the next time and Herman telling him he could try until the breweries ran dry, with me still wowed by that beer-tasting stunt. Before we reached the car, I asked, "How'd you learn to do that?"

Herman was maybe somewhat tanked up on Olde Rhine Lager, but his answer was as sober as it comes. "Job I had in old country. Story for another time, when you want your hairs raised. Get in, Donny. We must go home and face the Kate."

13.

NERVOUS AS A cross-eyed cat, I took my place across the card table from Aunt Kate. It was the fateful turn of Herta Schepke, seated to my left, to host the weekly canasta party and she had really put herself into it, the heavy old dark living room furniture burnished with polish, the rose-and-thistle-patterned rug vacuumed until every tuft stood and saluted, the "nibbles" plate impressively stacked with Ritz crackers spread with pimento cheese. Even the parakeet in a cage by the window shone dazzlingly, preening its green and gold feathers in the sunlight as it squawked and whistled for attention.

"That's some bird," I thought I'd make polite, safe conversation while Gerda shuffled and reshuffled the fat deck of cards in expert fashion and Aunt Kate inaugurated the nibbles plate with an *Mmm mm* and two bites that did in a cheese-topped cracker. "What's its name?"

"Big Tiny Little Junior," replied Herta, although I wasn't sure I had heard right. She took pity on my mystified expression. "Oh my, don't you know? Big Tiny Little Junior is the *most* divine piano player with the Lawrence Welk orchestra. They make 'champagne music' and play here every year for the Fourth of July observance in the park and at the county fair and everything of the sort. And the name Big Tiny Little Junior just seemed *so* right for a parakeet. The little dear is a budgerigar, you know." I didn't have a clue that was what a shrunken parrot was called, and my face must have given me away because Herta gave a little giggle of compassion and spelled out, "So there you have it, don't you see? Biggie the budgie. He even knows his name." To prove it, she twittered across the room, "Pretty bird, who's my pretty bird?" The wild-eyed parakeet cocked its head and squeaked, *"Big-ee, Big-ee"* over and over.

During this, Gerda was dealing out cards with mere flicks of her fingers, faster than I could pick them up. We had barely started and already I was scared half sick at the way this so-called game was shaping up. Characters such as Old Shatterhand in Herman's shoot-'em-ups faced situations all the time where a person's fate could be decided on the turn of a card. But in real life, my future with Aunt Kate rested just as precariously on my gameness, to call it that in all possible senses, to cope with great big handfuls of canasta cards.

For it had dawned on me during the hen party chitchat before we sat up to the card table why she was so determined—savagely so, I thought at the time—to drill canasta into me. From the evidence of framed family photographs lined up over on the glistening sideboard, Herta was the matriarch of a whole slew of sharp-looking Schepkes, and Gerda ever so casually kept working into the conversation remarks about the latest achievement of a grandson here, a granddaughter there, the cream of her crop no doubt rising in the world. And Aunt Kate was stuck with me, her lone such twinkling star of the younger generation, supposedly bright enough to read by at night, to be shown off at last. If I didn't prove to be too dim to grasp a card game old ladies played like riverboat gamblers. By now I knew Aunt Kate well enough that if that were to happen, any attempt at shining me up to match Herta's and Gerda's golden offspring would be doused at once and she would devote her efforts to conveying to the others what a complete moron she was nobly putting up with. She could go either way. I was in big trouble if I did not play my cards right.

. . .

NO SOONER had Gerda finished dealing than she reached down for the purse beside her chair and took out a roll of coins, plunking it down beside her. Aunt Kate simultaneously did the same, each woman thumbing open the bank wrap to spill a stock of quarters in front of them.

"Time to feed the kitty," Aunt Kate said musically, evidently a usual joke.

"We'll see about that, Kittycat," Gerda declared.

"Here's my half, Gerd," Herta thrust a five-dollar bill across the table, which vanished into Gerda's purse. I blinked at that transaction, which indicated each roll of quarters was ten dollars' worth, plopped down here casually as if this were a game of marbles.

"Are we playing for blood?"

My shrilled question, straight from bunkhouse poker lingo, made all three women recoil. It was up to Aunt Kate to set me straight, the pointed looks at her from Gerda and Herta made plain.

"If you mean are we gambling, dearie, *you* most certainly are not," she set in on me with a warning frown. "I am standing your share, aren't I," underscoring the point by picking up a wealth of quarters and letting them trickle from her hand. "The Minnie share, we can call it."

The other two tittered appreciatively at that. "As to our teensy wagers," Aunt Kate spoke, as if this might be hard for me to follow but I had better try hard, "we are simply making the game more interesting, aren't we, girls. To liven things up a little, mm?"

So saying, she shoved a quarter each for herself and me, the would-be Minnie Zettel, out next to the deck to form the kitty, Gerda did the same for her and Herta, and that was supposed to be that.

WITH MONEY RIDING on the game, added to all else circling in my head as I stuffed cards into my hand fifteen deep, I sneaked looks right and left, sizing up our opponents. Both women were cut from the same cloth as Aunt Kate, which was to say spacious. Gerda was squat and broad, Herta was tall and broad. The halfway similar names and wide builds aside, they were not sisters, merely cousins, and old acquaintances of Aunt Kate from some ladies' club way back when, I gathered. Both were widows, Herman holding the firm belief that they had talked their husbands to death. Widders, in the bunkhouse pronunciation I had picked up. *Melody Roundup* on the Great Falls radio station sometimes played a country-and-western song that backed Herman's theory to a considerable extent: *"Widder women and white lightning, what they do to a man is frightening."* That tune crazily invaded through my head, too, as I tried to force myself to remember the countless rules of canasta.

Almost as if peeking into my mind, Herta right then chose to ask with a certain slyness, "Are you *musical,* like your auntie who even *talks* like there's a song in her voice?"

"Oh, now, Hertie, don't get carried away," Aunt Kate responded, as if she were being teased with that as well as me.

I answered up to Herta's dig or whatever it was. "Naw, I'm the kind who can only play one instrument. The radio." I fell back on the old joke, which did not go over as big as I'd hoped.

"Are we playing cards or musical chairs?" Gerda asked pointedly.

"Don-ny," Aunt Kate prompted, with a smile seeking forgiveness from the Herta-Gerda partnership, "any red threes to meld?"

Not a good start. "Sure, I was just about to."

I grabbed the trey of hearts I had stuck at the far end of my hand without a thought and flopped it on the table. Aunt Kate leaned back and smiled at me with a hint of warning in her eyes that I had almost cost us a hundred points by not playing the damn three in the first place, and Gerda looked at me slyly as she flipped me the replacement card. "My, my, aren't you something, you're beating the *pants* off us already," Herta said in the same dumbed-down tone she used in talking to the bird.

After that I tried to keep my mind fully on draws and discards and Herman's eye-deas for bushwhacking and the rest, but the hen party combination on either side of me, not even to mention Biggie the budgie squealing away, was really distracting. Herta actually clucked, making that *thwock* sound with her tongue against the roof of her mouth when she exclaimed over something, which was often. That was bad enough, but her partner presented an even worse challenge. The last name of Gerda was Hostetter, which was so close to Horse Titter that I couldn't get that out of my mind, either. I had learned by way of Gram to call grown-ups I didn't know well Mr. and Mrs., and every time I addressed the widder to my right it came out something like "Mrs. Horssstetter."

"Oh, don't, snicklefritz," she killed that off after the first few times. "Just call me Gerda, please." Making a discard that I had absolutely no use for, as she uncannily almost always did, she idly glanced at me, saying, "I understand you're from a ranch. Is it one of those fancy dude ones?"

"No-o-o, not exactly. It's more the kind with cows and horses and hayfields," that last word came out wistfully.

"I suppose you're glad to be here because there's not much for a boy like you to do there," said Gerda, as if that were the epitaph on my ranch life.

"Aw, there's always something going on," I found myself sticking up for the Double W. All three women were eating the cheese-and-cracker nibbles as if they were gumdrops, so it must have been their obvious devotion to food that brought what I considered an inspiration. "You know, what's really fun on a ranch is a testicle festival."

That stopped everyone's chewing and drew me full attention from three directions, so I thought I had better explain pretty fast.

"It happens at branding time, see, when the male calves have to be taken care of. It's nut cutting, there's no way around calling it anything but that. Well, castration, if you want to be fancy. Anyway, all these testicles get thrown in a bucket to be washed up and then cooked over the fire right there in the corral. There's plenty to feed the whole branding crew. Two to a calf, you know," I spelled out, thinking from the blank expressions around the table that maybe they weren't that knowledgeable about livestock.

"Don-ny," Aunt Kate spoke as if she had something caught in her gullet, "that's very interesting, but—"

Herta blurted, "You actually *eat* those?"

"Oh sure, you can guzzle them right down. Rocky Mountain oysters, they're real good. You have to fry them up nice, bread them in cornmeal or something, but then, yum."

"Yum" did not seem to sit well with the ladies. Thinking it might be because they were used to nibbles, as Aunt Kate called the candy gunk, which bite by bite didn't amount to much and Herta's crackers-and-cheese treat that tasted like dried toast and library paste, I kept trying to present the case for Rocky Mountain oysters despite the discreet signals from across the table that enough was enough. Not to me, it wasn't. I had an argument to make.

"Honest, you can fix a whole meal out of not that many nu—testicles—see. They're about yay long," I held my fingers four or so inches apart, the size of a healthy former bull calf's reproductive items.

Herta seemed to take that in with more interest than did Gerda, who just looked at me as if sorting me out the ruthless way she did cards. Apparently deciding I could be coaxed off the topic, Herta crooned in practically birdie talk, "That tells us *so much* about ranch life. Anyway, aren't you cuter than *sin* in your cowboy shirt."

Without meaning to—much, anyway—I gave her the full snaggle smile for that, the one like I might bite.

"Heavens!" She jerked her cards up as if shielding herself from me. "What in the world happened to that boy's t—"

"He fell while he was working on the ranch." Aunt Kate wisely did not go into the roundup tale. "They have a favorite dentist back there and his grandmother is taking him to be fixed up good as new, the minute he gets home from the summer to Montana," she topped that off smooth as butter. This was news to me, but not the kind intended. My supposedly no-nonsense aunt could story as fast and loose as I could.

AFTER THAT PERFORMANCE on my part, as I knew Aunt Kate was going to level the word at me later, the game dragged on with the score steadily mounting against us and the quarters in the kitty regularly being scooped in by Gerda. It turned out that livening things up a little, as Aunt Kate called it, included many an ante during play as well as the payoff for winning each hand. Natural canastas, without wild cards, brought groans and a forfeit of quarters, as did things Aunt Kate characterized as Manitowoc rules, such as melding all black aces. I watched with apprehension as Aunt Kate's stake of quarters dwindled. In bunkhouse terms, we were up against sharpies. Gerda was a terrifying player, seeming to know which cards each of the rest of us held as if she had X-ray vision. Herta was no slouch, either. As I desperately tried to keep up with what cards were played and the passel of rules, I was concentrating nearly to the point of oblivion when I heard the word *green*, followed by *stamps*.

I snapped to. Herta was going on about a certain lawn chair featured in the window at the Schermerhorn furniture store downtown. "It has the *nicest* blue plastic weave and is so light, made of aluminum, and you can fold right down *flat* in it to sun yourself," she enthused. "It costs something *fierce*, though. So I'm hoping I can get it if I can build up my Green Stamps before *too* awfully long, while summer is still going good."

"Oh, those, I never bother with them," Aunt Kate pooh-poohed the trading stamps. "They're so little use, you can't even trade them in for decent clothes."

"We all have *ravishing* clothes, Kitty," Herta responded with a bland glance at Aunt Kate's muumuu of many colors. "What I *want* is that lawn chair. *Free* and for *nothing* and with not even a *fee*, as the saying is." All three tittered at that. Then Herta sighed and consoled herself with a nibble. "I've been saving up and saving up, but it's a slow process."

"You watch and see," Gerda put in, "you'll be eligible for that lawn chair about the time a foot of snow comes. I'm with Kitty, those silly stamps aren't worth the trouble. It's your draw, snicklefritz," and, bang, we were right back at playing canasta for blood.

I watched and waited for the discard pile to grow, while dipping my hand into my pants pocket to work on the lucky arrowhead. Gerda noticed me at it, as she did everything, and asked none too nicely, "What's the attraction down your leg there?"

Before I could make up an excuse, Aunt Kate spoke up. "Oh, he insists on carrying some piece of rock he thinks is his secret lucky charm, it's harmless."

Luckily enough, that took care of that, and on the next go-round, my ears ringing with Herman's advice—*Hold back, discard one like you don't got any use for it, and watch for same kind of card to show up on pile in your turn. Bullwhack the hens*—I discarded one of the five seven-spots I had built up. Sure enough, two rounds later, Gerda the human card machine operated on memory and tossed onto the pile what should have been an absolutely safe seven of spades. Saying nothing and maintaining a poker face if not a canasta one, I produced my double pair of sevens and swept up the pile.

There was a stunned silence from Gerda and Herta and a tongue-in-cheek one from Aunt Kate as I pulled in the rich haul of cards.

Finally Gerda could not stand it and said, in a tone very much as if she had been bushwhacked, "Just as a point of the obvious, you do know you discarded a seven a bit ago."

"Uh-huh," I played dumb although I also kept spreading sevens and other melds across the table, "but this way I got it back." Aunt Kate conspicuously said nothing, merely watching me meld cards right and left as if our good fortune was an accident of luck, which it was, but not in the way she thought.

THAT AND A few other stunts I came up with that drew me black looks from Gerda and surprised ones from Aunt Kate saved our skin and our stake somewhat, but I was running out of tricks according to Hoyle and Herman, and several hands later Aunt Kate and I still trailed on the score sheet, and worse, in the kitty. Another ridiculous thing about canasta was that the game went on and on until one set of partners had scored a total of five thousand points. The way this was going, Herta and Gerda would reach that in another hand or two and wipe us out good and plenty. My partner across the table wore an expression of resignation tinged with exasperation, and I did not look forward to the ride home with her. Before the next hand was dealt, though, we were temporarily saved by the luck or whatever it was of me sneaking the last cracker-and-cheese and downing it.

"Goodness, we've gone through the *nibbles*, haven't we." Herta immediately noticed the empty plate and felt her hostess duty. "What do you say we take a wee little break and I'll fix some more."

"And a little wee break," said Aunt Kate, surprisingly reckless, as she pronto headed out to what in these circumstances seemed to be called the powder room. Gerda called dibs on the next visit, and went over to wait by cooing to the parakeet.

Here was my chance, slim as it was. As if merely looking around,

I wandered into the kitchen, where Herta was industriously dipping a table knife into a freshly opened jar of pimento cheese spread and daubing some on cracker after cracker to build a pyramid on the plate. She glanced around at me with an eyebrow raised, humorously maybe. "After all that talk of *oysters*, too hungry to wait, are we?"

"Huh-uh. It's not that." I peeked back into the living room to make sure we couldn't be overheard. Gerda was babytalking to the parakeet, which answered her with unending screeches of *"Big-ee, Big-ee."* "Those stamps you were talking about, the green ones? You know what? I've got some that aren't doing me any good."

"Oh, *do* you?" A glob of cheese spread had smeared onto the edge of the plate and she cleaned it off with her finger and ate it, with a wrinkle of her nose at me that said it would be just our secret, wouldn't it. Thinking I was making too much of too little, she kept her voice low in saying, "You must have been with Kitty or that *husband* of hers at one of those gas stations where they give out a few for a fill-up, is that it?"

"Uh-uh. I have a whole book, pasted in and everything."

She sucked her finger while studying me with deepened interest. "What's a boy like you doing with *all those*?"

Sixteen hundred and one hard-earned miles on the bus, that was what. But I only said, "I got them with my ticket here. So I was wondering if we could sort of make a trade, since they're called trading stamps, right?"

"A *trade*, you say," she inquired in a lowered voice, nibbles forgotten now. "Such as?"

"Well, see, I know how much you'd like to have that lawn chair. And you know how much Aunt Kate likes to win. If you could help that along a little, so she and I come out on top today, I could bring you my book of Green Stamps next time we play. That way, you get your free lawn chair and I don't get my fanny chewed about canasta all week."

"Goodness gracious, you *do* have a way of putting things." She thought for a couple of seconds, calculating what she would lose in the kitty against the fierce price tag on the lawn chair, then craned her neck to check on the living room, with me doing the same. Gerda was taking her turn in the powder room, and Aunt Kate now was stationed at the birdcage, whistling at Biggie and receiving squeaks and scratchy *chirrups* in return.

Clucking to herself as clicking onto a decision, Herta leaned all the way down to my nearest ear and murmured:

"It *would* be a good joke on Kittycat, wouldn't it."

"A real funnybone tickler, you bet."

"*Just* between us, of course."

"Cross our hearts and hope to die."

She giggled and whispered. "We'll *do* it."

SINCE THERE WASN'T much time to waste before Herta and Gerda would reach a winning score just in the ordinary way of things, at the first chance I had when the discard pile grew good and fat and all three women were waiting like tigers to pounce and pick it up, I discarded a deuce, the wild card under Manitowoc rules, crosswise onto the pile.

Aunt Kate leaned over the table toward me. "Honeybunch, that freezes the pile, you know."

"I know."

"You are sure that is the card you want to play, that way."

"You betcha." The spirit of Herman must have got into me to sass her that way.

"Mmm hmm." Stuck for any way to dislodge me from my stubborn maneuver, she tried to make the best of it by shaking her head as if I were beyond grown-up understanding. "Girls, it appears we have a frozen deck."

"Doesn't it, though," Gerda said through tight lips. "Someone has been putting ideas in this boy's head." Aunt Kate sat there looking like she couldn't imagine what got into me, nor could she. "Well, we have no choice, do we," Gerda reluctantly conceded. "Your draw, Hertie."

The pile built and built more temptingly as we all drew and discarded several more times, until Herta drew, stuck the card away and as if distracted by Biggie's latest rant of chirrups, discarded an ace of spades. Immediately she went into flutters and the full act of "Oh, did I play *that* card? I didn't mean to!"

She made as if to pick it back up, which Aunt Kate headed off so fast her hand was a blur as she protected the pile.

"Oh no you don't. Against the rules, Hertie, you know perfectly well." Tossing down her natural pair of aces, she gobbled up the whopping number of cards and began melding, the black aces side bet and rainbows of other high-scoring combinations across half the table, canastas following canastas, while Gerda squirmed as if enduring torture and Herta tried to look remorseful, although with little glances sideways at me marking our secret. I pressed my cards to my chest with one hand, nervously rubbing the arrowhead in its sheath with the other to summon all the luck I could. It must have worked. Finally done laying down cards, Aunt Kate looked around the table with a smile that spread her chins.

"Guess what, girls. Donny and I seem to have fifty-one hundred points, also known as out." She reached for the stream of silver Gerda was unhappily providing by yielding up quantities of quarters while Biggie screamed as if celebrating our triumph.

I FELT LIKE a winner in every way as my triumphant partner, humming away as pleased as could be, started to drive us back to the house. Victory over the canasta hens! Herman would get a great kick out of that. And winnings, actual money, the first gain of that kind since I had alit in Manitowoc. Manitou's town itself was even showing a more kindly face, leafy streets and nice houses surrounding us as Aunt Kate took a different way than we had come because of the "nasty traffic" of the shift change at the shipyard.

So I was caught by surprise when my attention, racing ahead of the DeSoto's leisurely pace, suddenly had to do a U-turn when I heard the words "Donal, I have something to say to you, don't take it wrong."

In my experience as a kid, there wasn't much other way to take something that started like that. I waited warily for whatever was coming next.

She provided it with a look at me that took her eyes off the road dangerously long. "Has your grandmother ever, *ever* suggested circumstances in which you should"—she paused for breath and emphasis and maybe just to think over whether there was any hope of changing my behavior—"hold your tongue?"

Was I going to admit to her that frequent warning of Gram's, *Don't be a handful*? Not ever. "Naw, you know how Gram is. She calls a spade a shovel, dirt on it or not, like she says, and I guess I'm the same."

From her pained expression, she apparently thought that described her sister all too well and me along with it. She drew a breath that swelled her to the limit of the driver's seat and began. "I'm not laying blame on your grandmother, I know she's done the best she could under the"—she very carefully picked the word—"circumstances."

That could only mean Gram putting up with my redheaded behavior, and now I was really wary of where this was heading. Once more Aunt Kate took her eyes off the road to make sure I got the message. "So this is for your own benefit"—which was right up there in the badlands of being a kid with *don't take this wrong*—"when I say you are a very forward youngster."

I hadn't the foggiest notion of what that meant, but I risked: "Better than backward, I guess?"

She stiffened a bit at that retort, but a lot more when I couldn't stop myself from saying, "And I can't help it I'm a *young*ster."

"There's the sort of thing I mean," she emphasized. "You're Dorie, all over again. Chatter, chatter, chatter." She took a hand off the wheel to imitate with her arched fingers and thumb something like Biggie the budgie's nonstop beak. "One uncalled-for remark after another."

Ooh, that stung. Was my imagination, as she seemed to be saying, nothing more than a gift of gab?

I was getting mad, but not so mad I couldn't see from her expression that I had better retreat a little. "Yeah, well, I'm sorry if Herta and Mrs. Horssstetter took the testicle festival the wrong way. I thought they'd be interested in how we do things in Montana." Figuring a change of topic would help, I went directly to "Anyhow, we beat their pants off, didn't we. How much did we win?"

"Mm? Ten dollars." She reached down to her purse between us on the seat and shook it so it jingled. "Music to the ears, isn't it," she said with a dimpled smile that would have done credit to Kate Smith.

"And how!" I couldn't wait one more second to ask. "When do I get my half?"

"Sweetheart, it is time we had a talk about money." The smile was gone that fast. "To start with, I was the one who put up our stake, wasn't I. By rights, then, the winnings come to me, don't they."

"But we were partners! We won the canasta game together! And I didn't *have* any money to put up, remember?"

That accusation, for that's what I meant it to be, only made her wedge herself more firmly behind the steering wheel of the DeSoto. "Now, now, don't make such a fuss. If I were to give you your share, as you call it, what would you spend it on? Comic books, movies, things like that, which are like throwing money away."

Things like that were exactly what I wanted to spend mad money on, and I tried to say so without saying so. "I can't go through the whole summer just sitting around the house doing nothing."

"That is hardly the case," she didn't give an inch. "I'll take you shopping with me, you can be my little helper at the grocery store and so on. Then there's the jigsaw puzzle now that you've learned canasta, and always the greenhouse to visit, isn't there." Her voice went way up musically as she said the next. "Don't worry, bunny, you won't lack for entertainment if you just put your mind to it. And here's a surprise for you." By now she was cooing persuasion at me. "On the Fourth, we'll go to the park, where they'll have fireworks and sizzlers and whizbangs and all those things, and hear that wonderful Lawrence Welk orchestra Herta talked about. Won't that be nice?"

Talking to me that way, who did she think I was, Biggie the budgie? But before I could think up a better retort, she let out an alarming sigh as if the air were going out of her. I saw she was stricken, for sure, but not in an emergency way. Everything about her appeared normal enough, except her eyes were not on the road, her attention seized by something we were passing.

"I'm sorry, buttercup," she apologized in another expulsion of breath, "but the sight of it always almost does me in."

I jerked my head around to where she was looking, expecting a hospital or cemetery at the worst, some place ordinarily sad to see. But no, I saw why the sight so unnerved her, as it did me. The forbidding old building set back from the street was spookily familiar, even though I was positive I had never seen it before. The sprawling structure, rooms piled three stories high, each with a single narrow window, seemed leftover and rundown and yet clinging to life like the skinny little trees, maybe a failing orchard, that dotted its grounds like scarecrows.

"What is that place?" I heard my own voice go high.

"Just what it looks like," Aunt Kate responded, speeding up the car to leave the ghostly sight behind. "The poorhouse."

THE WORD STRUCK me all the way through as I stared over my shoulder at the creepy building. Put a rocky butte behind it and weather-beaten outbuildings around it and it was the county poorfarm of my nightmares. As if caught up in the worst of those even though I was awake, I heard Aunt Kate's pronouncement that made my skin crawl.

"And that's another reason I must be careful, careful, careful with money and impress on you to do the same. I sometimes think we'll end up there if a certain somebody doesn't change his ways."

"Y-you mean Herman?"

"Him himself," she said, squeezing the life out of the steering wheel.

"But—why?" I was stupefied. "How's he gonna end you up in the poorfarm—I mean house?"

"Have you ever seen that man do a lick of work? If only," she said grimly. Another sigh as if she were about to collapse scared me as much as the first one. "To think, what a difference it would make if Fritzie was here."

"Huh? Who?"

"Oh, the other one," she tossed that off as if it were too sad to go into.

No way was she getting away with that. My burning gaze at her was not going to quit until she answered its question, *The other what?*

She noticed, and said offhandedly, "Husband, who else?"

I gaped at her. She seemed like the least likely person to believe the plural of spouse is spice, as I'd overheard grown-ups say about Mormons and people like that.

"You've got another one besides Herman? They let you do that in Wisconsin?"

"Silly. Before Brinker, I mean." She gazed through the windshield. "Fritz Schmidt. A real man."

Herman seemed real enough to me. "What happened to him? The other one, I mean."

"I lost him." She made it sound as if he had dropped out of her pocket somewhere.

Not satisfied, I again stared until she had to answer. "Storm, slick deck."

"Really?" Strange how these things work, but Herman's shake of the sugar bowl that spilled some over the side when he was showing me the fate of the *Badger Voyager* combined with her words to make my pulse race. Trying not to sound eager, though I was, I leaned across the seat and asked, "Like when the Witch of November came?"

"He's been filling your head out there in the garden shed with his old sailor tales, hasn't he. All right, you want the whole story." No sighing this time, actually a little catch in her voice. "My Fritz was bosun on the *Badger Voyager.* Washed overboard in the big November storm of '47."

I thought so! The same storm and ship that took Herman's eye! That Witch of November coincidence inundated me in waves of what I knew and didn't know. Her Fritzie was Herman's best friend on the doomed ore boat. No problem with that, I could savvy the pair of them as bunkhouse buddies or whatever the living quarters were on a ship. But then how in the world had someone she would not even call by his first name get to be the replacement husband? Someone she thought was so worthless they'd end up in the poorhouse? Where that embattled matchup came from, my imagination could not reach at all.

All this whirling in my head after her news about Fritzie's sad fate, I miraculously managed to hold my exclamation to a high-pitched "That's awful!"

"Yes, it's a tragedy." She gazed steadily ahead at the road. "But that's in the past, we have to put up with life in the here and now, don't we," she said, as if she didn't want to any more than I did. As if reminded, she glanced over at me and patted her purse enough to make it jingle again in a sort of warning way. "You did fine in today's game, honeybunch, but stay on your toes. Next time, the party is at our house and we'll do as usual and play two out of three."

14.

Dear Gram,

The dog bus was really something, with all kinds of people like you said. Aunt Kate, as I call her but everybody else says Kitty, and Uncle Herman, who does not go by Dutch anymore, found me in the depot fine and dandy and we went to their house and had what they called a Manitowoc dinner, what we call supper. It takes some getting used to here.

Gram had made me promise, cross my heart and so on, to write to her every week, but doing so when she was in the middle of complications after her operation stayed my hand from so much I really wanted to say, none of it good news as far as I was concerned. Carefully as I could, I was doctoring, so to speak, life with Aunt Kate. If word ever came from that intimidating nun, Sister Carma Jean, that the patient was better, maybe I could somehow sneak a phone call to let Gram know I was being bossed unmercifully, from being kept flat broke to being stuck in the attic. On the other hand, what could she do about it from a hospital bed when Aunt Kate was right here, always looming, seeming as big as the house she dominated top and bottom and in between.

Already she had stuck her head in to make sure I was keeping at it on a space of the card table that didn't have presidents from Mount Rushmore staring at me with scattered jigsaw eyes. She left me to it but not before singing out, "Don't forget to tell her the funny story of mistaking me for Kate Smith, chickie," which wild horses could not drag out of me to put on paper. Instead:

> *Aunt Kate and I play cards some, not pitch like we did in the cook shack but a different game I'll tell you about sometime.*

Herman wore a broad grin when I told him he and Hoyle had bushwhacked Herta and especially Gerda, to the Kate's satisfaction. "Did you know they play canasta for money?"

"For two bitses, *pthht.* Hens play for chickenfeed, notcherly."

It was laborious to fill the whole page of stationery with anything resembling happy news. Herman's greenhouse gave me a chance to list vegetable after vegetable growing under glass, which helped, and I recounted the antics of Biggie the budgie as if Aunt Kate and I had simply paid a social visit to old friends of hers. There was so much I had to skip not to worry Gram in her condition—the Green Stamps secret deal with Herta, Herman's out-of-this-world talent at tasting beer, my impressive broken front tooth from the scuffle with the campers, and most of all, Aunt Kate heedlessly throwing away every cent of my money—it would have filled page upon page of writing paper. But if *Reader's Digest* could condense entire books, I supposed I could shrink my shaky start of summer likewise.

> *The Fourth of July is coming, and Aunt Kate is taking me to the big celebration here where they will shoot off fireworks of all kinds and a famous band whose leader is Lawrence Somebody will play music. It should be fun. I hope*

you are getting well fast and will be up and around to enjoy the Fourth like I will.

Your loving grandson,
Donny

"Oh, I was going to look it over to check your spelling." Aunt Kate clouded up when I presented her the sealed and addressed envelope for mailing. The look-it-over part I believed, which is why I'd licked the envelope shut.

"Aw, don't worry about that. I win all the spelling bees in school," I said innocently. "Miss Ciardi says I could spell down those Quiz Kids that are on the radio."

"Well, if she says so," Aunt Kate granted dubiously. "All righty, I'll stamp it and you can put it out in the box for the mailman. There now, you can get right back to your puzzle, mm?"

THE REAL PUZZLE, of course, was how I was going to endure a summer of thousand-piece jigsaws, old *National Geographic*s, and canasta without being bored loco or something worse. Especially seeing as once I'd paid off the bribe to Herta by slipping her my Green Stamps, I was going to be no match for the merciless sharpies in not one canasta game but two, and it took no great power of prediction to guess Aunt Kate's reaction to that. The Witch of November in a muumuu was on that horizon.

So the next couple of days after writing Gram how fine and dandy everything was in Manitowoc, I hung around with Herman in the greenhouse as much as possible to keep my morale up. He was good company, better and better in fact, as he read up some more from Karl May and other books in his corner stash and gabbed with me about cayuses and coyotes—relying on me to straighten him out on which were horses and which were canines—and the wonders of Winnetou as a warrior and the spirit of Manitou living on and on and making itself felt in mysterious ways. "Here you go, Donny, Indians believed Manitou lived in stones, even, and could come out into a person if treated right, if you will imagine." With the fervor of an eleven-year-old carrying an obsidian arrowhead in his pocket, I certainly did turn my imagination loose on that, seeing myself riding the dog bus west sooner than later to a healthy and restored Gram, her with a job cooking on some ranch where the rancher was no Sparrowhead, me back at things I was good at like hunting magpies and following the ways of cowboys, poorfarm and orphanage out of our picture. In other words, in more luck than I was used to lately.

IT IS SAID a blessing sometimes comes in disguise, but if what happened in the middle of that week was meant to be any kind of turn of luck, it made itself ugly beyond all recognition when it came.

At first I thought it was only the household's usual ruckus at breakfast while I was parked on the living room couch as usual, reading a *National Geographic*, this time about "Ancient Rome Brought to Life," where according to the paintings shown, people sometimes went around even more naked than in Bali. I was pondering an illustration of a roomful of women mostly that way and the caption with some ditty from back then, "Known unto All Are the Mysteries, Where, Roused by Music and Wine, the Women Shake Their Hair and Cry Aloud," those mysteries unfortunately unknown to me except for that smackeroo kiss Letty and I exchanged, and I did not notice her shaking her hair and crying aloud from it.

Just then, though, I heard a woman definitely roused, but not that way.

"Have you lost half your brain as well as that eye?" Aunt Kate was shouting in the close confines of the kitchen.

"Does not take any much brain to know you are talking crazy," came Herman's raised voice in return.

"Oh, I'm the one, am I. I've told you before, don't be filling his head with useless things. When I was out seeing what flowers I could cut for our next little party, I heard you telling him more of that Manitou nonsense."

"Is not nonsense. You think you are more smart than Longfellow? Not one chance in a million." Herman went on the attack now. "You are the one filling him up with canasta nonsense and putting him on spot in your hen parties. Let the boy be boy, I am telling you."

In a kind of stupor as I realized the knock-down, drag-out fight was about me, I crept to the hallway where I could peek toward the kitchen. They were up on their feet, going at it across the table. I'd heard them having battles before, but this sounded like war. More so than I could have imagined, because as I watched in horror, Aunt Kate leaned across the table almost within touching distance of Herman and shrieked one of the worst things I had heard in my life.

"Don't get any ideas about who's in charge of our little bus passenger for the summer! You're not wearing a Kraut helmet anymore, so don't think you're the big boss around here!"

Herman's face darkened, and for a few frightening seconds, I wondered whether he was going to hit her. Or she him, just as likely, given the way her fists were clenched.

Then Herman said in a voice barely under control, "What I am, you did not care when you wanted your bed keeped warm after Fritz." With that, he turned his back on her, heading out to the refuge of the greenhouse. Aunt Kate followed him far enough to get in a few more digs before he slammed the door and was gone.

Shocked nearly senseless as I was, by instinct I scooted for the stairs and scuttled up to the attic while she still was storming around the kitchen. I would have retreated farther than that if I could, after what I had heard. Before long, Aunt Kate's voice was raised again, this time in my direction and straining to sound melodious.

"Don-ny. Yoo hoo, Donny, where are you? Let's go for a little outing and do the grocery shopping, shall we?"

I stayed absolutely still, gambling that she would not labor up the stairs to seek me out. And if I could make her think I was at the greenhouse with Herman instead, she likely wouldn't want another shouting match out there. Silence, rare as it was tried in this household, might save me yet. After some minutes, I heard the DeSoto pull away, and so hurt and mad at being deceived that I could hardly see straight, I raced down the stairs two and three at a time, bound for a showdown in the greenhouse.

"YOU LOOK NOT HAPPY, podner," Herman said beneath his usual cloud of cigar smoke. The only sign that the battle royal in the kitchen might still have him agitated was the sharp strike of his spoon against the pot rims as he fed fertilizer to the cabbages. "Something the Kate did, hah?"

I wanted to holler at him, *No, something you did, turning out to be a German soldier!* Swallowing hard, I managed to restrict myself to saying, "I—I heard Aunt Kate bawling you out in there."

"Habit," he wrote that off and tapped his cigar ash onto the floor. "She wouldn't have nothing to do if not yelling her head off at me."

I had to know.

"Did you really fight on the Kraut side, like she said?"

Wincing at that language, he looked up at me in surprise. "She should wash her tongue and hang it out to dry." The big shoulders lifted, and dropped. "But, ja"—which I finally heard for what it was, instead of *Yah*—"that is one way to put it."

"So you really truly are a"—I had trouble even saying it—"a German?"

"Ja, double cursed," he said, as if life had done him dirty at the start. "The name 'Herman' even means 'soldier' in German language, if you will imagine."

"But then how come you don't talk like they do in the movies?" I demanded to know, as if his squarehead accent was a betrayal. "The Nazi bad guys, I mean."

"Pah, those Nazi bigwigs, they speak like they are chewing a dictionary," he dismissed that. "I am from where we talk different German than that. Emden, on the North Sea. Netherlands is next door, the Dutchies are a spit away, we say."

"So aren't you sort of Dutch, any?" I seized on what hope there was. "Like when you were called that before it went down with the ship?"

"No-o-o," he drew the answer out as if calculating how far to go with it. "'Dutch' was sailor talk for 'Deutsch,' which means 'German.' Better than 'Kraut,' but not much."

That clinched it. A Kraut by any other name, even his shipmates recognized it. Imagination did me no favors right then. My head filled with scenes of landing craft sloshing to shore under a hail of gunfire from Hitler's troops, and sand red with blood, and a figure on crutches in the hallways of Fort Harrison hospital trying to learn to walk again, which was not imaginary at all. Giving Herman the German, as he now was to me, the worst stink eye I was capable of, I demanded:

"Tell me the truth. Were you one of them at Omaha Beach?"

"Hah? What kind of beach?"

"You know. On D-Day. Were you there shooting at my father, like the other Germans?"

Realization set in on him, his face changing radically as my accusation hit home. "Donny, hold on to your horses. I am not what you are thinking. The Great War, I was in."

What, now he was telling me it was great to have been in the war where my father got his legs shot to pieces? I kept on giving him the mean eye, hating everything about this Kraut-filled summer and him along with it, until he said slowly so I would understand, "World War *Eins*. One."

I blinked that in. "You mean, way back?"

He looked as if his cigar had turned sour. "You could say. I was made a soldier thirty-seven years ago," which I worked out in my head to 1914.

Slowly I sat down on a fruit box as he indicated, a whole different story unfolding than what I had imagined. "No choice did I have, Donny, back then." He gazed up at the photographic panes of glass holding olden times in the poses of the portrait sitters, as if drawing on the past from them. "You have heard of the draft, where government says, 'You, you, and you, put uniform on,' ja? Kaiser Wilhelm's Germany in the Great War was very drafty place." The joke made a serious point. "There I was, young sailor on the North Sea, and before I knowed it, foot soldier wearing a pickle stabber." He put his hand on top of his head with the index finger up, indicating the spiked helmet of Der Kaiser's army.

Comical as that was, I was not deterred from asking, "So, were you in any big battles?"

He puffed out cigar smoke that wreathed a rueful grin. "With my corporal, many times."

"Aw, come on, you know what I mean. Real fights. Like Custer and the Indians."

"Shoot-them-ups, you want," he sighed. "Karl May should write Western Front westerns for you."

At first I thought he was not going to answer further, but finally he came out with, "I was at Höhe Toter Mann, was enough."

That didn't sound bad, nothing like Omaha Beach. Disappointed at his evidently tame war, I said just to be asking, "What's that mean, Ho-huh whatever you said?"

He half closed his good eye as if seeing the words into English. "Dead Man's Hill, about."

That sat me up, all attention again. "Yeeps! Like Boot Hill, sort of?"

"More ways than one," he evidently decided to give me Herman the German's side of the war. "Höhe Toter Mann was fought over time after time, back and forth, forth and back, Germans and French killing each other all they could." He grimaced, and after what he said, I did, too. "You could not see the ground, some places, dead men or parts of them was so thick."

I'd wanted to know the blood-and-guts truth about him being a soldier, had I. That would do. "H-how come you weren't killed there?"

"The shovel is sometimes better friend than the rifle," he said simply. "Learned to dig such foxholes, I did, could have given fox a lesson." He paused to frame the rest of that story. "Here is a strange thing soldiers go through. The more of my comrades died on Höhe Toter Mann, the more it saved my life. My outfit, I think you call it?"—I nodded—"Second Company, lost so many men we was moved to rear guard duty. Behind the lines, we had chance to survive the war." His face took on an odd expression, as if skipping past a lot to say, *And here you see me, in America.*

"Yeah, well, good," I spoke my relief that he had been in a separate war from my father. Now I could be curious about things less likely to bring the whole summer crashing down. "My dad was a private first class—what about you?"

"Private no class, my soldiering was more like," he told me, memory turning toward mischief now. "Not what you might call hero. Mostly, behind the lines I was chicken hunter."

"Uhm, Herman, that sounds awful close to chicken thief."

"In peacetime, ja. In war, is different. When rations are short, you must, what is the word, when cattles go here and there to eat grass?"

"Forage?"

"Sounds better than 'thief,' don't it," he went right past that issue without stopping. "Same eye-dea, though. Go find what you need to survive. 'Sharp eyes and light fingers' was the saying. When night came, so did chance for hunting. You must understand, Donny"—he could see I still was trying to sort this out from chicken thievery—"we was being fed a pannikin of soup like water and slice of bread per man, day's only meal, before armistice came. Starvation ration, too bad it don't rhyme better." He looked contemplatively at his private garden of vegetables under glass. "I grew up on little farm at Emden, cows lived downstairs from us and chickens loose outside, so I understanded where food could be rustled."

We heard the DeSoto jouncing up the bumpy driveway. "Tell you what, podner," Herman suggested rightly, even if it was not what I wanted to hear, "go help the Kate with the groceries, hah? Keep her off the warpath for once."

I WENT THROUGH that day of Aunt Kate's bossy supervision—*here, honeybunch, help me with this; there, sweetums, do this for me*—with Herman's words outlasting anything she had to say. *Sharp eyes and light fingers*; there is no switch you can reach in your brain to turn something like that off. It fit with me, for if I hadn't been what he called a hunter, the black arrowhead still would be on the hall table at the Double W instead of within the touch of my fingers in the security of my pocket. Even after a suppertime so tense I wondered whether one of them might throw the sauerkraut at the other, and another march to bed when I was wide awake, a tantalizing possibility kept coming to mind, like an echo that went on and on: *Go find what you need to survive.*

When I went to bed, my eyes not only wouldn't close in favor of sleep, they barely blinked. Put yourself in my place, doomed to screeching bedsprings and attic confinement for the rest of the summer and no mad money to see a great movie like *Tomahawk* or do anything else that was halfway interesting, and see if your mind doesn't become a fever field of imagination and you don't turn into an eleven-year-old desperado. I ignored the plaque on the wall that preached getting down on my knees and praying as the one-and-only answer, and instead saw through the house, to put it that way, to the sewing room. Where Aunt Kate kept her purse and maybe significantly more. Those quarters that jingled all the way home from the canasta party had to live somewhere.

IT IS TOO MUCH to say I waited for the cover of night the way Herman had poised himself behind the lines to go out into the dark of war to forage, but I did make myself hold back, tingling to go and do it, until long after everything in this battling household went quiet.

Finally swinging out of bed, I hurried into my clothes, Tuffy-wrapped arrowhead in my pocket for luck, and slipped into the moccasins. Cracked the door open, listening for any sound downstairs. There was none whatsoever except that nighttime not-quite-stillness of a house holding people deep asleep. Quiet as a shadow I crept down and into the sewing room. I didn't know what I was going to say if I got caught at this. Something would have to come. It usually did.

Almost the instant I entered the small darkened room, I blundered into the cot, barking my shin on the metal frame and causing a thump that seemed to me loud as thunder.

Sucking in my breath against the hurt, I froze in place for what seemed an eternity, until I convinced myself the sleepers had not heard. Burning up as I was to get this done, but not daring to put on the lights in the room, I waited until my eyes adjusted to the dark and the furnishings in the room took form, if barely. What I was after had to be somewhere in here. Aunt Kate's purse hung next to the door as always, but I knew better than to risk going into it. Tightfisted as she was, she would keep track of every cent she was carrying. No, in any household I knew anything about, there was a Mason jar where loose change, the chickenfeed, was emptied when people cleared out their pockets or purses of too much small silver.

Normally kept in a kitchen cabinet or on a bedroom dresser, but from what I had seen, not in this case, undoubtedly to keep even the smallest coins out of Herman's reach. That stash must be, ought to be, *had* to be in here in the vicinity of her purse, something like hunter instinct insisted in me.

I cautiously hobbled over to where the sewing machine was located. If I was right, a Singer model this fancy might have a small light beneath the arm of the machine to shine down on close work. My blind search ultimately fumbled onto a toggle that switched on a small bulb above the needle and router, perfect for my purpose. In its glow I could pick out objects shelved around the room, stacks and stacks of cloth and pattern books and such. But nothing like a jar holding the loose change of canasta winnings.

Doubt was eating away at my courage pretty fast—maybe I was loco to even try this and ought to sneak back upstairs to bed. Instead, Manitou or some similar spirit of the miraculous guided my hand into my pants pocket, where I squeezed the arrowhead for all the luck it might have. That steadied me enough to take another look around the room. My last hope, and it did not appear to be much of one, was a standard low cabinet next to the sewing machine, designed to hold thread and attachments. Quietly as possible I pulled out drawer after drawer, encountering a world of spools of thread and gizmos for making buttonholes and ruffles and so on, until finally I reached a drawer that jingled when I opened it.

I dipped my fingers into the discovery, very much like a pirate sifting gold doubloons in a treasure chest. This was it, coins inches deep and loose and rattling to the touch, nickels, dimes, and quarters, quarters, quarters, some in bank wrap rolls. My heart rate and breathing both quickened like crazy. There was so much accumulated small silver, a dozen or so quarters and the rest in chickenfeed would scarcely make a dent in it.

Biting my lip in concentration, I sorted out onto the platform of the sewing machine in the pool of light about the same proportion of quarters and dimes and nickels to make the drawer's holdings seem as even as ever. There. I had it knocked, my rightful five dollars of the hard-won canasta pot. I was wrapping my withdrawal, as I saw it, in my hanky and about to pocket it for the journey through the dark back up to the attic, when the voice came:

"Are you done, you little thief?"

She was practically filling the doorway, in a nightdress as tent-like as the muumuu and wearing those fuzzy slippers that were noiseless on the living room rug. At first my tongue did fail me as I stared at a greatly irate Aunt Kate and she at me, an outpouring of words no problem for her. "I was on my way to the bathroom when I noticed this funny little glow from in here. It's not like me to leave the sewing machine on like that, is it. And what do I find, Mister Smarty Pants, but you stealing for all you're worth."

I didn't know anything to do but fight back. "Why is this stealing when I won the pot in the canasta game just as much as you did, remember? I bet Minnie Zettel got her share every time the two of you won. So why can't I?"

"I went over that with you in the car—"

"And you told me you and Herman were headed for the poorhouse, but looky here, you have money you just throw in a drawer."

"—will you listen, please." She was growing loud now. "You need to get used to not having your own way all the time. I hate to say it," but it was out of her mouth as fast as it could come, "Dorie has spoiled you something serious, letting you behave like a bunkhouse roughneck or worse."

That infuriated me, not least for her picking on Gram while she was fighting for her life in the hospital. "Gram's done the best she can, and I am, too, here. But you treat me like I'm a bum you took in. If I had that money you threw in the garbage, none of this would've happened."

"That is no excuse for stealing," she said loftily, advancing on me with her hand out for the hanky-wrapped coins.

"I don't think it's stealing," I cried, "when you won't give me anything and I'm only taking my five bucks of what we won as partners. Why, isn't it stealing, just as much, for you to keep it all for yourself?"

"Donny," she warned, all her face including the chins set in the kind of scowl as if she were battling with Herman over toast, "you are getting into dangerous territory and had better mind your manners, or—"

"The boy is right. Why do you have to be money pincher so much it is ridiculous?"

The figure in the doorway now was Herman, in pajama bottoms and undershirt.

Aunt Kate lost no time in turning the furious scowl on him. "Brinker, this does not concern you."

"Pah. Why do you talk so silly? You like being wrong?" A thrill went through me when he didn't back down, one hunter of what was needed to survive coming to the aid of another, if I wanted to get fancy about it. "I live here, Donny lives here, and as far as anybody in whole wide world knows, he is my grandnephew, too." I couldn't sort out the tangle in the middle of that sentence, but it didn't seem to matter as Herman kept at her. "You talk big to him about behavior, but you should fix up your own while he is our guest."

Aunt Kate had to work her mouth a few times to get the words out, but inevitably she managed, double-barreled. "That is enough out of both of you. We will sort this out in the morning. Donny, put that money back and go to bed. As for you, Brinker, keep your opinions to yourself if you're going to share my bed."

Neither of us wanting to fight her all night when she showed no sign of being reasonable, we complied. Herman waited at the doorway and put his hand on my shoulder as I trudged to the stairs, saying low enough that Aunt Kate couldn't hear as she fussed around with the sewing machine and the change drawer, "Don't let silly woman throwing a fit get you down, podner."

IT DID, THOUGH. The next couple of days were a grind, with me sulking in my attic version of the stony lonesome or spending every minute I could out in the greenhouse with Herman.

Saturday came, after those days of Aunt Kate and I being as cautious as scalded cats around each other, and I could hardly wait to go with Herman again on his "medicine" run for a change of scenery, not to mention atmosphere. This morning, she was more than fully occupying her chair in the kitchen as usual but fully dressed for going out. Herman was nowhere around, but that was not out of the ordinary after their customary breakfast battle. In any case, Hippo Butt, as I now thought of her, actually smiled at me, a little sadly it seemed, as I fixed my bowl of soupy cereal, and naturally I wondered what was up.

I found out when she cleared her throat and said almost as musically as ever:

"Donny, I have something to tell you. After breakfast, pack your things. I'm sending you home."

Home? There was no such thing. Didn't she know that? Why else was I here? I stared at her in incomprehension, but her set expression and careful tone of voice did not change. "Hurry and eat and get your things, so we don't miss your bus."

"You can't just send me back!" My shock and horror came out in a cry. "With Gram laid up, they'll put me somewhere! An orphanage!"

"Now, now." She puffed herself up to full Kate Smith dimensions as she looked at me, then away. "This hurts me as much as it does you," which was something people said when that wasn't the case at all. "After the sewing room incident, I wrote to your grandmother saying I have to send you back, without telling her that was the reason, so you're spared that. I didn't tell you before now because I didn't want you to be upset."

Talk about a coward's way out. She did the deed by letter instead of telephone so there could be no argument on Gram's part. And to keep clear of that starchy nun Carma Jean asking where her sense of charity was. And "upset"? How about overturned and kicked while I was down?

"But, but, it's like you're sending me to jail, when you're supposed to let me be here all summer." Life had flipped so badly I was desperately arguing for Wisconsin.

She had the decency to flinch when I flung that charge at her, but she also dodged. "Donny, dear, it won't be as bad as you think. We have to believe that your grandmother will recuperate just fine and be able to take care of you again, don't we. But in the meantime, there are foster homes that take in children for a while." I knew those to be little more than a bus drop stop on the way to the orphanage. "To make sure, I went to the county welfare authorities here and got a list of such places in Great Falls. It's all there in the letter I sent. Your grandmother will only have to fill out a form or two, and you'll have a temporary home until she gets well."

I must have given my now sworn enemy a gaze with hatred showing.

"Please don't look at me that way." She fussed at creases in the newspaper that needed no fussing at. "The nuns will help out if need be. They'll have to, when you show up. Now eat up, and we'll have to be going."

I pushed aside my breakfast, too sick at heart to eat, and went for my suitcase for hundreds upon hundreds of miles of travel agony ahead.

. . .

WE WERE AT the car before I came out of my shellshock enough to realize the missing part in all this. "Wh-where's Herman? Isn't he coming with us?"

"You shouldn't ask." She sure couldn't wait to tell me, though, as she impatiently gestured for me to climb in the DeSoto. "He sneaked off on the city bus for that 'medicine' of his. Threw the car keys to me and told me to do my—my dirty work myself."

She got the rest off her chest, more than a figure of speech as she heaved herself into position behind the steering wheel and said over the grinding sound of the starter, "That man. He says he can't bear to tell you good-bye. I don't know why not, it's just a word."

Another piece of my heart crumbled at that. Abandoned even by Herman the German. I meant less to him than a couple of beers at the Schooner. Brave survivor of Höhe Toter Mann, hah. If there was a Coward's Corner on Boot Hill, that's where he deserved to end up.

AT THE BUS DEPOT, everything was all too familiar, benchfuls of people sitting in limbo until their Greyhound was ready to run, the big wall map of THE FLEET WAY routes making my journey loom even longer. Forced to wait with me until my bus was called, Aunt Kate turned nervous and, probably for her sake as much as mine, tried to play up what lay ahead of me. "Just think, you'll be there in time for the Fourth. They'll have fireworks and sizzlers and whizbangs of all kinds, I'm sure."

"I don't give a rat's ass about whizbangs," I said loudly enough to make passing busgoers stare and veer away from us.

"Donal, please." She looked around with a false smile as if I were only being overly cute. "This is the kind of thing I mean. You can see it just isn't right for you here."

It would take a lot to argue with that, but before I even had any chance, she had her purse up and was diving a hand into it. "Oh, and take this." She pressed some folded money into my hand. In amazement, I turned the corners of the bills back, counting. Three tens. The exact same sum as had been pinned inside my discarded shirt.

"What—how come—"

"No, no, don't thank me," she simpered, while all I was trying to ask was why she hadn't done this in the first place, like maybe as soon as we both realized she had thrown my summer money in the garbage.

All at once she burst into tears. "Donny, I wish this would have worked out. But you see how things are, Herman and I have all we can do to keep ourselves together. I—I may be a selfish old woman, I don't know, but my nerves just will not take any more aggravation. Not that I blame you entirely, understand. It's the, the circumstances." Still sniffling, she pulled a hanky from her purse and blew her nose. "This is the best thing all around. You'll be back there where people are more used to you."

Yeah, well, it was way late for any apology, if that's what this amounted to. All it did was delay us from the departure gate where passengers already were piling onto the bus with MILWAUKEE on its roller sign. For me, there'd be another one with WESTBOUND after that. I did not look back at her as I handed my ticket to the driver for punching, left the wretched old suitcase for him to throw in the baggage compartment, and climbed aboard to try to find a seat to myself.

IF SHE HADN'T CRIED, I would have given in to tears. As it was, I sat there trying to hunch up and take it, one more time. Two days and a night ahead on the dog bus, doom of some kind waiting at the Great Falls depot. Convinced that everything that could go wrong was going wrong, I sent a despairing look up the aisle of the bus. All the situation needed now was something like that bunch of hyena campers to torment me. But no, my fellow passengers mainly were men dressed up for business, a Manitowoc *Herald Times Reporter* up in front of someone like a last mocking farewell reminder of Aunt Kate, and a few couples where the women were as broad-beamed as seemed to be ordinary in Wisconsin. Nothing to worry, I thought bitterly of Herman's wording.

The bus was at the outskirts of Manitowoc, the radius of my summer failure, when I heard the *oof* of someone dropping down next to me. Oh, swell. Exactly what I did not need, a gabby seat changer. With so much else on my mind, I'd forgotten to place my jacket in that spot and now it was too late. Two full hours ahead to Milwaukee yet, and I was in for an overfriendly visit from some stranger with nothing better to do than talk my ears off. Goddamn-it-all-to-hell-anyway, couldn't life give me any kind of a break, on this day when I was being kicked down the road like an unwanted pup? I didn't even want to turn my head to acknowledge the intruder, but sooner or later I had to, so it might as well be now.

"Hallo."

Out from behind the newspaper, Herman the German was giving me the biggest horsetooth smile.

I rammed upright in my seat. "What are you doing on here?"

"Keeping you company, hah?" he said, as if I had issued an invitation. "Long ride ahead, we watch out for each other."

"Y-you're going to Montana with me?"

His shoulders went way up, the most expressive French salute yet. "Maybe not to Big Falls. We must discuss."

So flustered was I trying to catch up with things in no particular order, I craned my neck back toward Manitowoc as if Aunt Kate were on our trail. "Does she know you're here?"

"Puh." That translated different ways, as "Of course not" and "It doesn't matter," take my choice. "Left her a note saying I am gone back to Germany, we are you-know-what." *Kaput?* I goggled at him. Just like that, he could walk out of a marriage and hop on a bus in some other direction from where he said he was going? Man oh man, in comparison I was a complete amateur at making stuff up.

"Today was last straw on camel's back," he said. I listened open-mouthed as Herman continued in a more satisfied tone. "The Kate will run around like the chicken with its head chopped off awhile, but nothing she can do. I am gone like the wind." He looked at me with the greatest seriousness. "Donny, this is the time if I am ever to see the West and how it was the Promised Land for people. I must do so now, or I am going to be too soon old." To try to lighten that heavy thought, he winked at me with his bad eye. "So, we are on the loose, ja?"

"I guess *you* are. But Hippo Butt—I mean the Kate—got it all set up that my grandmother has to stick me in a foster home ahead of the orphanage as soon as I get to Great Falls and—"

"No, she does not. Silly eye-dea. I kiboshed."

He had to repeat that for it to make any sense to me. As best I could follow, what it came down to was that he had guessed what she was up to when he saw her writing a letter. "Unnotcheral behavior," he sternly called it. The rest was pretty much what you would think, him sneaking around from the greenhouse after she put the letter to Gram out in the mailbox, swiping it and reading it and, he illustrated triumphantly to me by fluttering his hands as if sprinkling confetti, tearing the thing up. "Evidence gone to pieces, nobody the wiser, hah?"

IT SANK IN on me. No one in the entire world knew that the two of us were free as the breeze. Herman wasn't merely flapping his lips; we really were footloose, crazily like the comic strip characters in *Just Trampin'* who were always going on the lam, hopping on freight trains or bumming rides from tough truck drivers to stay a jump ahead of the sheriff. Or at least bus-loose—the fleet of Greyhounds ran anywhere we wanted to go. It was a dizzying prospect. Good-bye, battle-ax wife, for him, and no Hello, orphanage, for me—it was as simple as sitting tight in a bus seat to somewhere known only to us, the Greyhound itself on the lam from all we were leaving behind.

I tell you, scratch a temptation like that between the ears and it begins to lick your hand in a hurry. "You mean, just keep going?" As excited as I'd ever been, the question squealed out of me. "Like for all summer?"

"Betcha boots, podner. Who is to know?"

"Yeah, but, that'll cost a lot." A shadow of reality set in. "I don't know about you, but I've only got thirty dollars."

"Nothing to worry. I am running over with money." Seeing my disbelief, he patted the billfold spot in the breast pocket of his jacket, where there did seem to be a bulge.

"Really truly? How much?"

"Puh-lenty," said he, as if that spelled it out for me. "Cashed in all my settlement, I did, then went to the bank and taked my share from there. Half for her, half for me, right down center. What is the words for that, same-sam?"

"Uhm, even-steven. But I thought from what Aunt Kate said, you guys were about broke."

"Pah. Woman talk. We will live like kings, Donny. Here, see." He took out the fat wallet from inside his coat and spread it open for me. Lots and lots of the smaller denominations, of course, but I hadn't even known fifty and hundred bills existed, as maybe half the wad consisted of. "Outstanding!" I yelped at the prospect of money raining down after my spell of being flat broke.

There was a catch to simply taking off into the yonder, though, isn't there always? "See, Gram has me write to her every week," I fretted. "She'll know right away I'm not back there with you and Hippo—the Kate—like I'm supposed to be, if those are mailed from any old where."

Even before I finished speaking, Herman had that look that usually produced eye-dea, but this time what came out was scheme. "Mailed from Manitowoc, they can be. Ernie owes me favor." He spieled it as if it were a sure thing, me writing enough letters ahead to cover the rest of the summer, the batch then sent to the bartender at the Schooner with instructions to mail one each week. "I stick ten dollarses in with, Ernie would jump over moon if I ask," he impressed upon me. "Your *grossmutter* hears from you regular, what you are doing," he finished with infectious confidence. "Postmark says Manitowoc if she looks."

"You mean," I asked in a daze, "make up the whole summer?"

"Ja, tell each week the way you like. Make it sound good so she is not to worry."

And that clinched it. The chance to condense the disastrous season spent with Aunt Kate entirely according to my imagination was too much to resist.

"Woo-hoo, Herman!" I enlisted in his plan so enthusiastically he shushed me and took a quick look around at the other passengers, luckily none close enough to have overheard. Whispering now, I asked eagerly, "But where will we go?"

With a sly grin, he leaned back in his seat as if the dog bus were the latest in luxury. "Anywheres," he said out the side of his mouth so only I could hear. "Just so it is"—he made the cocked-finger gesture and pointed that pistoleer finger toward the west—"thataway."

THE PROMISED LAND

June 30–August 16, 1951

15.

LIKE A STUCK compass needle, Herman's fixation held us to a single arrow-straight direction. To the Karl May territory of Indian knights and pistoleer cowboys, if you were Herman. To anywhere out there short of "the other side of the mountains" and a poorfarm for kids called an orphanage, if you were me. To the west, or rather, the West, capitalized in both our minds as the Promised Land, where we could be rid of the Kate and her bossy brand of life.

Old gray duffel bag on his shoulder, my new companion of the road marched through the crowd in the waiting room of the Milwaukee depot without deviating an inch either way, the wicker suitcase and me trying to keep up, dead-ahead until reaching the long and tall wall map topped with COAST TO COAST—THE FLEET WAY. Over our heads loomed the outline of America, which, I swear, seemed to grow as we stared up at the numerous Greyhound routes extending to the Pacific Ocean.

Our silent gawking finally was broken by a thin voice. Mine.

"So where do we start?"

"Big question," said Herman, as if he didn't have any more of a clue than I did. I could see him giving the subject a little think. "Maybe takes some *Fingerspitzengefühl*, hah?"

Unable to get my ears around that, I started to tell him to talk plain English because we didn't have time to fool around, but he got there first, more or less. Tilting his head to peer down at me as much with his glass eye as his good one, he uttered—and I still was not sure I was hearing right—"You got *Fingerspitzengefühl*, I betcha."

My hands curled as if he had diagnosed some kind of disease. "That doesn't sound like something I want to got—I mean, have."

"No choice do you have. It comes notcheral, once in great while," he said, as if it were perfectly normal to be singled out by some crazy-sounding thing. "Generals who think with their fingers, like Napoleon, born with it. Clark and Lewis maybe, explorers like us, ja?" The more he spoke, the more serious he seemed to grow, and I could feel my goose bumps coming back. Passengers overhearing him while they checked out their routes on the map were giving us funny looks and stepping away fast.

"Captain Cook, how about, sailing the world around and around." He still was cranking it out. "Must of had *Fingerspitzengefühl*, or *pthht*, shipwreck."

I SINCE HAVE LEARNED that what he was trying to describe with that jawbreaker word might best be called intuition in the fingertips, something like instinct or born genius or plain inspired guesswork tracing the best possible course up from map paper there at the end of the hand. A special talent of touch and decision that comes from who knows where.

HE COCKED that glass-eyed look at me as if I were something special. "You are some lucky boy, Donny, to got it."

Unconvinced and uncertain, I rubbed my thumbs against my fingertips, which felt the same as ever. "And wh-what if I do?"

"Easy. You find us where to go." In demonstration, he waggled his fingers as if warming up to play the piano and shifted his gaze to the map over our heads.

I did not want any part of this. "Herman, huh-uh. Even if I stand on a bench I can't reach anything but Florida, and that's way to hell and gone in the wrong direction."

"Tell you what," he breezed past my objection, "I get down, you get up." Then and there, he squatted low as he could go.

I realized he wanted me to straddle his shoulders. Skittish, I couldn't help glancing at people pouring past in as public a place as there was, a good many of them staring as if we already were a spectacle. "Hey, no, really, I don't think I'd better," I balked. "Won't we get arrested?"

"Pah," he dismissed that. "America don't know hill of beans about arresting people. You should see Germany. Come on, up the daisy," he finished impatiently, still down there on his heels. "Pony ride."

Feeling like a fool, I swung my legs onto his shoulders and he grunted and lifted me high.

Up there eight feet tall, the West was mapped out to me as close as anyone could want, for sure. Finger-spitty-thinger or not, I had to go through the motions. Pressing my hand against the map surface, I tried to draw out inspiration from one spot or another, any spot. Certain the eyes of the entire depot were on me, I felt around like that blind man exploring the elephant. Easy, this absolutely wasn't. If Herman's Apache knight was anywhere around Tucson or Albuquerque, he didn't answer the call. Nor did any Navajo cousin of Winnetou, around the four corners where Arizona, New Mexico, Utah, and Colorado all met. Automatically my hand kept following the bus routes traced in bright red, drifting up, on past Denver, Salt Lake City, Cheyenne. Whatever the right sensation of this silly Hermanic stunt was supposed to be, it was not making itself felt.

By now I was stretching as far as I could reach, the Continental Divide at my elbow, with Herman swaying some as he clutched me around the legs.

"Donny, hurry. Getting heavy, you are."

"I'm trying, I'm trying." At least my hand was, moving as if of its own accord. I could tell myself I didn't believe in the finger-guh-fool stuff all I wanted, but all of a sudden my index finger went as if magnetized to the telltale spot over the top of Wyoming.

"I got it!"

"Whereabouts?"

"Montana!"

"Good! Where in Montana?"

"Down from Billings a little."

"What is there?"

"Crow Fair."

"Hah? Go see birds? Donny, try again."

"No! Let me down, I'll tell you about it."

16.

"THESE CROWS ARE INDIANS, see, and Crow Fair is their big powwow." Back to earth, or at least the depot floor, I talked fast while Herman listened for all he was worth. "They always hold it between the strawberry moon and the buck moon, something to do with when berries are done growing but buck deer grow new antlers." I could tell I had lost Herman more than a little there. "That's this time of year, get it? We learned a bunch of Indian stuff like that in social studies class at Heart Butte. Anyhow," I rushed on, absolute grade-school expert that I was on such matters, "Crow Fair is really something, it lasts until they're powwowed out after about a week, and I bet we can get there while it's still going on."

Fingerspitzengefühl notwithstanding, he squinted dubiously up at the little red artery of Greyhound route to the Crow Reservation, way out west from Milwaukee certainly, but also in the apparent middle of nowhere, until I kicked in, "And all kinds of Indians show up for Crow Fair, honest."

Herman's thick glasses caught a gleam. "All kinds Indians? You are sure?"

"Sure I'm sure. Hundreds of them. Thousands."

"Even Apaches like Winnetou?"

"There's gotta be," I professed. "They wouldn't stay home from a powwow like that, the other Indians would think they're sissies."

That settled it. Declaring there could be no such thing as sissy

Apaches, Herman nodded decisively. "Crow Fair is where we go. Pick up your suitcase, Donny."

IN MY EXPERIENCE, there is no other thrill quite like disappearing, the way Herman and I were about to, aboard the dog bus. Who would not be excited at the prospect of walking away—no, better, riding away at high speed almost as if the racing hound beneath our side window was carrying us on its back in some storybook—from what we faced in that household where you couldn't even eat toast in peace? This is hindsight, always 20/20, but given my nearly dozen years of living more or less like an underage vagabond in construction camps and cookhouse, I had been through enough to grasp that with every mile flying past we would be borne away from Palookaville existences—Manitowoc ruled by the Kate in his case, foster home and orphanage limbo in mine—to life of our own making in the wide-open map of the West. An idea as freeing as a million-dollar dream and a whole hell of a lot more appealing than waiting on your knees for your soul to be snatched to heaven, right? So I still have to hand it to Herman, vanishing as we did was an inspiration right up there with the Manitou walkers going about their business in ghostly invisibility.

Not that erasing ourselves from where we were supposed to be was as easy as a snap of the fingers and the two of us gone in a cloud of tailpipe exhaust. Right away there in the Milwaukee bus terminal, Herman had me keep out of sight while he did the buying of the tickets to the map dot called Crow Agency—as he said, so any busybody would not remember us traveling together. "No tracks behind do we leave," he told me as if we were as stealthy as the Apaches themselves.

WHICH HELD TRUE only if Apaches greeted anyone sitting across from them on a Greyhound bus with "Hallo, you are going where?"

Something I had not counted on was that my newly conceived comrade in travel would be an adventure himself on the long trip west. This came through to me almost the minute our fannies hit the bus seats, when Herman struck up a conversation with whoever happened to be seated opposite us, or for that matter, in front or behind. Evidently he had stored up bushels of talk those hours in the greenhouse all by his lonesome, and did he ever let the surplus out now, much of it given to bragging up the two of us as adventurers of the highway.

"My nephew, some traveler he is," time after time he presented me, grinning back skittishly through my freckles, to whatever listener happened to be captive at the moment. "Seeing the land, we are."

Now, I had palavered plenty with total strangers on my trip to Manitowoc, for sure, but I was not trying to cover my tracks at the time. So while I was constantly jumpy about us somehow being tracked down—fairly or not, in my imagination the busybody who might do so had the plentiful face of Aunt Kate—Herman without a qualm gabbed away along a tricky line of conversation to maintain, keeping things approximate enough to be believed yet skipping the troublesome truth that we amounted to voluntary fugitives.

Runaways, when you came right down to it, as the mean little Glasgow sheriff had wrongly accused me before I was even out of Montana on my first cross-country journey. It does make a person think: Had the runty lawman with his sour squint spied something in me that I didn't recognize in myself? Being seen through is never welcome, and thank heaven or Manitou or whatever weird power seemed to guide Herman, because despite my nerve flutters, whenever someone expressed curiosity about where we were going, he always derailed the question with a goofy grin and the observation "Somewheres south of the moon and north of Hell, if we are lucky."

. . .

AND SO, state by state, as the bus rolled up the miles then and beyond, if we were remembered at all by the young honeymooners giggling their way to Wisconsin Dells or the retired Mayo Clinic doctor and his pleasant wife who reminded me of the kindly Schneiders or the Dakotan couple off the hog farm to shop in town, any of the Greyhound riders across the aisle would have recalled the pair of us only as a pared-down family of tourists out to see things.

That, at least, held a lot of truth, because with Wisconsin behind me I belatedly was ready to heed Gram—although not nearly in the manner she had so strenuously advised back there in the cookhouse—and step out in the world eager for new scenes and experiences, while Herman was as complete a sightseer as a one-eyed person can be. "Donny, look!" he'd point out any stretch of land open enough to hold a horse or cow. Even across cactusless Minnesota, he declared the countryside the perfect setting for a Karl May shoot-'em-up.

Then about the time I'd had all of those exclamations I could stomach, I would glance over and he'd be snoring away—literally in the blink of an eye he could sleep like a soldier, anytime and anywhere—restoring himself for the next stint of gabbing and gawking. But no sooner would I be taking the quiet opportunity to snack on a Mounds bar or pull out the autograph album to coax an inscription from some promising passenger than I'd hear from beside me, "You got work done, Donny?"

The yawning question as he came awake would be my signal to sigh and get back at what needed to be done, thanks to his big eye-dea on our ride out of Manitowoc. That is, corresponding with Gram from well into the future. I will say, when Herman put his mind to something like that, he did it all-out. In the shop at the Milwaukee terminal that sold everything from toothpaste to shoelaces, he had bought me a tablet with stiff backing, envelopes, and stamps, everything needed "for you to write like a good boy." Then, of course, it was up to me, the storier that I hoped Gram would be more glad of this time than others. As towns and their convenience stops came and went—Fond du Lac, Eau Claire, Menomonie, the Twin Cities, where I made damn sure we caught the next bus in plenty of time—I composed letter upon letter describing how my summer in the company of Aunt Kitty and Uncle Dutch was supposedly going. Creating my ghost self, I suppose it could be said, existing with the Manitowocers roaming around in the afterlife.

If my imagination and I were any example, there may be something to the notion that life on the road lends itself to rambling on the page. Putting the Kwik-Klik into action, I would begin with some variation of *Dear Gram—I am fine, I hope you are better. The weather here in Wisconsin is hot. I am having a good time.* Then I'd bring my foe into the picture, week by week disguised as the swellest great-aunt ever. *For the Fourth of July we went to the park where they played music like "God Bless America" and shot off fireworks and everything. . . . Today Aunt Kitty took me to the circus. Those acrobats are really something. . . . Guess what, Aunt Kitty bought a collie dog named Laddie to keep me company. She is always doing things like that. . . .*

I scarcely mentioned Herman, not wanting to get into his change from Dutch and the glass eye he could play a tune on and all that, and he seemed not to mind being left out. He read each of my compositions with his finger, very much as Gram would do when it arrived to her, occasionally questioning a word—"Looks funny, trapeze is spelled with *z*?"—before sealing it up and putting it in precise order in the packet to go to Ernie, the Schooner bartender, for mailing onward to the Columbus Hospital pavilion in Great Falls once a week. And I would go on to make up the next feature of my pretended summer on the Lake Michigan shore where Manitou held sway. *Aunt Kitty and I went to the Manitou Days celebration. It is a big deal here, with a parade like at a Montana rodeo and everything, because back in Indian times he was their Great Spirit, sort of like God to them, maybe. You know how the Blackfeet go on vision quests, up to Chief Mountain or someplace wild like that, to see if they can get visited by a spirit of some kind. That's like a dream when they are not sure they are asleep, if I savvy it right. I know it sounds spooky, but Aunt Kate said if we can't believe in that, we can at least believe in Indians. . . .*

Old Hippo Butt would have been surprised all the way to her back teeth at the number of kindly endeavors my imagination provided her.

I CAN'T ACTUALLY call it a waking dream that proved real, but definitely a visitation of the spirited sort sought me out that first night of our journey, in the most ordinary of dog bus circumstances. As happens in the monotony of night travel, passengers up and down the aisle had gradually nodded off until the bus was stilled to the sounds sleeping people make, Herman leading the chorus. While I dozed off and on, I was too keyed up by our daring escape from Aunt Kate and all she represented to really conk off. Somewhere in the long stretch beyond the Twin Cities to the even longer stretch of South Dakota, around three in the morning, I came to once again, with a strange little comet of light joining my reflection in the pitch-black window beside me. Blinking at its mysterious appearance there, I realized it was coming from inside the bus rather than up in the sky.

I sat up to look around, and across from us, where a couple who must have got on at a recent stop was sitting, a narrow beam of light poked down into the lap of the man in the aisle seat. The woman next to him was curled up kittenishly as she slept, while he was writing for all he was worth, just like I'd been during the day, but into a slick-looking hardbound notebook with sky-blue pages. While the rest of the bus was thoroughly dark, his fancy writing gear was illuminated by that tiny spotlight from someplace. At first I couldn't figure it out, but as my eyes adjusted, I realized he had a penlight, about the size of my Kwik-Klik, clipped to his shirt collar and aimed down. This stranger kept on writing like a demon, his hand never stopping to change or erase anything, a lit-up page no sooner filled than he flipped to the next and was giving it his all.

Holy wow. This was too good to pass up. I nudged Herman awake with a start. *"Hsst.* Trade seats with me."

"If it makes you happy," he mumbled grumpily, and we switched in that clownish way when there is not enough room to maneuver. Herman at once slumped against the window and back into slumber. He'd have to sleep for both of us, I was not going to miss out on this. More wide awake than ever, I half hung over the arm of the seat, in a way designed to catch the man's attention.

When the ceaselessly writing passenger felt my eyes on him and turned my direction to look, the flashlight dimly revealing our faces to each other, I whispered eagerly, "Hi. Do you do that a lot? Write on the bus, I mean."

"Funny you should ask, man," he replied in a heavy smoker's voice, low enough not to wake the curled-up woman. "Got the divine curse." Shoulders on him like a football player, he shrugged comically nearly up to his ears. "The old itch for which the only cure is pencil-in."

"Wow." I was impressed in more ways than one. His playful way with language reminded me of Gram somehow. Feeling an immediate kinship, I kept right on: "So are you gonna write all night?"

"Until the brain runs dry, let's just say." From the look of him, like he'd had too much coffee, that could be a real long while yet. He patted the open notebook on his lap. "Have to resort to tabula rosy here, because my machine is in the baggage."

My silence must have told him I was trying to decipher that. "My typin'writer." He grinned fast and friendly. "Old Hellspout."

"Oh, sure." Ceaseless writing gave me my opening, sort of. "I wrote a whole bunch myself, today. To my grandmother. She's in the hospital, back in Montana. She had to have an awful operation, and send me away"—I nodded toward snoozing Herman in more or less explanation of the two of us together—"until she gets better."

"That's a tough go, buddy," this man I had never seen before was all sympathy right away. Full face to me now, he took me in intently, yet with a sort of gentleness, as if we were old companions on the hard road of getting by. What he offered next could not be called encouragement exactly, yet I heard a kind of call to courage within it. "Life is what it throws at you."

That fit pretty well with *Hunch up and take it*, I thought. Stranger that he was, he seemed to instinctively understand a loco time like this summer of mine, so much so that I had no qualm about getting personal with him. "Can I ask? When you're writing like that, do you ever make stuff up, a little?"

Amused, he cut a quick caper with the pen-size light, pretending to write wildly in the air with its beam. "Anything goes, when you razz the matazz into one of those alphabet boxes called a book."

Book! That was way beyond any number of letters. My excitement grew. "Ever write those *Reader's Digest* ones? Condensed Books, I mean?"

"Phwaw," he expelled air like a hair ball. "That's a pregnant thought." From his expression after that burst I couldn't tell whether he was grinning or grimacing. He had a face like that, more than one thing going on at a time. In the glow of the penlight, his high forehead shown pale and his nose seemed to come down straight from it, but with a mashed look at the end, as if he'd been worked over in a fight. He had quick eyes, like a cat's, as he met mine. I couldn't be sure, but he might have winked in answering, "Condensation is only fog on the windshield for me. What I write, man, is as long as this highway."

"Whoo, really?" About then the woman at his side stirred in her sleep. I couldn't see much of her except quite a bit of bare leg. But emboldened by the dark, I asked, "Is that your wife?"

That set him off into another "Phwaw" exclamation. Shaking his head as if it was a question he had never been up against before, he speculated, "Only in the cosmic sense, bride of the slave to lust, you might say." He reached around and tickled her approximately in the ribs. "Aren't you, Sweet Adeline."

"Mmm." In a sleepy pout she leaned his way and gave him a kiss right in the ear. "Aren't you done scribbling yet?" the woman teased, still going at the ear. "You need to rest up for better things, Jean-Louis de K." She snuzzled—if that was a word, because it sure looked like it fit what she was up to—herself into his side until she was practically joined on to him, before drowsing off again with another pouty "Mmm."

Gazing broodily across to me, he spoke perfectly man-to-man. "The ladies. You know how it is. Can't do without 'em, can't do with 'em."

He said a mouthful there. Out of nowhere, which was just like her, Aunt Kate abruptly clouded out Letty, and I hurried to change the topic. "How far are you and the, uh, lady going?"

"Califrisco, Sanifornia," he quacked it, which if I wasn't mistaken was the address of Scrooge McDuck in the funnies, or at least I laughed like it was. He quit clowning right away, though, soberly thinking out loud in that tobacco-smoked voice. "Babylon by the Bay, yowser. We'll crash with some of the Frisco cats awhile, then drop down to Big Sur. The little lady here"—if I wasn't mistaken, he was tickling the inside of her thigh now—"has never seen the blue Pacific, west of the West." Although the tickle, tickle, didn't stop, his voice deepened, I'd almost say darkened. "Been a while for me, too, to see where it all begins and ends, kerplosh."

To the best of my geography book knowledge, I worked out where they were headed. "Isn't this sort of out of the way?"

"A standard deviation," he replied, which I didn't get at all. As if reminded of the extent of highway ahead, he leaned into the aisle to peer toward the windshield and the stretch of blacktop lit by the bus's headlights. Restlessly passing a hand through his hair, which started at a widow's peak but turned so thick and dark it made up for it, he asked, as if I'd been keeping better track than he had: "Where are we, anyway? Shouldn't civilization be showing up?"

The way the bus was keeping to eternal bus speed, we still had a lot of South Dakota to go yet, so I gave that the French salute. "He'd say," I pointed over my shoulder to Herman, "we're somewhere south of the moon and north of Hell."

"That's solid, man," my partner in conversation let out, as if he wished he'd thought of it first. His exclamation roused the sleeping woman, who wriggled against him in a way that couldn't help but get his attention. "*Excusez-moi*, buddy," he apologized in a whisper, closing his notebook and putting a hand to her somewhere I could not quite see. "Need to tend the home fire."

"Uh, first, since you're writing so much anyway, could you put something in my autograph book just real quick?" I asked before the chance slipped away. He gazed at me across the aisle again, question replacing mood in his deep-set eyes. "It has Senator Ridpath in it and everything," I hurried to say. "He's called the cowboy senator because he's from Montana."

"Well, bust my britches," he faked a cowboy drawl. "Hand that there thang over, pardner."

Curiosity getting the best of him, he focused his little flashlight on the album pages and read a couple at random. With a hand on his drowsing ladyfriend's thigh marking his place there, he split his attention to keep paging through the inscriptions and signatures, smiling here and there at the purple penmanship. Totaling up the contents, he whistled softly. "You laying this on people wherever you go?"

"Betsa bootsies I am," I answered boldly, as one inspired traveler to another, the darkness helping my courage. "I want to collect so much of what they write it'll make *Believe It or Not!*"

"Man, that's so far out it's in," he said wisely, or at least I interpreted it that way.

Next thing I knew, he was rapidly filling the album page with slanted handwriting. At the speed he was giving it, I grew alarmed that he might fill a whole bunch of pages.

But finally he signed off near the bottom with a last burst and handed the album back to me. "*Toot sweet and adoo*, buddy," he excused himself to tend to business at his side. "See you down the road." The penlight snapped off, leaving me in the dark.

> *You think about what actually happened, you tell friends long stories about it, you mull it over in your mind, you connect it together at leisure, then when the time comes to pay the rent again you force yourself to sit at the typewriter, or at the writing notebook, and get it over with as fast as you can.*
>
> *Advice free for the taking if you want to live life as she be in this mad bad buggered old contraption of a country called Uhmerica. Hang in there, buddy, and take it as it comes.*
>
> *It evens out in the end.*
>
> *Jack Kerouac*
>
> *On the road somewhere south of the moon and north of Hell*

17.

"'BUGGERED.' BAD LANGUAGE."

Herman wore an upset expression not entirely due to the South Dakota version of bus depot breakfast as he read over what, unbeknownst to either of us in the literary dark back then, would turn out to be as famous a set of words as I could ever hope to coax into the autograph book.

"He must have meant 'boogered,' don't you think?" I stuck up for my fellow long-distance writer. "Sort of snotted up like with a bad cold, maybe?"

Herman opened his mouth, but chose not to enlighten me. By then I was already on to the next thing that threw me, that signature, the strange name which sort of quacked its way around in the alphabet. "I thought from what the lady said he was John Louie de Something."

Herman gave it that salute. "The French."

By then we were in the linoleum-floored cafe section of the otherwise dead Greyhound depot in Aberdeen, the breakfast stop before the long remainder of South Dakota ahead. To my disappointment, the fully named Jean-Louis de Kerouac and his Sweet Adeline had vanished. If I had to guess, to an accommodation more horizontal than a bus seat.

I DID NOT THINK anything much out of the ordinary in bus depot experience when our none-too-appetizing meal arrived. My stack of hotcakes was burned to a crisp around the edges, and the ham and eggs must have come from tough pigs and pygmy chickens. Nonetheless I tied into the victuals, because food is food. Herman at his, though, turned out to be what Gram would have called a pecky eater, and then some.

That is, when his order of scrambled eggs and toast arrived, he ate the somewhat runny eggs in regular enough fashion, but then I noticed him nibbling away and nibbling away at an overdone piece of toast. More accurately, taking bites tinier than nibbles, whatever those might be, which was quite a sight with his chisel-like teeth.

While this peculiar performance across the table did not cause me to throw a fit as it so regularly did Aunt Kate at Manitowoc breakfast times, I do have to say such behavior was sort of disturbing, hard to watch and harder not to.

Herman kept at it, turning the toast this way and that to take those squirrelly little bites, discarding crust onto the edge of his plate, until finally putting down what was left of the slice and sitting back in apparent satisfaction. Figuring it was none of my business if a person wanted to eat a piece of toast like it was bird food, I worked away at my singed hotcakes without saying anything.

He wasn't letting me off that easy. "So, Donny, look," he prompted, indicating the remains of his meal. "Where is it, do you think?"

What kind of nutty question was that? Giving him a funny look, I pointed my fork at the limp remainder of toast, so chewed over it had ended up vaguely like the outline of a discarded boot, nibbled-out instep between heel and toe and all. "What, are your peepers going bad?" I spouted off, not the best thing I could have said to someone with a glass eye. "I mean, what you were chewing on is right there in your plate, if it was a snake it'd bite you."

"Hah-uh. Think bigger." When I didn't catch on, he hinted: "Gee-oh-graphy."

Still perplexed, I peered harder at the crustless gob of toast. Then it dawned on me, not vague at all when a person really looked.

"Italy?"

Herman slapped the table in triumph. "Smart boy. You got it, first try."

Where Aunt Kate thought his way with toast was disgusting, I was totally impressed. "Out the far end, Herman! Can you do other countries?"

"Everything in the book," he claimed grandly. "On ship and in army, you pass time best you can, so I learned world of toast." He grinned about wide enough to fit a piece of it in. "Winned lots of bets that I could not do Australia or somewheres, too."

Add that to playing a tune with a spoon on his glass eye and chicken-hunting behind the lines at places like Dead Man's Hill and surviving the Witch of November in the Straits of Mackinac and recognizing any beer at first taste and stocking up on Indian lore from Gitche Gumee to Winnetou, and I realized I was in the company of someone whose surprises just did not stop coming. This was a treat of a kind I could never have dreamed of, but also a challenge. Life with Herman was a size larger than I was used to, like clothing I was supposed to grow into.

COME SUPPERTIME, it was my turn to do the surprising. Almost from the start of the trip, Herman kept pestering me to know, "When are we in the West?" That evening, when we had reached Miles City, far enough into Montana that the neon signs on bars showed bucking broncs kicking up their heels, I finally could give the answer he wanted to hear. "Guess what." I pointed out the window of the cafe section of the Greyhound depot to that evidence. "We're there now."

"Hah!" said Herman, his eyes lighting up and following mine to the flashing sign on The Buckaroo bar across the street, with a rider waving his cowboy hat back and forth with the bronc's every blinking jump. "Feels different already! Map of Montana at breakfast, I make."

I'll say for myself that I knew inspiration when I saw it. "Guess what again." I caught Herman's attention by gobbling the last of my piece of pie and shoving the plate away. "Now that we're here, we need hats like that guy's. C'mon, the bus isn't leaving for a while yet."

Herman was like a kid on Christmas morn as we rushed across to the WRANGLERS WESTERN WEAR, conveniently right next to the bar with the flashing bronc and rider. As we went in the store, he was gamely peeking into his wallet until I told him, "Put that away, this is on me." It was rambunctious of me, because I had handed over my thirty dollars to him for safekeeping since I had no safety pins and a history of money somehow getting away from me. But the smaller sign I had spotted on the storefront was irresistible: S&H GREEN STAMPS ACCEPTED. Tough luck about that lawn chair, Herta, but fate made our deal kaput.

In the merchandise-packed place of business, one of those rambling old enterprises that smelled like leather and saddle grease and spittoons, every manner of western regalia from ordinary cowboy boots to fancy belts slathered with turquoise was on display and I had to herd Herman closely to keep him from stopping and exclaiming at each bit of outfit. But I managed to navigate us to the redemption desk at the back of the store, where the clerk, a bald man with a sprig of mustache who looked more like he belonged in Manitowoc than Montana, pooched his lip as my pages of stamps counted up and up. Finally he pushed a catalog across the counter, fussily instructing us that we needed to shop through it for what we wanted—I saw with dismay it was page after page of lawn chairs and the like—and as soon as the item was shipped in we could return and pick it up.

"No no no," for once I simulated Aunt Kate, waving off the catalog as if batting a fly. "We're not interested in mail-order stuff, we want hats."

"Cowboys ones," Herman contributed.

"In-store merchandise is outside the redemption program," the clerk stated.

"That's not fair," I said.

"It's policy," said the clerk.

"Proves it is not fair," said Herman, the veteran of Der Kaiser's army.

"Folks, I just work here," the clerk recited.

To my surprise, Herman leaned halfway across the counter, the clerk gravitating backward as he did so. "You maybe know who Karl May is," Herman leveled at him curtly. "Writes famous books about the Wild West?"

"I've heard of the person, of course," the clerk tried to fend, his mustache twitching in a rabbity way. "The Zane Grey of Germany or something like that."

"Austria, but does not matter. You are looking at him in the face." Now the clerk appeared really worried, running a hand over his bald head. "Sane Grey, pah," Herman puffed up in righteous Karl May indignation. "I can write whole story about Old Shatterhand while Grey fellow is taking a leak in the morning."

The clerk was speechless, kept that way by Herman's spiel about how I, favorite nephew accompanying him on one of his countless trips from Vienna to the land of Old Shatterhand and the like, had collected Green Stamps all the way across America with my heart set on obtaining cowboy hats for the two of us when we reached the real West, which was to say Miles City, and now here we were and being offered rubbish like lawn chairs instead. "I hope I don't got to tell my million readers Green Stamps are not worth spitting on."

I held my breath, watching the clerk shift nervously. "Mr.—uh, Herr May, let's be reasonable," he pleaded. "The problem is, it takes a special transaction form to substitute anything for catalog merchandise. It's only done when the item you want is out of stock, but that doesn't quite fit this—"

"Close enough, I betcha," Herman closed him off. "Let's have action form, my nephew will fill it out in big jiffy."

I did exactly that, and the defeated clerk led us over to the selection of Stetsons. Quickly I picked out a pearl-gray Junior Stockman model, the dress-up kind without a high crown or wide brim—even President Truman had one like it—while Herman glommed on to a white floppy ten-gallon type until I convinced him he'd look like the worst duded-up greenhorn this side of Hopalong Cassidy in it, and talked him down to about an eight-gallon one in sensible tan. Without a whimper the clerk shaped the hats for us, working the brims in the steam machine until we each had what we wanted—mine with a neat downward crimp in front, Herman choosing to have his curled up on the sides like the cowboys on the cover of *Deadly Dust*.

Next to each other, we gazed at ourselves in the full-length mirror. "Get you," I laughed to Herman. "You look pretty good in Mr. Stetson's shade."

"Not so bad your own self," he grinned back at me in the reflection. "We can go be punchers of cows now, ja?"

"Huh-uh, not quite yet," I declared. Whipping out the autograph book, I laid it open on the counter, startling the clerk morosely compiling the paperwork of our transaction. All the cross-country letter writing had kept me too busy to hunt inscriptions on the bus to the extent I wanted and I was bound and determined to make up for it. Seeing what I was up to, Herman started to say something, but held back. "People have been putting stuff in it for me all during our trip, see," I reeled off to the clerk staring at the spread pages in confusion. "I'm getting a real good collection, but I don't have any Green Stampers in it yet, so can you write something?"

The clerk stood on one foot and then the other, as if he couldn't decide even that much. "I've never been asked for this before. I don't know what to put in it, except—" He dipped his head shyly. "There's our song. We sing it at company picnics. Will that do?"

"Sure! Anything!"

Oh, S&H, S&H,
What would I do without you
To stretch my wage?
To trade for stuff
Page by page?
Everybody craves 'em,
I bet even Jesus saves 'em.
Little green stamps, little green stamps!
Sperry & Hutchinson
Does wonders for my purchasin'.
My book is full at last,
I better spend 'em fast.
I'll get that lamp with the frilly shade,
I'll fill the tub with free Kool-Aid.
Oh, those bonus-givin'
Guaranteed high-livin',
Super-excellent little green stamps!

18.

I SPOKE TRUER than I knew when I assured Herman we had reached the part of the country to take our hats off to. The next day, the Fourth of July, he and I hopped off the local Greyhound at Crow Fair, and into a vision of the West that Karl May and Zane Grey at their most feverish could never have come up with.

As if to greet us, what appeared to be a mile of Indians slowly riding in file was headed in our direction. At last! There we were at the fabled gathering, the tribal heart of the Indian world. Herman looked as happy as a tabby in catnip. As was I. We grabbed a spot along the parade route with several thousand other paleface onlookers to watch the approaching procession.

It was led by the flag-bearing color guard of war-bonneted Crow veterans marching in khaki, the same army uniform my father had worn, and those of us with hats held them over our hearts as those modern warriors passed. Then, as parades go, this one spared no form of horsepower. First came ranch trucks and hard-used pickups turned into floats with bales of hay as seating for the participants, the sides of the vehicles draped with handprinted banners.

THE CROW NATION

WELCOMES

ITS INDIAN BROTHERS AND SISTERS

AND

WHITE FRIENDS

CROW FAIR

A PROUD TRADITION

SINCE 1904

CROW FAIR PRINCESS 1951

VALENTINA BUFFALO CHILD

SPONSORED BY THE WIGWAM CAFE

And so on. The genuine thing for us, though, was the Crow nation saddled up in its glory, the horses' hooves stirring up little eddies of dust as the spectacular column of riders approached. The Crows were dressed top to bottom in powwow regalia, men in beaded leather vests that caught the sun in brilliant dazzles and women in red velvet dresses decorated with elk teeth. Even the Appaloosas and dappled ponies the riders were mounted on glinted with finery, dazzling beadwork on saddlebags and rifle scabbards.

"Whoo," I let out in awe as the long, long horseback procession continued, while drums kept up a constant beat we could almost feel in the ground, and the air vibrated with the chant of "Hey-ya-ya-ya, hey-ya-ya-ya" from every side. Herman was simply speechless, taking in the Indian world like a dream come true.

We watched until the last decorated pony and lordly rider of the cavalcade passed. Such is fascination, the spellbinding moment of imagination coming true. I can only speak for myself, but surely Herman, too, felt like a spectator into a world beyond any dreaming that day. Back then, the term "Native Americans" had not come into common usage, but definitely the traditions of the people who were here before Columbus, like the first owner of my precious arrowhead, were on living display beyond anything museums could capture. As far as we were concerned, "Indian" was word enough to carry the magic of the past, and here it was on full show, as if just for us.

"OH MAN, that was as good as it gets!" I still was giddy afterward. "Did you see those saddle blankets, even? They use Pendletons!"

I rattled on until Herman said, "Ja, I telled you *Fingerspitzengefühl* works like charm," as if the bus ride all the way from Milwaukee had been merely a matter of giving it a little think.

Already feeling like we'd had one of the great days of our lives, after the parade the two of us followed the flow of the crowd to the ticket booth at the fairground entrance, where the rest of the day's events were chalked on a slab of blackboard.

"Fancy dancing, Donny."

"Rodeo, Herman."

I was impatient to get in and start to see everything worth seeing, but he took his time peeling off money for our entrance fee, asking the ticket seller, an Indian of indeterminate age with a single feather sticking straight up out of his hair, if we could stow the duffel bag and suitcase in the booth since we hadn't had time to find a place to stay. "Hokay, I'll keep an eye on 'em." He jerked a thumb to the corner of the booth and I dragged our luggage there and turned to go.

"Donny, wait." Herman was grinning nearly back to his ears. "One thing more. Put moccasins on, hah?"

Why hadn't I thought of that? With my purple rodeo shirt with the sky-blue yoke trimming and now my pearl-gray cowboy hat, my outfit lacked only the moccasins. Swiftly I swapped out of my shoes, my feet grateful in the softness of the buckskin, and in an inspiration of my own, I tucked the autograph book under my belt like a hunter's pouch. Then off Herman and I went as if the beadwork fancy-dancers on my feet were leading us to the real thing.

We still were on the same earth as Manitowoc, but the world changed as we headed for the fenced-in area of grandstand and corrals and chutes and arena where the rodeo would be held. Tepees by the hundreds populated the encampment bordering the fairground, white cones sharp against the blue sky like a snowy mountain range, all the same precise height. Drummers and chanters there kept up the "Hey-ya-ya-ya, hey-ya-ya-ya" beat as if it was the pulse of the seasons of the strawberry moon and the buck moon. Herman and I tried not to rubberneck amidst it all, but failed laughably. Fully half of the rodeo-going crowd around us was Indian families, the fathers wearing braids and the mothers sometimes not, excited children dribbling after in colorful shirts while trying to look as swayve and debonure as I felt. Herman was like a keyed-up kid, too, asking this person and that if they happened to be Apaches and not discouraged by the steady answer "They're not from around here."

Then we were funneled into the rodeo grounds—surrounded by a horse-high hog-tight woven-wire fence with the gate conspicuously manned by sharp-eyed tribal police; rodeo crowds are not exactly church congregations, and the Crows were taking no chances on drunks and other unwelcome sorts sneaking in—and the pair of us virtually walking on air filled with the aromas of fry bread and sizzling steak amid the lane of food booths and craft displays of jewelry and woven blankets and wearables set up next to the arena.

"Karl May would not believe his eyes, hah?" Herman chuckled to me when we passed by a homemade camper, SLEWFOOT ENTERPRIZES painted on the driver's door, where a bearlike Indian man seated on the running board was driving belt holes into some piece of paraphernalia with a leather punch and chanting, "Made to order, folks, best dancing rigs this side of the happy hunting ground, same price as they was a minute ago, git 'em right here and now." And as if he had conjured them, suddenly ahead of us at a refreshment stand were fancy-dancers everywhere, costumed as if they were under a spell that made them halfway to birds.

THE SIGHT CAST me into a spell of my own. The day's fancy-dance exhibition, according to the printed program we had picked up at the gate, would take place between the bronc-riding events, and this batch of selected dancers—many of them not a day older than me, I noticed enviously—were waiting around, drinking pop and eating candy bars until called on to perform. I hung back and gaped at their costumes, which covered them almost entirely, from beaded moccasins to a feather or two sprouting out of equally beaded headbands. I mean, *fancy* only began to say it. Fuzzy Angora goat hide step-ins were wrapped around the bottoms of their legs, and fringed vests long as aprons draped down that far. Anklets of sleigh bells jingled with their every step. The upper part of the body was the real story, though. Strapped on each dancer's back was a great big spray of feathers, like a turkey's tail in full display. What lucky kids they were in all that getup, I thought with a pang, ready to dance their hearts out. It may have been my imagination, but my moccasins seemed to twitch as we passed the dancers by.

Coming out of my trance as everyone but us was flocking to the grandstand on the far side of the arena, I had the presence of mind to say the next magic word to Herman.

"Cowboys."

"Ja? Where abouts?"

He gawked all around, as if expecting pistoleer angels wearing Stetsons and boots to materialize. Here I was on familiar ground, steering us to the area behind the bucking chutes, knowing that was where anything interesting happened until events in the arena got underway.

BACK THERE in the gathering place between where horse trailers and other vehicles were parked and the pole corral of the arena, it was as busy as could be wished, big-hatted Indian contestants and those from the professional rodeo circuit clustered behind the chutes, working on their riding rigging, fastening their chaps on, joshing one another about how high the bronc they'd drawn would make them fly. Calf ropers were building their loops and making little tosses at nothing. Teenage girl barrel racers exercised their horses, leaving behind increasing islands of manure. In the background, Brahma bulls bawled in the holding pens and saddle broncs snorted and whinnied as they were hazed into the bucking chutes.

Herman and I meandered through, taking in the whole scene as if we were old hands at this, our Green Stamp Stetsons blending right in with the cloud of rodeo hats. This was the best yet, hanging around the "choots," as Herman called the chutes.

Then I saw it. If I were telling this story from long enough ago, I suppose it would have been the chariot of a god touched golden by the fire of the sun. As it was, the gleaming purple Cadillac convertible parked at the very end of a row of horse trailers and pickups stopped me in my tracks.

"Herman, look at that!" Recovering, I rushed over to the chrome-heavy car with upswept tail fins and peeked in. The seamless leather seat covers were the same deep purple as the exterior. Likewise the floor mats and door panels. And the crowning touch—on the inlaid-wood steering wheel, even the necker knob was that color. I was so excited I was forgetting to breathe. All but certain who had to be the owner of this modern heavenly chariot, I checked the hood ornament.

And yes, wonder of wonders, there it was, exactly according to reputation. The shiny replica of a livestock brand replacing the Cadillac's stylized flying figure.

◇

"SEE, IT IS!" I gushed to Herman as he came up behind me. "It's his!"

"Ja?" He eyed the gaudy car as if it was unique, all right. "Whose?"

"Rags Rasmussen's! The champion bronc rider of the world! He's the most famous cowboy there is! That's his brand, he puts it on everything—the Diamond Buckle." The symbol of his world championships, in other words. "He's just the greatest," I attested as Herman puzzled out the hood ornament for himself. "My folks and me saw him ride at the Great Falls fair. I tell you, he turned that horse every way but loose."

Babbling on like that about what a famous cowboy we were going to be lucky enough to watch in the saddle bronc go-round, I happened to look past Herman and the air sucked out of me as I gasped, "Here he comes!"

Tall and lanky except for squared-off chest and shoulders like the box the rest of him came in, the champ rider was moseying toward us with purple chaps slung over an arm. No one else in the world walks like a real cowboy, a sort of devil-may-care saunter, as if the ground was unfamiliar territory but he was making the best of it. "Would you look at them long legs on Rags," some admirer over at the chutes remarked. "The Lord took his time when he split him up the middle."

The object of all attention continued on his way toward the bucking chutes as if cloudwalking, his black boots with the inlaid Diamond Buckle emblem freshly shined, his lavender Stetson spotless, his plum-colored gabardine pants sharply creased. Completing his outfit, I was thrilled to see, was a shirt nearly identical to mine, emphatic purple with a blue yoke and pearl snap buttons. Talk about suave and debonair for real, he carried it on his back in a naturally fitting way that made me wish I was him so hard it hurt.

Blinking along with me at the elegant sight, Herman whispered, "Why is he called Rags?"

"That's easy. He's always got his glad rags on when he rides." Herman still didn't get it. "Look how dressed up he is."

"Hah," he understood and more. "Like a knight, he puts on his best for the tournament, what you mean."

"The rodeo, you bet," I confirmed breathlessly. "That makes him the slickest rider there is in every way, see."

The female population of the rodeo grounds conspicuously thought so, too. Barrel-racing beauties in tight blue jeans and a performing troupe of blond cowgirls astride matching palominos called out flirtatious hellos, no small number of these contingents so-called buckle bunnies, who had an eye for winners. "Later, ladies," the famous bronc stomper sent them with a lazy smile.

By now the immaculate lanky figure was nearing the chutes and being greeted by fellow contestants. A calf roper looping out his lariat called out, "How's it hanging, Rags?"

"Long as a bull snake," the champion bronc rider of the world said back, loose and easy. "Got to be careful I don't step on it."

Now, that was man talk. Imagine how my vocabulary would increase around somebody like him. Swamped with hero worship, I could think of only one thing to do, and I did it—a little frantically, but I did it. "I'll be right back," I yipped to Herman, and charged over to the most famous cowboy there was, yanking the album out from my belt as I ran.

"Rags? I mean, Mr. Rasmussen. Can I get your autograph, huh, can I?"

He broke stride enough to give me a curious glance.

"I'm helluva sorry to bother you," I bleated, the pitch of my voice all over the place. "I know you're getting ready to ride and everything, but this is maybe the only chance to put you in my book and I'm trying to get really famous people in it and you're right here and—please?"

Amused at my prattling, he smiled and offered up in the same easy drawl as before, "Guess I don't see why not, if it's gonna put me in such highfalutin' company."

He handed me his chaps to hold, taking the autograph book in return, a swap so momentous it nearly made me keel over. A kid in Cleveland with the pitcher's glove of Bob Feller bestowed on him, an eleven-year-old New Yorker gripping Joe DiMaggio's bat—it was that kind of dizzying moment of experience, unexpected and unforgettable, a touch of greatness tingling all through the lucky recipient. Resting the autograph book on the front fender of the Cadillac, Rags Rasmussen started writing. Not merely his signature, I saw with a thrill. An inscription, from the way he was going at it! World championship words, right in there with the observations on life by the night writer Kerouac and the sage old Senator Ridpath. At this rate, the autograph album was headed for *Believe It or Not!* fame in no time.

"Hey, Rags," a hazer at the nearest bucking chute hollered to him, "better come look over your rigging. You're up in this first go-round."

"Great literature takes time, Charlie. Be right there."

> ***When you lift your hat,***
> ***to ladies and that,***
> ***make sure you have something upstairs***
> ***besides a collection of hairs.***

"There you go," he said, his signature and all the rest on the page in Kwik-Klik purple ink magically matching his riding chaps—clear as anything, a sign to me this was meant to happen. Lucky arrowhead, happy coincidence, the spitzen finger that had put Herman and me in this place at this time, something finally was working in my favor this loco summer. Sky-high about my newly found good fortune, I heard, as in a haze, Rags Rasmussen talking to me almost as an equal. "Seen that little ditty on the bunkhouse wall at the old Circle X ranch down in the Big Hole country, a time ago. Wasn't much older than you when I started breakin' horses for outfits like that." He gave me a look up and down and a long-jawed grin. "Figured it was worth passing along to somebody who knows how to wear a rodeo shirt."

"Wow, yeah! I mean, thanks a million," I fumbled out my appreciation for his supremely generous contribution to the autograph book, hugging it to myself as though it might get away. Unwilling to let go of these moments of glory with him, I blurted, "Can I ask, what horse did you draw today?"

He shifted from one long leg to the other. "Aw, sort of a crowbait—" He broke off into a rueful laugh and scratched an ear. "Guess I hadn't ought to use that word around here. Anyway, I pulled out of the hat a little something called Buzzard Head."

Hearing that just about bowled me over. Talk about a *Believe It or Not!* moment. Buzzard Head was famous—the notorious kind of famous—as the most wicked bucking horse on the rodeo circuit, the bronc that had never been ridden. Through the years, contestants at Cheyenne, Pendleton, Great Falls, Cody, Calgary, all the big rodeos, had done their best to stay in the saddle for ten seconds aboard Buzzard Head, and had eaten arena dirt for their trouble. Here was the matchup that people would talk about ever after, the bronc that threw them all and the rider who was never thrown, and Herman and I, as fate and luck and blind coincidence would have it, were on hand to see history made.

When I had my breath back, I said with more fervor than diplomacy, “Good luck in riding to the whistle.”

“Might need it,” Rags Rasmussen said agreeably. “Get yourself a good seat and enjoy the doings.” Flopping his chaps over a shoulder, he strolled off to meet the meanest horse imaginable as if he hadn’t a worry in the world.

Herman had come up behind me and laid a hand on my shoulder. “Some man, he is. Like Old Shatterhand, cool custard, hah?”

“Cool customer,” I fixed that, still idolizing the strolling figure in his riding finery. “Look at him, not worried at all about that cayuse in the chute.”

“Buzzard Head does not sound like merry-go-round horse.” Herman cocked an inquisitive look at me.

“He’s the worst,” was all I could say. “C’mon”—I still was on fire from the miraculous encounter with my hero Rags—“I know the best place to watch him ride, if they’ll let us.”

“YOU ARE SURE this is good eye-dea? Dangerous place, if we fall?” Herman shied away as far as he could from the bronc pawing at the bucking chute beside us, as he crept after me on the narrow plank stairs.

“Then don’t fall,” I gave him the cure over my shoulder. “Shhh. Leave this to me,” I cautioned further, keeping on up the midair steps that led to the shaded platform beneath the announcer’s booth.

When we popped our heads through the opening in the floor of the platform, what awaited us was pretty much as I expected from other rodeos I’d been to. Clustered there where the arena director and anyone else who counted in running the events could keep track of things at close hand were several Indian men in snazzy beaded vests and the darkest sunglasses made, beside big-hatted rodeo circuit officials and a few other white guys in gabardine western suits who had to be the livestock contractors supplying bucking horses and Brahma bulls for big shows like this one. As I scrambled onto the perch with Herman stumbling after, the only personage paying any particular attention to our arrival was a Crow elder, lean as a coyote, with braids like gray quirts down over his shoulders, who gave us a freezing stare.

"We're friends of Rags and he told us to get a good seat to watch him ride," I said hastily, as if that took care of the matter. "My uncle here is from, uh, out of the country and this is his first rodeo"—Herman wisely only grinned wide as the moon and did not ask if there were any Apaches around—"and it'd be a real treat for him to see it from up here like this and we'll stay out of the way, honest, and just—"

"Welcome to Crow Fair, don't get too close to the horses." The gray-haired Number One Indian made short work of us and swung back to overseeing the commotion in the chutes beneath our feet where the rigging crew was wrestling saddles onto thrashing broncs.

Establishing ourselves at the far end of a long bench softened by gunnysack cushions filled with cattail reeds—boy, these Crows knew how to do things—Herman put his attention to the printed program that listed saddle bronc riding, calf roping, steer wrestling, barrel racing, bareback riding, and of course, the fancy-dancing exhibition. "Same as circus, many acts," he expressed in satisfaction as I read over his shoulder. But then, coming to the names of the broncs the riders had drawn, Widowmaker and Funeral Wagon and Dive Bomber and similar ones, he nudged me in concern. "Sounds like war, this buckjumping."

I had no time to reassure him on that as the saddle bronc riding explosively got underway almost beneath where we sat, with an Indian contestant named Joe Earthboy sailing out of the chute on a nasty high-kicking horse called Dynamite Keg. Earthboy and airborne animal became a swirl of dust and leather and mane and tail as the crowd cheered and the announcer chanted encouragement. A full few seconds before the timer's whistle, the rider flew up and away from the bronc as if dynamite had gone off under him, all right. "Ow," Herman sympathized as Earthboy met the dirt, gingerly picked himself up, and limped out of the arena.

Which set the tone for that go-round, contestant after contestant getting piled without coming close to completing the ride. By now it was obvious Crow Fair did not fool around in staging bucking contests. Deserving of their blood-and-guts names, these clearly were the biggest, meanest, most treacherous horses available on the professional circuit, as veteran in their way as the career rodeo cowboys who tried to master them. Watching these hoofed terrors with Herman swaying next to me as if he felt every jolt in the saddle himself, I couldn't stop my nerves from twanging about Rags Rasmussen's chances on the monarch of them all, Buzzard Head.

ALL THE WHILE, I also was having the time of my life. Beside me, Herman was entranced in a Karl May knights-of-the-prairie way as he ohhed and ahhed at the spectacle of cowboys and broncos whirling like tornadoes in the arena. We were sitting pretty in the shade in the best seats in the rodeo grounds, comfy as mattress testers, while an acre of sunburn was occurring in the sweltering grandstand across the way. The announcer's steady patter overhead was as soothing to my ears as a cat's purr, filling time between bucking contestants by joking with the rodeo clown down in the arena as he went through his antics in overalls six sizes too large and a floppy orange wig. Like committing poetry to memory, I took in every word of their beloved old corny routines, as when the clown hollered up to the booth that he hated to leave such a good job as dodging broncs and Brahma bulls but he needed to move to Arizona for his seenus trouble. "Hey, Curly, don't you mean 'sinus' trouble?" I could have recited the deep-voiced announcer's line right along with him.

"Nope." The clown made the most dejected face ever seen, and I knew this part by heart, too: "The trouble is, I was out with another fellow's wife, and he seen us."

Hooting and hollering, the crowd reliably responded as if that were the height of humor, while Herman slapped me on the back and nearly fell off his gunnysack seat guffawing and I laughed as hard as if I hadn't heard that mossy joke at every rodeo I had ever been to. Life can tickle you in the ribs surprisingly when it's not digging its thumb in.

ALL OF WHICH is a way of saying, what an emotion came over me in that precious space of time at Crow Fair. For the first time that unhinged summer, I felt like I was where I belonged. Around horses and cattle and men of the ranches and reservations, and the smell of hay in the fields and the ripple of a willowed creek where magpies chattered. Most of all, I suppose, because he was the author of this turnaround of our lives, in the company of halfway wizardly Herman, the pair of us blest with freedom of the road wherever the dog bus ran, enjoying ourselves to the limit at this peaceable grown-up game of cowboys and Indians. This is not the prettiest description of a perfect moment, but it was a king hell bastard of a feeling, filling me almost to bursting.

EVEN THE INTRODUCTION of danger as the next rider was announced—"Here's the matchup we've all been waiting for," the announcer's voice hushed as if on the brink of something colossal, "down in chute number six, the reigning world champion in this event, Rags Rasmussen, on a pony that has never been ridden, Buzzard Head!"—felt like it fit with the fullness of the day. Secretly, I would have given anything to be in those Diamond Buckle boots snugging into the stirrups down there on the notorious horse that the riding champ of all mankind was easing onto. A fantasy like that knows no logic and common sense, of course, because the most treacherous hazard in all of rodeo was hanging up a foot in a stirrup while being thrown and getting dragged by a saddled bronc determined to kick the life out of its trapped victim. While my imagination naturally pasted me into Rags Rasmussen's place as he rode to the top of his profession, I nonetheless fervently fingered the arrowhead in my pocket for whatever luck it might bring in his matchup against the killer horse.

Herman looked as breathless as I felt, on the edge of his seat as we craned to see into the chute below, watching Rags make his preparations, his purple chaps vivid against the buckskin flanks of the waiting horse. Buzzard Head plainly deserved its name, with a big Roman nose and cold, mean eyes at the end of a droopy neck. Rags took his own sweet time getting ready, joking to the chute crew that they might at least have dabbed some chewing gum in the saddle to help him stick on, casually pocketing his world championship diamond ring so it wouldn't catch in the rigging and yank his finger off, tugging his hat down tight, flexing his boots into the stirrups until it felt right. Then, every motion easy but practiced, one hand gripping the hackamore rope and the other high in the air according to the rules, spurs poised over the point of the bronc's shoulders, he leaned back almost sleepily in the saddle, balanced against the catapult release he knew was coming. Throughout this, the glassy-eyed horse stayed deathly still, according to reputation saving itself up to attempt murder in the arena.

The tense chute crew stood ready until the man in the saddle said, cool as can be, "Open."

Then the gate was flung wide, and the bronc erupted out of the chute, twisting its hindquarters in midair that initial breathtaking jump. Buzzard Head alit into the arena practically turned around and facing us, as if to convey, *You wanted to see what a real horse can do, here it is.* Instantly the buckskin bronc went airborne again, throwing itself full circle in the opposite direction from the first maneuver, snapping Rags from one side to the other like cracking a whip.

"Damn, it's a sunfisher," my fear found words.

Herman needed no translation of that, the crazily bucking creature contorting in its leaps as if to show its belly to the sun. He worried in return, "The picker-ups, they can't get to Rags neither if he don't fall."

I saw what he meant. The pair of Indian pickup men, whose job it was to trail the action at a little distance and swoop in on their spotted horses to pluck the rider off after the whistle blew, were driven away by the bronc's hind hooves cutting the air wickedly at every unpredictable twist and turn. Buzzard Head plainly hated everything on four legs as well as two. Now even if Rags survived atop the murderous horse for the full ride, he would have to get out of the trap of stirrups by himself. "Meat wagon," the gray-braided Crow in back of us issued flatly, sending one of the other Indians swiftly down the steps to the arena gate where the ambulance and its crew waited outside.

An *Oooh* ran through the crowd as the bronc levitated as high as a horse can go, the ugly head ducking from side to side, trying to yank the rope from Rags's grasp. Possibly the only person there on that never-to-be-forgotten day who thought the rider stood a chance as Buzzard Head writhed and twisted and plunged through its bag of tricks was Rags himself, athletically matching split-second reactions to those of the bronc, his long form rebounding from every dodge and dive as if he was made of rubber. I suppose a question for the ages is, What is so spellbinding about watching a man ride an uncooperative horse? Probably something that goes far, far back, the contest between human will and what it finds to match itself against. At least that is the justification for the sport of rodeo, if it needs any. I was rubbing the obsidian arrowhead so hard my fingers went numb as we watched the sunfishing horse do its best and worst, but Rags stayed in the saddle, even as his hat flew off, bouncing onto the horse's rump, then to the ground as if Buzzard Head meant to throw the man off his back piece by piece.

Time never passed so slowly. But at last, after the ten-second eternity of Rags Rasmussen's immortal ride, the whistle blew.

"Jump, right quick!" Herman shouted, as carried away as I was, watching the pickup men futilely trying to spur in on the furiously kicking bronc.

Then, in a feat as unlikely as sticking in the saddle the way he had, Rags shed the stirrups in a lightning backward kick and simultaneously vaulted off in a running dismount. Before Buzzard Head could locate and trample him, the pickup men forced their horses in between, letting Rags saunter to the safety of the chutes, picking up his hat on the way and sailing it up to the pretty woman whistle judge in the announcer's booth.

That great ride, I knew even then, was the legendary kind that would have people saying for years after, *I was there that day*, and by the luck of the arrowhead or some other working of fate, now I was one of them, forever. It was left to Herman to put the moment into words.

"That was bee-yoot-iffle."

THEN CAME THIS, all because I had to use the rodeo version of a convenience, one of the outhouses behind the corrals.

During a break in the action while the chute crew saddled the next round of broncs, I excused myself to Herman and trotted off to do the necessary. Naturally there was a long line there at the one-holer toilets, but I scarcely noticed the wait, my head filled with the dizzying experiences of the day, topped by the purple presence of Rags Rasmussen himself in the memory book. On my way back from the outhouse visit, I still was caught up in such thoughts, trying to decide whether to press my luck and ask the head Crow there on the platform to write himself in, too. He looked kind of mean behind those darkest dark glasses, but at last getting an Indian into the autograph album would make the day just about perfect, wouldn't it. Couldn't hurt to try, could it? Maybe if I said to him—

Whomp, the sound of hooves striking wood next to my ear sent me sideways. Startled, I reeled back from the corral alley I was passing. In the confusion, it took me a moment to catch up with what was happening. Horses were being hazed in for the bareback riding, and barebacks generally were unruly cayuses fresh off the range and not accustomed to being corralled as the saddle broncs were. This first one being herded through from the holding pen was spooked by the cutting gate that would send it to a bucking chute and was trying to kick its way out, hind end first. Almost crosswise in the narrow corral enclosure with its rump toward me, the snorty bronc kept on kicking up a ruckus despite the swearing efforts of the corral crew. "Whoa, hoss," I contributed uselessly as I backed away farther, ready to continue on my way. But then. Then the agitated horse turned enough that I caught sight of the brand on its hip, the double letters registering on me as if still hot off the branding iron.

I stood there like a complete moron, unable to take my eyes off the *WW* in the horseflesh. It didn't take any figuring out that the same would be on all the broncs in the bareback bucking string. No way had this ever entered my mind, that Wendell Williamson, livestock contractor to rodeos though he was, might furnish Double W bucking stock to this one all the way across the state. But perfectly like the next thing in a nightmare, here came the familiar braying voice in back of the milling broncs and the frustrated corral crew. "Don't let 'em skin themselves up on the cutting gate, damn it. These nags are worth money, don'tcha know."

In horror, now I could see the chesty figure through the corral rails. Sparrowhead, flapping a gunnysack at the hung-up bronc and barging in on the hard-pressed corral wranglers. My blood drained away.

"Here, let me handle the sonofabitching thing myself—" He broke off a hotter streak of swearing and scrabbled up onto the corral to run the cutting gate. Instinctively I backed away fast, but he spotted me. The beady expression of recognition on the puffy face expanded into something far worse.

"Hey, you, Buckshot! Get your thieving butt over here, I want that arrowhead back!"

I bolted.

Behind me I heard Sparrowhead hollering for the tribal police. Luckily I was able to dodge out of sight around the corrals and back to the arena before the gate cops knew what was up. Every lick of sense told me, though, it would not take long before they tried to sort me out of the crowd. Heart beating like a jackhammer, I scrambled up the stairs beside the bucking chutes to reach through the platform opening and grab Herman's ankle. "Hah?" I heard him let out, before he had the good sense to glance down and realize it was me.

He descended as fast as I had gone up, ducking behind a head-high trash bin of the kind called a green elephant where I was hiding. "Donny, what is it? You look like losing your scalp."

"We're in trouble up the yanger," I whimpered.

"Don't want that, I betcha." Herman waited for translation and explanation, hanging on every word as the story tumbled out of me about how I took the arrowhead when I left the ranch and Sparrowhead now wanted it back to the extent of siccing the Crow cops on me.

When I was finished, he poked his hat up as if to get a closer look at me. Too close for comfort.

"Took. As means, stealed?"

"No! I found it in the creek, fair and square. You said it yourself, sharp eyes and light fingers. I mean, Sparrowhead thinks it's his because he owns the whole place, but why isn't it just as much mine, for seeing it in the creek when nobody else had since before Columbus and—"

He held up a hand to halt any more explanation. "Let's think over. Maybe give it him back?"

"No." I moaned it this time. "Herman, listen. It's like when you were a chicken hunter. Didn't you take only what you needed? I—I can't really explain it, but the arrowhead is like that to me. Something I need to have."

"Different case, that is." His expression changed, in my favor. He cast a look around the rodeo grounds and that horse-high, hog-tight fence. "We must get you away."

There was this about Herman. When he really gave something a think, you could see him generating a brainstorm until his eyes lit up, somehow even the glass one. That happened now, as I listened with every pore open to hope while he assuredly outlined the *eye-dea* to me. Anything was better than being arrested and branded a thief and handed over to the authorities who would send me to the poor-farm for kids the other side of the mountains and I'd lose Gram and my life would go right down the crapper. But Herman's plan set off all kinds of fresh worries in me.

"You—you're sure that'll work? I mean, they'll *know*, won't they? I don't think I can—"

"You betcha you can." He had more than enough confidence for both of us, not necessarily a good sign. "Come on, no time is there to waste."

Scared half out of my wits as I kept looking for the trooper hats of Crow cops to show up, I stuck tight by his side as we sifted along the arena corral where people were watching the rodeo from the backs of pickups and the fenders of their cars, blending in as best we could.

At last safely reaching the area of food booths and crafts tables and so on, we made straight for the homemade SLEWFOOT ENTERPRIZES camper, where the bearlike Indian man sprang up from his leatherwork when he saw us coming.

"Howdy. You fellows collectors, maybe? 'Cause I got some nice things stashed in the camper here. Buffalo skulls and like that."

"Hah-uh." Herman shook off that approach, glancing over his shoulder in one direction while I nervously checked over mine in the other. "Something else, we are in hurry for."

"In a hurry, huh? Funny, you don't look like fugitives from a chain gang." Humorous as that theoretically was, there was small-eyed suspicion behind it as the Indian vendor studied the pair of us trying too hard to compose ourselves. "Anyhow, the something else. What might that be?"

"Your help, ja?" So saying, Herman extracted a twenty-dollar bill from his billfold but held on to it.

"Huh, twenty smackers," the Indian acknowledged the sight of the cash, "that's starting to look like the price on something else." He jerked his head toward the rear of the camper. "Step around the tepee on wheels here and let's palaver."

Back there out of sight, I breathed slightly easier. Waiting to hear what we had to say, the Indian stood there broad as a bear. Even his head looked like a grizzly's, round and low on his shoulders. Herman couldn't wait to ask. "You are Apache, maybe? Winnetou, you know about?"

"Winnie who?"

"Not now, okay?" I hissed to Herman.

"Apaches aren't from around here, friend," the Indian helped me out in putting us past any further Karl May enthusiasms out of Herman. "I'm Blackfoot. Louie Slewfoot, to boot," he introduced himself, Herman and I shaking hands with him the proper soft Indian way while keeping our eyes off his clubfoot that jutted almost sideways from the other one.

Briskly he got down to business. "What can I do for you to loosen your grip on poor old Andy Jackson there," he indicated the twenty-dollar bill in Herman's fist. "Look, he's turned green."

Herman glanced at me, I endorsed what he was about to say with a sickly smile, and he spoke the momentous words that would either save my skin or not.

"Dress up Donny like fancy-dancer. Long enough to get him out from here."

"Whoa, no way." Louie Slewfoot backed away a lame step, laughing in disbelief. "These costumes are sort of sacred to Indian people, you can't just wear them for Halloween." He gave me a sympathetic wink. "Nothing personal, cowboy, but them freckles of yours are a long way from Indian."

"Hey, that's not fair," I bridled. "I have an Indian name even, Red Chief. Nickname, I mean."

"Sure you do," he rolled his eyes, "and I'm Tonto."

"And look at my moccasins, don't they count? They're Blackfoot, like you." His heavy dark eyebrows drew down as he took a good look, but that was the extent of it. "And I went to school some at Heart Butte with Indian kids," I persisted insistently, "and—"

"Yeah, yeah, yeah," he butted in, "all of that gives you full standing in the Whooptydoo tribe, chiefie, but I can't go around duding up a white kid in—"

"How about this, then," I butted right back, reaching the arrowhead out of my pocket and peeling back enough of its condom sheath to flash the slick black obsidian to him in my palm.

"Wah." Silent now, he put a hand toward the shiny black stone, but didn't touch it. "That's big medicine. Where'd you git it?"

"It's, uh, been in the family."

"Tell him all, Donny," Herman warned before wisely hustling off toward the front of the camper to keep a lookout.

I spilled the whole tale of arrowhead and Sparrowhead, Louie Slewfoot listening without ever taking his gaze off the obsidian gleam of it.

When I was done, he laughed over the Tuffies as Herman had, saying, "Pretty smart, but the problem with them things is they can spring a leak and you end up with something you wasn't expecting." That explained it! Why the arrowhead sometimes worked like a charm and sometimes didn't, if its luck could leak out like that. Louie had the way to fix the matter, reaching onto his table of leather goods and tossing me a small leather sack on a buckskin thong. "Let's git it out of its cock socks and into a medicine pouch, hokay? Hang it around your neck and treat it right if you don't want to lose the big medicine."

At the end of that, he growled deep in his throat. "That wampus cat, Williamson. He runs the Gobble Gobble You like the whole earth is his. We have to chase its goddamn cattle off the rez land all the time. The rich sonofabitch sure to hell don't need any big medicine like that." With something like an animal grin, he sized me up in a new way. "Dearie dearie goddamn," he expressed, which went straight into my cussing collection. "How did I git myself into this, fixing you up as a fancy-dancer? Gonna take some doing." He laughed so low it barely came out. "But it'd be a helluva good joke on these Crows, wouldn't it. They was on Custer's side, you know. Bastard scouts for Yellow Hair."

"Po-leece is com-ing." Herman's soft singsong reached us from his sentry post up front.

I just about dissolved at that, but it galvanized Louie Slewfoot. "Git in," he half helped, half shoved me into the back of the camper, with him clambering after. In there, in the semi-dark, everything was a flurry as I undressed and was dressed all over again by the grunting Louie slipping a long apronlike skin shirt and a beaded harness that hung way down and woolly leggings—"Them other kids can have their plain old goatskin, this here is pure angora"—and jingle bell anklets and a bunch more onto me. As he draped a sort of harness made up of shiny disks bigger than a silver dollar around my neck, I wondered, "Are these real silver?"

"Naw, snuff box lids. Stand up straight, can't you."

I was starting to feel as weighted down as a deep-sea diver, but he kept on digging out items and fastening me into them, until we both froze in position at the sound of a voice with the flat cadence of the Crows asking Herman where the custodian of the booth was.

"Hungry, he is. Gone for the frying bread. I am minding for him," said Herman, as if glad to be of help.

"When he comes back, tell him to keep an eye out for a red-headed punk kid in a purple shirt and give us a shout if he spots him. Some kind of sneak thief we need to turn in to the sheriff," the Crow cop finished his business and could be heard moving on. Sheriff! The memory of the mean little Glasgow lawman who arrested his own brother gripped me like a seizure, the vision of what all sheriffs must be like.

Louie Slewfoot had his own pronounced reaction. "You would have red hair." He pawed through his stock of costumery, and the next thing I knew, I was top-heavy in a turban-like feathered headdress that covered my hair and came halfway down to my eyes. "That's better. Now we paint you up good." Working fast, he smeared my face and hands with some oily tan stuff. "The half-breed kids use this, it makes them look more Indian to the dance judges."

Along with a knock on the back door came Herman's urging, "Coast is clear, better hurry."

"Yeah, yeah. We're about done. Turn around a half mo, Red Chief." When I did so, Louie strapped something large and feathered on my back, patted me on a shoulder epaulet the size of a softball, and told me, "There you go, chiefie. The rest of this is up to you."

"Donny, is that you?" Herman met me with astonishment when I hopped out of the camper. Overcome with curiosity myself, I stretched my neck around to glimpse the thing on my back, and blinked at the unmistakable mottled black-and-white feathers arrayed almost to the ground, fanned out as if in full flight.

"Holy wow! The bald eagle wing thinger!"

"You been to Heart Butte basketball games, sure enough," Louie Slewfoot granted. The Heart Butte Warriors had cheerleaders in swirly skirts like any other high school, but also—famously or notoriously, depending on your point of view—a boy dancer, rigged up pretty much as I was and stationed at the top of the stands every game, who at crucial points would whirl around and around, letting out the hair-raising staccato eagle screech, *Nyih-nyih-nyih.* Before a player on the other team was about to shoot a free throw, preferably.

"Never been able to sell the bald eagle getup to these cheapskates down here," Louie was saying philosophically, "so you might as well give it a little use. See if you can git its medicine going for you." Turning to Herman, he rubbed his thumb and forefingers together. "Speaking of medicine, where's that twenty?"

HERMAN PAID UP, but we weren't done with Louie Slewfoot yet, nor he with us.

"Hokay, now we need to git Fancy Dan here past the rodeo chief," he instructed as he set off toward the bucking chutes, motioning us on behind. "Remember now, you're not Donny the wanted kid, you're my nephew Marvin." He cautioned Herman, "Leave the rodeo chief to me. Henry Swift Pony. He's not a real chief, but he's a bossy SOB even for a Crow and somebody has to run the show."

With my outfit jingling and jangling and Herman fretting that he hoped nothing happened to the moccasins in this, we trailed after Louie's slewfooted gait, both of us unsure how this was going, especially when he did not turn aside at all as the biggest Crow policeman imaginable, black braids down to his shiny badge, appeared from the back of the chutes and beside him, complaining loudly about the lack of arrest of a certain thieving runt of a kid, Wendell Williamson.

The shaking of my feathers and ankle bells had nothing to do with dance steps. I was convinced my life was going to end then and there, amid horse manure and moccasin tracks. In that big word *incarceration*, one way or another.

"Th-that's Sparrowhead," I quavered to Herman, wanting to turn and run.

"I guessed so," he grunted back, keeping right on toward Louie and the oncoming lethal pair. "Don't be horrorfied," he bucked me up, as if being scared to death was that easy to be rid of. "This is where you are Red Chief, brave as anything." I swear he sounded straight off a page of Karl May. "Big medicine in your pouch, remember." His words made me feel the presence of the arrowhead resting against my chest. "Walk like Winnetou and Manitou are with you, the earth is your hunting ground." I couldn't match his steady stride, but I did square my shoulders beneath the epaulets and skin shirt and work my eagle wing rig as if flying on the ground and marched to the jingle of my bells.

Still, as Louie barreled along on his collision course with Sparrowhead and the Crow version of a harness bull, I said tremulously out the side of my mouth, "Is he gonna turn us in?"

"We find out. Keep walking like you got no business but dancing fancy, Red Chief."

Of all things, Louie planted himself in the path of the oncoming two men. Hunched like a bear spotting prey, he gave the Crow policeman a wicked grin and said:

"Howdy, Constable. Glad to see you keeping the peace. No ghosts of Custer around or anything."

The big Crow cop glared, snapped, "I don't have time for fool talk," and stepped around him. Giving the Indians an exasperated look, Wendell Williamson sidestepped along with the cop while Herman and I swept past, unnoticed.

"THAT WAS SORT of close," Louie Slewfoot remarked when he caught up with us at the bucking chutes. "Hokay, next act. Git in back of the green elephant there and stay out of sight until I tell you." He pointed me to a big trash bin, and as for Herman, "You can make yourself useful by standing at one end and sort of blocking the view. Pretend like you're watching the rodeo and you don't know him or me from Sitting Bull."

We took our places, and Louie clomped around to face the platform above the bucking chutes, cupping his hands to his mouth. "See you about something, Henry?" he hollered up to the man in charge. "Won't take time at all."

Peeking past the edge of the trash bin, I could see the rodeo chief turn to him, stone-faced behind the dark sunglasses, his braids more than ever like whips of authority down over his shoulders. "You again, is it, Slewfoot. I gave you the booth spot you pestered the crap out of me for. What's eating you now? If you weren't so frigging good at the squaw work, I wouldn't let your blanket-ass butt in here."

"Big frigging *if*, Henry, and you know it," Louie gave no ground. "Don't be giving me a bad time when I'm trying to perk up your rodeo with something special, huh? My nephew, Marvin here. Brung him to show you spazzes how dancing's done at Heart Butte."

Henry Swift Pony laughed without any humor whatsoever. "Pull my other one, Louie. Nothing doing, we have all the entrants we need." Herman, nearly toppling over in their direction to hear this, looked as anguished as I felt.

Louie ignored the turndown and called out to me, "Marvin! Come show Mr. Swift Pony what a fancy-dancer looks like."

I stepped out from behind the green elephant.

From his platform perch, the head Crow looked me over for half a minute, whipping off his dark glasses to see if the feathered rig on my back was truly the bald eagle wing outfit, and stopping at my moccasins. My heart thumping a mighty rhythm, I jigged enough to make the eagle feathers shimmer and the anklet bells ring-a-ling-ling. Helpfully or not, Herman abandoned his fixed casualness of staring into the arena to turn around and exclaim, "Some outfit!"

With a dip of his head, Henry Swift Pony had to agree, conceding to Louie: "He's got it all on, for sure. Fine, chuck him in with the other kids. But at the tail end."

THE GAGGLE of fancy-dancers that had been at the refreshment stand was now bunched at the passageway gate beyond the chutes, where the rodeo clown and anyone else who needed access to the arena could come and go. Wishing me luck—"Git out there and show 'em how the cow ate the cabbage," said the one; "Let Manitou be in moccasins with you, hah?" said the other—Louie and Herman left me to it, and so, ankles tinkling and snuff lids clattering, I shuffled down the passageway to join the gaudily outfitted assemblage.

Not that the group of them, waiting for their time of glory in the arena, could particularly hear me coming. They jigged and jangled and jiggled and jingled—maybe other jittery *j* words, too, but I don't know what those would be. These were some wound-up kids. Nonetheless, I couldn't help but be noticed as I tucked myself in with them. The biggest one of the bunch, an ornery-looking high school kid with a jackknife face, spotted me at once, my black-and-white wing outfit standing out amid their feathers of the mere golden eagle, dime a dozen out there on the plains. Enviously he looked down that long blade of nose at me, his eyes narrow as the rest of his unwelcoming mug. "Who're you? Little Beaver?"

Ordinarily those were fighting words, but these were not ordinary circumstances. Trying to make nice, I started to respond, "Donny Cam—" and just in time managed a coughing fit. "Sorry, frog in my throat," I barely rescued the name situation. "Anyway, Donny, but my dancing name is Slewfoot."

"Tanglefoot is probably more like it." The ornery kid, head and shoulders taller than me, suspiciously eyed what he could see of me under all the costume. "So, Donny Frog in the Throat, where'd you dig up the bald eagle rig?"

There comes a point, in something like this, where you just do not want to take any more crap. "That's for me to know and you to whistle through the hole in your head to find out," I retorted to Jackknife Face.

"Gotcha there, Ferdie," the other rigged-up kids hooted, more curious about me than hostile. Giving me a good looking-over, they concluded: "You're not from here."

"That's for sure," I verified, and let drop: "Heart Butte."

"Blackfoot," Jackknife Face snickered. "That explains a lot."

The others, though, were as impressed as I'd hoped. "Whoa, the war whoop hoopsters, like in the papers! Neat! You play basketball?"

"Damn betcha." I may have fluffed my feathers some in composing the brag. "We shoot baskets for an hour after school every day. Everybody does, even Shorty the janitor."

"Bunch of crazy gunners," my skeptic tried to dismiss Heart Butte's famous basketball proficiency. The others hooted again. "Yeah, they shot the living crap out of you, Ferd. What was that score the last game, about 100 to 20?"

The jackknife-faced one was back at me. "So, baldy. What are you, an apple in reverse?"

Not up on that in Indian talk, I dodged. "Ever hear of speaking English?"

"Come on, pizzlehead, you know—white on the outside and red on the inside?"

"Oh, that. Sure, why didn't you say so." That fit fine. Maybe he was going to acknowledge me as an honorary Indian after all, and that would be that.

"I still don't go for this," Jackknife Face took a turn for the worse, though. "We've practiced our butts off together and you just show up to do the eagle dance, big as you please? Why should we let you horn in?"

Uh oh. That didn't sound good. If I got kicked out, I was right back to being searched for all over the rodeo grounds by every Indian policeman. In a fit of desperation, I started to protest that the rodeo chief himself had let me into the fancy-dancing, but Jackknife Face was not about to give that a hearing. Pointing to me, he called out to the dance leader waiting at the gate, a tribal elder with a skin drum, "Hey, Yellowtail, how come he gets to—"

He was drowned out by a shout from Henry Swift Pony, up on the platform. "You there, bird boy! I thought I told you to stay at the back."

"See you at the dancing," I told Jackknife Face as I scooted to the rear of the bunch.

"And now, a special treat, courtesy of Crow Fair," the announcer's voice crackled in the nick of time, "for your entertainment, the fancy-dancers of the Crow nation, junior division!"

"Here we go, boys, do yourselves proud," the dance leader intoned, simultaneously starting up a rhythm with his drum like a slow steady heartbeat, and the entire group of dancers—with one exception, me, the straggler in more ways than one—burst into "Hey-ya-ya-ya, hey-ya-ya-ya." I caught up, more or less, as the whole befeathered and jinglebob collection of us pranced into the arena, and in the soft dirt each began to dance to the chant and drumbeat.

DID I HAVE any idea of dance steps to do, fancy or otherwise, there in front of thousands in the packed grandstand and the eyes of the Crow nation and the world-beating bronc rider Rags Rasmussen? No, yes, and maybe. For although I was merely a make-believe Indian in pounds of costume, I did remember the whirling and twirling of the Heart Butte mascot while he scared the neck hair off opponents at basketball games with the high-pitched eagle screech, and may have invented swoops and swirls of my own as I swept rambunctiously around in jigging circles with my arms out like wings and the array on my back aquiver in every beautiful black-and-white feather. Caught up in the drum music and the *hey-ya-ya-ya*, but most of all in the moment where imagination became real, I danced as if my flashing beaded moccasins were on fire. I danced as if the medicine pouch with my arrowhead in it was a second heart. I danced for Gram in her hospital bed and wheelchair, danced for Herman the German and his monumental little thinks, danced for shrewd Louie Slewfoot, danced for the threesome of soldiers fated to Korea and for Leticia the roving waitress and for Harvey the romantic jailbreaker and for the other traveling souls met on the dog bus and inscribed in the memory book, all of us who were hunched up and taking it while serving time in this life.

So, I suppose I was me, nerved up to the highest degree, but in the moment I was also Red Chief, and who knows, maybe some kind of ghost of Manitou bursting out of wherever a spirit walks through time. Possessed as I was, my moccasined feet knowing no boundaries and my high-pitched eagle shrieks of *Nyih-nyih-nyih* puncturing their chant, I spooked the other fancy-dancing kids away from me as I plain and simple outcrazied them.

By now I could hear as if in a dream the announcer singling me out, calling, "How about young Woolly Leggings there, part angora and part bald eagle, quite the combination! Look at him go! He's got more moves than a Scotchman trying to sneak under the door of a pay toilet. Folks, what you're seeing here today holds special meaning. These dances go back a long way—"

On the dust cloud raised by the pack of dancing kids, my moment of fame forever with me, I jigged my way from the arena as the exhibition ended and on out the gate of the rodeo grounds, still hopping and writhing, past the stern-faced Indian police watching for a purple shirt and red hair.

HERMAN WAS WAITING a little way beyond the gate, and immediately gathered me in front of him, herding me to the parking lot near the tepees. "Quick fast. Louie has camper out, you can change there."

Sweat running off me in streams, as tired as I had ever been, I stood there slack like a horse being unharnessed as Louie took the costume off me piece by piece.

"You did pretty good for a redhead," he allowed. As I slowly dressed in my own clothes, he excused himself, saying he had to try to wangle the same booth spot out of the Crows for the next day, it was a sort of lucky location.

That left Herman, sitting on the narrow bunk at the front of the camper cabin with his arms folded across his chest, saying nothing as he watched me button my rodeo shirt and settle my Stetson on my head. The last thing I did was to make sure the freed arrowhead hung straight in the medicine pouch under my shirt, where it felt like it belonged. My watcher still had said nothing. Timidly I broke the silence.

"Are—are we gonna keep on?"

Herman took off his glasses, breathed on one lens and then the other and cleaned both with deliberation, using the tail of one of Louie's costume garments lying there. Settling the eyeglasses back in place, he gazed at me as if newly clear-sighted. "On with what, Donny?"

"On with our trip?" My voice was uncertain. "On the bus?"

Deliberately or not, he kept me in suspense a while more. Finally he said, "More to see out west here, there is. Dog bus is how to git"—natural as breathing, he had absorbed the word from Louie—"there, ja?"

Overcome with relief, I still had to make sure. "You're not too mad at me for getting us in that fix? By taking the arrowhead, I mean?"

He shifted on the bunk, his glasses catching what light there was in the cabin. "I am giving it a think, sitting here while you was putting clothes on. You know what, Donny? Not for me to decide, how right or wrong you taking the arrowhead comes to. You are some good boy where it counts, by sticking with me. I must do same by you, hah?"

I just about cried with—what, gratitude, happiness? Some feeling beyond that, inexpressible elation that he and I would hit the road together again? In any case, it was the kind of situation where you duck your head because there is no way to say thanks enough, and move on.

"Yeah, well, gee, Herman—what do you want to see next?"

"Something without police breathing on us," he thought. "Notcheral wonders, how about."

19.

For another twenty smackers, Louie Slewfoot's going rate for saving our skins, he drove us to Billings, a safe distance from Crow Fair and its cops in braids, and dropped us at the Greyhound station there.

"You fellows sort of make a full day," he remarked as he handed down the now dusty suitcase and duffel bag from the back of the camper, with dusk giving way to dark. Life with Herman packed a lot into the hours, I was definitely finding out.

"Take good care of that arrowhead, chiefie, so it'll take care of you," Louie advised me with a sly wink as he took his leave of us with a slam of the camper door. But not before, big medicine or whatever doing its work, I coaxed him into an autograph and more.

Say, do you remember the time
I slipped on a banana peeling
and hit the ceiling
while wondering why
I had a stye in my eye
and how in hell
my nose runs while my feet smell?
Oh, I was in tough condition

because life's a rough proposition—
but at least it makes a nice rhyme.
Louie Slewfoot
Off the rez and on the go—

"Not Longfellow, but not shabby," Herman approved, reading over the inscription from a genuine Indian that I had finally proudly attained. "More to him than meets an eye. Too bad he is not Apache."

Handing me back the autograph book, he switched his attention to the old standard, the red-webbed route map on the Greyhound depot wall. "Scenery everywheres, I betcha," he observed about the many roads trending west. "So, Donny, what does your fingers say?"

This was almost too easy. On tiptoes, I jabbed a finger to the most famous spot west of Crow Fair.

"Yahlahstone," Herman ratified thoughtfully, looking over my shoulder. "Old Faithful geezer is there?"

Fixing his pronunciation, I assured him that besides geysers there were bound to be natural wonders popping up all over the place in Yellowstone National Park.

"Not only that," it must have been the big medicine still working in the pouch around my neck that had me thinking so expansively. "See there, then we can go on through the park"—my finger confidently traveled down the spine of the West, arriving in Arizona—"all the way to where the Apaches live, how about."

"Now you are speaking," he enthusiastically took up the prospect.

First thing was to get us on our way, and I drew Herman's attention to the schedule board, showing that the bus we wanted was about to go. "C'mon, or we're gonna miss it."

"Donny, wait," he held back, concerned. "We have not had bite to eat since breakfast."

"Never mind," I took care of that, seasoned bus hopper that I was, "we'll grab candy bars."

. . .

SCRAMBLING ONTO THE BUS at the last minute with a handful of Mounds bars apiece, scanning the rows of mostly filled seats in that game of chance of where to sit, we even so were not the last to board. Just as the driver had shut the door with the departing *whoosh*, there was a polite tapping on it, and here came a wisp of a man, hardly enough of him to withstand being blown away by the wind; gray-headed and with a silvery mustache sharp over his lip like a little awning; well-dressed in a mild way, his plain brown suit obviously far from new. He thanked the driver kindly for letting him board, and evidently to make no more fuss deposited himself in the first seat available, which happened to be across from us.

As the bus pulled out, for once someone got the jump on Herman, with the latecomer leaning across the aisle and inquiring in a cultivated voice, "Where are you gentlemen headed, may I ask?"

"Yahlahstone Park, next on list," replied Herman, triggered into his usual spiel that he and I were out to see the West, but perhaps in deference to the man's oh-so-polite demeanor, he left off the part about ending up somewhere south of the moon and north of Hell.

"Oh, good for you and the young man there." His visitor approved our intentions with an odd click of his mouth. "Endless things to see in the park," he went on in that same refined tone but clickety at the end of each string of words, "all the marvels of nature. I'm passing through there myself, on my way to visit my daughter in Salt Lake City." By now I had caught on that his false teeth clacked.

"Ah-huh," Herman stalled, like me thinking over the prospect of several hours of clickety-clack conversation like this from across the aisle. "You got some big miles to go."

"So I have, you put it so well." The fine-boned man, on second look maybe not as elderly as he first appeared, smiled under the cookie-duster mustache. "But that's the story of life, isn't it. Keeping on across the unknowable distances that at the end of it all add up to that mystical figure of three score and ten," click-click.

I had heard Herman's gabs with strangers across the aisle so many times I was only half listening to this exchange, more interested in devouring Mounds bars and catching my breath, mentally at least, after the narrow escape from Sparrowhead. But that sizable serving of heavy thought from the little gent drew my attention. By now Herman, too, was cocking a speculative look at him.

"Please forgive me," this daintiest of passengers touched the area of the knot of his tie. "There I go again, with my preaching collar on. You see, I'm a minister. Answered the call all those years ago"—a smile peeped from under the mustache again—"those big miles ago, and even though I'm retired, the pulpit still beckons at odd moments." He laughed at himself, ever so apologetically. "I suppose folks like you unlucky enough to listen to my ramblings are my congregation now. I didn't mean to intrude, my heart was simply warmed by the sight of the pair of you traveling together."

Back there at the word *minister*, I stiffened. *Dearie dearie goddamn. Why this, why now, why why why?* On one of the biggest days of my life, the question of my taking the arrowhead had attached itself to me like a telltale shirttail that hung out no matter how I tried to tuck it. I mean, I still believed I in no way amounted to a real thief, whatever grabby-guts Wendell Williamson thought, because discovering the arrowhead after it had lain there unclaimed since before Columbus amounted to my luck and his loss, didn't it? And I deserved half of our canasta winnings just as much as Aunt Kate, didn't I? Shouldn't old Hippo Butt and Sparrowhead both know when they were beat, and fold their cards like canasta losers? Yet if the situation was that clearcut, why did it keep bugging me? Now *whoosh*, and right here on the dog bus the latest stranger proved to be a man of the cloth, as I knew from something I'd read such people were called, whose occupation it was to provide answers to things like that, in church and out, from the looks of it.

OLD-TIMER ON THE DOG bus that I was from sixteen hundred and one miles going back east to Wisconsin and now many hundreds more westward with Herman, I had the crawly feeling that this particular passenger across the aisle was too close for comfort. This was way worse than the nun at the start of my trip to Manitowoc or the attic plaque of the kid on his knees bargaining with death in the night, this was as if the big mystery called God was using the bus-hopping minister like siccing a sheepdog onto strays. *"Go get 'em, Shep, herd them close. Nip 'em good. Here, take this new set of teeth."* Maybe a limited dose of religion never hurt anyone, but bumping into the small-fry minister this way bugged me. For some reason, the wispy figure an arm's length away reminded me of the little sheriff who'd arrested Harv. Trouble came in small sizes as well as large, I was learning.

"NO, NO, IS OKAY," Herman was busy assuring the kindly minister he wasn't intruding on us, although he sure as hell was, pardon my French. I could tell Herman, too, was thrown by the religious wraith's sudden appearance. For if my conscience had a few uncomfortable things on it, the one in the seat next to mine must have been considerably weighted down with the phony tale of going back to Germany and this entire disappearing act he had thought up for the two of us.

"May I ask how you two are related?" the minister pressed on. "I see such a striking resemblance."

He did? Was I growing to be like Herman that much? Oh man, there was another weighty question—good or bad, to take on the homely yet compelling characteristics of somebody so one-eyed, horse-toothed, and, well, Hermanic?

"Great-uncle only, I am," he postponed the matter as best he could, with a glassy glance at me. "Donny is best grandnephew ever made."

"How fortunate you are, sir," a click and a chuckle from across the aisle. "Great by dint of the fruit of the family tree."

"No bad apples on our branch, hah, Donny?" Herman fended.

"By the way, my parishioners called me Reverend Mac" came next, with an extended hand of introduction. "It's from my middle name, Macintosh," which had quite a clack to it as he said it.

Seeing no way out of it, Herman and I shook hands with him and introduced ourselves back, and the Reverend Mac promptly followed up with just what we did not want to deal with.

Smiling to the fullest under the rim of mustache, he made the modest gesture toward his collar again. "A contribution I can still make to the good cause is to distribute Bibles into hotel rooms," he confided. "I have been doing so in Billings, which needs all the salvation it can get." He gave another clickety chuckle, Herman and I trying to politely match it with heh-hehs. I think we both were a little afraid of what was coming, rightfully so. Slick as a carnival barker, the man of the cloth or whatever he was now pulled out a black book with gilt lettering, unmistakably a Bible, saying, "I happen to have an extra, and would be gratified if you gentlemen would accept it as a gift from a fellow traveler."

With it deposited on him that way, Herman had to take the offering, mumbling a thanks and shoveling the Bible along to me as if I were its natural audience. I gave him a look, but he wouldn't meet my eye, attending instead to the minister's rambling about the inevitable good that the Good Book would do in those dens of sin, hotel rooms. What he gave us proved to be a flimsy paperback version with typeface about the size of flyspecks, but it still unnerved me enough that I didn't want it paired with the autograph book, and quick as I could, stuck it in my opposite coat pocket.

"It does provide its rewards, spreading the good word." The minister still was holding forth to us as if we were in a church on wheels. "And that brings me to a question, if I may"—Herman and I both braced, now really knowing what was coming—"are you followers of the Lord, in your own way?"

The bus saved us, barely, gearing down into the town of Laurel at that moment, followed by the driver's announcement of a ten-minute stop to pick up passengers. As the Greyhound pulled over at the hotel serving as depot, I pleaded to Herman, "I need to go," although the urge wasn't really about using the convenience. "Real bad."

"Me, too." He was out of his seat as if his pants were on fire, with me right after.

"I'll mind your seats for you," Reverend Mac obligingly called after us.

MAKING USE of the restroom since we were there anyway, we spraddled side by side to discuss the minister matter. Escaping a preacher may not sound like the worst problem there is, but you have to admit it is among the trickier ones.

"Sky pilot, Old Shatterhand would call him," said Herman, buttoning up.

"Nosy old Holy Joe, Gram would call him," I said, doing the same.

"Ja, he is sniffing awful close to us."

"Guess what. I've got an idea."

Hearing me out as we headed back to the bus, Herman brightened up and paid me the ultimate compliment, saying I had a good think.

"You do it first, then I do same," he whispered before we stepped on. As we took our seats, Reverend Mac, his hands peacefully folded, welcomed us back.

He looked as if he'd been jolted in his prayer bones when, first thing, I leaned across Herman and thrust the autograph book at him, asking him ever so nicely to contribute some words of wisdom.

"My goodness, this is quite an honor," he recovered quickly enough, "and I had better make the most of it, hadn't I." He stroked his mustache as he studied the opened album, apparently sorting through holy thoughts. Then he began to write, surprisingly like a schoolboy toiling away at a handwriting exercise.

The Good Book is a stay against the darkness
a source of wisdom
and a comfort in troubled times.
Yours in the fellowship of man
Isaac M. Dezmosz

"Written with a pen of iron and with the point of a diamond. That's biblical," he said, handing me back the Kwik-Klik with that click of his own. "Hallelujah, brother, I thank you for the chance to get those words down." It seemed to me sort of a preachy inscription and didn't even rhyme, but what else could I expect, I figured.

"I see you wondering about the last name," he provided next, noticing Herman's puzzlement as he studied the inscription over my shoulder. No wonder the man went by Reverend Mac, was my own reaction to what looked like a line from an eye chart.

"A touch of Poland in the family, way back." He smiled as if we all knew what a tangle the family could be. "Mankind is such a mixture sometimes."

Herman could readily agree to that, yawning prodigiously some more as he had made sure to do while the reverend wrote.

Yawns are of course catching, and following his, mine were absolutely epidemic, according to my plan. "You know what," I stretched drowsily, which did not take much pretending, "I'm all in but my shoelaces."

"Ja, we are feeling it," Herman did his part, patting away another yawn as if doing a war whoop. "South Dakota is a long ride," he borrowed the jackrabbit territory of the day before.

If the Reverend Mac was disappointed in not pinning us down about whether we were with the Lord, he did not show it. "By all means, go to your rest." He could not have been more gracious about excusing us to slumber. "Bus travel takes it out of a person."

He said a mouthful there. Naturally Herman was asleep almost the instant he shut his eyelids, and I was more than ready to doze off as well, with the bus heading due west through the Yellowstone valley into a sunset of colored clouds and shafts of sunlight that had the driver pulling his windshield visor all the way down. The dainty minister sat back, smiling to himself, one more Bible inflicted on potential sinners or proven ones, to his evident satisfaction. The last thing I remember before sleep claimed me, he was humming to himself, more than likely a hymn.

"OLD FAITHFUL INN, the Waldorf Astoria of Yellowstone National Park. You may disembark if you so wish—"

Herman and I alit in the dim parking lot after the driver's done-it-a-hundred-times announcement with a cluster of tourists already exclaiming over this and that. Still trying to yawn ourselves fully awake as we waited for our baggage to be dug from their mountain of suitcases, I looked around for the talkative minister, suspicious that he would hop off to stretch his legs and have another go at us. But there remained no sign of the soul-hunting demon, to mix terms in an unholy way. The little Bible-pusher had disappeared from the seat across from us whenever I cracked an eye open from my series of naps as the bus traveled through the dark, probably to farther back in the aisle where religious pickings might be better, and I figured he must be staying aboard to work on some poor Salt Lake City–bound soul who needed directions to the Lord.

Hallelujah, brother, now the Reverend Mac was digested into the memory book, and that was enough of him for me. Quickly putting aside the churchy bus experience, Herman and I turned to our much-awaited surroundings. Smell that piney air, feel that high altitude! We had made it to glorious Yellowstone, free as knights and Apaches and other roaming spirits, and in silent agreement we grinned at each other and took a minute to marvel at it all.

Some distance away, with black forest as a backdrop, floodlights picked out a mound of earth, nearly as white as salt, which we divined must be where the famous geyser would make its appearance. Out and around in what looked like a geyser kitchen, steaming water bubbled out of the ground as if from gigantic boiling pots. Oh man, nature was really cooking here, in all senses of the phrase. And magically, a star brighter than all the others—probably the planet Venus, I now realize—was pinned right there over the geyser site, as Mae Schneider's ditty in the autograph book promised. Yellowstone already was putting on a show for us, as Herman's mile-wide grin attested. Nearly as splendid as the natural wonders for our current purpose was the colossal Old Faithful Inn overlooking all this, several stories high like an elaborate fortress made of logs, with gables everywhere and a sloping roof as long as a ski jump. By now it was long past suppertime and a place as grand as that surely would have a menu fit for the gods, or at least us, and then a nice warm room for the night.

"Notcheral wonders and fancy eats and feathery beds, hah, Donny?" Herman exulted as he shouldered his duffel bag and I hefted my suitcase.

"Yeah, finger-spit knew what it was doing, didn't it," I crowed happily as we started off after everybody else to check in to the fancy Inn and head for supper.

"Donny, wait!"

What I heard in Herman's voice stopped me cold. When I

glanced back, he had dropped the duffel bag and was clutching his chest. Having never seen a heart attack, I nearly had one myself at this sight.

"Herman!" In a stumbling panic, I rushed to him. "Y-you're not gonna die on me, are you?"

"No, not that. My wallet." He kept searching his coat pockets over and over. "Is gone."

"How can it be? Didn't you put it down the front of your pants when you were sleeping?"

"I didn't think."

I could barely squeak out the next. "Was all our money—?"

"Ja."

"Fuck and phooey, Herman!" my voice came back. "You mean we're skunk broke?"

"Hah?" He looked so anguished I was afraid he really might have a heart attack. "If that means all gone, ja again." He slapped his pants pocket, which did not jingle one bit. "Spent the chickenfeed on candy bars, even," he moaned.

I still was in shock. This was a hundred times worse than the ex-convict trying to steal my suitcase at that Minnesota Palookaville. "Who—how—" We needed to do something, but what? "Let's ask on the bus, maybe Reverend Mac saw somebody—"

"Not just yet, hah-uh," he stopped me. He still looked stricken but in a different way. "Something is tickling my mind. Quick, your book. Let me see."

Blankly I handed over the autograph album, and peered along with him in the barely lit parking lot as he flipped pages to Reverend Mac's inscription. With some kind of swearing in German, he put his thumb next to the signature, *Isaac M. Dezmosz.*

"Should have seen. Dismas was thief crucified with Christ." It took me a moment to put together the initials with that pronunciation and come up with it: *I Am Dismas.*

"Lying in his false teeth, he was," Herman bleakly summed up the so-called Reverend Macintosh.

I blew my top. "The smart-ass little sonofabitch of a thief! Distributing Bibles, my butt! C'mon, we'll show him troubled times."

I tore across the parking lot to where the bus was idling, ready to go, Herman galloping after me. I banged on the door, and Herman joined in as if he would tear it open with his bare hands.

The driver opened and considerately asked, "Forget something, boys?"

Without answering, I lunged up the steps and into the aisle, Herman right behind, both of us furiously searching for a distinctive gray head and silvery mustache.

Neither of which was in evidence on any of the remaining passengers, from front of the bus to the back as I careened up the aisle in search, Herman blocking the way in back of me in case the little Bible-spouting weasel tried to make a break for it. "Where'd that goddamned preacher go?" I demanded at the top of my voice, glaring at the rows of startled faces, none of them the right one.

"Who, the nice little minister?" the driver called down the aisle to us, perplexed by our invasion. "He got off at Livingston, a ways back. Said he had a train to catch."

"Sinked, we are," Herman said huskily, putting a hand on my shoulder to steady me, or maybe himself.

Retreating to the front of the bus, we laid out our situation to the driver, who could only shake his head as if now he had heard everything and offer the commiseration, "Tough break, boys, better report it at park headquarters and they'll get the sheriff in on it."

20.

STILL AS MAD as could be, I piled off the bus to do that very thing, my view of law enforcement having come around full circle in the past few minutes, with Herman more slowly following.

"Hurry up," I called over my shoulder, half frantic or maybe more, as he lagged on the way across the parking lot, "let's get some kind of cops after the thieving bastard."

"Donny, hold back. Over here, please."

Disconcerted by the detour, I uncertainly trailed after as he veered off to the gigantic wooden deck at the geyser side of the Inn, where people could sit out to watch Old Faithful display itself, although at that time of night we were the only ones anywhere around.

He dropped his duffel bag in a corner away from where everyone else was sitting, so I set my suitcase there, too, until it would become clear what this was about. More and more unnerved, I whispered when I didn't have to, "Why're we wasting time here when he's getting away with—"

"Shhh, notcheral wonder is coming," he gently shut me up.

Unstrung as I was anyway by Herman behaving this way, now I was hearing what sounded like low thunder and heavy rain mixed together, although the night sky remained cloudless. I thought I felt the earth tremble, but it might have been only me. We turned together toward the source of the sound, a boiling hiss from the whitish mound, and, as we watched, in its center what looked like a giant fountain started up, the cascades of steaming water billowing and falling, but steadily and incredibly shooting higher and higher, until the ghostly white column stood taller than the tallest trees, almost touching the single bright star, it looked like.

Yet magnificent as the sight was, it did little to change my anxious mood. Old Faithful was an eyeful, for sure, but so what? It faithfully would be blowing off steam again in an hour or so, after we'd had time to spill our story to whatever passed for cops under these circumstances, but Herman was making no move whatsoever in that direction.

Instead, he motioned wordlessly for me to take a seat in the deck chair next to the one he claimed. Scratching a match on the arm of the chair, he lit a cigar and gazed fixedly at Old Faithful's rising and falling curtains of water as he puffed. Had he gone loco? This I could not understand at all, the two of us planting ourselves there, sightseeing the geyser fading slowly back into the ground, while the thief who'd left us skunk-broke except for a cheap Bible was making a getaway free as the breeze.

Finally he extinguished his cigar and murmured, as if coming out of his deepest think yet, "Guess what, Donny. Not a good eye-dea, to go to police."

"Not a—? Sure it is. We've got to, they're the ones to chase down the sonofabitching phony religious—"

"Many questions, they will have."

"So what?"

"Donny, listen one minute."

Something in his voice warned me to prepare myself for what was coming. Not that I possibly could, because what he was leading up to saying was:

"I am not American on paper."

That took some digesting. At first I didn't know what to make of it. "Then what are you?"

"German."

"Well, yeah, sure, we been all through that. But who cares about something of that sort anymore?"

"*Citizen* of Germany, yet," he spelled out, his voice growing strained. "Here I am something called alien."

Giving this news what I thought it deserved, the French salute, I asked what was wrong with being one of those, whatever they were.

"*Enemy* alien," he fit the two words together with a grimace.

That hit me where it counted. It put things right back to when I learned he was Herman the German and feared he was one of the Hitler demons who shot my father's legs to pieces at Omaha Beach. Was I right the first time?

Fearfully I trembled out, "How—how are you an enemy?"

He threw up his hands. "By not showing my face when World War *Zwei*"—wincing, he corrected that to *Two*—"got America in. Some big danger I ever was, hah?"

I LISTENED DUMBSTRUCK to the rest, how having had enough of war in the first one, the second time around he quietly shipped out on ore boats like the *Badger Voyager* where no questions were asked as long as you could shovel heaps of coal, keeping himself at sea or whatever the Great Lakes were, and, beyond that, essentially hiding out in plain sight. "Manitowoc is German sort of place, you maybe noticed," he said whimsically. "Government was not going to declare whole town an enemy."

The meaning was sinking in on me now, all right. "You're not supposed to be in this country at all? They'd kick you out?"

"Not at first," he raised my hopes. But then: "Put me in prison, they would."

I was horrorfied, as Herman's word best said such a thing. "You're that much of an"—I couldn't bring myself to say *enemy*—"alien?"

"By stupid law, ja," he spat out. Given how law enforcers seemed to automatically side with Sparrowhead against me, I couldn't blame him for feeling picked on. "But if you're still stuck being a—a German," I was back to circling in confusion, "how'd you get here at all?"

He laughed, the hollow empty kind.

"Took French leave."

Unsteadily I told him I didn't quite know what that meant.

"Long story, Donny."

"HITLER, PAH. Too bad I did not break his neck when he was close as me to you, that night."

And so in the next unforgettable minutes, there in an American national wonderland, I learned that "French leave" meant desertion, although in this case not from any army but an entire country. Germany, that is, when it was falling to pieces after losing World War One and the Nazis were coming out of the woodwork. As his searching words led me through, my imagination transformed the hunched figure clasping his hands between his legs into a young veteran like my own father coming home from combat. Aunt Kate may have thought Herman had no ambition, but it sounded to me as if he had been smart as an Einstein in his choice of livelihood after his term as a soldier on the losing side: making beer where they drank it like water. "In Munich were beer halls like you would not believe, big as this, almost." He pointed a thumb to the whopping Inn behind us. "And Oktoberfest there, two-week festival of foods and beers." He gave that hollow laugh again. "Crow Fair for drunkards. Good place to be a *Braumeister*." From what he said, that was a vital task in the brewing of beer, sampling and comparing to the competition, and he had enough knack at it to work up to a job at a famous place, although I had never heard of it until his chilling telling.

"The Buergerbraukeller, biggest in Munich." He paused, the night just before Armistice Day in 1923 coming back to him as it brought me to the edge of my deck chair. "Not always a good idea to be where history gets made." He ducked his head as if dodging too late. "Packed hall that night, thousands drinking beer, government people there to say the country is not going to the dogs, if anybody would believe them. I am notcherly curious, so I come out from where brew vats are, to listen. Bring stein of beer for myself, why not, and sit at table near the back, where people have left." All of a sudden he flung an arm up as if firing a pistol at the sky, making me nearly jump out of my hide. "Right in time for Hitler to come through door and climb on table and shoot in the air, like some cowboy. Close as me to you," he repeated, shaking his head at how history brushed past him. "But when I try to reach across table to grab him, pull the feet from under this crazy person up there shooting, make him fall on his face like fool he is, Hitler keeps dancing around like cat on a stove, he is so nervous, and I miss him this far." He held his fingers inches apart. "Before I can try again, whole bunch of brownshirts with guns out jump on me and others around, goverment people and all." Drawing a breath, he husked out the rest of the recitation. "Hitler takes those to a room, the rest of us is held at point of guns, told shut up and drink beer. When myself and some others say what is happening is not right, we get knocked around and told we are now on list to be shot." Talk about spellbound; I was as much all ears as when he'd told about being swept up by the Witch of November, only this November rough weather was called Adolf Hitler.

"A putsch, it was," which he defined as a gamble at taking over everything. "Did not work that time, Nazi march on rest of Munich failed the next day, so putsch collapsed, good thing. But I had two eyes then," he made a wan face, "and did not like look of things in Germany. Beer hall bullies, Hitler bunch was, but maybe more than that if they ever got hold of government, hah? On list to be shot reminded me too much of Höhe Toter Mann"—the specter of Dead Man's Hill sent a chill up my spine. "*Pthht*, to that," he rid himself of his homeland. Leaning toward me as if that would bring me nearer to understanding, he tapped his temple, where little thinks came from. "Listen, Donny, this is the how of it. Find a safe harbor, is good saying. In Germany then, that meant small ports on the Baltic, where Nazis was not thick on the ground yet. Always ships going out the Baltic Sea, to all places of the world." This I could follow almost as though I were at his side escaping from the Nazis and that sonofabitch of all sonsofbitches, Hitler. "I give the ship engineer a little something," he went on, rubbing his fingers together in that familiar gesture meaning money. "He lets me hide in tool room, down where boilers are. Nobody topside comes ever, and I make friends with stokers by helping out. Learn to shovel coal. When we dock in America, jumped ship, I did."

IN THREE PARAGRAPHS, there it was, not so long after all. One for *Believe It or Not!*—the man who came within the length of his fingers of stopping Hitler. Not only that, the history that had made him an enemy of Germany for real and an enemy of America on paper, both at the same time.

Almost dizzy with the size of the fix he was in—*we* were in—one more thing I had to check on.

"Jumped ship. Is—is that against the law, too?"

"Could say so," came the not unexpected reply. "Stowaway, is that word," he ruefully added it to the growing list of other offenses charged to Herman Brinker.

"Aunt Kate," I whispered again, for no reason but the weight of the question, "was she in on this? You being an alien and all?"

He nodded slowly. "She knew, all the time. Had to. House in her name, car in her name. She is the one that counted, on paper." He shrugged, helplessly resigned to the one-sided situation. "No identification papers can I show for anything."

And she had called *me* a storier? What about living under false pretenses with a husband who was not anything he appeared to be? Busy piling that up against her, it took a few moments for that last part to fully register on me. I thought we were bad off when we simply didn't have any money. Now we didn't even have a real Herman.

He turned to me, his expression the most serious yet. This next, I will never forget.

"Donny, I am so much sorry"—if spoken words ever shed tears, it happened now in his broken apology—"for what is happened. Miles from anywheres, we are, and money gone, trip kaput." In that moment he looked so much older, the way people do when they are terribly sad. I felt as awful as he looked.

"Hey, it wasn't just you," I felt compelled to take my share of the blame, "it was my bright idea for us to go to sleep to get rid of the goddamn minister. If I hadn't thought that up—"

"*If* is biggest word there is," he saved me from myself. Or maybe himself along with it. As I watched, he dry-washed his face, holding his head in his hands while trying to think. For some moments I held my breath, until he came up with "No sense beating ourselfs like dead horse, hah?"

Just like that, he straightened up, unhunching his shoulders for the first time since the words *enemy* and *alien*, and tipped his cowboy hat back, if not the Herman of the dog bus again a pretty good imitation of it. "We got to git in for the night"—cocking his good eye toward the fancy Inn—"into the Waldorfer, someways, Donny."

"But what are we gonna do after that?" I spread my arms helplessly.

He gazed off into the distance, as he must have gazed countless miles that way since that night in a Munich beer hall. "We take a leap of fate."

Believe me, I have looked this up, and the roots of *fate* and *faith* are not the same. Nonetheless, I picked up my wicker suitcase to follow Herman the German into the Old Faithful Inn.

. . .

EVER STEPPED into an aircraft hangar? The lobby of the elaborate old Inn was like that, only roomier, largely higher. In the big open area I had to tip my head way back to count balcony after balcony held suspended by beams thick as logs, the supports all the way to the towering roof peak positioned each on top of the one below like those circus acrobats standing on one another's shoulders. Incredibly, except for a mountainous stone fireplace, every single thing in the Inn—walls, balcony railings, chairs, benches, ashtray stands, light fixtures—seemed to be made of timber, actual trees, freaks of the forest according to the fantastic twists and turns of some of the trunks and limbs. Dimly lit only by old electric candles that threw about as much light as Christmas tree bulbs, the place struck me as creepy, as in those fairy tales where bad things happen to travelers in shadowy old inns.

Herman seemed unperturbed. "Like the Kaiser's hunting lodge, but built by beavers" was his estimate of the pine-forest lobby as we entered, baggage in hand.

"So, Donny, do like I told," he whispered as we headed toward the front desk. "Pretend you own the place, whole schmier is your vacation palace." Before coming in, he had dug down in the duffel bag and found his tie, the out-of-date one with mermaids twined coyly in seaweed, but a tie. He similarly dressed me up by making me put on my moccasins. "Now we are not looking like hoboes so much," he appraised us with a lot more confidence than I felt.

Or for that matter, the sleepy night clerk, who blinked himself more alert at the sight of us, glancing with a growing frown at his reservation book and our approach. He did take a second look at my impressive moccasins, although that may have been canceled out by his beholding Herman's dangling mermaids. Whatever he thought, he cleared his throat and addressed our coming:

"Checking in late, sir? Name, please?"

"No, no, got room this afternoon." Herman waved a hand at the first question and simultaneously erased the second. "*Der Junge* can't sleep, so watched the geezer go off and off, and now we are bringing his souvenir collection from the car and laundry bag along with," he accounted for our conspicuous odd suitcase and duffel. "Back to room we go, everything fine and jimmy-dandy."

"Oh, say, Grandpa," I spoke my part, as we had to march right by the clerk's still inquisitive scrutiny, "did you lock the Caddy?"

"Ja, don't want bears in the Cadillac, hah?" Herman laughed in such jolly fashion it infected the clerk.

Chuckling, the man behind the desk all but ushered us past. "You're a hundred percent right about that, sir. Good night and sleep tight."

Up the plank-wide stairs we went, climbing to the absolute top and darkest balcony and passing by rows of rooms until reaching a far corner, as Herman had calculated, out of sight from the front desk. Also as he had counted on, there was more of that wildwood furniture, massive chairs made out of lodgepole, along the balcony for lobby-watching. Grunting and straining, between us we wrestled two of those into our corner and tucked the duffel and suitcase in behind. Ourselves we tried to fit into the rigid wooden seats in some semblance of bedtime positions. "Beds a little hard tonight," Herman tried to joke, patting the tree limbs under the not very thick cushions.

"About like sleeping on a lumber pile, yeah," I muttered, squirming in vain to get comfortable at all, missing the upholstered seats of the dog bus as if they were the lap of luxury. But I had to admit, we were in for the night, flat broke though we were.

HERMAN SHOOK ME awake when the first hints of dawn shown in the upmost windows of the timbered lobby, whispering, "Up and at. Outside we must get before hotel people come around."

After peering cautiously into the canyon of the lobby to make sure a different desk clerk had come on duty, we headed down, with Herman saying, "Leave to me. We must go out like kings."

Or freeloaders to be arrested on sight, I thought to myself.

As we approached the obstacle of the front desk again, I tried to appear as prosperous as royalty who went around in Blackfoot moccasins, meanwhile hoping the clerk would be impressed by a matching suitcase woven out of willows.

Striding as if he genuinely did own the place, erect as the timber of the lobby and his nose in the air, Herman gave the clerk the barest of nods and a guttural *"Guten morgen."*

"Ah, good morning to you, too. May I help—"

"Checked out, we already are," Herman growled impatiently, throwing in some more gravelly German. "How you say, grabbing early bus."

"Wait, your room number is—?"

Herman threw over his shoulder some rapid incomprehensible number in German and a farewell wave. *"Auf Wiedersehen."*

WITH THAT, we were outside in the fresh Yellowstone morning, fresh enough to make my teeth chatter.

"Lived through the night, hah, Donny?" I could see Herman's breath as he made this pronouncement.

I simply looked the real question to him: *Now what?*

A *whoosh* growing louder and louder in the still air, Old Faithful percolating out of the mound again, spared him from answering that. "Notcheral wonders we are not short of, anyways," he stuck with, gazing at the plumes of hot water shooting skyward.

Yeah, right. Stranded and broke in a natural wonderland was still stranded and broke. Stiff and sore and tired of Old Faithful butting in every time I pressed Herman for some way out of the hot water we were in, I was feeling out of sorts. Doubly so, actually. Because along with our predicament, something about Yellowstone itself kept tickling my mind, to put it in Herman's terms. One of those itches in the head that a person can't quite scratch. Some out-of-this-world fact from *Believe It or Not*? Something digested way too deep from a Condensed Book? But whatever the teaser was, it kept refusing to come out from behind the immediate matter of Herman and me being the next thing to hoboes and maybe even having crossed that line.

AS IF to rub it in, the tourist world was comfortably coming to life, people moseying out onto the deck from breakfast, while my stomach was gnawing my backbone, and tour buses were pulling up in front of the Inn with baggage wranglers busily piling suitcases into luggage compartments. I watched the buses with envy, another gnawing sensation, longing for a Greyhound to take us somewhere, anywhere.

Herman read my mind. "Better look for a safe harbor, hah?"

"Right," I said crankily, "let's go see where we could go if we only could."

Trying to appear like travelers actually able to buy tickets, we hefted our baggage over to the loading area, skirting a line of chattering tourists boarding to see mud volcanoes and other sights, as we made our way to the extensive bulletin board where in routes of red sheeted over with weatherproof plastic, THE FLEET WAY once again was promised.

"Guess what, Donny," Herman began as we approached the map, waggling his fingers piano-player fashion to encourage mine, "time for you to—"

"Huh-Huh-Herman!" I gasped. Unable to get out the actual word. *"Look!"*

I pointed an unsteady finger, not at the map but toward the opposite end of the bulletin board.

Like me, he stared in disbelief, then shock. There, past the park's announcements of the day's activities and its lists of don'ts and tacked-up tourist messages to other tourists, was a lineup of FBI MOST WANTED posters of the kind that kept a gallery of criminals scowling from the wall of every post office in the land. Prominent in its glossy newness was the one featuring HERMAN "DUTCH" BRINKER in bold black letters, full-face on. The photo was many years old, without glasses or for that matter a glass eye, back when he was a Great Lakes seaman, but the similarity to the Herman stunned motionless at my side popped out all too clearly.

A soft strangled sound, which I suspected must be the German cussword of all cusswords, escaped from his lips. Recovering before I did, he glanced around and around, pulling me close as he did so. Whispering, "What we must do, quick, quick," he rapidly told me how to proceed, and I followed his instructions as blankly as a sleepwalker, edging along the bulletin board as though every piece of paper was of surpassing interest, with him leaning over my shoulder. Reaching the MOST WANTED lineup, he shielded me with his body, checked around again to make sure no one was looking, and when he whispered, "Now!" I ripped down the poster with the awful words ENEMY ALIEN and VIOLATION OF and CONTACT YOUR NEAREST FEDERAL BUREAU OF INVESTIGATION OFFICE AT ONCE IF YOU SPOT THIS SUSPECT and stuffed it inside my jacket.

DEED DONE, we grabbed up our luggage and retreated to the deck of the Inn yet again, depositing ourselves in a corner farthest from the latest batch of sitters waiting for Old Faithful to live up to its name, which I could have told them it relentlessly would. With a ragged sigh, Herman held out his hand for the poster. Both of us studied the slightly crumpled likeness of the sailor Dutch, as he was then, and the paragraph of official language fully describing him and his offense. He shook his head in despair at the MOST WANTED treatment, definitely the wrong kind of being famous. "You would think I am Killer Boy Dillinger, Public Enemy Number *Eins*."

"One," I automatically corrected. "But why are they after you so bad?"

He passed a hand over his face as if to clear something away, although from his expression it wouldn't go. "Wisconsin has a senator, like they say, who sees Red anywheres he looks. 'Foreign' spells 'Communist' to him. And here was I, mystery man with no proof of being American, under his nose all this time?" He bit out the next words. "The FBI, excuse how I must say it, is kissing this Senator McCarthy's hind end by making me big fugitive."

"Yeeps, Herman! That's not fair!"

"No, is politics gone crazy." He fell silent, looking downcast, the WANTED poster trembling a little in his hand. At last he said almost inaudibly, "Turned me in, she did."

It took me a moment to gather that in. "Aunt Kate? Aw, she couldn't, could she? I mean, isn't there a law or something? What the hell, Herman, she's your *wife*."

He stared at the WANTED poster in his big hands as if asking the same of it, then looked away from the photo of his younger self, from me, from anything except the question that invaded the beautiful park, taking over his voice.

"Who said we are married?"

YOU COULD HAVE knocked me over with the blink of an eye. Speechless at first, I tried to get my mind around the pair of them living under the same roof, sleeping in the same bed, fighting the same battle every breakfast, all these years without ever—as the saying was—disturbing the preacher.

Thickly I managed to stammer, "But she's a Brinker, like you. You've got to be married for that, don't you?"

He shook his head. "She took the name, is all. Easier that way.

Keep people from thinking we are living"—he really gave his head a shake now, as if trying to clear it—"in sin, hah. More like, in duty. Drafted soldiers, both of us, if you would imagine," he put it in starkest terms. "From time of Witch of November when—"

THE STORY WAS, when Fritz Schmidt was lost in the storm that sent the *Badger Voyager* to the bottom of Lake Michigan and Herman survived but with an eye gone, the new widow Kate, stranded now in her waterfront waitress job, came to see him in the hospital. "All broke up, crying like cloudburst. Tells me she knows what friends Fritz and I was, how hard it is for me, like her. And this"—he tapped alongside the substitute eye—"meant I was without job." You can about hear her, he mused, declaring this was too much on both of them, it wouldn't hurt them one time in their lives to do something out of the ordinary. "Said if I wanted place to stay," he drew the tale to an end, "I could come to the house." Gazing off, maybe looking back, he shrugged. "Never left."

Bewildered anew, I blurted, "But all the time I was there, the two of you fought like—"

"—alley cats at table scraps. Not at first," he tempered that, his look at me a plea for understanding. "But you think about it, the Kate was used to Fritz away most of time, on boat. I was not away, ever, and it got on nerves. Me on hers, her on mine, fair to say." He spread his hands, as if balancing choices. "Not good way to live together, but both too stubborn to give in to situation. Until—"

He did not have to say the rest. Until I showed up, a stranger off the dog bus, bringing with me old baggage in more ways than one for Gram's sister and a jolt of imagination for the man going through life not being Dutch, not being an actual husband, not really grounded in much of anything but dreams of adventure in the Promised Land, out west.

Feeling I was to blame, while trying strenuously to deny it to myself, I started to throw a fit. "Goddamn-it-all-to-hell-anyway, why didn't you and her get married in the first place like you were supposed to and we wouldn't any of us be in this fix and, and—"

My tantrum dwindled as the answer caught up with me. "The alien thinger?"

"Ja," he acknowledged wearily. "Marriage license could not be got without notcheralization paper. Not worth the risk to go and say, after all the years, here I am, how do I make myself American?" With a last blink at the WANTED poster, he creased it to put in his pocket, still speaking softly. "The Kate believed same as I did, more so, even. As much her eye-dea as mine, pretend we're married. Worth it to have a man around, she telled me, somebody she can boss like she is used to with Fritz. Joke at the time," he sighed, "but she meant it, you maybe noticed."

I was listening for all I was worth, but Aunt Kate's bossy tendency that had driven both of us batty shrank to nothing compared to picking up the phone and turning in her imitation husband to the FBI. That truth rattled through me—the clank of a jail door closing behind Herman—shaking me to the core. The hard knocks of history were not done with him yet. Or for that matter, with me. Eleven going on twelve abruptly seemed way too young to be the seasoned accomplice of a fugitive, or when you came right down to it, a criminal whom the FBI put up there with the bank robbers and murderers as some breed of desperado. But what else was I?

The one thing clear was that the face of Herman the German, enemy alien, was plastered here, there, and everywhere on bulletin boards throughout Yellowstone National Park, as public as the sun. "Now we really need to get out of here," my voice broke, Herman chiming, "Ja, ja, ja," as I scrambled to my suitcase and he to his duffel. That was as far ahead as either of us could think. That and the FLEET WAY map back at the bulletin board.

. . .

SKIRTING THE TOUR bus lines and trying not to notice the bare spot among the MOST WANTED posters, seeming to gape with guilt pointing our direction, we edged up to the Greyhound map in search of inspiration as much as destination. We needed a fortunate break in some direction, north, south, east, west, it didn't matter. Somewhere to hole up, until people's possible memories of a horse-faced man with a German accent waned. But where? Make a run for the coast, to Portland or Seattle or Frisco? Hide out in some Palookaville? Hightail it to Canada, on the chance that up there they wouldn't know an enemy alien when they saw one?

Still putting his faith in *Fingerspitzengefühl*—not that we had much else to draw on—Herman began waggling his fingers again to encourage mine. "Ready, Donny? Find us somewheres to git to?"

"Nothing doing." I tucked my hands in my armpits. "You choose this time. My finger-spitting got us into this."

"Then must git us out, hah?" Herman said a little testily.

Hard to argue with that. But *Fingerspitzengefühl* and its outcomes unnerved me and I determinedly kept shaking my head—*Nothing doing, absolutely not,* you *do it for a change*—when a certain dot of all those on the map caught my attention. Before I quite knew what I was doing, my finger flew to it.

"Here," I said, decisive as Napoleon or any of those, "this is what we want."

STARTLED BY my abrupt choice, Herman peered at the map as if my finger were pulling the wrong kind of trick. Making sure of the small lettering beside the tiny red dot of a bus stop, he turned huffy. "Funny as a stitch, Donny. No time for piddling around, please."

"I'm not!" My exasperation at his shortsightedness, both kinds, boiled over. "You're the one who's piddling!"

He retorted to that, and I retorted to his retort, and in no time we were in a slam-bang argument, the kind where tempers go at one another with all they have until someone's hits its limit and backs off. In this case, Herman's.

"You are not making joke like I thought, hah?" he finally more or less conceded. "And maybe your finger is on the nose about where we must git to," he went even further, after I'd insisted that the arrowhead in its pouch under my shirt was showing it was big medicine.

"Powerful sure about spot on map, you are." Eyeing me in my most rambunctious red-in-the-head state of mind, Herman spoke very carefully. "Big question is, Donny, how to git anywheres." He glanced over his shoulder at the busloads of tour groups coming and going as free as the four winds. "Can't talk sweet to a driver, don't we wish it was easy as pies, and go on dog bus like seeing the sights, tra la la," he said with a deep and helpless longing for our old days as comparatively innocent cross-country passengers.

WHO KNOWS how these things happen, what whiz of a trick the mind will pull when you're least expecting it. Suddenly my thinking apparatus was jogged, the teasing smidgen about Yellowstone standing out clear as purple ink on the white paper of the autograph book. "Herman, I've got it! What you just said! Idea!"

Misunderstanding me, he shook his head so hard it was a wonder his hat didn't fall off. "Donny, no! We cannot go begging drivers for tickets or sneaking on bus or such. They will report us, snap like that"—he snapped his fingers like a shot—"to rangers and rangers to sheriff and sheriff to FBI and I will be locked up until cows trot home and you, you will be put in—" He hesitated to even speak my jail word, *orphanage*.

"Huh-uh, that's not what I meant," I feverishly shook off his concern in turn. "I just finally got reminded of something. Listen up, okay?"

Duly hanging on my every word as I explained my brainstorm, he couldn't help still being dubious.

"It better work right. Or *ptfft*—" He nodded an inch, plenty indicative, to a passing pair of park rangers looking as seriously loaded with authority in their flat hats and badges as any Crow cops.

WITH NO OTHER real choice, he accompanied me to the park headquarters, and in we went to the WONDERS OF YELLOWSTONE exhibit, and up to the information counter manned by a gray-headed ranger who no doubt had heard every possible tourist tale of mishap, including the one we were about to try on him. It didn't help, either, that despite my coaching, Herman pronounced what we needed as the *infirm-ary.*

Maybe his sympathy was simply feigned, but the ranger did peer over the counter as I made myself look miserable as possible, and accorded me, "Oh, the poor kid." Poor, yeah, little did he know. Anyway, he directed us to the infirmary, and down a couple of hallways and around enough corners, we came to a door with that sign on it.

As he found a place to sit and wait outside the office, Herman had some last jitters about me doing this alone, but I pointed out that we didn't want the enemy alien matter to crop up somehow due to a mess of paperwork, did we, and he had to agree he'd better stay absent. "Be brave as anything, like Winnetou and Red Chief," he resorted to again. I fished the necessary item out of the duffel and into my jacket pocket, and with heart pounding, bravely I hoped, stepped into where they treated the infirm.

In the waiting room, a full-lipped and generously lipsticked young woman who reminded me strongly of Letty, except her crisp uniform was a nurse's and I could not spot her name stitched on in the best place, was busy opening up for the day. Probably figuring I had taken a wrong turn in seeking the restroom, she smiled at me in a seasoned way. "Hello there, can I help you find something?"

"Fishbone," I croaked, pointing to my throat.

"My goodness"—her manner changed that quick—"we need to take care of that, don't we." Plucking up an admittance form and sitting right down to administer it, she peeked past me, beginning to look perturbed. "Isn't there anyone with you?"

"They're at the geyser." I gagged some more. "I was supposed to catch up. Slept late, breakfast was slow."

The perturbed expression did not leave her, but she dropped the form. "We'll have to get you on paper afterward, it sounds like. Right this way." Her uniform swishing, she escorted me to the office off the waiting room and stuck her head in. "Throat case, Doc, the rainbow trout special strikes again. Give a shout if I'm needed, I'm still catching up at the desk."

The doctor was slipping on his starchy-clean white office coat as I entered the medical inner sanctum trying to keep my chin up like the bravest Indian who ever walked in moccasins. Not anything like I expected, with a surprising amount of gray in his crew cut and a twinkle in his eye, he greeted me with a smile as professional as the nurse's even though I was a surprise patient.

"Hello, buddy. Don't I wish the dining room would stick with hotcakes and eggs for breakfast." Busying himself with a tray of instruments to explore my throat, he maintained a soothing manner, observing that swallowing a fishbone was not a good way to start the day but at least I was not scalded or mauled.

Ready, he patted the operating table that I couldn't help looking at without thinking of Gram. "Hop up here, friend, and open wide so I can have a look."

"Uhm," I jerked back to reality, "it's no use." The doctor stopped short at picking up a tongue depressor so he could go to work down my gullet. "I mean, I didn't swallow a fishbone or anything."

Accustomed as he must have been to all kinds of odd cases, he nonetheless scrutinized me with a puzzled frown. "Then what's your problem, hmm? Nothing broken, I hope?"

"Yeah, that's it! Me," I seized my opening. "Flat broke."

"Are you telling me," his tone turned as starchy as his medical coat, "you came in here to ask for—"

"Eleven dollars and forty cents, is all." I made it sound as reasonable as possible.

That brought me a stare nearly strong enough in itself to throw me out of the office. "Starting kind of young, aren't you?" he said along with it, more sternly yet. "At bumming?"

"No, no, this isn't that!" I protested, my voice taking off toward the high country. Prepared as I thought I was in asking for the money as nicely as I could, I fell apart at being thought some kind of a moocher.

"What it is," I sort of whimpered out, "I know Mae and Joe." Shakily I pointed to the nameplate on his desk identifying him as PAUL SCHNEIDER, M.D., his gaze following my gesture uncomprehendingly. "Your mom and dad?" I provided as if he needed reminding of the fact.

He still looked so baffled that I yanked out the Bible in desperation. "See, I'll swear on it." I clapped a hand over the chintzy paper cover. "We were friends right away fast. They were awful good to me, took my side against the dumb bus driver and everything, so I thought maybe you would be, too, at least a little bit, and really, all I need is eleven dollars and—"

"Whoa, slow down." A strapping guy as big as both of his parents put together, Dr. Schneider bent way down with his hands on his knees as if I needed closer examination. "The folks? Where do they come into this?"

"On the dog bus. Just before the rollycoaster." Herman's lucky mention of the Greyhound driver community and seeing the sights, tra la la, popped the happily traveling Schneiders from that itch spot in my mind, along with their vital mention of a son who fixes up people who fall into hot pools or get mauled by grizzlies in Yellowstone. None of what I'd tried to say so far enlightened the doctor son nearly enough, I could tell, but desperation sometimes grows into inspiration. "Here, look, they wrote in my memory book."

To some extent, amusement replaced bafflement in his expression, I was relieved to see. "You're a regular traveling library, aren't you," he kidded—at least I took it as kidding. Carefully grasping the autograph album, he studied the pair of inscriptions while rubbing a hand through his iron-gray bristle of hair. "That sounds like the old man, all right. And that mother of mine—" He silently read over the neatly composed lines, as did I, my eyes moist.

I won't say her contribution to poetry ranks up there with Longfellow, but I still think Mae Schneider's tidy verse is beautiful.

When twilight drops a curtain
and pins it with a star,
Remember that you have a friend
Though she may wander far.

After that, again bending close to listen when I told of getting robbed on the last Greyhound by the sonofabitching phony preacher, whom I barely restrained myself from calling that and more, the doctor frowned as if still working on his diagnosis. "Then where's this uncle of yours? Why isn't he here with you?"

"Uhm, he's sort of, you know"—I twirled my forefinger at my temple—"from the war. Scared of people in uniform. Like rangers. Or your nurse, even. What do they call it, 'nervous in the service'?"

He *mm-hmmed* the way someone does to acknowledge they've

heard what you've said, whether or not they believe it. "Why eleven dollars and forty cents?"

"Bus fare. Like my uncle says, we're just trying to get someplace south of the moon and north of Hell."

"Your uncle has a strange sense of geography," he was half laughing. Turning serious again, he parked his hands in the side pockets of his office coat the way doctors do when they're about to deliver the news, good or bad.

"I've had some dillies come in here, but you beat all." I swallowed real hard at that. Then that twitch of a smile showed up on him again. "Nellie," he called out to the front desk. "I've invented a new cure. Bring me a ten and a five from the cash drawer, please."

Looking at me curiously, the nurse swished in, handed him the money, gave me another look, and left. Dr. Schneider started to pass me the ten-dollar bill and fiver, but then hesitated, giving me a heart flutter. "If you're so confounded broke, what are you eating on?"

"Nothing, really."

"Nellie," he called through the doorway again, "the case has grown more serious. Bring me another five."

Adding that fiver, he handed me what amounted to a junior fortune, compared with my situation a minute before. Thanking him six ways to Sunday, I pocketed the money in a hurry and held out the autograph book. "Write down your address, please, huh? We're gonna pay you back, honest."

"Are you. When Uncle Wiggily gets over being nervous in the service, hmm?" Skeptical as he may have been, he wrote his name and address in, topping it with what he said was a prescription for a condition like mine.

I met a boy with hair so red
it lit up whatever he said.

He does not need a lucky star,
his gift of gab will carry him far.

Passing the album back, Dr. Schneider gave me a last curious look as if still searching for a diagnosis. "You haven't told me, buddy, where that bus fare is supposed to take you."

When I did so, he half laughed again, ending up with what I hoped was just a snatch of philosophy or something. "Good luck and Godspeed. Normally it takes most of a lifetime to reach there."

21.

HERMAN HARDLY LET our newfound wealth rest in his hand before buying bus tickets out of the natural wonderland of Yellowstone, but then tucked away the remainder of the money, this time in a shirt pocket that buttoned tightly, with the firm pronouncement "Belly timber must wait, up the road. No candy bars even, until we git where we go."

SO IT WAS that we arrived worse for wear, inside as well as out, several hours and a couple of bus changes and long stretches of highway later and not done yet, at the Greyhound terminal in Butte, of all places, with Herman unshaven and me in a rodeo shirt showing every sign that I had been living in it day and night. Grooming was not foremost on our minds, however. Hunger was making me so cranky Herman had to relent on the candy bars, and he wolfed into the first of his as readily as I did mine while we hustled from the newsstand on into the waiting room. For once, we did not have to run eyes and fingers over the almighty map lettered COAST TO COAST—THE FLEET WAY for our connection and destination. Up on the Departures board along with bus times to Denver and Seattle and Portland and Spokane and other metropolises of the West was all we needed to know.

3:10 TO WISDOM.

. . .

"DONNY, NO TIME to smart ourselves up like Einsteins," Herman had scolded me in our slambang argument outside the Old Faithful Inn when I blurted that what we needed was Wisdom. "They throw me in the stony lonesome, like you say," he grumbled with another furtive look over his shoulder. "I will have plenty time to git wise."

"No, no, not that kind," I held rock-solid to my inspiration, surer than sure. "Wisdom is a real place we can go to, honest! See, it's a town called that." My finger had punched the map dot beside the name as if it were the doorbell button to the Promised Land. "Wisdom must amount to something, it has a bus depot and everything, way down there in the Big Hole."

Leaning in and skeptically adjusting his glasses, Herman tried to fathom all this. "Something been digged deep, and the town fell in?"

"Huh-uh, the Big Hole is a sort of a—oh, what do they call it—a nice long valley out away from everything. It's famous in Montana, honest."

"Famous, what for?"

"Hay."

THAT HAD SET him off again. "Cow food? Donny, are you lost in your mind? What good is hay to us? We cannot be cow farmers."

He continued to balk like that until I managed to spell out to him jobs on a ranch in the best hay country under the sun. "That's the really great thing about the Big Hole," I pressed my argument. "There's hay up the yanger there, they'll be putting it up the whole rest of the summer. Time enough for—"

"Killer Boy Dillinger to go away from public eyes," he thought out the rest for himself, nodding his head. "I take back that you left your mind, Donny," he apologized with a sort of laugh dry as dust. "Let's go to Wisdom place. Maybe some rub off, hah?"

. . .

SO HERE we were, only a pair of dog bus tickets short of the half-hidden town that was the gateway to hay heaven. I couldn't wait to get there, brimming as I was with visions of driving the stacker team on some well-run ranch with no Wendell Williamson to say *Nuh-huh, horsepower over horses*, the birdbrain, while Herman was hired on as—well, that would have to be determined. Now that we had made it as far as Butte and one last change of buses, the ride of what appeared from the route map to be only a couple of hours at most should be a snap of the fingers for seasoned travelers like us.

On the other hand, the distance to the ticket office on the far side of the jam-packed waiting room gave us both cause to pause. From the moment we stepped in through the ARRIVALS swinging doors, the Butte bus depot looked like a tough proposition. Throughout the waiting room, hard-eyed men with bent shoulders and faces with an awful lot of mileage on them, the best description was, were slouched on benches that would never be mistaken for church pews, and the women perched next to them in their none-too-good Sunday best for traveling did not look much better. Even more unsettling to me were scruffy boys my age roving through the crowd, shrilly hawking newspapers at the top of their voices. *Orphans!* was my immediate thought, captives of the state orphanage right here in the infamous mining city. Around the corner with its door wide open and just waiting . . .

Looking back I realize that citizens of a famously tough copper company town with neighborhoods called Muckerville and Dublin Gulch, where miners with names like Maneater Duffy and Monkey Wrench Mike and Luigi the Blaster and hundreds of others worked in mines such as the Destroying Angel and the Look Out, were not likely to be a greeting committee of fashion plates. But we were not mistaken in there was a prickly feeling that we had better watch our step—that was Butte for you, if you were an outsider—as we cautiously moved off from the Departures board toward the ticket office.

And then we both saw it at once. The bulletin board alongside the ticket window with all manner of things posted as usual, but standing out like a billboard to us the bold black lettering NEW THIS WEEK FROM YOUR FBI and that lineup of posters with Herman's mug prominent on the very end.

STOPPING DEAD in his tracks, he stared at himself across the distance of the long waiting room. "Are they after me everywheres?" a whisper of despair escaped him.

Did it ever seem so, at our each and every turn, but since then I have caught up with the lore that the dictatorial boss of the Federal Bureau of Investigation at the time, J. Edgar Hoover, used Butte as a Siberia for agents who had fallen out of his favor. Having too little else to do, this band of exiles was notorious for plastering the city and the country around with the latest MOST WANTED posters, apparently in the hope of netting criminals in the backwaters of Montana. It was simply our rotten luck of the moment that, with his face here, there, and anywhere, their most likely catch was Herman the German.

"**HERE.**" I tried to disguise him by handing him what little was left of my candy bar. "Hold this in front of your face and pretend to eat it while we go across there. We're running out of time to get tickets." Queerly, the schedule board did not show any Wisdom bus beyond the one, even the next day. If I had learned anything from experience, it was to catch the bus first and deal later with whatever came along.

Herman may have agreed in principle, but as we set out to edge through the waiting room without attracting notice, all at once he faded like a shadow into the men's restroom, leaving me abandoned with "Donny, wait here. I be right back."

. . .

OH, GREAT. The worst possible time for a call of nature. Now I was stranded there trying to seem inconspicuous while minding the duffel bag and wicker suitcase, both of which looked suspiciously ratty even alongside the Butte mode of dusty old luggage. Right away I caught Herman's case of jumpiness. My imagination could feel the entire depot population looking at me, especially those sharp-eyed newsboys roaming the waiting room like coyotes on the hunt.

"Hey, looka the greeny," one of them jeered as they circled past me.

"Yah, fresh off the boat," laughed another. "Probably got that willow yannigan from his granny in the old country."

Determinedly looking casual, I tried to kill time by gazing around and around the terminal with surpassing interest except at the incriminating bulletin board. No Herman, no Herman, as minutes ticked away. What the hell was he doing in there all this time? Had he been rolled by some thug?

At last, thanks be, Herman emerged, still in one piece. Although not quite. I had to look twice to be sure of what I was seeing. Surprise enough, he did not have his eyeglasses on, which he all but slept with. But the shocker was that he had taken out his glass eye.

Face squinched out of shape to stretch the eyelid down and cheek skin up to cover the empty eye socket, he looked different from his WANTED picture, for sure. More like a sideshow freak winking gruesomely.

Words failed me as he said out of the twisted corner of his mouth, "Ready to git, Donny."

Talk about walking like Winnetou and Manitou in the tracks of braves through all time—I was overawed at the amount of guts it took to bring out that grotesque wound for the world to see. I could not help staring, and no doubt people would. But chances were the only resemblance anyone could take away would be to a beached, one-eyed pirate in *Treasure Island*.

I barely got out, "Didn't know you could do that with your peeper."

"All kinds advantages to have glass in your head, ja," he said tartly. "Hurry, let's buy tickets before somebody sees Killer Boy Dillinger under my hat."

AT THE TICKET COUNTER, the clerk idly doing a crossword puzzle took in my suitcase and Herman's duffel with a bored glance as we stepped up. The missing eye didn't faze him a bit. "You boys for the special?"

I answered with a question. "How do you mean?"

"The special," the clerk recited as if it were common knowledge. "Last bus to Wisdom."

The last?

That makes a person think. As in, last chance ever? Or something like dead last, some kind of bus especially for unswift customers who missed out on the real thing?

I still was trying to digest the meaning, Herman now squinched up in thought as well as one-eyed nearsightedness, when the clerk put down his puzzle and pencil and took fresh account of the two of us and our ratty luggage. "Or am I seeing things, and you aren't that sort?"

"Uhm, sure, that's where we want to go. To Wisdom, you bet."

"Then let's see the color of your money, gentlemen." As Herman dug out the fare, which may have been special but still took nearly all of what we had left, the clerk spun on his stool and called to an arthritic-looking man dabbing away at paperwork in the cubbyhole office behind the counter. "Two more, Hoppy."

"The merrier," the man croaked, clapping on a battered-looking Greyhound driver's hat and strapping on the holster for his ticket punch. "Makes a full house, Joe. Any other 'boes are gonna have to hoof it." Rounding the counter with a hitch in his gait about like Louie Slewfoot's, he jerked his head for us to follow him. "Let's git to gitting," he said, instantly winning Herman over.

AS WE TRAILED the gimpy driver past departure gate after departure gate to the loading bay at the very end of the depot platform, I was more than curious to see what was up with this special bus. As we neared, it became evident this was not one of the sleek modern fleet, but a stubby early model that had seen more than its share of miles—even the galloping greyhound on its side looked like time was catching up with it, its coat of silver dimming to dusky gray—and plainly was brought out only as a spare. That description probably fit the aged driver hopscotching along ahead of us as well, Herman and I realized with a glance at each other.

What really caught our attention, though, was the horde waiting to board. It was all men. If we thought the Butte waiting-room crowd were tough lookers, they were an Easter parade compared with this ill-assorted batch of customers, lounging around on bedrolls that looked none too clean and smoking crimped roll-your-own cigarettes, giving every appearance of having come straight off freight train boxcars. Most of them wore the cheap dark gray work shirts known as Texas tuxes, which didn't show dirt, but even so, the wearers appeared to be badly in need of a wash day.

The driver halted under the overhang of the depot just out of earshot of the mob and gave us a dubious look.

"Free advice, worth what it costs, but maybe you gents ought to find some other way to git to Wisdom. 'Gainst regulations, but I can sneak you a refund." He inclined his head toward the squat old bus. "This is what's called the hay wagon, unnerstand. These scissorbills aim to hire on in haying, down there in the Big Hole."

"Yeah, well," I spoke right up, Herman backing me with vigorous nods, "that's us, too. Haymakers."

"I dunno." The driver looked us over even more skeptically. "Nothing personal, but one of you seems sort of young and the other one pretty much along in years, to keep up with fellas like these."

To my surprise, Herman now said a piece. "Not to worry. Ourselfs, we are from Tough Creek, where we sleep on the roof of the last house."

Whatever western he had that from, it was enough to make the driver croak out a laugh and stump off toward the bus. "Join the fun, then. Let's go."

I didn't, though, holding Herman back by his sleeve, too. A vision had come to me from the funnies, unsought but vividly there, of PeeWee the dim-witted little bum and his shabby pals mooching along in *Just Trampin'*, from the looks of it about like these hard-boiled excuses for humanity we were about to join. The question quavered out of me.

"W-wait. Are all of them—bums?"

Quick as I said that, the driver turned to us in a sort of crowhop. "You got that all wrong, sonny," he schooled me, "bums don't ride buses. Tramps, now, they maybe might if somebody was to give them the money," he furthered my education. "Been known to happen. But these fellas"—our gaze followed his to the waiting men—"are hoboes, whole different thing. They ain't your total down-and-outers, more like hard-luck cases. Got to hand it to them, they travel around looking for work. Seasonal, like. Apple glommers, almond knockers, sugar beeters"—Herman's expression skewed even more as he tried to follow the driver's tally—"what hoboes do is follow the crops. Haymakers, about now, tough a job as any," he added pointedly, with another skeptical look at the pair of us. "You better unnerstand, living rough like they do, hoboes by nature are a hard lot. Have to be. For them, it's root, hog, or die."

He paused to make sure the lesson was sinking in on us. "That refund is still ready and waiting."

Herman must have given that the quickest think in history, for I immediately felt his bolstering hand in the middle of my back, making our decision. I spoke it, in our biggest leap of fate or faith yet. "Nothing doing. We're going with on the what's-it. The special."

Shrugging as if our blind determination was water off his back, the driver crowfooted away toward the waiting bus. "Hop on."

22.

THE LAST TWO seats were way at the back of the bus, which meant the entire hobo contingent had a chance to look us over from stem to stern as we wove up the aisle. Stepping aboard right after us, from tossing my suitcase and Herman's duffel into the baggage compartment with a collection of bedrolls and what looked to me like bundles of belongings but for some reason were called bindles, the driver sang out, "Okey-doke, final call. Last bus to W-I-S-D-O-M, for those of you who know the alphabet."

"We're all scholars of the Braille sort," a man taller and brawnier than the rest called out.

"I bet you've put the touch on many a thing all right, Highpockets," retorted the driver, counting heads to make sure the total matched the number of tickets he had punched. "Talk about faces a person can't forget even if he tries. Druv the majority of you scissorbills at this same time last year, if I don't miss my guess."

"That's us, Hoppy, last but nowhere near least," a scrawny old fellow with a cracked voice was heard from next. "Had a chance to take drivin' lessons since then, have ye?"

The driver snorted and made as if to fling his cap at the offender. "I have druv longer than you been off your ma's hind tit."

"That makes you older than the pharaoh's dick, don't it, Hop," the fellow plenty far along in years himself cracked back, to hoots of encouragement and cries of "Lay it to him, Skeeter." Of course, I was following this like a puppy lapping milk, until Herman tugged my ear to bring me close enough for a whispered "Phoo. Rough tongues. Don't listen too much."

"Let's can the mutual admiration and get this crate goin'," the one called Highpockets spoke with authority. "Else the best kips are gonna be taken at the Big Hole Riviera."

"Birds like you can always roost in the diamond willows," the driver responded crossly. Nonetheless he dragged himself into place behind the steering wheel, managed to find the clutch and brake pedal with his feet, fiddled around some on the dashboard, and eventually ground the starter—it growled so much like the DeSoto back in Manitowoc that Herman and I couldn't help trading amused glances—until it eventually caught, and the bus bucked its way out of the depot driveway as if hiccupping.

Hoppy mastered the gearshift somewhat better on the downhill run from the Butte business district and away, I could now hope, from the nightmarish orphanage. Herman was breathing easier, too, as the bus hit the highway, with the splash of MOST WANTED posters receding behind him. The tortured side of his face missing its eye relaxed a little, even.

PRETTY QUICK we had something new to worry about as Highpockets, who by all indications was some sort of topkick of the hoboes, made his way to the rear and squatted in the aisle by us. Up close, he showed more wear and tear than at first appearance, what Gram called weary lines at the corners of his hooded eyes. Some time back, his nose apparently had been rearranged by a fist, and he bore a sizable quarter-moon scar at the corner of his mouth. But I would not want to have been the other guy in the fight, strong as his unrelenting gaze was and the rest of him more than enough to back it up. Cordial but direct, he asked, "You fellows going calling on the near and dear, down in the Hole? Or what?"

Or what required some answering on this bus, all right, as it bucketed along making exhaust noise as if it needed a new muffler, or maybe any muffler. Catching on to the situation if not the conversation level, Herman intuitively sealed his lips in favor of mine.

"Huh-uh, we're going haying like everybody else," I launched into. "See, I'm a stacker team driver, and my grandpa here is a sort of a roustabout, good at lots of stuff. But you need to excuse his not talking"—the story built as fast as I could get it out of my mouth—"he's straight from the old country and doesn't savvy English very much. He's over here taking care of me because"—I had to swallow hard to move from invention to the real answer about near and dear relatives—"my parents passed away, and we're all each other has." That at least was the truth of the moment, although Gram was due a major mental apology for substituting Herman for her in the larger picture of life.

Highpockets heard me out with scarcely a blink, his scrutiny all the more unnerving for that. More than a few of the other hoboes were swung around in their seats, taking all this in. Like them, Highpockets had on a shapeless old hat that signified rough living and outdoor labor, more than likely the mark of being a true hobo. Sitting back on his haunches, he skeptically eyed our fresh Stetsons and my fancy rodeo shirt. "You trying to tell me you and Gramps are on your uppers?"

Fortunately I had enough bunkhouse lingo to answer, "We're not broke, but we can see it from here." All the honesty I could summon seemed to be called for. "What it is, we got robbed blind. Back on the dog bus, the one from Billings." Herman, who had gone stiff as a coffin lid at my designation of him as grandpa, unbent enough to bob his head in confirmation of "robbed blind." I plunged on. "A sonofabitching phony preacher gyppo"—my vocabulary gleaned from the Double W riders fit right in with this audience, it seemed—"picked Gramps's pocket and wiped us clean, so that's why we're on here with you." I made myself shut up, praying that was just enough and not too much or too little.

It at least worked with Highpockets, who relaxed and bounced on his haunches a bit, glancing around at the other listening hoboes. "Their bad luck to run into a fingersmith, pulling the old sky pilot dodge, eh, boys? Seen that one put over on many a pilgrim." He slapped my knee, startling the daylights out of me, and gave Herman that round O sign of forefinger touching the tip of the thumb, the rest of the fingers up, which means OK. Herman smiled weakly in return. "Stealing isn't our style," Highpockets was saying, his gunsight gaze sweeping around to take in the whole set of rough-and-ready men, "at least from each other." Unfolding to his full height, nearly scraping the ceiling of the bus, he gestured around. "You're gonna be with us, better howdy up with the boys."

Right then the bus jolted off the highway, slewing somewhat too fast onto a gravel road headed south. Highpockets grabbed a seat-back to keep his balance, laughing. "Hold on to your stovepipes," he advised about our Stetsons, "here comes the real haywagon ride." Another of the hoboes yelped to the driver, "Kick 'er in the ribs and let 'er buck, Hoppy!"

"I'll do the driving, you do the sitting with your thumb up your butt, how about," the driver hollered back, wrestling the steering wheel as the shuddering bus adjusted to the gravel surface, more or less. Which had suddenly narrowed to what my father the construction catskinner would have scoffed at as a goat trail, so much so that Herman and I now were peering almost straight down the steep bank of a fast-flowing river on our side. I gulped, and Herman narrowed his good eye in concern. I know it wasn't possible for the rear tires to be traveling on thin air over the water, but that's how it seemed.

Unconcerned about the Greyhound flirting with the fishes, Highpockets got back to introductions up and down the aisle. The

Jersey Mosquito. Oscar the Swede. Midnight Frankie. Snuffy. Overland Pete. Shakespeare, who looked to me like any ordinary human being.

"Then there's Fingy." Highpockets pointed to a squat swarthy man who gave Herman a comradely wink and waved a hand short of two fingers.

The roster of the last bus to Wisdom went on pretty much like that. Bughouse Louie. Pooch. Peerless Peterson. The California Kid, who was the most gray-haired of the bunch. So many others of the sort that I was having trouble keeping track, and Herman looked swamped from the first by the roll call of nicknames.

No sooner had Highpockets finished than the scrawny one with shoulder blades jutting high as his neck, the Jersey Mosquito known familiarly as Skeeter, leaned into the aisle and addressed me. "That's us, to the last jot and tittle. Now, who be ye?"

At least I had no trouble figuring this out, although I had a pang at forsaking Red Chief.

"I'm Snag." My jack-o'-lantern smile showed off the jagged reason. "And him here," I indicated Herman, "is One Eye," no explanation needed there, either.

"Good enough for me." Highpockets credited us both and flashed that OK sign again. "Welcome to the Johnson family," he left us with, and worked his way seatback by seatback up front to where he sat, the aisle a lot like the deck of a rolling ship as the bus galloped along on the unpaved road.

To my relief and no doubt Herman's, the other hoboes took his lead, everyone settling in for the ride, which may have looked short on the map but wound along the twisty river, which would head one direction and then another, with timbered mountains hemming it in so close it was hard to see the sky. I began to wonder about this route that hardly seemed to rate being marked in red on a map. Why were there no towns? Or ranches? A forest ranger station, even. Out there in back-road nowhere, I grew more jittery as every riverbend curve threatened the Greyhound's groaning springs and Hoppy's straining grapple with the steering wheel, the water always right down there waiting for a bus to capsize upside down.

Soon enough, I had something else to worry about. When a swerve around a pothole the size of a washtub swayed Herman halfway into my seat, he glanced around to make sure no one was watching, then took me by the ear again, this time with a harder pinch. His whisper was all that much sharper, too. "Why am I *Grossvater* all the sudden?"

Uh oh. I didn't have to understand German to know he was put out about being designated grandfather.

"It's to cover our tracks," I sped into rapid-fire explanation as low as I could whisper. "See, this way, if anybody ever picks up our trail and starts nosing around, you're not on the spot for being my great-uncle, like they're looking for, you're just my grandpa in the natural order of things." Herman's deep frown did not move a muscle. Casting around for anything that might thaw him, I invoked the Apache method or what I hoped might be. "I bet Winnetou did this all the time, scrubbing out his trail with a batch of sagebrush or something, so his enemy couldn't run him down. That's all we're doing, you being the grossfather is just our, uh, scrub brush, sort of."

Herman did not buy my interpretation entirely, his grip on my ear not letting up. "Your eye-dea, this Wisdom bus is." He cast a dubious look around at our fellow passengers. "Now look who we are with, one step from bums."

"Two," I said, wincing from his hold on me. "Tramps are in between, remember."

He still didn't relent. "What is this Johnsons family?"

I took a guess. "Maybe it means all the hoboes, sort of like a tribe?" This time I harked back to Crow Fair. "Like the Indians we saw in the camp there, but without tepees or braids or moccasins—"

"No fancy-dancing, I betcha, either," he said, pretty sarcastic for him.

"Herman, listen," I persevered, ear pinch or no ear pinch, "like it or not, we have to stick with these guys. Think about it, okay?" I managed to flash the hobo sign for that. "You can tell by looking they aren't ever going to turn you in, are they. They've got their own reasons to avoid the cops."

Wrinkled in concentration, Herman followed my logic around all the corners he could, finally shaking his head. "If you say so, Donny. I don't got a better eye-dea." He pressed against his seatback as if bracing himself. "Let's go be hoboes, Gramps will live and learn."

NO SOONER had our whispered conversation ended than a shout from down the aisle roused the Jersey Mosquito, sitting across from us. "Hey, Skeeter, you old skinflint, pass the bugle," the Johnson family member known as Peerless Peterson, if I remembered the roll call right, piped up, spitting a tobacco plug onto the floor, evidently to clear his mouth.

Not for the purpose it sounded like, though. "I'm the man what can, ye damn moocher," Skeeter yipped back, but instead of a musical instrument he fumbled out from somewhere something long and slim wrapped in a paper bag. Seeing me onlooking in confusion, Skeeter paused to explain, "Hoppy ain't supposed to see any bottles on the bus. This way, he don't. Right, Hop?"

"You have got the only Greyhound driver with blinders on," Hoppy agreed to that, perilously close to the truth according to the way he hunched over the wheel to peer fixedly through the windshield as the bus shimmied on the washboard road.

Skeeter, proper host, was screwing the top off the hidden bottle when he noticed Herman craning over in curiosity along with me. "Hey there, One Eye, you want a swig? This is giggle juice you don't get just any old where, it's—"

"Wait, don't tell him," I jumped in barely in time. "He'll tell you."

Herman received the sacked bottle from the surprised Skeeter, nodded his thanks, tipped it up like sounding the bugle charge, and chugged enough of a drink to swirl in his mouth good and plenty. He swallowed as if the contents were tough going down, but when he got his voice, he announced without a shade of a doubt:

"Fruit wine, plenty fermented. Wild Irish Rose, I betcha."

"Damned if he ain't right," Skeeter said, pop-eyed with awe. "How'd ye do that? Boys, we got a miracle worker here. At the hooch store I asked for Rosie in a skirt"—he displayed the bagged bottle Herman had without hesitation handed back to him—"I was gonna have some fun with you fellas whose tongues has been worked to leather by too much Thunderbird. But One Eye nailed it first taste. Beat that!"

Highpockets, who didn't seem to miss anything, shifted in his seat and pinned a penetrating look on me. "What's more, his English improves around a bottle, eh? Usually that operates the other way."

"Yeah, well"—I didn't have time to think up any other explanation for Herman's tasting talent as displayed in the Schooner and now in these circumstances, so a sample of the actual story had to serve—"in the old country he worked in one of those places where they make beer, see, and that was part of his job, guzzling all the other beers to see how those stacked up against theirs. It tuned up his taster, you might say."

"That's the job I want in the next life," Fingy was heard from, clasping his hand and a half in prayer.

GENERAL ACCLAMATION FOLLOWED that, along with the bottle passing to ready volunteers turning bugler until it ran dry. I sat back to collect myself, the already more than full day, which was winding to somewhere along a tightrope-wide back road pressing in on me, filling me with that feeling of being transported in more ways than one. This back-road trip was not the longest of my life, yet was taking me farther than I had ever dreamed. Letty's inscription in the autograph book promised *Life is a zigzag journey*, and as she said, truer words were never. By now Manitowoc, the Crow rodeo grounds, the marooned time at Old Faithful, scary Butte, each and every one was in the memory book in my head as well as the one in my pocket, while an unforeseen chapter waited ahead. On the one hand, what was happening now tingled in me as a kind of off-kilter excitement, similar to that dreamy daze between sleep and waking in the morning, when what is real and what the mind has manufactured in the night are not clearly divided. At this point, Gram would have told me not to get red in the head and over-imagine things, but this last bus carrying Herman and me and our rough-and-ready gang of new companions inevitably made my mind fly around. Here we were, on a journey my imagination couldn't resist playing with, like being on a stagecoach—if the dog bus didn't qualify sufficiently as the modern version, the Rocky Mountain Stage Line and Postal Courier surely did—packed with the equivalent of owl hoots, the roamers and ramblers, taking new names for themselves as they pleased, out to experience everything of the West.

MY REVERIE was broken when Peerless Peterson, whose nickname became self-evident as he stuffed a chaw in his cheek from a packet of Peerless tobacco, leaned toward me and asked confidentially:

"Hey there, Snag, what was it that happened to your grampop's peeper?"

"Knife fight."

That impressed all those listening in as much as I'd hoped. Herman, as surprised as anyone, thought fast and joined the spirit of things. He took me by the ear one more time but only to tug me close so he could go on at whispered length. I almost could not believe what he was coming up with. It was perfect! Herman at his absolute little-think best beat Karl May by a mile, and when he was finished now, I gave my brightest snaggy smile and reported:

"Gramps says to tell you our last name is Schneider, not that it counts for anything in the here and now, we savvy. But he wants you to know *Schneider* means tailor in the old country, so all he did was cut the other guy some new buttonholes. In his hide."

The whole busload roared approval of that description, which no doubt went straight into hobo lingo. Relieved, I sat back, surreptitiously stroking the medicine pouch beneath my shirt, thanking the arrowhead for the luck of encountering Mae and Joe and the generous doctor and their fortunate name, while Herman accepted accolades for the tale with a grin halfway back to Germany.

Things settled down then, the passengers trading gripes about railroad bulls who patrolled the switchyards like it was a sin to climb onto a perfectly inviting empty boxcar, and countless other indignities the Johnson family had to suffer. I started to relax somewhat, deciding maybe the bus was not going to topple into the river and drown us just yet, although I did not quit stroking the arrowhead every little while to ward that off. But then, as I kept catching snatches of conversation as the Jersey Mosquito yakkety-yakked with Fingy while Overland Pete swapped observations on humanity with Oscar the Swede, a certain feeling came over me. It was unmistakable, and it had me clasping what lay half forgotten in my coat pocket as if it were a precious rediscovery. I had hit the jackpot, I realized. An entire busload of all kinds, here for the taking with a Kwik-Klik.

Excitedly I nudged Herman, drawing a grunt and an inquisitive look. "You know what?" I said close to his ear, resisting the urge to grab it as he had grabbed mine. "I need to get these guys in the autograph book. Nobody else has names anything like them."

"Except maybe racehorses," he spiked that with a guttural laugh. "Ja, fill your book with odd Johnsons." He yawned, the Wild Irish

Rose perhaps having its effect. "Busy day. While you are gitting them to write, I am going to catch winks."

I still don't know how he could do it, popping off to sleep like that aboard a bus snorting its exhaust and rattling like crazy on the washboard road, but there he went, soundly slumbering by the time I had my pen and album ready and intentions sorted out.

I had brains enough to start with Highpockets, and staggered my way down the aisle to his front seat as the bus bucked along. Ordinarily nothing seemed to surprise him, but this did. He eyed the white album none too trustfully as I squatted by him and reeled off my request known by heart. "If I was to dab something in for you," he questioned, "how would you want it signed?"

"Just with, you know, your moniker." Then I got inspired. "How about *Highpockets, on the last bus to Wisdom.*"

"Fair enough." He took the Kwik-Klik and, as I had hoped, made a little music on the page.

There's a land somewhere
so pretty and fair,
with rivers of milk and shores of jelly,
where every man has a millionaire belly.

"There you go, the hobo anthem, verse number about a hundred and fifty probably." He loosened up into almost a smile as he shifted the album back to me.

"It's nice. I like it." Now I had to try Bughouse Louie sitting next to him, who had been feigning disinterest all the while Highpockets was writing. First, though, I needed my curiosity satisfied. "Can I ask you something?" I stuck with Highpockets. "How come you and the other ho—haymakers wait to take the last bus?"

"I might ask you and One Eye the same," he said mildly, but still giving my heart a flutter as the MOST WANTED poster loomed into the picture. "But I won't."

He leaned back, his big frame squashing the seatback cushion, and with the practiced eye of a lifetime traveler, scanned the hard-used and unmaintained interior of the bus, which in that respect matched its exterior. "Not exactly soft, swift, and smooth, is it, going by dog in the last of the pack." The bus shuddered across the metal rails of a stock crossing in answer. "But the reason we hold off," he resumed, "to catch this old crate on its last run is because that puts us past the green hay, when ranchers who never learn any better start mowing too soon and try to stack the cut before it dries like it ought to. Haying is tough enough without the stuff being heavy and slippery." He glanced at me to see if I knew that, which I did.

"Uh-huh, real smart," I confirmed, thinking past that seasonal maneuver to the larger matter of Wisdom and the Big Hole and the reputation as a valley of prosperity. "But don't any of you ever, ah, hole up there? I mean, stick around in jobs besides haying?"

Highpockets emphatically shook his head. "Hoboes don't stick," he put it in simplest terms. "We're not barnacles."

Bughouse Louie backed that with a smile that displayed gums instead of teeth. "I sure ain't."

Their point fully made, I thanked the one for honoring my album and was about to ask the other to do the same when I was flatly turned down. "Can't possibly," Bughouse Louie cramped a hand to show me. "Got the arthritics."

DISAPPOINTED BUT EXPRESSING my sympathy, I moved on from what would have been that terrific name on the page to someone I figured would have no such trouble wielding a pen, the plain-looking hobo called Shakespeare. By appearance, he might have been anything from a bank teller to an actual whey-faced minister but for his hat stained dark from sweat and the faded gray Texas tux work shirt. Accepting the album as if by natural right, he scanned the verse Highpockets had written and sniffed, "Pockets sticks to the tried and true." Not him, according to the way he waved the pen over the waiting page while he thought, his lips moving, straining his brain from the looks of it. Then when he had the rhyme or rhythm or something, he wrote lines like a man possessed.

The king called for his fiddlers three.
He bade them, "Play for me your fiddle-diddle-dee."
The fiddlers cried, "Oh no, sire, not we!"
The queen giggled and said, "They only fiddle that with me."
—an original rime by Shakespeare

Sort of dirty though that seemed to me, I minded my manners and thanked its author—you don't get the name Shakespeare in an autograph book just any old day—and let the sway of the bus carry me to the next candidate along the row, Overland Pete. Seeing me coming with the Kwik-Klik and the open album, he shook a hand as pitiful looking as Bughouse Louie's. "I'll pass. Arthritis is acting up something fierce."

Huh. I had never heard of an epidemic of that, but it seemed to be hitting half the people on the bus. Before I could choose my next candidate, I heard an urgent *"Psst."* The Jersey Mosquito several seats back crooked a finger at me.

When I went and knelt by him, he brought his face of crinkles and wrinkles down almost to mine to confide, "Ye want to be a leetle keerful with that book of yours, Snag. The learnin' of some of the boys didn't happen to have readin' and writin' in it."

"I'm sorry." My face flamed. "I should have thought of that. B-but I really want to get anybody I can."

"Then all's you need to do is wait till payday and keep an eye out then," the man known as Skeeter counseled. "Them that takes their wages in hard money prob'ly can't write their names to endorse a check. The rest of us is regular scholars enough to cash our skookum paper right there in the Watering Hole, that's the bar in town. More eefficient that way."

I thanked him for that vital lesson and scooted back to my seat. Goddamn-it-to-hell-anyway, I hunched there stewing to myself, was there no limit to what I had to learn by hand, this summer like no other? Feeling sorry for myself and the autograph book, I was fanning through the empty pages that would never know Overland Pete and Bughouse Louie and maybe too many others to make the pursuit worthwhile, when Herman came to the rescue.

"Donny, nothing to worry. Other people will write in your book up to the full, I betcha." I hadn't even known he was awake—it was twice as hard to tell, after all, with only one eye to judge by—but now, same as ever, he took in the passing landscape as if the West still was the Promised Land, rough road to get there or not. "Tell you what," he eased my disappointment, whispering low to not attract further attention from the hoboes in their rounds of bottle and gab, "I will say to you by heart an old German verse and we will make it into English, or something like." That sounded like it was worth a try, and I perked up as he and I went back and forth over how words looked and what they meant, until we were both satisfied.

When you take a look in your memory book
Here you will find the lasting kind,
Old rhymes and new, life in review,
Roses in the snow of long ago.

"Wow, that's pretty nice," I said when the final version stood out on the album page in Herman's scrawly handwriting, "although I'm not sure if I get it all."

"Nothing to worry, you will someday." He stretched from the exertions of this day, but grinning as he did so. "Last bus is gitting somewheres at last. See, looking more like Promised Land." He drew my attention to a broad gap ahead that the river and the road both relaxed into, so to speak, the landscape turning into the best ranching country I had ever seen. In life along the Rocky Mountain Front, I was used to unbroken cliffs and crags always towering to the clouds in the west, but here the mountains circled the entire skyline, an unforgettable surround of peaks painted beautiful with streaks of snow and the blue of distance. My heart dancing, I gazed around and around at the ring of natural wonders, always coming back to the long valley of ranches and their patterns on the land, where the first hayfields lay tawny in the sun.

23.

THE SCATTER OF buildings the bus pulled into at our destination did not look like much of a town. Much of anything.

While the tired dog bus chugged along a wide spot in the highway that was the main street, I tallied a couple of gas stations, a mercantile, a farm equipment dealership, a post office, the Watering Hole saloon as mentioned by the Jersey Mosquito, a supper club that looked like it had started life as a hash house, and a sprinkle of houses around. I had to admit, I'd seen Palookavilles that amounted to more. Yet the community of Wisdom famously carried one of the best names ever, by way of Lewis and Clark, who were thinking big when they passed through on their expedition and grandly dubbed three nearby rivers the Philosophy, the Philanthropy, and the Wisdom. None of those graftings lasted through time and local reference—the Wisdom became simply the Big Hole River, which proved to be the roundabout torrent our road had hugged so closely, and still was flowing good and wide here at our destination—but the little town picked up the name and used its remote location to good advantage as the provision point for the great hay valley; the nearest municipality of any size, Dillon, was sixty-five miles away through a mountain range.

I mention this only because there was something about Wisdom, scanty as it looked from a bus window, that immediately appealed to me. Anticipation can cause that, but somehow I felt Herman and I had arrived at a place that did not make too much of itself nor too little, and that felt about right. So, I was alarmed when Hoppy the driver did not even slow down as we passed the black-and-white enameled GREYHOUND sign hung to one side of the mercantile's display window.

"Hey, wait, he missed the depot!" I burst out, Herman jerking to attention beside me.

Overland Pete and the California Kid and some others hooted as if that were the funniest thing they'd ever heard, but Skeeter again rescued me from further embarrassment. "We ain't there yet, Snag. The one thing special about this excursion is, Hoppy dumps us off right where we're puttin' up for the night."

Soon enough, those words bore truth. The bus jounced off the highway onto a stub dirt road, heading straight for the brush along the river. "We want the beachfront accommodations down the road, Hoppy," Highpockets ordered up. Which drew the peevish response, "I know, I know. How god-many times have I druv the passel of you there?"

Not far from town, near a hidden-away clearing in the thick diamond willows, we rolled to a stop. "Everybody off, far as the golden chariot goes," the driver recited, as I'd have guessed he did every year.

As everyone piled into the aisle and out, Herman and I were the last off the bus, and the final ones to have our belongings hurled out of the baggage compartment by Hoppy, who wished us luck with a shake of his head. We turned to have our first good look at a hobo jungle.

Herman, who had witnessed the Depression, chewed the side of his mouth before saying, "Hooverville without shacks, even."

The poorfarm without walls or a roof, was my own spooked reaction to the scene of rough-dressed men strewn around a campfire in the dusk as our own bunch from the bus joined them, pitching their bindles and bedrolls into whatever nooks in the brush they could find. I was horribly afraid Herman was going to remind me it was my eye-dea that brought us to this—he sure was entitled to—but he confined himself to "Find ourselfs a place for the night, we better."

Since we were too broke to afford a room even if Wisdom had any, our only course of action was staring us in the face. "Okay, we're gonna have to jungle up with the rest of them." I shook myself out of my poorfarm stupor. "First thing is, we don't look right."

Pulling him behind a clump of brush where we were out of sight from the campfire, I rolled up our pants cuffs to the tops of our shoes and generally mussed our clothes up, pulling our shirttails out some to look baggy and so on.

Lifting my Stetson off, I punched my fist up into the crown to take out the neat crimp and make it more like what the hoboes wore. I held out my hand for Herman's eight-gallon pride and joy.

"Do we got to?" he groaned.

"Damn betcha," I said, reaching up for it so he wouldn't have to commit the crime against it himself. "We don't want to stand out like dudes at a testicle festival."

I beat up his hat against the willows, then rubbed it in the dirt for good measure as he watched in agony.

"There you go." I handed him the limp, abused Stetson and clapped my own on my head. "Ready?" I inclined my head to the campfire.

"One Eye is with you, Snag," he said, as if swallowing hard.

HATS BEATEN UP and hearts beating fast, we headed into the hobo jungle in the brush beside the Big Hole River. The kip, as they called it, turned out to be a gravel bar down from a state highway department gravel pit and storage area, where culverts and bridge beams and steel guardrails were stacked. Bunched there in the open-air kip, maybe twice as many as were on the bus with us, was a band of men sitting around rolling their smokes in brown cigarette paper. Like beached pirates, was my thought, to go with Herman's roguish missing eye. Imagination aside, it was written in the sparks flying upward from the open campfire and the bubbling of the blackened stewpot hung over the flames that we were joining the bottom end of society, manual laborers with leather gloves stuck in a hind pocket, maybe their only possessions beyond a bindle and a bedroll. Now I was the one swallowing hard.

Blessedly, Highpockets intercepted us before we reached the campfire circle.

"Now, I'm not saying you two don't know how to take care of yourselves," that point made itself in his tone of voice. "But after dark here, it's colder than old Nick." Night was fast coming on, and I was remembering the gripping chill outside the Old Faithful Inn. Highpockets shifted his gaze significantly to my scanty suitcase and Herman's sagging duffel. "I don't notice any bedroll makings on you. Better do something about that."

"Ja, what is your recommend?" Herman surprised us both.

"Doesn't speaka the English, eh?" Highpockets gave me an unblinking look. "That's your own business. Uptown at the merc, they sell bedroll fixings, old army blankets and the like."

"I will get fixings," Herman startled me further. Chicken hunter he may have been, but Wisdom did not seem to offer much prospect along that line.

I would worry about that later, right now I had a basic concern about getting any kind of shelter over us for the night. "Ah, Mr. Highpockets, I was wondering—"

"No misters in the Johnson family," he said not unkindly.

"Okay, sure, uhm, Pockets. Do you suppose Gramps and me could have dibs on one of those culverts?"

"That's inventive, anyway. Sling your plunder in there to stake your claim," he gave his blessing, turning away toward the kip. "Then better come on down for mulligan before it's gone."

I hustled to the nearest steel shelter with my suitcase, Herman following with his duffel and looking thoughtful at the prospect of the metal tunnel just large enough to hold us if we slept end to end. "Go be acquainted," he more or less shooed me to the hobo gathering. "I will be a little while in town."

Another worry popped out of me. "What are you gonna use for money? We're just about broke again, remember?"

"Nothing to worry. I have eye-dea."

WHATEVER IT WAS, I left him to go to town with it, in all meanings of the phrase, while I made my way down to the kip and its inhabitants. But beforehand, at the edge of the brush I encountered Pooch hunched over like a bear as he scrounged dry branches along the riverbank for firewood. When I asked if I could help, he replied, "Damn straight," without looking up, and I started tromping downed cottonwood limbs in half until I had a good armful.

I don't know that it would be in any book of etiquette, but I was a lot more welcome walking into the hobo gathering with an armload of firewood than if I had merely strolled in with my face hanging out. "Good fella," said Midnight Frankie, stirring the black pot of mulligan, a stew found in no recipe book. I dumped my armload on the firewood pile and retreated to the farthest spot on one of the logs that served as seating surrounding the campfire, wishing Herman was with me to provide moral support or at least company.

"For any of you who didn't have the pleasure of his company on the last bus, this here's Snag." Highpockets did the honors of making me known to the other batch of hoboes and them to me. Similar to our busload, they had names all over the map, Candlestick Bill and Buttermilk Jack and Dakota Slim and the Reno Kid—not to be confused with the California Kid—and Left-handed Marv, who had an empty sleeve where his right arm should have been, and so on through enough others to confuse St. Peter at the gate. My presence as a kid with no kind of a capital *K* did not seem to bother anyone since Highpockets vouched for me and he clearly was the topkick of the whole bunch. The Big Ole, as I soon learned this unelected but acknowledged type of boss was called. Why the hobo community fashioned an oversize Swede as the last word in leadership, I hadn't the foggiest idea—it was their lingo, not mine—but in any case, Highpockets saw to things that needed seeing to, including keeping the peace now when Peerless Peterson and the Reno Kid scuffled over which of them had claimed the spot under a favorable cottonwood first. With that settled by Highpockets's threat to knock their heads together, things went toward normal, the wine bottles appearing out of bindles every so often lubricating a general conversation that ran toward the unfairness of a world run by fat-cat capitalists and sadistic small-town sheriffs.

By now I was nervously glancing out into the dark, wondering what was delaying Herman and kicking myself for not going with him into town and keeping him out of trouble, or at least being on hand when it happened. Goddamn-it-to-hell-anyway, could even this remotest of towns conceivably be plastered with MOST WANTED posters, and had he been thrown into whatever variety of jail the Big Hole held? I was torn between holding our spot in the campfire community and plunging into the darkness to go searching for him.

In the meantime, the hoboes were loosened up by the circulating bottles to the extent there was now a jolly general demand. "C'mon, Shakespeare, give us one."

"My kingdom for a source," that individual half comically, half dramatically put a hand to his brow as if seeking inspiration. Mimicking a high-powered thinker—or maybe there was no mimicking to it, with him—he pondered aloud, "Now, what immortal rhyme would a distinguished audience of knights of the road wish to hear, I wonder?"

"Quit hoosiering us and deliver the goods, Shakey," Highpockets prodded him.

"As you like it, m'lord," the response pranced out, over my head and probably all the others as well. Crossing his legs and leaning on his knees with his arms, the learned hobo lowered his voice confidentially enough to draw his listeners in, me included.

"There was an old lady from Nantucket—"

Audience cries of "Hoo hoo hoo" greeted this promising start.

"Who had a favorite place to tuck it."

The way this was going, I was momentarily glad Herman was not there.

"It slid in, it slid out—" The recital bounced the springs toward its climax, there is no more apt way to say it. I could see Pooch moving his lips in repetition to catch up with the words, while Midnight Frankie smirked like a veteran of such moves. Other hoboes banged fists on their knees along with the rhythm of the limerick or leaned back grinning expectantly. By now I was thankful Shakespeare's contribution to the autograph book was only vaguely smutty.

"Slick and sure in its route—" An artful little pause to build suspense, I noted for future reference. Then the culmination:

"Under the bed. Her night bucket!"

"Ye damn fancifier, here we thought we was gettin' somethin' educational," the Jersey Mosquito called out while other critics hooted and kicked dirt in Shakespeare's direction and told him where to stick the old lady's chamber pot. As the merriment went on, I was giggling along until I glanced over my shoulder for any sign of Herman yet and saw a flashlight beam headed straight for our culvert.

I knew it! Herman had been nabbed uptown, and here came a

cop to confiscate our belongings. With a feeling of doom, I slipped away from the campfire circle and stumbled up the road embankment, frantically rehearsing pleas to the law officer now shining his light at the mouth of the culvert and pawing around in there.

And found it to be Herman, stowing two sets of blankets and wraps of canvas to roll them in. He kept dumping goods from his armload. A Texas tux work shirt for each of us. Leather gloves, ditto. Changes of underwear, even. Not to mention the flashlight. "So, Donny," he said after a flick of the beam showed him it was me panting up to the culvert. "We have fixings to be haymakers."

"Holy wow, how'd you get that much? Weren't we next thing to broke?"

He fussed with a bedroll a bit before answering. "Old-timey wicker will just surprise you, how much it brings."

It took me a moment for that to fully penetrate, but when it did—

"You sold the suitcase? Gram will skin me alive!"

"Don't be horrorfied," he begged. "It was that or the moccasins. No choice did I have. Had to get bedrolls, can't sleep bare on something like this." He knocked a knuckle against the corrugated metal culvert, making it ring hollowly. "Take it from an old soldier who has slept on everything but bed of nails, ja?"

"I guess so," I muttered, taking it a different thing from having to like it. "But my moccasins and the rest—what'd you do with my things?"

"In duffel." He messed around with the bedroll a bit more without looking up. "I selled my Karl May books, too, to make room."

So we both had sacrificed mightily, for the privilege of living like hoboes.

24.

We reached the campfire circle in time for mulligan, served in tin billies from a stash somewhere in the kip, along with spoons that no doubt were missing from many a cheap cafe. Both of us feeling starved—candy bars had been a long time ago—we dug into the stew nearly thick as gravy and featuring chunks of potato and lumps of some meat everyone knew better than to ask about. Amid the concentrated eating and mild conversing, Highpockets suddenly lifted his head, Skeeter doing the same. Clicks of someone walking on gravel could be heard, and across the campfire from where we sat, a rangy man stepped out of the night into the fireshine. He had something about him that made the circle of hoboes stir nervously.

"Got room for one more?" he drawled in a spare way I'd heard before.

I blinked, but he didn't change. It was Harv the jailbreaker. Who was supposed to be in that stony lonesome at the far end of the state.

Highpockets responded by unfolding to his full height, hitching up his pants, and maybe even standing on this tiptoes a little, the Big Ole to the life, but he still didn't match the height and breadth of Harv Kinnick.

But doing what he had to, he challenged: "You smell the grub and figured you'd mooch? Or you got something more permanent in mind?"

"Might have," said the newcomer, still as a statue.

"Sort of a nightbird, aren't you," Highpockets spoke the guarded curiosity of the hobo contingent.

"Takes a while to get here by boxcar and thumb," Harv mentioned.

Highpockets gazed across the leaping flames of the campfire at the taller man for some moments, sensed the unspoken vote of the group, and said, "If you're bunking rough like the rest of us, there's enough of the great outdoors to go around. Come on in and plant yourself. Any scrapings in that pot for him, Midnight?"

As the man who looked like Gregory Peck if you closed an eye a little strode in with that purposeful amble of a town tamer and took a seat on a community log when the resident hoboes shifted over for him, the Jersey Mosquito recited the who-be-ye. The newcomer considered the question with that distant look of a soldier or, as Herman's nudge and whisper conveyed to me, a knight, and came up with:

"Harv will have to do, I guess."

All eyes except his shifted to Highpockets again, who could be seen weighing whether an actual given name was up to hobo code.

"Whatever a man wants to go by is his own business, I reckon," he decided.

Peerless Peterson couldn't stop from meddling a little. "You don't have any too much to say for yourself, do you."

"Still waters can bust dams," Harv drawled, spooning into the billy of stew remnants Midnight Frankie had handed him. After an unsure moment, general laughter broke out. "Stick that in your rear aperture and smoke it," the Jersey Mosquito joshed Peerless, who grinned painfully and retreated into silence while conversation built back up to normal among everyone else. Harv in the meantime silently kept at his mulligan.

"Come on," I tugged at Herman, "let's scooch around there to him."

He was as intrigued as I was. "Ja, he is some man, you can see from here."

I circled around, Herman on my heels, and edged down on the log next to the newest hobo on earth, making us into old-timers. "Hi again."

He chewed a bit before saying, "You're the kid with the autograph book."

"Sure thing, Mr. Kinnick," I swiftly used his name to emphasize I full well remembered who he was, back there in handcuffs, too.

"Harv," he corrected quietly but in a way that told me not to forget it.

Herman cleared his throat, a signal that prompted me to introduce him as One Eye, my grandfather from the old country and so on, and on a hunch that we would be wise to have on our side someone with a knack for evading lawmen, I leaned close as I could to Harv, considerably above my head as he was, and confided, "Gramps is sort of staying out of the way of the, uhm, authorities, too."

Herman stiffened at first, then caught up with my thinking and Harv's apparent circumstances. "We are not much liking jail, either."

"Then we have a lot in common," Harv said, proffering a hand even larger than Herman's outsize mitt.

After the handshakes, I had to ask. "How'd you spring yourself from Wolf Point this time?"

"Wasn't that tough, as jailbreaking goes," the veteran at it reflected, both of us listening keenly but Herman with real reason to. "They have a habit there of making the prisoner mop the cell, and when Baldy, that's the deputy," he said, as if the jailer was an old acquaintance, "had to go to the toilet, I reached the key ring off the wall peg with the mop handle. I was out and hightailing it down to the tracks by the time Baldy pulled his pants up, I guess. Caught the next freight going west and linked up with Lettie after her shift at that Le Havre." The mention of his girlfriend brought a pining expression, which he resolutely shook off. "Had to move on from Havre, of course," summing up in an aside to me. "You can guess how Carl is when he heard I'm out free again." Did I ever, the half-pint sheriff on the bus suspiciously grilling me as if I were a runaway when I wasn't—yet—still a memory I wished I didn't have.

From Harv, this had grown to a speech of practically Bible length, and he wasn't through yet. "I sort of wish Carl would take it easy on me for slipping jail, when it's not even his," he said, as if there was more than one kind of justice.

"Yeah, he's a mean little bugger," I said boldly, Herman's good eye policing me not to go too far. "He sure did you dirty, back there on the bus to Wolf Point."

"Aw, Carl maybe means well," said Harv out of brotherly, or at least step-brotherly, loyalty. "It's just that you put a big badge on a little guy, his head swells along with it."

After that evident truth, he turned reflective again.

"Still and all, he had something there on the bus, that I should go haying. Taking him up on it, though he doesn't know it," he concluded. He shifted attention to us. "Do I savvy you're here to make hay, too?"

"You bet I am. I mean, we are," I hastily included Herman.

"I thought you were getting sent someplace back east."

"That, uh, didn't work out. See, One Eye is my closest relative from back there, and he wanted to see the West."

"Ought to be able to get your fill of it around here." Harv smiled a little.

"Can I ask"—I maybe shouldn't have pressed the question but he was the one who had racily all but drawn her into the autograph album—"what about Lettie? I mean, you're here and she's there, all the way up in Havre."

That cast him into silence for some seconds, evidently dealing with his longing until he could put it into words. "We're working on that. I'm going to save my wages and she's putting away her tips, and after haying we'll get married and find some way where I'm not running from jail all the time."

Herman looked as if he would have liked to add advice to that, but only nodded silently.

AT THAT MOMENT—I'll never forget it, it is clocked into memory as if with a stopwatch dividing that night of my life—came an outcry from Fingy, stumbling into camp still buttoning his pants from taking a leak in the bushes. "We got company! The town whittler."

The atmosphere around the campfire changed like a gun had gone off. Certain hoboes evaporated into the willow thicket on the riverbank, others sat up rigid in a collective stare toward the road, where a black-and-white patrol car with a big star on the door luminescent in the moonlit night was pulling up. Harv stayed as he was, as though none of this turn of events applied to him, and Herman and I were caught up in his example, whether or not we should have taken to the brush.

Right away, Highpockets was on his feet and in charge. "Anybody been yaffled lately?"

"I done a jolt a little while back," Buttermilk Jack, the oldest of the hoboes except for Skeeter in our bunch, owned up to. "Fifteen days, vag, in Miles City."

"Good time, or did you scoot?" Highpockets pressed what must have been the most veteran vagrant to be found anywhere.

"Served my sentence honest and true," the old hobo swore. "Then they run me out of town. If anybody's on the lam, it ain't me."

No, it was the trio of us at the other end of the log from old Jack who fit that description up, down, and sideways. Fear gripped me so savagely I could scarcely breathe. Would my all too readable face, between Harv's imperturbable one and Herman's contorted one, give us away, first of all to Highpockets? He had no stake in us, and as the Big Ole, his responsibility was toward the bunch he traveled through the fields of the West with, the Johnson family compressed into that last bus. He could dust his hands of strays like us to any inquiring lawman, to everyone else's benefit but ours. I am sure my eyes were rabbity and my freckles gone pale as I watched Highpockets read faces in the firelight.

Just before he reached ours, Peerless Peterson spat a sizzle of tobacco juice into the fire. "Why can't the bastards let us alone? We got as much rights as anybody, but they treat us like dirt when we're not sweating our balls off doing the work for them."

"Shut your flytrap," Highpockets snapped at him, "until we see what this is about. You go poking Johnny Law like that and he's likely to poke back with a billy club, you ought to have learned that by now."

The circle around the campfire went tensely silent as he checked from man to man. "Anybody else the bloodhounds might be after, for anything? No? Let's make sure or we're all in for it." On one side of me, Harv looked on innocently, and on the other, Herman somehow was an equal picture of guiltlessness. For my part, I had to sit tight and try not to appear as guilty as I felt about landing the pair of us in this fix. Luckily, Herman's whisper put some backbone in me. "Remember, big medicine you have. Makes you brave." Newly conscious of the arrowhead and whatever power it carried, there next to my heart, I managed to guilelessly meet Highpockets's eyes as his gaze swept over the three of us, lingered, then moved on.

"All right, we seem to be in the clear. We've lucked out, some," he reported in a low voice as he recognized the advancing lawman in the moonlight. "It's Mallory, the deputy sheriff over here. He's not the worst as hick dicks go." But he still was some kind of sheriff and Herman still was featured on a MOST WANTED poster, and I still was his accomplice or something, skating on thin ice over the bottomless depth of the orphanage. I gripped the arrowhead pouch through my shirt, my other hand clasped in Herman's to tie our fortune together, good or bad.

THE DEPUTY and Highpockets acknowledged each other by name as the local lawman stepped into the circle of light cast by the campfire. They did not shake hands, which would not have set well with either of their constituencies. This officer of the law was half again bigger than Harv's banty-size Glasgow nemesis, somewhat beefy the way people get from sitting behind a desk too much, but without that air of throwing his weight around unnecessarily. He did not look overly threatening except for the pistol riding on his hip. That six-shooting symbol of authority, however, was more than enough to draw resentment, loathing, hatred in some cases, from men harried first by railroad bulls and then the lawmen of communities that wanted them gone the minute their labor was no longer needed. The shift of mood in the encampment was like a chilly wind through a door blown open.

"Only checking to make sure you boys are comfortable." Mallory spoke directly to Highpockets but all of us were meant to hear.

"There ain't nothing like it, bedroom of stars and the moon for your blanket," Skeeter contributed ever so casually, as Peerless spat into the fire again. "Care to kip with us for the thrill of it all?"

"I think I heard a feather bed call my name," Mallory chose to joke in return with a hand cupped to his ear. No one laughed. Heaving a sigh, the deputy got down to business. "Speaking of relaxation, maybe it'd help everyone's mood to know I'm only coming back from a hearing at the county courthouse over in Dillon, not on the lookout for anyone in particular. But"—he paused significantly—"I figured I'd stop by Highpockets's old stomping grounds here just to keep myself up-to-date. Any new faces I ought to be acquainted with, on the odd chance they'd show up in town on Saturday night and I wouldn't recognize them as haymakers instead of plain old drunks?"

Several of the hoboes who were already at the kip when our bus bunch arrived grudgingly owned up to being first-timers in Big Hole haying. The deputy made a mental note of each, then raised his eyebrows as he came to Harv and Herman and me. Harv merely nodded civilly to him. I was tongue-tied, and Herman did not want to sound the least bit German. In these circumstances, muteness could be construed as guilt—we certainly had a nearly overflowing accumulation of that among the three of us—and just as the silence was building too deep, Highpockets stepped in.

"Snag and his gramps there, One Eye, have been with us since we were apple-knocking, over by the Columbia. The big fella, too. They're jake."

"If you say so, Pockets." The deputy apparently could not help wondering about me, though. "Say there, Moses in the bullrushes. You're sort of young to be hitting the road like this. What brings you to hay country?"

"My s-s-summer vacation. From school."

"Some vacation." Mallory was growing more curious, the audience around the campfire restless with his lingering presence. Highpockets was looking concerned. "These your folks here," the deputy persisted, "this pair of specimens?"

Herman's hand firmed on mine, helping to take the quiver out of my voice. "You guessed it. My Gramps, here, and my, uh—"

"Cousin," said Harv offhandedly. "First cousin." He glanced at the deputy sheriff barely an instant as if that were the issue.

Mallory's jaw came up an inch, but he did not challenge Harv's version of family life. He turned to Herman, studying the ruined side of his face where the eye had been and the facial wrinkles that looked deeper than ever in the flicker of the firelight. "Must be nice to have a helper in raising the youngster out in the rough like this, huh, old-timer?" His question was not without sympathy.

Giving the lawman a sad sweet smile, Herman uttered, "Ja,"

which for once I was really glad sounded close enough to good old American "Yeah."

"Well, I've seen worse bunches of renegades," the deputy tried joking again, making a move toward leaving but not before a conciliatory nod to Highpockets and a general one to the rest of us. "Just don't tear the town up on Saturday night and you won't see my smiling face again."

"HERMAN?" MY VOICE sounded hollow in the confine of the culvert where we were stretched feet to feet. "Do you think that deputy sheriff believed Harv?"

"Does not matter much." He, too, sounded like he was at the bottom of a well.

"Mister Deputy made believe he did. Sometimes make-believe is as good as belief, hah?" I heard him shift inch by inch to try to get anywhere near comfortable on the corrugated metal, the bedrolls literally saving our skins. "Better catch winks, Donny. Tomorrow might be big day."

25.

THEY ALL WERE big days, in the Big Hole. And I was among the first to see this one come, at least as represented in human form.

Herman and I crawled out of the culvert at earliest daylight, stiff in every joint and sore in corrugated bands across our bodies, the morning chill making us ache all the more. Were we ever thankful that down at the kip Skeeter was already up—hoboes do not sleep late—and rebuilding the fire while Midnight Frankie was working on mush of some kind in the mulligan pot. The encampment was gradually coming to life as its inhabitants groaned their way out of their bedrolls, abandoning the bed of earth to face another day. Harv could be seen rolling up a bedroll no doubt provided by loyal Lettie. As we crossed the road to head on down for whatever this day would bring, Herman blearily said he was going to the river to wash up, while I needed to take a pee so badly after the night of confinement in the culvert that my back teeth were swimming. Off he went to the gravel bar and I ducked into the brush below the road.

I was relieving myself when someone came thrashing through the willows, swearing impressively, right into the path of what I was at. He cut a quick detour, giving me an annoyed look. "Hey, Pee-Wee. Watch where you're aiming that thing."

"Oops, sorry."

Still swearing enough to cause thunder, he plowed on through the brush toward the encampment, leaving me red with embarrassment, but what was worse, slapped with that tag. There it was. Pee-Wee, peeing in wee fashion in the bushes, homeless as a tumbleweed. Nowhere near making *Believe It or Not!* but already dubbed into the funnies. My shameful fallen state in life, a tramp, a shrimpy one at that.

No, damn it, a hobo. A haymaker, I resolved nearly to my bursting point, if anyone would just let me. Buttoning up quickly, on a hunch I set off after the visitor crashing his way toward the campfire.

AS HE BURST through the brush into the clearing with me close behind, the tandem of us drawing the attention of the entire kip, I saw he was wearing good but not fancy cowboy boots and a stockman Stetson with a tooled leather hatband complete with a miniature clasp. He probably was around forty years old, although his brown soup-strainer mustache was tinged with gray. Halting on the opposite side of the campfire from where Highpockets and Harv and others were lining up for Midnight Frankie's version of breakfast, he held his palms toward the blaze to take the chill off. "Morning, men."

"We can agree with both of those," Highpockets acknowledged, the rest of the hoboes risking no commitment beyond silent nods. "What's on your mind otherwise?"

"Putting up hay fast and furious, what the hell else?"

By now Herman had silently joined me, ruddy from the cold water of the river and with his glass eye in and his eyeglasses on. I can't say he looked like a new person, but at least he looked like the old Herman the German, the one ready to hop a bus for the Promised Land somewhere south of the moon and north of Hell. His strong hand on my shoulder lent support as we found a place in the growing circle of hoboes crowding around to hear what came next from the man warming himself by the fire.

Identifying himself as foreman on a ranch plentiful with those

Big Hole hayfields, the new arrival glanced around the circle, right over me and past Herman, sorting faces with his quick eyes.

"I'm hoping some of you are the genuine haymaking article, unlike your pals next door." He jerked his head in disgust toward some kip farther up the river. "They don't want to hear about anything but tractors and power mowers. You'd think they were all mechanical geniuses." He paused, studying the waiting faces more intently. "What I'm saying, we're still a horse outfit."

Can a person jump for joy standing still? Not really. But his words set off that kind of upspring of elation in me. At last! Surely an outfit like that would need a stacker team driver, wouldn't it? If only one of the older hoboes didn't beat me out for the job. In an onrush of anxiety at that and wild with desire at the same time, I seesawed so nervously that Herman couldn't help but notice my agitation and whispered, "Stand steady as a soldier, Donny."

"We don't have anything in particular against horses so long as they don't have anything against us," Highpockets was saying. "Am I right, boys?" Amid answers such as "Pretty much" and "More or less," Peerless took care to specify, "Although we ain't no bronco busters, either."

"Don't worry, that's taken care of." The ghost of a smile visited under the foreman's mustache. "Here's the setup," he brusquely went on. "The spread I work for used to be the Hashknife—maybe some of you put in some time there?" On our side of the campfire, someone muttered, "That sure as hell fit the grub there. All knife, no hash."

"Don't get your feathers up," the foreman forged on. "The spread is under new management. Fresh owner, wants things done right. I was brought in to cut loose anything that wasn't working, which meant just about every stray sonofabitch on the place. So, but for a few riders summering the cows and calves up in the hills, my crew is out of whack."

"Enough said," Highpockets took over. "Try us."

"First of all, I'm looking for a man who isn't allergic to hay by the load and hard work."

A number of the hoboes took a half step forward. "What's the work?"

"Stack man."

The Jersey Mosquito, who looked like it would be all he could do to push around an empty pitchfork let alone one shoving swads of heavy fresh hay into place, asked possibly out of pure mischief, "Do ye favor building them haystacks big as Gibraltar?"

"Sizable" was as close to that as the foreman would come, but it was admission enough.

The hoboes, even Highpockets, stepped back to where they were. "A strong back and a weak mind, is what he means," Shakespeare expounded.

"Donny, what are they talking?" Herman whispered worriedly. "Nobody wants haymaking job?"

"Shh. Watch Harv."

Without twitching a muscle, the fugitive from the Wolf Point stony lonesome still seemed to be studying the first pronouncement, before the strong back and weak mind wisecrack. Then, slowly he stepped forward as if to take the world on his shoulders. "I suppose that'd be me. Up top of that Gibraltar."

The foreman sized him up as if he were too good to be true. "You've stacked hay before?"

"Tons of it."

Inasmuch as any haystack held several tons, that was not as impressive as it might have been. But seeing no chance of a miraculous stack man materializing among the rest of us, the foreman made up his mind. "Well, hell, you look the part anyhow. What's your name?"

"Harv."

The foreman waited, then gave up. "If that's the way you want it,

I guess I can stand the suspense until your first paycheck to find out if that's a first name or a last or what you call yourself when the moon is full." The wisp of a smile appeared under his mustache again. "Who am I to talk? I go by Jones myself, one hundred percent." Even to the hobo nation that mocked society by calling itself the Johnson family, going through life as just a Jones sounded like quite a dare, but the man by the fire wore the moniker with bulldog authority.

With that out of the way, Jones scanned the collection of ragtag individuals beyond Harv, his gaze passing me—did he show a flicker of interest at how I was all but falling out of my shoes with eagerness?—as he briskly ticked off on his fingers. "Now, I need two mower men and a couple of buckrakers and dump rakers each and a scatter raker. Any of you balls of fire ambitious enough some for that?"

"Bucking," Highpockets got his bid in. Followed by Peerless Peterson: "I can handle a mower team if they ain't runaways."

The Jersey Mosquito laid his claim. "Maybe it don't look it, but I c'n still climb onto a rake seat." Pooch mustered, "Damn straight. Me, too." Midnight Frankie chose driving a mowing machine and Fingy, the simpler task of riding a dump rake, while Shakespeare, the last person I would have picked out as a teamster, announced he was a buckraking fool. So tense that my skin felt tight, I prepared to spring up the instant when the man doing the hiring would realize he was one haymaker short and announce he lastly required a stacker team driver.

Instead came the awful words "Good enough. That finishes the crew, so let's get a move on. The pickup's parked up the road." Jones gestured beyond the brush of the hobo jungle. "Come on up when you've got your bindles together and I'll pull out the daybook to talk wages and catch whatever you're using for names. Soon as we're squared away on that, we'll go make hay."

. . .

As Highpockets and Harv and the others started making their farewells to Oscar the Swede and Snuffy and Overland Pete and Bughouse Louie and the California Kid and the others from the last bus who would wait for other haying jobs to come along, I turned as numb as a cigar store Indian. This was clearly inconceivable, that a Big Hole horse outfit would not use a teamster but some automotive monstrosity like a Power Wagon on the stacker. Yet it all too evidently was about to occur that bright-as-a-new-penny Jones was committing the same kind of sin against common sense as dumb Sparrowhead on the Double W. Some lofty writer who probably had never held an honest job once claimed that the ability to grapple with two contrary facts at the same time was the mark of higher intelligence, but I must not have been marked that way. Trying to do so only made my head swim.

Seeing how stricken I looked, Herman leaned down anxiously, telling me there were other ranches, nothing to worry, we would be haymakers yet somewheres.

Then I glimpsed it when the foreman stopped to check on something with Highpockets and turned his head a certain way, the wink of morning light as the sun caught the small silvery clasp, not much bigger than a locket but distinct as anything, that held his fancy hatband together.

I grabbed Herman's arm so fiercely he drew back from me in a pained squint. "We absolutely have to get on this crew."

"Hah? How?"

That, I had no idea of, but I knew our best chance in the Big Hole was about to be lost if we didn't try something. "C'mon, grab our stuff, we need to catch up with him."

We did so, crashing our way out of the hobo jungle so loudly the foreman looked around at us in surprise as he reached his pickup.

"Hey, wait, Mr. Jones, sir. Didn't you maybe forget you need a stacker team driver?"

The ranch honcho leaned against a rear fender, crossing his arms at my challenge. "Not really. I figure to handle that myself, be right there at the stack with the crew that way."

"But then what if there's a breakdown and you have to go to town for parts or somebody's cows get into a field and you have to go and dog them out or there's a runaway and a dump rake goes all skoogey from hitting a ditch and maybe the raker does, too?" I started down a well-remembered list of the Double W haying mishaps. "Or what if the cook throws a fit and quits and—"

"Hey, hey, I have enough keeping me awake at night already," the foreman put a stop to my onslaught.

Thinking over what I'd reeled off, he pushed away from the pickup and turned to Herman, who was trying to encourage our way onto the crew with nods and shrugs and grins while keeping a silence and leaving things to me. "Your boy here makes a pretty good argument for you. It's not necessarily nutty to have somebody else drive the stacker team and free me up for whatever the hell else happens. You do look like you've had experience of some kind"—maybe too much experience, from his tone as he eyed Herman's lined face and general muss from sleeping in a culvert—"but where'd you last do your teamstering?"

"Not him," I rushed the words before Herman could say something guaranteed to confuse the issue. "Me."

"Yeah?" Jones laughed. "You're the horseman of the family?"

"Oh sure, you bet. I've been a stacker driver since I was eight. On a big ranch. Up north."

"Eight, huh." He played that around in his mustache as he studied me. "Just how old does that make you as we're standing here on the green earth?"

I was perpetually being told I was big for my age. Wasn't it logical for that number to grow to catch up with the rest of me, in this instance? "Thirteen," I said. He looked skeptical. "My next birthday." The next after that, at least. An approximation.

He waited for me to say more, but when I didn't, he let it go. Now he scanned Herman from his city shoes to his eyeglasses. "How about the mister here, who you seem to do the talking for? I don't hear him owning up to advanced years like some."

"He's my grandfather, but he married young." I hoped that would help in my fudging away from whatever Herman's age was. "See, we're all each other has," I laid that on thick while Herman instinctively stayed mute, "and we're sort of on hard times. We really, really need jobs."

The foreman still hesitated. "Nothing against you, but you're still just a kid, and you can't have been around workhorses any too many years, whatever you say."

"Make you a deal," I scrambled to come up with. "If I can't harness a team the way you like, as fast as anybody else on the place, and show you I can handle the reins, you can fire me right away and we'll walk back to town."

The man called Jones settled his hat and perhaps his mind. "Now you're talking about something. I could stand that kind of guarantee on this whole damn crew—these hoboes are sometimes the teamsters they say they are and sometimes not. You're on. Toss your stuff in the pickup and I'll test you out soon as we're at the ranch."

He started toward the pickup cab for his daybook as Highpockets and Harv and the others emerged from the kip in the brush, swinging their bindles and bedrolls at their sides. "One more thing," I said quick, stopping him in mid-reach for the door handle. "My grandfather has to come with me. Watch out for me and so on. I'm a, you know, minor."

"Damn it, you're going to have me hiring the whole hobo jungle before you're done." He thought for a second. "All there'd be is grinding sickles and mending broke-down stuff, sort of second fiddle to the choreboy. Not much of a job, general handyman is what it amounts to."

It was going to take some serious stretching, but I was about to try to make the case that Herman, who never in his life had been on a ranch outside the Germanic pages of Karl May, could somehow be generally handy, when he startled us both with the exclamation "Sickles!" and gave the hiring foreman the thumb and finger OK sign. "Ho ho, handled hundreds sickles in the old country."

Both the foreman and I drew back our heads to look at Herman in a new way, Jones eyeing him now with curiosity or suspicion or both. "I thought your grandkid here did the talking for you. That sounded like you found your tongue all of a sudden."

"I talk broken, but apprehend some, the English," Herman said blandly.

I pitched in, "He means he pretty much savvies what you're saying."

"That's welcome news." He looked hard at me and then at Herman. "You can talk American, but he can't? How's that come to be?"

"My granddad hasn't been here that long from the old country," I made up offhandedly. I still was worried about Herman at large on a ranch. "There's a little something maybe you better know." I dropped my voice. "He needs to keep out of the way of the livestock. See, he doesn't speak enough of our language for the horses to understand him, just for instance."

"What old country is that, anyway?" Jones demanded. "I'd have thought 'Giddyup' and 'Whoa' were pretty much the same anywhere."

"Switzerland," I chose willy-nilly out of Herman's world of toast maps.

"No hooey? A yodeleer, is he?" The foreman seemed entertained by the idea, insofar as I could tell past his mustache. "All right, you're both hired, long enough to prove yourselves, anyhow. Let's get you down in the daybook." He reached into the seat of the pickup for a big ledger. "Start with you, teamster whiz. You're—?"

"Snag." I bared the sharp stump at him in what I hoped was a grin.

His mouth twitched. "When you're not being a knight of the road."

"Scotty." He waited for more and I produced, "Scotty Schneider."

With a sense of wonder or something very much like it, I saw that instant new name go into ink as he wrote it down. "And what's his?"

"Uh, Gramps."

"You got to do better than that."

"Fritz Schneider, I am," Herman spoke up, and if I kept a straight face, I don't know how.

"There, you're both on the payroll." The foreman jotted down Herman's alias or whatever it was to join mine. Done with us at last, he turned to do the same for the rest of the crew waiting in curiosity at the rear of the pickup, first sorting out me and Herman. "Youth and beauty up front with me. The rest of you, dump your plunder in back and jump in."

"THAT WAS A GOOD think by you," Herman murmured as we settled into the pickup seat to wait for our new employer. "Some Swiss speak German."

"They do? I figured they talked Switzer or something. Whoo, that was lucky."

"Luck is the star we steer by," he invoked for the how manyeth time. I was in agreement for once.

"You know what, Herman?" My mood was so high it was a wonder my head wasn't hitting the roof of the pickup. "We've maybe got it knocked, once and for all."

"Donny, you are extra happy. These jobs are that good?"

"Didn't you see the clasp in his hatband? The livestock brand?"

The French salute, meaning *No.*

"It's the Diamond Buckle. Guess who owns the ranch."

26.

ALL BUT EXPLODING with excitement, I managed to pass the harnessing test—I will say, avoiding a ten-mile walk back to town is no small incentive—even though in the team of workhorses I was given, I had to stretch higher than I thought possible to struggle various straps into place on the lofty back of the huge mare, Queen.

Panting as I finished up on the other workhorse, a sleepy-looking black gelding called Brandy, I couldn't help asking about the gray mare looming out of her stall like the giant mother of the horse race. "How come she's called something nice like Queen instead of Big Mama or something?"

All during my flinging on of harness and scrambling to buckle up this and that, Jones was leaning against the barn wall with his hands in his pockets, critically observing. "The owner's idea, from cards," he replied, appropriately poker-faced. "Named her that way because he always draws to a queen, thinks it brings him luck. Worthwhile females being as scarce in poker as they are in life generally, according to him."

"Hah, he is some thinker." Herman, nervous spectator, took that way of warning me not to point out half of that problem could be solved with the French bible deck in his duffel.

Curiosity got the best of me, all this talk of "the owner" as if it were some deep dark secret. Feeling invincible after my harnessing success, I rashly brought the matter out into the open.

"Is Rags around?"

The foreman looked at me sharply, then included Herman. "All right, geniuses. How'd you already figure out the place is his? Most of these 'boes could be working for Hopalong Cassidy, for all they know."

When I related sighting the purple Cadillac at Crow Fair and what ensued, and with Herman chiming in about what a bee-yoot-iffle ride Rags had made, Jones relaxed his scrutiny of us somewhat. "Well, good for you. I don't advertise who owns this outfit, right off the bat, because guys can get the idea somebody like Rags ought to pay higher wages. No worries about that with you two who are just lucky to be here, am I right?" He secured headshakes from Herman and me as if *Oh no, any notion of a larger paycheck would never cross our minds.*

"Anyway, Rags is riding the circuit" the topic was finished off. "He'll pull in here big as life sooner or later." Shoving off from the wall, the foreman headed out of the barn saying gruffly, "Leave the team tied up until I get the rest of this world-beating crew lined out on their jobs. Come on, let's go to the bunkhouse and settle you in."

MY FEET BARELY tickled the ground, I was on such a cloud as I crossed the yard of the ranch owned by the champion saddle bronc rider of the world. Was this perfect or what? Miles better than my try at talking Gram into letting me hang on at the Double W back at the start of summer. Look at all that had happened since—in the giddiness of the moment I folded the high points of dog bus life over the low ones—and hadn't I gained not only the black arrowhead that was big medicine, but Herman, who was something of a found treasure himself except for being a few kinds of a fugitive? Out here he was hidden away, in hobo company, where nobody inquired too closely about one's past. To top it all, even if I didn't have a framed certificate to prove it like the gallant Twin Cities newspaper van driver, I now was a teamster!

Accordingly, I was half into another world, one totally without any Bible-dispensing pickpocket nor MOST WANTED posters nor the kid prison called an orphanage—nor for that matter, Aunt Kate—when Herman gradually dropped back a few steps behind Jones's purposeful strides toward the bunkhouse and I heard a significant *"Ssst."*

Slowing until I was next to him, surprised at his perturbed expression, I whispered, "What's the matter?"

"We are hired, ja?" he made sure in a return whisper. "Knocked, we have got it?"

"Yeah! Out the far end!"

"Good, good. But one something is on my mind," he fretted, quite a change from his usual *Nothing to worry.*

Before Herman could go on, Jones glanced back at the pair of us. "Just to scratch my curiosity itch, where do the pair of you fetch up after haying? Where's home?"

"Oh, where we live when we're not with the Johnson family, you mean," I had to do my best to field that because Herman's face went as lifeless as a MOST WANTED poster. "About the time school starts we'll have to go back east to—" Herman went even more rigid. "Pleasantville. It's around New York, you know. Gramps has a job there, he's the handyman at the *Reader's Digest* place."

Jones chewed his mustache as he contemplated us. "So he's got a job there and a job here, does he. Lucky, lucky him." Reciting straight out of the put-upon ranch foreman's book of rules on dealing with the odder elements of a crew, he let us know, "Out here, we're not big on previous, wherever or whatever a person comes from, understand? Just so's you can do this job."

"Ja, we savvy," Herman forced out more loudly than needed. I gave him a look, wondering what could be spooking him when everything was going so slick.

Before I could nudge him aside and ask that question, Jones halted us, saying, "Hold on a sec, here's somebody you might as well meet and get it out of the way." He called across the yard to a man limping along toward the chickenhouse carrying a pan of feed. "New hands, Smiley, come get acquainted."

The choreboy, as I recognized him to be and Herman was destined to find out, swerved toward us swinging a leg held out stiff. *Holy wow,* I thought to myself, *first Louie Slewfoot and then the gimpy bus driver Hoppy, and now this lame specimen, all in one summer.* Yeeps. Maybe they came in threes, like when famous people died, according to Gram.

NOW CAME OUR INTRODUCTION to Smiley, former rodeo clown, whose name outside the costume might as well have been Cranky as Hell. Clowns as I have known them, essential performers at rodeos in drawing bulls and mean horses away from bucked-off riders at the risk of their own lives, those entertainers in baggy overalls and whiteface makeup stayed physically fit from all the running and ducking and dodging in the soft dirt of the arena. This one had gone to flab and deeper ruin from the look of him, with a beer gut that might have looked comical in a costume but in ranch jeans hung precipitously over his belt. Facially he seemed to be sucking on something sour all the time, lips twisted and eyes narrowed. An encounter with a Brahma bull, we discovered soon enough from bunkhouse gossip, left him with what is called a cowboy leg, crooked and off at an angle, causing that stiff-limbed gait. He seemed to resent the world of the able-bodied with every step he took. Certainly he acknowledged Herman and me with minimum enthusiasm, muttering, "How ya doin'" without interest and immediately turning to Jones to demand, "When you gonna let me shoot that cow?"

"How many times do I have to tell you," the foreman gritted out, "no one is shooting any livestock on a ranch owned by Rags Rasmussen. He'll can you so fast your head will swim. Waltzing Matilda is the best milker on the place, so don't you touch her except pulling those tits," Jones went on, as if this had been said too many times before, too.

"A bitch from hell, is what she is," Smiley whined. "Shat on me again." The evidence was fresh and green all over the bottom half of his pant leg. "Did her best to kick me, too. I tell you, she's a killer."

"It is your job to milk the cows, no matter what. Waltzing Matilda included. Enough said," Jones declared.

Unsatisfied, Smiley scowled—a severe contradiction in terms, but that was Smiley for you—toward a pasture next to the barn where three cattle were grazing as peacefully as a Wisconsin dairy picture, or rather two of them were. The other was a bony brown-and-white Guernsey with jutting hip bones and a sort of outlaw longhorn look about her, even though she had been dehorned to stubs. Merely from the way she swished her tail, as if spoiling for a target to use it on, I would have bet solid money that was Waltzing Matilda. Herman, maybe from his own alien notoriety, studied the scandalous cow with interest.

"I have some actual good news for you, if you'll simmer down a minute and listen," Jones informed the would-be cow shooter, who dubiously clammed up and waited. "You're off of grinding sickles. One Eye here will be handling that chore."

"Ja," Herman put in, as if sickles were his ordinary diet. "Like in the old country."

"He's welcome to all those sonofabitching things in the whole god-blasted world as far as I'm concerned," Smiley accepted that with a fresh twist of the lips and lumbered crookedly off to the chickenhouse, bawling in a voice that had not lost any of its arena volume, "Chick, chick, chick, come and get it, you damn feather-dusters."

Well, evidently not everyone thought the Diamond Buckle ranch was perfect.

ALTHOUGH HERMAN was furrowing his brow again after the encounter with Smiley, it took more than a used-up rodeo clown to dent my spirits, and I nearly trod on the foreman's heels into the bunkhouse. The one long single room was the ranch standard in those days, never any bargain, with discolored tan beaverboard walls and bare wooden floor and iron-frame cots in two rows and a potbellied stove and a battered table with chairs that had rungs missing. Merely quarters for drifting laborers who came and went with the seasons, the bunkhouse for me was a palace where I'd be in with grown men, actual haymakers, a full-fledged member of the crew. Beat that, at eleven going on twelve.

Gab stopped as the foreman stepped in, the hoboes apparently not short of conversation anytime and anywhere. As Herman and I closely followed Jones in, I looked around real quick in concern about the bunk situation, and saw there were two empty ones off in a corner. Highpockets told me with a simple shift of his eyes in that direction that he had saved those for us, and we lost no time in unrolling our bedrolls and chucking the duffel out of the way.

"We'll get going on the machinery pretty quick, the mowers and stacker can be greased up and the rakes can have new teeth put in, any fix-up you see that needs doing," the foreman was addressing us all. "First order of business, though, is right here." Reaching into his hip pocket, he began handing out small leather belts of a kind Herman and I alone recognized.

"What's these for?" Peerless asked suspiciously, turning his over like it was a snare of some sort.

"Those beat-up lids of yours," Jones made plain with a tap to his own trim Stetson. "Diamond Buckle hatbands. The owner thinks these'll add a bit of style, he's big on that. Give you the feeling of working on a first-class place."

There was a general moment of uncertainty, going back to the rants in the hobo jungle about the rich with their heel in the face of the poor. This was a step up from that, for sure, but even so it took some thinking about wearing another man's brand on yourself.

"Might as well tell you the rest now that you're signed on," the foreman said into the general silence. "It's Rags Rasmussen that owns this spread. World champion bronc rider, got the diamond belt buckle to prove it. Heard of him, haven't you?" he appealed to Highpockets.

"More or less," Highpockets squared himself up as the Big Ole for the hobo contingent. "We don't exactly ride in the same fashion, boxcars instead of broncoes."

Peerless couldn't keep from harping. "If I had any kind of a diamond and this Rasmussen had a feather up his butt, we'd both be tickled."

"You're bellyaching over nothing," Highpockets shut him down. "If you'd ridden as many killer horses as that man must've, you might have something to show for it, too." He returned his attention to Jones. "We can maybe stand a little fancying up, if that's all there is to it," he decided for the hobo group after a glance around at how the hatbands were being received. Midnight Frankie was scratching the back of the clasp of his with a jackknife to see if it was real silver. "Imagine, the head that wears the crown sharing a touch of it," Shakespeare said, installing his band on a hat that had seen thousands of suns and the grime of countless fields. Pooch watched to see that it was all right to put his on. Harv pondered his, taking no account of what anyone else was doing, then shined the buckle up on his sleeve and fitted the band on. Herman and I had no qualms about dressing up our battered Stetsons, proud to share the Diamond Buckle, even it was the size of a locket. All we lacked now was the owner of that championship brand, and of the hay land that would give us work and wages and withdrawal from the treacherous world for the rest of the summer.

"ALL RIGHT, let's get to work." Jones led the way out of the bunkhouse, the crew so various in so many other ways in hatbanded unison as we followed him across the yard toward the machine shed, a structure open on one side so the workhorses could be backed in to the tongues of the mowers and dump rakes and buckrakes and hooked up right there under shelter, a perfect setup most ranches were too lazy to do and left the haying equipment scattered around to rust in the weather. Let's hear it for the Diamond Buckle, my head sang with the help of my hatband. I had to stop myself from skipping, everything in me going pitty-pat about this haymaking dream come true.

Until Herman once again dropped back, motioning me to come close enough for a whisper. When I did, he made my heart stop by asking:

"Donny? What are sickles?"

27.

"THEY'RE THE THINGERS you cut hay with!" I had trouble keeping my voice down when I really wanted to screech, *"Fuck and phooey, Herman, you have to know what sickles are or we're fired and kicked off the ranch to walk to town and right back to where we started in the hobo jungle, only worse off because Highpockets and the others aren't there to stick up for us and that deputy sheriff could come back and recognize you from a poster and then we're sunk."*

Instead, I sort of hissed desperately, "Didn't you have sickles of some kind to cut hay with in Ger—the old country?"

His face lit up. "Scythes, you mean, I betcha." He gestured as if swinging that oldfangled curved implement Father Time is always carrying in cartoons.

"No, no!" I bleated. "Nobody has used those since the Pilgrims or somebody. Sickles, see, go in mowing machines," I tried frantically to assemble an explanation of modern haying, "and cut back and forth like crazy when the horses pull the mowers, and there's all these teeth that need sharpening a couple of times a day, and that's what you're supposed to do, what they call riding the stone."

"Sorry as all git out"—Herman wrinkled up, trying to imagine—"but riding some kind of rock, I do not savvy."

"It's a *grind*stone, get it?" I practically chewed the words up for him. "There's a seat on it and you sit there and pedal it like you would a bicycle and it makes the stone go around fast and—"

I was growing a little hysterical, trying to conduct a lesson in sickle sharpening, with Herman not comprehending that his chore was the absolutely essential first task in haying. As sure as Murphy's Law, the heavy green hay would clog the mowing machines if the teeth were dull when Peerless and Midnight Frankie pulled in to the first field to start cutting, and we'd be hoofing it back to town on that long road, right back to being on the run. And wouldn't you know, with the rest of the crew busy on their machinery with grease guns and oil cans and general fixing up, now here came Jones to deal with us.

"One Eye"—the foreman was in his usual hurry—"let's get you squared away at the blacksmith shop so you can start right in on the sickles." As for me, he jerked his head toward the towering wooden framework of the beaverslide stacker parked behind the shed. "I guess you know where you're headed. Give all those pulleys a helluva good oiling."

"Uhm, I'll get right at it," I claimed, not moving an inch. "Maybe it'd be a good thing for me to stick with Gramps a little bit while you get him started, though? To, ah, translate, sort of."

"Come on, the both of you," Jones said, as if it were his own idea, "I don't have time to parley voo in some other lingo." He set off in his bustling stride toward a low old log building near the barn. Trailing him just out of his hearing, I managed to whisper to Herman to simply watch me when we reached there.

The way things were done in haying season, the grindstone had been moved out of the inside of the shop into the big open doorway for space to handle the sickles, which were nearly as long as a man is tall. Herman caught on to this part of it quick enough as I hopped into the seat and with false enthusiasm—"Oh man, I wish we could trade jobs, Gramps!"—pedaled madly to set the wheel-like grindstone spinning at top speed. I could also see it dawning on him that the wicked-looking limber spans of metal propped against the wall in the cluttered blacksmith shop, each with treacherous teeth from end to end presenting countless chances to cut a finger off, must be the sickles, and he had no idea in this world how to handle the dangerous objects.

Jones noticed his hesitation, too. "This is the sort of thing you did in the old country, right? Up there in the yodeleer meadows?"

"Ja. Sure. Might be rusty some, like the siskles—"

"Sickles, Gramps, rhymes with tickles." I hopped off the grindstone seat and behind Jones's back pantomimed to the best of my ability, grabbing a sickle from the back by the bar that the teeth jutted from and carrying it the do-or-die way a tightrope walker uses a pole to keep his balance.

With something like numb determination written all over him, Herman gingerly approached the sickles and picked up one the excruciatingly careful way I'd shown, while I silently cheered him on.

"Sharpen the bejesus out of the first couple of those," Jones ordered, "so I can send the mower guys out to the field. And don't round off the goddamn points, like Smiley tends to do. It wears them down too fast." The foreman whirled to go, impatiently glancing over his shoulder at me. "That stacker is still waiting."

"I'm just about to be there," I maintained, waltzing wide around the sickle as Herman shakily balanced it while climbing onto the grindstone seat. "I need to tell Gramps one last thing about how we do it in this country."

"Hurry up about it," Jones warned. "Standing around gabbing doesn't put up any hay."

As he departed, I pulled the medicine pouch out from under my shirt and over my head. "Here, I'll leave this with you a while to go by," I told Herman, unsheathing the arrowhead and placing it on the frame of the grindstone in front of him. "This is what he means about sharp and not rounded off, see? Grind them until they have an edge like this and no more, savvy?"

"Like maybe so?" He tentatively pedaled and sent sparks flying from the bevel of steel meeting the grindstone. Then, though, he halted the encouraging screech of the grinding to pick up the arrowhead and feel its whetted edge with his thumb.

"Lucky one more time, you and it, Donny," he said so softly I didn't correct him to *Scotty*. Holding the charmed piece, he gazed around at the prosperous-looking buildings of the ranch and the shielding mountains beyond and past even that horizon, I believe, to the ups and downs the dog bus had carried us through all the way from Manitowoc. Then at me, the hunted look gone from him at last. "Knocked, we have still got it, ja?"

"Close call," I expelled in relief, relaxing back into the haze of well-being that came with a Diamond Buckle hatband. "But yeah, we still do."

IN THAT SUMMER of flying calendar pages, Big Hole haying was a streak of time, when I take account of myself then, that I can scarcely believe packed so much into my life in so short a period. I suppose it would be like a kid of today thumbing through the holdings of some smartphone that shows him himself and realizing that a couple of years and robust inches have been slipped onto his pouty eleven-year-old self without notice. Electrifying, to use a word that still holds true of such a shot of overnight growing up.

Exactly as I had seen myself when I ventured into Wendell Williamson's lair to offer myself as stacker team driver in Double W haying before the sparrowhead turned me down in favor of a dumb truck, I proudly was in charge of my own pair of workhorses and a steel cable that the team pulled to hoist the stacker fork laden with hay, and—here truly was the weight of responsibility to rest on eleven-year-old shoulders—of halting the horses every time at just the right instant to drop the thick cloud of hay atop the stack wherever Harv indicated with his pitchfork.

In doing so, I had to manipulate a ton and a half of actual horses at the end of leather reins, back and forth the fifty-foot-length of the cable each time Shakespeare or Highpockets delivered an overflowing buckrake load onto the broad fork for sending up. Horses are not thrilled with walking backward—me either—yet that was half our job, backing to the stacker after the hay was dumped at Harv's altitude, and I needed to steadily cluck and coax and tug the reins just so to return us to our waiting spot for the next load. My salvation was Queen, as magnificent to me as the Trojan horse must have been in that age-old tale and as smart as she was grand, dutifully tugging Brandy—dumb as they come except when oats and the barn stall were involved—along with her in the pulling power that ran the stacker.

Love is a strong word to use anytime, but I loved that big gray mare, already taking a giant step or two before I could say "Giddyup" or "Whoa back," her big hooves largely responsible for the steady path we wore into the stubble beside each stack, like the front walk to the mansion of hay Harv was building with his pitchfork. Without Queen's steady horse sense, in the true meaning of that, I would have been sunk those first few days of trudging that same line of march over and over with the sun beating down and no rest for the weary, in Jones's unrelenting way of putting up hay.

All in but my toenails by quitting time, I was anxiously asked by Herman when I dragged myself into the bunkhouse to wash up for supper, "Tell the Jones it is too much for you, can I? He can put Fingy on stacker team and you on dumping rake, you can sit at your work like me."

"Don't you dare." I found the strength to sound offended. "I'll toughen in." Which I did, day by day, that path worn into the earth beside the haystacks leading me into the gritty line of Camerons and Blegens who had hunched up and taken it since time immemorial.

And see, by the end of the first week of Big Hole haying I held a triumphant mental conversation with Gram, *I'm not too young to live in a bunkhouse like a regular ranch hand.*

THE CAST OF CHARACTERS Herman and I joined were proof that the Johnson family tree had branches of all kinds. Midnight Frankie was from what he called Lousy Anna, and spoke with a deep southern accent. Shakespeare's tale was one of youthful indiscretions, when he became adept at what he called dialing the treasury, which amounted to safecracking, and it drew him an education written on jailhouse walls and in prison libraries. Peerless had hit the road during the Depression, starved out of an Oklahoma Dust Bowl farm to the California orchards, where the miserable Okie migrant camps turned him into an agitator and bunkhouse lawyer, and as aggravating as his mouthing off on practically anything could be, he was not often wrong. Skeeter went farther back in the workingman's struggle against the crapitalists, as he called them, when he fought the cops in the Seattle general strike of 1919 that got beaten down. Fingy never brought his background out except once when Smiley, obnoxious as usual, asked, "How'd you lose them fingers anyway? She close her legs on you too quick?" Fingy gave him a look as if about to squash a bug and only said, "Iwo Jima."

Then there was Pooch, who seemed to be the sad sack of the crew, his contribution to conversation almost entirely "Damn straight" and "You said it" as he plodded through life. At first I wondered at his lack of teasing by these often rough-mouthed men, because in a schoolyard anyone with a slow mind was in for it. But I overheard Highpockets take Jones aside in the barn and explain that Pooch had been seriously worked over by a notorious sap-wielding railroad bull in the Pocatello yards, and been a little off in the head ever since. Jones, to his credit, said nobody needed to be a mental giant to drive a scatter rake, and he'd make sure Pooch was given the tamest team of horses, after my own.

The one among them who did not share much about what turned him into a hobo was Highpockets himself. He did not need to, so obvious was he as a "profesh" who could make things happen in a collection of men otherwise as stray as cats.

And of course, Harv was Harv.

So, life in the bunkhouse was much like an extended version of that last bus to Wisdom, crowded and crude and somehow companionable almost in spite of itself. But also, with that many of us rubbing elbows in so small a space, an existence in which some friction was bound to occur.

READING MATERIAL in the bunkhouse never approached the Condensed Books level, and I was propped in my bunk after supper spending time with one of the pink *Police Gazette*s that were passed around until they fell apart. Ostensibly deep into "Is Marciano a Cheese Contender or a Legit Champ?" and the amazing number of secret lives of Elizabeth Taylor, I was all ears for Smiley's latest lustful tale of conquest. Herman was in the crapper, as the convenience with the toilet and sink and shower was always called in a bunkhouse, shaving as he did each evening to stay out of the morning crush for the sink, so I was free of frowns warning me not to listen too much. Smiley was a surprise candidate for rodeo Romeo, to call it that, with his moonface and globular belly, but to hear him tell it, he was God's gift to women.

This particular tale of lust involved a devastating Canadian blond fence-sitter at the Calgary Stampede who couldn't keep her eyes off Smiley as he went through his clown routine in the arena. To make a really long story short, he got word to her to meet him in back of the chutes while the chuckwagon race was being run, when he'd have a break from clowning. "And we hightailed off to the little trailer I traveled the circuit in back in them days," he finished, his rubbery face stretched into a triumphant leer. "Probably in record time, we done the deed every which way. Didn't even have to shed my overalls."

"Ye never even took off your clown outfit first?" Skeeter registered probably everybody's shock at the lack of etiquette. "What are ye, some kind of deviated prevert?"

"You're just jealous," said Smiley smugly, "of how them rodeo sweethearts liked to play rooty toot toot on my gazoot flute."

I was working on that rooty toot toot part and not really getting anywhere when Highpockets raised onto his elbows on his bunk and spoke up sharply. "Watch your mouth around the kid, can't you?"

"I ain't burning his ears off, am I, Snag," Smiley protested. "He has to learn the facts of life sometime."

"Sure, I'm kind of interested," I encouraged Smiley. "What's that flute business mean?"

This brought about a rare hesitation in the lady-killer choreboy as he studied me there propped on my bunk, rough-clad in a thousand-miler shirt like the rest of the crew but still plainly a youngster, although a husky one. Whatever other changes the summer may have produced in me, I had grown considerably, right past any semblance of eleven going on twelve. Even so, young was still written all over me, from freckles to boyish oversize feet, despite my efforts to camouflage it.

"Come on, everybody, it ain't nothing but the facts of life," Smiley defended his position to the bunkhouse in general but Highpockets in particular. "When I was his age, I knew plenty. Ain't it about time he learned about sailing around the world?" By now I felt like Herman when he'd listened to the hoboes rattling on in their lingo and asked me, "How many languages does English come in?" It was years down the line before I fully understood that Smiley's lip-smacking phrase meant something like learning the encyclopedia of sex by hand.

"It's up to One Eye," Highpockets ruled, sharp again. "None of your concern, so can that kind of mouthing off and—"

"The Pockets is right." Herman loomed into the room, there is no other word for it, knuckles clenched white on his straight razor as he fixed a snake-killing look on Smiley. "Scotty is good boy. I will take care of his educating."

"Don't get your dander up." Smiley backed down at the sight of Herman and that razor. "I was only funnin' with the boy, no harm in that, huh?"

"Do your funnying on somebody else." Herman's warning hit home on the now wordless Smiley, most of the rest of the crew sitting up and watching, with Highpockets and Harv half onto their feet to head matters off if that razor came into play. But Herman, with a contemptuous "Puh" at Smiley, crossed the room to his duffel bag and tucked the ivory-handled cutter away, snapping me to attention with "Let's catch air. Come help me with sickles."

Neither of us said anything as we crossed the yard to the blacksmith shop in the waning daylight, our long shadows mixing together on the ground in our strides. I felt guilty, although not sure why, and sneaking a look at Herman's set face was no help.

I trailed him into the blacksmith shop past the grindstone, sickles much too plainly not the first thing on his mind. He pulled out a pair of stout boxes from under the workbench and upended them for us to sit on. The sagging old shop, which had been a shambles at first, littered with stray tools and rusting pieces of metal and anything else that collects from breakdowns and repairs on a ranch, he had made tidy as a hardware store between his sessions of sharpening sickles. It has taken me until now to fully realize he had repeated the greenhouse, far, far from Manitowoc—an orderly haven for himself.

"Donny"—he made no pretense at Scotty or Snag—"I am having doubts about this place."

"W-why?" The Big Hole was showing off in the evening light, the mountaintops still goldenly sunlit while dusk softened the valley of hayfields to buckskin color, with the first town lights of Wisdom sparkling in the distance. To me, the Diamond Buckle ranch right then could not be beat, in any way I could think of.

Herman crouched forward toward me, as if making sure his words penetrated. "Bad company, you are keeping. Not your fault. My own."

"Aw, come on, Herman, don't let what happened in there get you down," I pooh-poohed the bunkhouse episode. "Smiley is as loose as the spool on a shithouse door and you shut him up good and that's that."

Herman passed a hand over his face. "There is some of what I mean. You are picking up language like from the garbage dump."

"So what?" If he was wrought up, so was I. "Goddamn-it-to-hell-anyway, this is what it's like on a ranch. I know the bunkhouse guys cuss like crazy and carry on like outlaws sometimes and all that. But they've been places and done things." I looked him straight in the eye, the good one. "Like you have."

"I have been"—his voice rose, then dwindled—"maybe too much places." He gazed off into the mountain shades of evening, as he must have gazed into many a night since that one in a Munich beer hall. "I am not example to follow. Life plays me big tricks—"

"Not your fault," I defended him against himself.

"—and I do not want same happening to you."

That jolted me. "Look at me here," he went on in the same grim tone, "and you with me, holed up like two Killer Boy Dillingers."

"But it's working out okay, isn't it?" I mustered in response. "We've got jobs, we're making wages, you're safe from the cops—Herman, what more do you want?"

He was searching so hard for how to say the next I could see it on him. "I am thinking you should go back to your *Grossmutter* some way."

That, I was relieved to shrug right off. "Well, sure, we both know that. After haying and when school starts, if Gram is . . . is herself again, I'll have to. But that's a real while yet."

"Now, I mean."

His Hermanic word *horrorfied* exactly fit my reaction. "Just up and leave you? W-why?"

Behind his glasses he was blinking hard, and I realized his eyes were moist. "I am doing poor job at being grandpa. You are living with men who have no home except the boxcars, and are always after by sheriffs, and speak I don't know what language, and the Smiley who is all dirty mouth. It can not be good for you, in bunkhouse. And I can not do anything about it except put the Smiley in his place once in blue moon."

"Skip it. I'm not leaving."

That stopped him cold. "Not yet anyhow," I rushed on to keep him that way. "Not until after haying, and then we can figure out what we're gonna do. Each." I was not far from tears, either, at the thought of going our separate ways. But that was not going to happen for as long as I could put it off. "Don't let the bunkhouse stuff throw you, okay? I won't listen any too much, I promise." I tried a ridiculous grin to help both our moods.

Herman wiped the corners of his eyes, blew his nose, sighed a deep surrender. "You are loyal. What can I do but try be same." He reached over and gripped my shoulder in a way that said more than words could. Both of us were one sniffle from breaking down.

He managed to be first at swallowing away the emotion, saying huskily, "Donny, if you are not going to your Gram, very least you must call her, ja? If she does not hear from you sometimes, she will worry too much and call Manitowoc, and there the Kate is and you are not. And then we are—"

"I know, I know. Kaput." Did I ever have that terribly in mind. Nun, Gram, Jones, they lined up like poles of the telephone line, and all scared me. One wrong word to any of them could do us in. Put yourself in my place: Gram was not even supposed to exist, according to what I had told Jones about me and Herman being all each other had, and any slipup on my part that let on to Gram about the Diamond Buckle ranch would be surefire disaster, and even Sister Carma Jean as suspicious keeper of the phone was no cinch to get past unscathed.

No surprise, then, that I lamely alibied to Herman, "I—I'm working on it. Gonna tackle Jones somehow about using the phone in the boss house, honest. Just haven't got around to it."

He appeared no more eager than me to tackle a foreman who was as gruff as any top sergeant, but gamely volunteered, "Ask him for you, can I, you think?"

"Better let me." I could see no way around the risky business of negotiating a phone call. "He still thinks you don't know diddly about things in this country and can barely spikka the language. We need to keep him thinking that."

"Ja, do not upset the cart of apples," Herman resigned himself to our situation. We stood up, man and boy and more than that through the bonds tying us together this life-changing summer, and he squinted wryly at the bunkhouse as if seeing through the walls to its inhabitants. "Sickles can wait until morning. Let's go be Johnson family."

Just as we were about to step into the yard, however, we heard the *whump* a car makes crossing a cattle guard too fast, then the crushy sound of tires speeding on the gravel road.

Putting a protective arm to me, Herman stepped back into the shop doorway exclaiming, "Emergency, some kind? Look at it kick up the dust."

The car swept into the ranch yard past the outbuildings, scattering the chickens Smiley had neglected to put to roost yet, and easy as the toss of a hat, glided to a halt in front of the boss house.

"Emergency, nothing," I yelped. "It's Rags!"

28.

THE PURPLE CADILLAC pulled up to the house and Rags climbed stiffly out from behind the wheel, still in his classy bronc-riding clothes. For once he was not the absolute feature, though, because with him was a black-haired beauty who instantly made me think of Letty, except that this one's uniform as she popped out of the convertible with a flounce and a laugh was a fringed white leather rodeo outfit like palomino troupe riders wear.

Herman and I tried not to gawk, without success. "Go on in and make yourself comfortable, darling," we heard Rags shoo her into the house with her ditty bag. "I need to act like a rancher a little bit. Catch up with you in no time."

"Promise?" said she, the word dripping with honey.

As she sashayed on in, Jones came hustling up to greet Rags. "Got a visitor, I see. Another buckle bunny?"

"Naw, she's a performer," Rags drawled, flicking a fleck of arena dust off his lavender shirt.

"I bet," Jones said with a straight face.

"Suzie Q there," Rags said offhandedly, "is only gonna be here overnight until we pull out for the Reno show, first thing in the morning. She's an exhibition rider, stands up in the saddle at full gallop and that sort of thing. Came along with me because she says she needs a refreshing whiff of country air."

Jones actually laughed. "Is that what it's called these days?"

"Don't have such a dirty mind, Jonesie," Rags drawled. Herman's expression said he wished he'd kept me in the man talk in the bunkhouse. "Saw on the way in you're managing to put up some hay," we heard Rags turn businesslike in his casual way. "How'd you make out on the hiring?"

"Old hands from the jungle, same as ever, except for"—Jones swept a hand toward where we were standing stock-still as doorposts in the shop doorway—"our Quiz Kid stacker driver and his one-eyed grandpa from the Alps."

"That's different. Gives the place a little foreign flavor." Rags cocked a look across the yard at Herman and me. "Let me take a wild guess," he said as he came over to shake hands, "which of you is the Alpine one-eyed jack."

"Hah! I fit that description, right up to the glass peeper," Herman proclaimed, delivering him a handshake that made him wince.

"Hey, be careful," Rags protested good-naturedly enough, "that's the hand I dance with."

Pumped up as I was in other ways, I took care to shake with him almost soft as Indian style, blurting, "We saw you ride at Crow Fair!"

"Did you now." Rags showed a long-jawed grin. "You had to look quick, the way that hoss had me coming and going."

"Buzzard Head!" Herman exclaimed. "You rided him until the whistler."

"I'm a fortunate old kid," the best bronc rider on earth said modestly. "Old Buzzard could have piled me half a dozen times in that ride, but I could feel every move he was gonna make just a hair ahead of when he'd do it. It's all in the timing, you know, making the right move at the right time."

HOLY WOW. Hearing the inside skinny from Rags Rasmussen on a winning ride had both Herman and me listening open-mouthed.

"Well, glad to have you on the crew," Rags said by way of excusing himself as he turned to head for the house. "Got company waiting."

"Tell you what," Herman said under his breath when Rags was just out of earshot. "Ask for making the phone call, before he goes in."

I was flustered. "Ask *Rags*? Right *now*?"

"He is like Winnetou, a knight of the West," Herman whispered into my ear, as if this were a sure thing, like *Fingerspitzengefühl*. "Hurry, ask."

"Uhm, can I please ask sort of a favor?" My voice was so loud and shrill it halted Rags halfway across the yard. "I need to make a phone call real bad. I mean, I won't get in your way with the company or anything, honest."

Jones had been heading for his own quarters, but my request whirled him back toward us. "Hey, you, anybody who's ever been on a ranch ought to know better," he put me in my place with a warning finger and simultaneously accused Herman with a scowl. "We can't run the damn outfit with every yayhoo in the bunkhouse trotting up here whenever he wants and tying up the phone and costing us—"

"Simmer down, Jonesie." Rags held up a hand to quell the outburst and asked me curiously, "What's all the hurry-up on a phone call?"

"To my sick grandma." Seeing Jones look suspiciously at Herman, supposedly my only relative, I hastily inserted, "On the other side of my family. She's in the hospital in Great Falls, from an awful operation she had to have. It's a way long story."

Rags rubbed his jaw, a gesture I have always associated with sharpening what comes out the mouth next, as smart guys seem to do it. "Sounds like you have reason enough to get on that phone. Come on in." He held up a soothing hand to stop Jones's sputtering protest. "It's all right, Jonesie. The exception proves the rule, or something like that."

On our way to the house, Rags limped more than a little, which alarmed me no end. Manners flung to hell, I outright asked the worst: "Did a bronc bust you up, there in Helena?"

"Naw, I drew a sidewinder hoss called Snow Snake that gave me a bad time and sort of banged my knee against the chute gate coming out, is all." He grimaced in a way that had nothing to do with the knee as we climbed the porch steps. "What's worse, I rode the crowbait, but only placed." He raised his eyebrows to indicate upstairs, where a certain somebody was getting herself comfortable. "Luckily a consolation prize was waiting."

Noticing my open-mouthed worship of his every word and move, he paused there on the porch to give me a pearl of wisdom. "Putting yourself on dodgy horses all the time is a tough go, amigo. I hope you don't have your heart set on being a bronc rider."

"Never. I mean, you're awful good at it and all, but I don't think I could be." His long legs and rider's body next to my chunky build pretty well confirmed that at a glance. "Can I tell you something, though? What I most in the world want to be is a rodeo announcer." I sent my voice as deep as it would go. "*Coming out chute four, it's Rags Rasmussen, champion of the world, on a bundle of trouble called Snow Snake.* Like that."

Then the most wonderful thing. The greatest rodeo cowboy on earth, who had heard announcers all the way from rickety roping-club arenas to Madison Square Garden, paused at the screen door and offered his hand. His grave experienced eyes met mine. "Let's shake on you making it to the top, son. I think you have the gift." In a trance, I shook his hand. "I'm sure not gonna bet against you."

IN THE MAGIC of that moment, the dream began to turn real. With his spirit in the world of rodeo as great as that of Manitou in the ghostland of the past, the vision never left me. I could foretell it clear as seeing into a mirror, the fancily painted broadcast crew bus with the bright red lettering emblazoned on its side where the silver dog used to run.

THE VOICE OF THE ARENA

SCOTTY CAMERON

BRINGS YOU THE WORLD OF RODEO

Fame and wealth, along with the cartoon tribute in *Believe It or Not!* For the hundreds upon hundreds of rodeos witnessed at the announcing microphone, those became within reach with that extended hand of Rags Rasmussen. I have had but to live up to what he called the gift.

Way ahead of that, I had to deal with a phone call I did not want to make, hiding my whereabouts and Herman's very existence from Gram.

NO SOONER were we in the house than a gale in woman form swept down the hallway to us. Not, unfortunately, the trick performer but the cook, Mrs. Costello, who liked to have her nose in everything.

"Oh, Mr. Rasmussen, you're home! What a relief, I always worry about you." A rawboned woman who looked like she could fight a bear with a switch, she normally ran a backyard laundry in Wisdom, but was a last-minute desperation hire by Jones. When Highpockets, on behalf of the crew, took the foreman aside after one too many servings of the cooked liver the hoboes called gator bait and asked if there wasn't better grub to be had somehow, Jones threw up his hands and said he had scoured all the way to Butte for a haying-season cook with no luck, they were all taken. Which left us with Mrs. Costello, as addicted to radio soap operas as Aunt Kate, chronically resorting to dishes featuring canned tomatoes, and making a racket in the kitchen as if the pots and pans were taking a beating while she hashed meals together. Milking time brought another uproar almost daily. She and Smiley hated each other, with her regularly complaining loudly about the splatters of manure on the milk buckets the choreboy would bring in after milking Waltzing Matilda. I have read that the finest Persian carpets would have one strand deliberately left astray, to avoid the sin of pride that perfection might bring. Mrs. Costello was something like that loose thread in the pattern of the Double Buckle, and of course I regarded her as poor material compared to Gram.

But that was neither here nor there; Mrs. Costello obviously had to be put up with, as I could read in Rags's face as she butted in on us now.

"Can I get you and your guest"—she didn't mean me—"some rhubarb pie with whipped cream and coffee?"

"No thanks, we'll save our appetites," Rags said politely. "Excuse us, we both have business to do."

With a final lingering curious look at me, off she went down the hall, next making an anvil chorus of pots and pans as she started doing the dishes.

Rags wagged his head and said something under his breath which sounded like "It takes all kinds." He pointed me to the wall phone and said to make myself at home, which was like telling me I had come a long way from a hobo kip in the willows. I wished Herman was in there with me to share the giddy experience.

Somewhere upstairs a radio was going, nice and soft. Rags winked at me and headed for the stairs, calling, "I'm coming, Delilah."

"DONNY? In the name of heaven as they say around here, is that you?"

"Yeah, hi, Gram."

Gram exclaimed over what a treat it was to hear my voice, and I stammered the same to her. My throat tight with emotion and apprehension, I blurted the question:

"H-how are you?"

"I'm sewn up like an old quilt, but I'll be good as new. It just takes time."

"Are you gonna be all right? I mean, like your old self?"

"You'll see. I'll be a holy terror again." She tried to sound like her old self, but the strain in her voice came through despite her best effort. My uncharacteristic silence made her try it over. "The only thing about it is, I have so many stitches that the doctor doesn't want me exerting myself any for a while yet."

A while yet. That was what I needed, too, to stick with Herman until haying was finished. Before I could think how to wish her well and simultaneously tell her to take her time at it, her voice rallied again. "Donny, this is quite some surprise, hearing from you like this."

"Yeah, well, Aunt Kate and I were wondering how you are, and she told me to pick up the phone and find out, just like that."

"Wasn't that thoughtful of her. Put her on please, I'd like to tell her so myself."

"Oh, she's not here." I had the receiver practically in my mouth and my hand over it to keep nosy Mrs. Costello from hearing. "She went to the grocery store for bread to make toast for breakfast."

"I'm glad you're getting along so well with her. She can be a handful." Hearing that, I was elated, justified in lighting out for the Promised Land with Herman. I was so jubilant I almost missed what Gram was saying next. "I'd ask what you've been doing, but your wonderful letters describe it all so well. How are you and Laddie doing?"

In that summer of many names, Donal and Donnie and Red

Chief and Snag and Scotty, and Dutch and Herman and One Eye and Fritz, not even to mention the hoboes' variety, I drew a blank on that one. "Uh, who'd you say, again?"

"The collie dog Aunt Kate got for you, it's right here in your letter, silly."

"Oh, *Laddie*. You know what, he ran away. Quit the country." I dropped my voice. "Couldn't take any more of Aunt Kate, I guess. She ordered him around all the time, poor pooch. Anyway, nobody knows where he went."

"That's awful," she exclaimed, "the poor thing just loose like that."

"Yeah, but maybe he's better off, without being bossed to death like that."

That carried us through, until we wished each other the very best and hung up until the next time.

29.

THE GOOD WEATHER of that Big Hole summer and the bountiful windrows of a record hay crop turned the Diamond Buckle crew into haymaking fiends, the loaf-shaped stacks rising in the fields fast enough to please even Jones. Harv really did prove to be a man and a half on the stack, handling many tons a day with his tireless pitchfork. Some days we skidded the stacker to three new fields, we were such scorching haymakers.

Those days fell away like fleeces, and I was caught by surprise when payday abruptly arrived, along with lifted spirits in the bunkhouse that it happened to be a Saturday night and time to go to town. Which of course meant to the Watering Hole.

I WAS ECSTATIC at getting my first paycheck. Until I looked at it and looked again, made out as it of course was to Scotty Schneider.

For an instant, Herman raised an eyebrow at Fritz Schneider on his, then grinned. "The Kate would have a cat fit, if she could see."

"Yeah, but," I still was seeing trouble, "what are we going to do with these? I mean, since they're not in our real names, isn't it forgery or something to cash them?"

"Ja, probably," he met that crime with the usual salute. "But no choice do we have if we want our money." Seeing that this didn't reassure me one least bit, he tried a lighter approach. "One more name maybe can't hurt, Red Chief."

"You're the one who made us into Schneiders," I reminded him shrilly.

"*Scotty*," he bore down on the word, "calm down some, please. All is not lost. Maybe they do not ask any too much questions in Watering Hole. Isn't that how they do in the West?"

"It still feels to me like something against the law," I muttered.

"Hah. Add to the list," said the most wanted man in the Big Hole.

GOING TO TOWN on a Saturday night meant spiffing up, baths having been taken in a galvanized tub filled from buckets on the stove—we cut cards for first water, and Midnight Frankie with mysterious inevitability won the right to squat and bathe in the clean tubful with the rest of us to follow in the increasingly gray bathwater. Now what passed for town clothes had been dug out, clean shirts and hair slickum so prevalent on the crew it was remindful of kids dressed up for the first day of school. Herman was the true fashion plate, sporting the mermaid tie, which drew winks and remarks about what he was fishing for with it. My rodeo shirt, somewhat faded and showing wear from its summer of long bus rides and strenuous occasions, was the best I could do, but I was trying to buff my stubble-scuffed shoes into respectability when I happened to notice that my moccasins were not where I kept them beneath the foot of my bunk.

Alarmed, I scrambled down onto hands and knees to search under the bed, but they were definitely missing.

Seeing me down there on all fours looking stricken, Herman caught on immediately. Jumping to his feet from his bunk, he shook the bunkhouse rafters with the outcry "Someone is thief! Scotty's moccasins is gone. I thought Johnson family does not take from its own."

Everything stopped. Skeeter and Pooch and Midnight Frankie and Shakespeare and Fingy and Harv halted in mid-motion at whatever they were doing, their eyes cutting to one another for some kind of answer to Herman's charge. It was bad luck that Highpockets had gone out to make sure with Jones that the crew would have a goodly amount of time to carouse in town, leaving Peerless to niggle at the moccasin matter as Herman stood there with clenched fists. "Now, now, don't get carried away, One Eye. Maybe them slippers just got misplaced. What makes you think any of us—"

"WAHHOO!" resounded from the crapper, and as we all jerked around in that direction, Smiley came prancing out, wearing only his shorts with a towel tucked in like an Indian loincloth, and my moccasins.

The spectacle was as grotesque as it was unexpected, his big belly jiggling over the scanty loincloth and his stark bony bad leg stuck out stiff, as if he were half tub of lard and half stick figure. Poking two fingers up behind his head like feathers, he cavorted around in a crazy lopsided dance, the beautiful beadwork fancy-dancers captive on his big feet with him warhooping and bellowing, "Wampum night! Hot time in town! Big chief Geronimo hitting the warpath!"

At first too stunned to do anything, the next thing I knew I had let out a howl of my own and launched into Smiley, grabbing him at the knees. Herman was right behind me, jamming him against the wall as I tried to wrest the moccasins off.

"Hey, don't you know entertainment?" Smiley croaked out, struggling against Herman's grasp. He was a large and fleshy man, almost too much for the two of us, but we heard Peerless warn the others of the crew, "Better stay out of it, this isn't any of our business."

"I'm making it mine," Harv's voice reverberated, or at least I felt it so. In no time the bigger, better-muscled man had Smiley squashed so tight against the wall he couldn't even squirm, as Herman lifted one of his feet like the hoof of a horse and I stripped the moccasin off, and we did the same on the other foot.

Right then coming through the bunkhouse doorway to be met by the three of us grappling with the various parts of the nearly naked Smiley, Highpockets let out, "What in tunket is going on?"

"High jinks of the wrong kind," drawled Harv.

"Joke not funny one least little bit," Herman attested.

"The dickhead swiped my moccasins," I made the matter clear.

"You're the crappiest audience I ever been around," Smiley complained, yanking the towel out from the vicinity of his private parts. "Hell, I was only trying to draw a laugh, get everybody in the mood for town."

"Ye dumb damn piece of maggot bait," Skeeter piped up. "Don'tcha know better than to put your meat hooks on somebody else's property in a kip like this? People've been knifed for less than that. Ain't I right, One Eye?"

Taking the cue, Herman drew down the eyelid over his glass eye and thrust a hand into his pants pocket as if fondling something there besides lint, sounding amazingly menacing in uttering, "Lost count of stitches I have *schneidered*, ja."

"Gramps means he's next thing to a killer," I furthered the bluff, rewarded by seeing the ex-clown's fat red face drain of color until it matched his lardy body.

"Nobody told me he packs a shiv," Smiley whined.

Highpockets took all this in and restored order. "Everybody shape up or Jones won't let us off the place. Throw some clothes on," he bossed Smiley, even though the choreboy did not belong to the hobo contingent, "and let's get to town."

THE RIDE INTO WISDOM was a carefully spaced truce, with Smiley hunkered broodily near the tailgate and Herman and me with our backs against the pickup cab and everyone else between as a buffer, and the miles down the valley of green haystacks passed as agreeably as a picnic outing, the soft and warm summer evening a rare pleasure for men who roughed it in the weathers of hobo life. Naturally Jones drove like the pickup was on fire, and quickly enough the little town made itself known, beer signs glowing in most colors of the rainbow at the Watering Hole, and the milk-white false front of the mercantile standing out in the dusk. Additionally, there were a couple of sheepwagons that hadn't been there before, prominent now in the vacant lot between the saloon and the gas station. Fingy was the nearest of our bunch to me and I asked in curiosity, "What're those doing here? I thought this was cattle country."

"It's where, ehh, some salesladies from Butte set up shop on Saturday nights," he answered delicately, and at least I knew enough not to ask what they were selling.

Jones pulled in right at the swinging doors of the Watering Hole. As the crew filed into the joint, joshing and laughing, I held back, uncertain. Herman had no such hesitation.

"Wages, remember, Mr. Scotty Schneider?" he said firmly, guiding me with his hand on my back to the entrance to I didn't know what.

THE WATERING HOLE inside stopped the two of us in our tracks, maybe even thrust us back a step and much farther than that in remembering. Festooned with lariat ropes and leather reins draped in graceful arcs from the ceiling and the side wall hung end to end with bridles and harness and tacked-up ten-gallon hats beyond their days and even angora chaps reminiscent of the leggings I had worn in the fancy-dancing exhibition, the ageless old saloon was like a western dryland cousin of the Schooner, back in Manitowoc. Herman made it official with the exclamation, "Is like home!"

As the crew trooped to the long bar, Skeeter by seniority took the lead, comically doffing his hat and holding it over his heart as he addressed the woman of about Gram's age standing ready at the cash register. "If it ain't Babs, my favoritest bartender in all of Creation."

"My, my, if it don't look like they let the rogues' gallery loose," she bantered back. "How's tricks, Skeets?" Spotting the Diamond Buckle hatband on him and the rest of us, she let out a teasing hoot. "Oh ho ho, fellas, you've come up in the world."

"We like to think so." The Jersey Mosquito dropped his hat on the bar to claim his drinking spot as the rest of the crew settled onto bar stools like a flock of birds alighting. "And just to prove it, tune up your cash register, Babs honey, we have got checks galore to cash."

"Again this year," the bespectacled bartender sighed, "fancy that." She fussed with her cash register, lifting out the coin drawer entirely for the fat stash of cash underneath. "Okeydoke, high rollers, the First National Bank of Babs is now open."

Herman still was gazing affectionately around at the saloon trappings, but I watched furtively as Pooch slipped his paycheck to Highpockets to endorse for him, recalling Skeeter's admonition on the last bus that certain people's education did not necessarily include reading and writing. Well, hell, that told me, if forgery was in the works we weren't the only ones, and I got on line with Herman close behind me.

Only to have the bartender pin my check to the bar with an unyielding hand before I could endorse it. "Uh-uh, not so fast." She peered at me through her wire-rim glasses. "What's the story here, Pockets, you taken on a mascot these days?"

"Our stacker driver," Highpockets right away spoke up for me, with Skeeter pitching in, "I's his age when I hit the road, so that just goes to show you he's a functionin' employee."

She was unmoved. "By rights, I'm not supposed to allow kids in here, let alone be shoveling money to them."

"Hey," I tried indignantly, "I'm thirteen." Herman nodded maybe too vigorously in backing that up.

"And I'm the Queen of Romania. Sorry, sonny, but I can't accommodate you."

"Aw, cut him a break, Babs, he's with us," Highpockets stuck up for me in the good name of the Johnson family insofar as that existed.

"Pockets, I can only cash checks for paying customers or I'd be bankering for the whole town right down to the dogs and cats."

"Nothing to worry," Herman asserted with the smack of a hand on the bar so loud everyone jumped a little. "Bar maiden, enough business for us both and then some, I will give you."

The bar maiden, gray-haired as could be, smirked with pleasure at the compliment, intended or otherwise. "You sound like you mean business, sure enough, buster," she allowed, looking him over from the mermaid tie to his strong eyeglasses that pretty much matched hers. "All right, everybody saw the miracle, the flower of youth here grew up while we were watching." She lifted her hand off my paycheck with the freeing instruction: "Dab your name on it and hand it over."

Fingers mentally crossed, I wrote *Scotty Schneider* on the back of the check. The bartender did not even look at the signature, simply stashed it in the cash register with the others and counted out my wages in nice green bills. "Here you go, angel."

Angel. That was a new one.

As I soaked that in, she cashed Herman's check the same way she'd done mine, and suddenly we were flush with money of the sort we had not seen since the fingersmith preacher robbed us. Herman now was in the best of moods, twirling his finger double speed at his temple as if strenuous thinking were required for the big decision he was making.

"Guess what, Scotty. I am having a schooner, hah"—he cocked his eye at the line of spigots along the bar with blazoned handles that were a far cry from the labels of the multiple beers of Great Lakes ports, but indisputably promised the same intoxicant—"to celebrate that we are haymakers, got the smackers to prove it." He dropped his voice. "And no posters of Killer Boy Dillinger out easy to be seen, I watched buildings careful on way in. Saving my neck, the Big Hole is." He grinned triumphantly. "Drink to that, let us."

Signaling the bartender from where she was busy setting up glasses of beer for the rest of the crew, he sunnily included me. "You want bottle of Crushed Orange, I betcha."

"Not now, maybe later." I had been weighing watching people guzzle beer against what was nagging at me, and conscience was winning out. "What I need to do is go call Gram. I haven't for a while, and Jones doesn't like me doing it at the ranch."

Herman shooed me toward the swinging doors. "Go, do. I will hold fort here."

AS I WAS PRETTY sure of, the Wisdom store had an arrangement common to mercantiles in those days before telephones were everywhere, a nook in the back where a wall phone was available along with an egg timer, so you could pay for the length of your call on your way out.

The familiar hum of distance, the suppressed ring at the other end, which always went on for a long time at the Columbus Hospital pavilion ward, until some busy nun set aside a bedpan or some other ministration for the nuisance of the phone, as I imagined it. Then Sister Carma Jean, who by now was getting used to my calls, briskly told me Gram would be there in a minute.

When Gram promptly came on and sounded like her old self in declaring she'd been waiting for me to call so she could share the nicest conceivable surprise with me, she skipped right past my hello to go right to her news. "I'm up and around and helping in the kitchen. Between you and me, nuns are terrible cooks."

"Jeez, Gram," my voice topped out in relief, "that's really terrif—"

"That's not the surprise, though," she busted right in as if the other news wouldn't keep. "You'll never guess who I've heard from." She could not have been more right about that. "Letty. She called me from Glasgow in her new job there."

I was boggled by that, the entire picture of the lipstick-implanted bus encounter scrambled in my head. "What happened to Havre?"

"A boss who pinched her bottom one time too many. Like once. Donny, why in heaven's name didn't you tell me in one of your letters you met up with her on the dog bus?"

"Uhm, I had a lot I was trying to get in the letters"—utterly true—"and must have missed out on that somehow."

"She thinks the world of you, anyway. Said you were real good company riding the bus together." My pride started to swell at that, but Gram was not nearly done spilling the surprise. "She's working at the Glasgow Supper Club now. Here's even better news. She can get me on as night cook."

"In *Glasgow*?" I asked dumbly. "Just like that?"

"Didn't I say so?" she retorted, as if I'd better wash out my ears. More of me than that needed clearing to hold what she said next.

"I know it's different country over there for us and we'd rather be on a ranch"—her voice turned honestly dubious for a moment—"but we'll have to tough through it. Letty and I have things worked out. There's an apartment right by hers. When you get home from Aunt Kate's for school, we'll be together under one roof. Doesn't that beat all?"

Yes, *no*, and *maybe* fought over that in me. There it was, imagination more or less come true, Letty embossed into our patchy family as niftily as the name on her blouse. And even better yet, maybe Harv, too, except he was a wanted man there in the jurisdiction of that snotty little sheriff. By and large, Gram's report was the jackpot of my wishes, but also a king hell dilemma. The best I could manage into the receiver was, "That's—that's really some news."

"You sound like the air has been knocked out of you," Gram said, perfectly pleased. "I can't wait to see you again—you'll have so much to tell me about your adventures back east there, won't you." Not if I could help it. "Donny? I think it'd be only fair if I let your Aunt Kate know how peachy the summer is working out, thanks to you being there with her and Dutch, don't you? Call her to the phone, pretty please."

"She's, uh, taking a bath," panic spoke for me. "She does that every night before bed. Boy, is she ever clean."

"I guess you'll have to tell her for me," Gram resumed. "Anyway, when the doctor turns me loose for good any day now and Letty helps me get established in that apartment and you can come home whenever you want, I'd like the great Kate to know how much your stay there has meant."

"Oh yeah, she'll know."

I PAID the merc clerk for the phone call and traipsed the darkened street of Wisdom back to the Watering Hole, weighed down with feelings that did not match up. Unspeakably relieved and glad though I was that Gram was herself again, nonetheless that emotion was shot through with remorse, already halfway to longing, for all I would be abandoning at the Diamond Buckle ranch and the Big Hole. The honest-to-goodness genuine job as haystack teamster. The bunkhouse hoboes who, in their coarse generous way, had taken me into the Johnson family right there on the last bus to Wisdom and ever since. The prestige of being a ranch hand for Rags Rasmussen, a source of pride I knew I would carry with me all my life.

Against those hard-won rewards, I now was free almost any time to go and be with Gram and Letty as well, a dream ready to come true. But only if I paid up with either deceit or confession about my time on the loose. Did I dare to simply show up in Glasgow, shiny as the silver greyhound forever fleet on the side of the bus, and start spinning extravagant tales about how terrific my summer in

Manitowoc had been? That felt treacherous. The truth had a nasty habit of coming out. At least sometimes.

Before any of that, however, dead ahead through the swinging doors of Wisdom's sole saloon was the matter of Herman. It was only fair to let him know I'd have to leave him sooner than later, wasn't it? Hadn't he brought it up himself, back there in the bunkhouse? So why was part of me wrestling so hard against telling him, at least yet?

THE ATMOSPHERE in the Watering Hole had turned very beery in my absence, the crew doing its best to drink the place dry in record time. Babs was behind in clearing away empty glasses as she filled fresh ones and scooted them along the bar to the hobo lineup laughing uproariously at some limerick Shakespeare had just composed. I was surprised to see two empties in front of Herman already, plus the one becoming that way in a hurry as he drank with lip-smacking gusto. Elbow to elbow with him there at the quieter end of the bar, Pooch was working on his latest golden schoonerful in his dim, deliberate way.

"Scotty!" Herman let out, as if we hadn't seen each other for ages. "Welcome back to Watering Hole, such a place. How is the *Grossmutter*?"

"Up and around," I hedged.

"Good, good. What a woman she is. Time for Crushed Orange, hah, to celebrate her recupery."

At his arm-waving signal, Babs worked her way along the bar to us and produced a bottle of Orange Crush for me, along with the announcement:

"Make way, boys, you got company. Here comes the Tumbling T crew."

Just as rowdy and ready for moonhowling as our bunch, the newcomers swarmed in and established themselves along the other end of the bar, brandishing their paychecks. There was no mistaking who was the Big Ole of this contingent of hoboes turned haymakers. The Tumbling T's leader was nearly Highpockets's height, but could not have been built more differently, with what's called a cracker butt, nothing back there as if that share of the anatomy had gone onto the front in his hanging belly. He turned out to be a boxcar acquaintance of the Jersey Mosquito, who called out to the Tumbling T's main man, "Deacon! You old sidewinder, c'mon over here and pretend you're social."

"Still pestering the world same as ever, are you, Skeeter." Deacon barked a laugh as he joined him. Quick as anything, he spotted the Diamond Buckle hatband on Skeeter's battered headgear. "But what's this?" His laugh became nastier. "You let the rancher slap his brand on you these days? What's next, holding hands and singalongs on the old rancheria?"

Overhearing, Highpockets said with cold control, "Rasmussen just likes to show off that world championship he won the hard way. I'd say he's entitled."

"If it don't bother you to have the boss's loop around your brain," Deacon responded with a slick smile, "it's no nevermind to me. Where's your hospitality, Skeeter, I could use a drink."

While that touchy reunion of sorts was going on, I sipped at my pop, pretty much matching Herman's and Pooch's downings of beer, while conscience worked me over from one direction and then another. I felt I couldn't hold Gram's news to myself, even though I hated to let it out, either. But driven to it at a more or less decisive moment, I mustered myself as much as I was able. "Herm—I mean, Gramps—I need to talk to you about something."

"Has to wait, please," he said, somewhere in another world as he hoisted his glass for an appreciative sip. "Pooch and me, we got big thoughts to think. Don't we, podner."

"Damn straight," Pooch said mechanically.

"Yeah, but I really need to tell you—"

"Saturday night is to howl," Herman formulated as if it had come from Longfellow. "And lucky us, here we are, south of the moon, hah?"

He shut me down with such a fond grin—for me, for the decorated saloon so much like the Schooner, for the company of our hobo pals—that I did not have the heart to tear him away. There are times when mercy cancels anything else.

AS HE AND POOCH lapsed back into their mute pleasure of imbibing, I tried to clear my head by seeing what else Saturday night in the Watering Hole had to offer, and it was then that I began to catch the drift of the Jersey Mosquito's earnest jawboning of the Tumbling T boss hobo.

"Haven't seen you since we was in that boxcar on the Ma and Pa"—the Maryland and Pennsylvania Railroad in hobo nomenclature—"and that Baltimore yard bull came callin' with a billy club in one hand and handcuffs in the other. I swear, Deac, never saw a man bail out the other side of a boxcar as fast as you. Left me to deal with that railroad dick by my lonesome, you sonofagun."

"Survival of the fastest," Deacon stated his philosophy smugly. The two of them batted boasts and put-downs back and forth like that until Skeeter sprung the trap I realized he had been baiting all along.

"I'm telling ye, Deacon, I know you think you're a helluva drinkin' man. But we got a fella who puts you to shame when it comes to lickin' a glass. Our man here can take the least leetle sip of anythin' captured in a bottle and tell you just exactly what it is."

"Skeets, you're so full of it your eyes are turning brown," Deacon dismissed that boast with a laugh.

"By the grace of whatever ain't unholy, I swear it's true, Deac,"

Skeeter persisted. “Seen him do it with my own two eyes.” Sensing a chance to hold forth, Peerless had moved in and backed that with “I’m a witness to that my own self. Damnedest stunt since Jesus turned ditchwater into muscatel.”

His interest piqued now in spite of himself, the Tumbling T haymaker peered along the bar at our crew carrying on in Saturday night fashion. “Where’s this miracle of nature you’re bragging up?”

“Sittin’ right there, answerin’ to the name of One Eye.” Skeeter pointed a skeletal finger toward Herman.

Deacon followed that up with a dubious look, then the even more skeptical inquiry to Herman. “So you’re this hipper-dipper sipper who can identify every beer this side of horse piss, huh?”

Herman drew himself up with pride. “Is true.”

“Tell ye what we’re gonna do, Deac,” Skeeter followed right on the heels of that, “if you got any guts left in that stewpot belly of yours. We’ll bet that our fella here can have a swig of any of these”—the sweep of his arm indicated the line of beer spigots half the length of the bar—“let’s say, oh, half a dozen just to make it sporting, and tell you like that”—a snap of his fingers like a starter’s gun going off—“whatevery by God one is, without him knowing aforehand.”

Deacon took another look at Herman, who gave him back a vague horsy grin and drained his glass as if in challenge, and it all of a sudden occurred to me just how many glasses he’d emptied. “Hey, though, he’s already had—” I tried to warn Skeeter, but Deacon overrode me with the shrewd conclusion, “Beer gets to be plain old beer the more you drink of it. What do you think, boys? Shall we call this windjammer’s bluff?”

That brought cries of “Hell, yeah!” and “I’m in!” from the Tumbling T crew.

“This suit you okay?” Highpockets shouldered in to make sure with Herman.

"Ja, betsa bootsies," said Herman with a wink at me, which I found alarmingly woozy. "Suits me to a T Tumbler!" he ambitiously tried a joke.

"Babs, set him up six of the Montana brews, shot glasses only," Deacon directed. "We don't want him swilling the stuff long enough to get familiar with it. The Muskeeter here claims he only needs a first swig anyway."

"STOP WITH EVERYTHING!"

Herman had resoundingly slapped a hand on the bar in a manner that indeed did slam the proceedings to a halt. Gesturing in rather grand fashion at the long line of beer spigots as everyone watched wide-eyed, he elucidated, "Not all of these wild woolly brewings am I acquainted with. Samples first, please, bar maiden."

Immediately Deacon was suspiciously accusing Skeeter and Highpockets of trying to pull a fast one by having our man wet his whistle too familiarly before the real taste test, while they hotly argued back that the man was new to Montana and it was essential to the bet for him to learn Babs's stock first so he'd have comparisons to go on. I could not deny the logic—even Pooch delivered "Damn straight" in recognition of it—but was leery of how much more beer Herman was taking aboard before the drinks that counted. I did not even know enough then to have the bigger worry, that in the era when almost every Montana city had its own brewery, the brewers almost to a man were of German origin, leading to a certain sameness of product. It had been nearly thirty years since Herman was testing steins of beer in Munich; did his sense of taste have that much memory of the Germanic tricks of the trade, such as they were?

We were about to find out, because Deacon and his side grudgingly gave in, and Babs, smiling to herself at all the fresh commerce, set up half a dozen shot glasses. As she named off each beer, I as our chosen representative in this—Highpockets was firm that Herman savvied me better than anyone else and we wanted no monkey business in making the individual beers known to him—wrote each on a cash register slip and put it facedown under the respective brew. Highlander, out of Missoula. Kessler from Helena. Great Falls Select. The beer from Butte, baldly named Butte Beer. Billings Yellowstone Brew. Anaconda Avalanche Ale.

Unsteady but unconcerned, Herman winked at me with his glass eye, wrapped a hand around the first shot glass, unleashed the toast "The Devil's eyedrops cure sorrow!" and lifted the Great Fall Select to his lips.

Eyes half-shut in concentration as I called out the name of each one, he sipped his way through the preliminary beers. When he was done and jovially declared that Montana beer at least was better than the product of any horse, as quick as the laughter died down Skeeter flapped some money under Deacon's nose and flopped it down on the bar as the start of the pot. "Now, about them bets, if ye haven't lost your nerve."

EXPERIENCE SOMETIMES lives up to its reputation as a teacher. From my time of hanging around the Double W bunkhouse and its card sharks, I was keeping an eye on Midnight Frankie. When he stayed perfectly poker-faced but flipped a nice fresh twenty-dollar bill into the pot—a lot of money, on our wages—saying, "Let's get some skin in the game," I tremblingly stroked the arrowhead pouch for luck and dug out twenty dollars from the front of my pants and secured the same from Herman's change lying on the bar without him noticing. Nor was I the only one following Midnight Frankie's lead. Highpockets thumbed out the sum with the declaration "I'm in for a double sawbuck, too," and Harv, thinking it over for a moment, silently did the same, followed in quick succession by Peerless, Shakespeare, Fingy, and Pooch.

"There's our chunk of the jackpot, Deacon," Skeeter crowed in challenge. "Decorate the mahogany or say uncle."

Faced with our crew's total backing of Herman, the Tumbling T outfit looked uneasily at one another, but when Deacon demanded, "C'mon, don't let this gang of broken-down blanket stiffs buffalo us," they all matched our bets. Just like that, nearly three hundred dollars lay in a green pile on the bar.

"All right, One Eye, hoist 'em and name 'em off," Skeeter led the roof-raising chorus of encouragement from our side. But before Babs could move to the taps to repeat the beers, Deacon stopped her and everything else with a shrill two-fingered whistle, evidently a hobo signal for something like stop, look, and listen.

In the immediate silence, the Tumbling T chieftain swelled up with the full attention he had drawn and sprang his demand. "Nothing against PeeWee here"—that again! I could have been put on trial for the murderous look I gave him—"but I want to handle them shot glasses and slips of paper myself, starting behind there at the taps. Just so there's no wrong impression of anything funny taking place along the way. You mind, Babs?"

The bartender backed away to lean against her cash register. "Since whichever bunch of you wins that jackpot is going to pay full price for shot glasses of beer, you can keep on all night for all I care."

Highpockets checked with Herman, who replied that as far as he was concerned, any fool who wanted to could pour the beer. Establishing himself at the taps, Deacon made a big deal of drawing the six small glasses of beer, as I hung over the bar watching to make sure he assigned the right slip of paper to each one. Then he arranged the setup on the bar, five glasses in a row in front of Herman with one held back, the hole card, so to speak, so Herman could not figure out the final sample by process of elimination. "We'll let him off with five out of six, if I have the option of switching this one in"—Deacon peeked secretively at the slip under it—"so he don't pull some memorization trick on us. Fair enough?"

Skeeter and Highpockets mulled over the proposition but could see nothing wrong with it, while Herman pitty-patted the bar impatiently to start the tasting. It was agreed that as Herman named off the brand of beer, I would read out its slip of paper to verify he had it right, or heaven and earth forbid, he didn't. With a flourish, Deacon mixed around the shot glasses, along with their accompanying slips, to his contentment and the great drink contest got underway.

Reciting "Ready on right, ready on left, ready on firing line!" in soldierly fashion, Herman reached for the first slug of beer, swilled it briefly before swallowing, and declared, "Bee-yoot!" which I verified as the Butte brew. "Attaway, One Eye!" and "Show 'em what the Diamond Buckle stands for!" came the shouts of encouragement from our crew, while the Tumbling T outfit groaned in disbelief.

So it went, down the line, each beer identified correctly at the first sip, until there stood the last two shot glasses, the one Deacon was holding back and the other resting in front of Herman.

Grinning tipsily but still in command of himself, he threw the challenge to Deacon. "Which one is to tickle my tonsils?"

"You're lucky so far," Deacon said sourly, "but let's see if that luck ain't due to run out about now." So saying, he switched the hole-card shot glass in for the other one.

This beer I couldn't even guess at. A darker, foamy brew than the others, it had to be either Yellowstone Brew or Avalanche Ale, but with everything riding on Herman's final feat of swilling a mouthful and identifying it, fifty-fifty odds all of a sudden didn't seem anything like a cinch. But quite nonchalantly, he raised the shot glass, said, "Bottoms upside," and in one motion swigged the mystery beer.

To my alarm, he chugged it too much, more of it going down him than the other beers had. Not for long, because what was left in his mouth he spewed onto the bar, his face contorted. Gagging and trying to speak, he was making a *k-k-k* sound like a car trying to start on a cold morning, as our crew watched in horror, me most of all. Whatever was wrong with him was calamity enough, but I could also see a major portion of our wages about to vanish in front of our eyes.

"Told you," Deacon crowed as he moved along the bar toward the pot. "Wore out his gullet after so many beers. Let's have that money and we'll even buy you a consolation round, Pockets." He couldn't hide his smirk.

"Herman, what is it?" I quavered as he kept trying to work his throat. "What's wrong?" Not knowing what else to do, I slammed him across the top of his back with my open hand as hard as I could.

The blow must have loosened up something somehow. "C-c-c-cough drop," he spluttered, pointing shakily at the offending shot glass.

"Deacon, you cheating bastard." Highpockets caught on to the dodge ahead of the rest of us, but not by much. "Grab him." Harv already had accomplished that, locking the protesting Deacon to his chest from behind as casually as gathering an armful of hay. "Frisk him good," Highpockets ordered, with Midnight Frankie and Shakespeare quick on the job.

Into sight came an orange box bearing the words OLD RECIPE MENTHOL COUGH DROPS LEMON FLAVOR.

"I'd say you just forfeited, Deacon," Highpockets pronounced, while I did my best to attend to Herman as he stayed bent over the bar, wheezing and still trying to clear his voice box.

"Can't you take a joke?" Deacon squawked in Harv's steely grip. "Let's call it a draw and just scrap the bet."

"Draw, my rosy-red butt." That brought Peerless into it in full mode. "You can't pull a fast one like that and crawl out of it like a snake on ice."

His Tumbling T equivalent argued right back. "Hey, your fella tumbled to the cough drop, but he never did name the beer. So by rights, we win the bet."

"Tell it in church, ye whistledick," the Jersey Mosquito put a stop to this. "We're claimin' the pot fair and square," he declared, whipping off his hat and scooping the pile of money into it. Then with surprising agility, he hoisted his bony old rump onto the bar, swung his legs over as the Tumbling T gang made futile grabs at him and Babs screeched a protest, and disappeared down among beer barrels and such, clutching the hatful of cash to him.

That set off general mayhem.

Each crew charged at the other, swearing and squaring off. Harv seemed to be in his element, flooring one Tumbling T opponent with a roundhouse punch and taking on the next without drawing a breath. Fingy and Pooch between them were fending with a burly member of the other crew. As befitted their leadership positions, Highpockets and Deacon singled each other out, locked together in a revolving grapple along the length of the bar that sent beer glasses shattering and stools tumbling like dominoes. Peerless and Midnight Frankie and Shakespeare each were honorably engaged in tussles of their own with Tumbling T bettors yowling for their money back.

Amidst the battle royal I saw Babs pull out a pool stick sawed off to the right length to make a good club and start around the end of the bar to put it to use.

Taking that as a signal this was getting serious, I tugged at Herman for us to clear out of there. Blinking his good eye at the melee around him, he resisted my pulling, saying thickly, "Wait, Donny. Oops, Scotty. You know who I mean. Let's don't go, I have to help fellas fight."

"Nothing doing. You've had your war," I gritted out, and hauled at him with all my might, yanking him off the bar stool in the direction of the door. In my death grip on his arm, he stumbled after me as we skinned along the bar, ducking and dodging swinging fists and reeling bodies as much as we could, out into the street to where the pickup was parked, and got him seated on the running board. "Don't move," I said. "Sing a song, say poetry, do something."

"Good eye-dea," he said dreamily, and began to recite the rhyme we fashioned on the last bus:

When you take a look in your memory book
Here you will find the lasting kind,
Old rhymes and new, life in review,
Roses in the snow of long ago.

Lovely sentiments, but I had to leave him deposited there while I raced off to the mercantile, on the chance Jones might still be in there buying groceries. I couldn't help looking wildly this way and that along the moonlit street of Wisdom, hoping that the deputy sheriff would not choose now to pay the hoboes another visit.

As I burst into the store, Jones glanced around in surprise from chucking an armload of loaves of bread onto the counter while the storekeeper kept tally. Before he could ask what my rush was, I stammered, "The fellas are ready to go back to the ranch."

"What, they drank the town dry already? Pretty close to a new record, I'd say." He turned away to grab boxes of macaroni off a shelf. "Tell them I'll be there by the time they can piss the beer out of theirselves. I'm not stopping every two minutes on the way to the ranch so somebody can take a leak."

"Uhm, if you could hurry. They're sort of in a fight. With the Tumbling T crew."

Jones swore blue sparks into the air, instructed the storekeeper to load the groceries in the pickup, and took off at a high run for the bar, with me trying to keep up.

"STOP IT!" he roared before he was even half through the swinging doors. "Or I'll see to it that every one of you sonofabitches of both outfits is fired and your asses run out of town before morning!"

That put a halt to everything, except a belated "Yow!" from Peerless, who had received the latest whack from Babs's pool stick. Sitting on Deacon's chest, where he had him pinned to the floor, Highpockets looked down at his adversary. "Your call."

Deacon squirmed as much as he could, very little, then managed to turn his head toward Jones. "Since you put it that way, we're peaceable."

"Us, too," Highpockets agreed, climbing off him. "You heard what the man said, boys. Let's take our winnings and evaporate out of here. Right, Skeeter?" He whirled around, looking in every corner. "SKEETER? Where the hell did he and that hatful of money go?"

The Jersey Mosquito popped up from behind the far end of the bar, grinning devilishly and holding the upside-down hat as if it were a pot of gold. "Just bein' our Fort Knox till you fellas got done socializin'. See you on the Ma and Pa sometime, Deacon," he called over his shoulder as he scampered out of the bar to jump in the back of the pickup.

FOLLOWING HIS LEAD, laughing and hooting like schoolboys, the Diamond Buckle crew piled into the box of the pickup, Jones counting us with chops of a hand like you do sheep. He came up one short. "Who's missing?"

Skeeter giggled. "Smiley, natcherly."

"He cut out of the saloon through the back door soon as his check was cashed," Peerless testified. "Wouldn't even stay and have one drink with us, the stuck-up bugger."

"Then where the hell is the knothead?"

Silence. Until Skeeter further provided:

"Gettin' his ashes hauled."

That puzzled me but not Herman, who let out a wild drunken

laugh. Revelation came when Highpockets swiped a hand toward the sheepwagons where the salesladies had set up shop.

Jones checked his watch. "Ever since we hit town, the sonofabitch has been at it? That don't take forever."

"More's the pity," said Shakespeare, to stifled laughs from the hobo audience.

Catching a second wind of swearing, Jones clambered into the driver's seat, saying the goddamn fornicator could walk back to the ranch with his pants around his ankles, for all he cared.

THE RIDE to the Diamond Buckle was riotous, as fight stories were traded on their way into legend. You would have thought the Watering Hole was the Little Bighorn, and our crew was the victorious Indians. Better yet, under the watchful eye of Highpockets the jackpot winnings were being counted out by Skeeter, hunched over so the cash would not blow out of his hat and carefully holding up greenbacks one by one in the moonlight to determine whether they were sawbucks or twenties, doling out the proceeds of the bet evenly among us. Fingy clutched his with all eight fingers as if he could not believe his good fortune. Pooch burst into more words than he ordinarily issued in a week: "First time we ever come back from town with more moolah than we went in with."

"Hee hee, stick with me and I'll have you boys livin' on the plush," Skeeter took all due credit. He judiciously handed a fistful of money to me instead of Herman, slumped against the back of the pickup cab singing softly to himself in German. "Here be your and his share, Snag."

For a long wonderful moment I clutched the winnings in triumph. Then, grinning back at the moon over the Promised Land that was the Big Hole, I stuck the folded bills down the front of my pants for safety.

. . .

THE CREW hit the bunkhouse still high as kites, but mostly from exuberance rather than what they had poured into themselves at the Watering Hole. The chilly ride in the back of the pickup had even sobered up Herman appreciably, so much so that he made it to his bunk without my help. He sank onto it, rubbing his head with both hands as if to get things operating fully in there. "Big night, hah?" he said thickly, blinking at me as I proudly patted the wad of cash pouched down there in my underwear. "How much did we winned?"

"Enough to get married on," Harv's serene answer took care of that, from where he was already fixing up an envelope to mail his windfall to Letty. The rest of the crew all were in the crapper at once, oddly enough. It sounded like some kind of hobo palaver going on in there, maybe something mysteriously connected to Skeeter's ability to generate a jackpot. Pretty quick, Highpockets could be heard checking with the bunch one by one—"You for it?"—and the answering "Yeahs!" and "Yups!"

They filed into the bunk room like men with a mission, Highpockets in the lead, the others crowding behind him with a mix of expressions, from Skeeter's crinkled countenance to Shakespeare looking wise to Pooch wearing an anxious attempt at a grin.

"The Johnson family has had a little powwow," Highpockets announced as the hoboes gathered around us. "One Eye, we're hoping you can stick with us after haying. Wheat country next, threshing out in Washington." His gaze shifted to me. "Snag is welcome to come along, too, if that's in the cards."

Herman was unable to say anything for some seconds. "Honored, I am," he finally got out. "Good eye-dea, for me." He struggled even more for the next words. "The boy"—he swallowed so hard that it brought an awful lump to my throat, too—"has somebody to go to."

"Any way you two work it out," Highpockets left it at and turned away. "Let's hit the sack, boys. Jones will be on a tear in the morning to make us earn those wages."

NOW HERMAN and I adjourned to the crapper. He put a steadying hand on the sink and studied his somewhat haggard reflection in the mirror, my drained one alongside his.

"Donny, it is for best if I go with them. When haying is over, no more sickles, and I am *pttt ht* here."

"I know."

"Will miss you like everything."

"Me, too. I mean, I—I'll miss you, too." It took all I could do to stay dry-eyed and keep my voice from breaking. "Walk tall, podner."

"You do same," he managed. Tall over me, he looked down at me, the miraculous glass eye and the good one blinking with the same emotion as mine. "We were good pair on the loose, Red Chief."

AMID THE SETTLED snores and nose-whistlings of the sleeping crew, I lay sleepless for a long, long time, as haunted as I'd been by that damnable plaque in Aunt Kate's attic. This time by life, not death. For the first time since the Double W cookhouse I whined, only to myself, but the silent kind is as mournful as the other. The miles upon miles of my summer, the immense Greyhound journey right down to the last bus to Wisdom, were simply leaving me torn in two, between Herman and Gram. She and Letty seemed like, what, mirages, distant and beckoning, but Herman had been my indispensable partner, from the depths of the Manitowoc stay to the ups and downs of the open road.

Imagination failed me as I tried to conceive of life without him, or his without me. How can you ever forget someone you will think of every time you eat a piece of toast? Or whenever you touch a map, your fingers bringing memory of red routes once followed to adventure of whatever kind? Or even catching the wink of an eye, sparkling as glass, from someone you are devoted to?

As bereft as I was for myself, I was just as afraid for what waited ahead for him, on the move with the hoboes and on the run at the same time, always with the threat of some yard bull or hick dick matching him up with a MOST WANTED poster, and without me and my tall tales there to rescue him.

As for counting on luck to help us out of our divided fate, phooey and you-know-what. In my misery I felt I might as well throw the black arrowhead into the Big Hole River. The cheerful sentiments in the autograph book seemed sickly against the true messages of life. Loco things happened without rhyme or reason, and that was that. The most hard-hearted set of words in the language, and the only ones that seemed to count in the end. Overwhelmed with these bleak thoughts, I gradually drowsed off, clinging to what I would possess forever, the time of dog bus enchantment when Herman the German pointed a finger west and said, "Thataway."

30.

IN THE BIG HOLE, there was something to the saying that when it rains, it pours, because sometime later that night, the heavens opened up, one of those sudden summer storms that flash through with crackles of lightning and rolls of thunder half drowned out by the downpour drumming on the roof. And the next morning came the deluge of the other sort, events cascading on the Diamond Buckle ranch as if the clouds had brought in every reckoning waiting to happen.

It began at breakfast, where black coffee was the main course as hangovers were nursed. I was groggy myself from the restless night of rainbursts and so much on my mind. Along the table, Skeeter had the shakes so bad he used both hands to lift his coffee cup, but still was grinning like the wisest monkey in the tree. Highpockets managed to look as capable as ever except for bloodshot eyes. The rest of the crew was in states of morning-after between those extremes. Except, that is, for Herman, who appeared not much the worse for wear, an advantage he had by always looking somewhat hard-used. Meanwhile Mrs. Costello made a nuisance of herself by nagging about the lack of enthusiasm for the runny fried eggs and undercooked side pork, until Jones snapped at her that the crew wasn't in a mood for hen leavings and pig squeals this morning, and she stomped back to the kitchen.

Despite the aftereffects, the triumphant night in Wisdom cast a good mood felt by everyone but Jones, grumpy over being rained out of haying. "Looks like the bunch of you have the day off," he conceded with a sniff at the weather, "mostly."

"What's that supposed to mean?" Highpockets was on the case at once.

Jones jerked a thumb at the empty chair next to his. "Smiley is no longer employed at the Diamond Buckle." That sank into me as almost too good to be true, my jubilant reaction mirrored on the faces around the table.

"So," Jones said, "I need a volunteer to be choreboy until I can drive to Butte and scare up a new one. The rest of you, sure, you can pitch horseshoes or lay around and scratch your nuts or whatever you want to do with the day, but somebody's got to step up and do the chores."

Peerless lawyered that immediately. "That would include getting a milk pail under Waltzing Matilda?"

"She's a cow," Jones tried to circle past that, "so she needs tending to like the others."

"I'm not milking any crazy cow," Peerless stated his principle.

Grinning, Fingy waved a hand lacking enough fingers to squeeze a teat. "I'm out."

Harv silently shook his head an inch or so.

"I'm allergic to titted critters," Skeeter announced, drawing a volley of hooty speculations about how far that allergy extended and when it had set in.

So it went, man by man, around the long table, no one willing to risk limb if not life in taking on the treacherous dairy cow. "Damn it," Jones seethed, "all in hell I'm asking is for some one of you to pitch a little hay to the horses, slop the hogs, gather the eggs—"

"—and milk an animal you won't go anywhere near yourself," Peerless inserted with a smirk.

"Now, listen here," Jones tried to shift ground from that accusation, "it's only for a couple of days. It won't hurt—I mean, embarrass—any of you to be choreboy that long."

He looked pleadingly at the one last figure that gave him any hope. "Pockets, can't you talk them into—?"

Highpockets was as firm as the others. "The boys are in their rights. We hired on to put up hay. Nothing else."

Whether it was that or inspiration circling until I could catch up with it, I suddenly realized: Wide open for the taking, the job of choreboy would not end with haying. Before the chance was lost, I crept my foot over to Herman's nearest one and pressed down hard on the toe of his shoe, causing him to jerk straight upright. Now that I had his attention, I cut a significant look toward Smiley's empty chair. He followed my gaze and after a squint or two, my thinking.

Clearing his throat as if he had been saving up for this announcement, Herman spoke out. "Nothing to worry. I am champ milker. Famous in old country."

"You are? I mean, are you." Jones turned to me, as he so often did when it came to figuring out Herman.

"Yeah, well, if Gramps says he can do a thing," I put the best face on it I could, "he generally pretty much can."

The foreman took one more look at Herman, sitting there with a grin skewed up toward his glass eye. "O-kay," he dragged the word out, "let's see how they do it in the old country. He can even yodel if he wants. Snag, go get the milk pails for him."

Need I say, the breakfast table was abandoned in a hurry and the barn gained a full audience to watch Herman take on Waltzing Matilda.

DAIRY COWS NORMALLY plod willingly to their stanchions, ready to stick their necks into captivity in exchange for being relieved of their milk. The other two cows did so, nice and docile, when Herman and I herded them in to the milking area, while the angular brown-and-white Guernsey lived up to her name by dancing sideways and snorting a shot of snot toward us and the stanchion. Bawling like she was being butchered, Waltzing Matilda then backed into a corner and rubbed a stub of horn on the barn wall as if trying to sharpen it.

"So-o-o, bossy." Herman approached her using the handle of a pitchfork to prod her out of the corner. I crept along right behind him, wishing he had the sharp end of the pitchfork at the ready. Giving another snort, Waltzing Matilda plowed past the two of us as we jumped back and, as if it were her own idea, plugged along to the waiting stanchion.

"There, see, that's half the battle!" Jones called from the safety of half the barn away, where he and the rest of the crew were clustered to watch.

"Stand back," Herman warned me as he sidled in to shut the stanchion on the cow's bowed neck. I thought I was, but still had to leap away when Waltzing Matilda shifted hind feet, flashing a kick that would have taken out a person's kneecap.

"Jeezus," Peerless cried, "watch yourselves, fellas. That critter's a killer."

Herman and I would not have disagreed with that as we huddled to consider our next move. "Any eye-dea?" he started to ask, interrupted by Waltzing Matilda loudly breaking wind and then letting loose as if to empty her bowels to the last degree. In dismay, we both stared at the switching tail now coated with manure, perfectly capable of swatting a person hunched on a milking stool.

"Puh," said Herman. "Maybe Smiley was right, a dose of lead is best answer to this creature."

"We have to do something about that tail." I was thinking hard, warily watching the crap-covered pendulum. "How about if we—" I outlined the only scheme that had popped to mind.

"Worth every bit of try," Herman agreed, both of us aware of

Jones prowling impatiently back and forth in front of the other spectators. "You go git the tool, I git the other. Bunny-quick."

I ran to the blacksmith shop and grabbed the longest tong off the forge, about two feet in length. While I was at that, Herman ducked into the tack room of the barn where saddles and such were kept, and came back with a pigging string, such as was used to tie up the legs of calves during branding.

Our audience craned their necks in curiosity, their mutterings and whispers not exactly a full vote of confidence. "No betting," Highpockets decreed, to the evident disappointment of Skeeter.

I made sure with Herman: "Ready?"

"Betsa bootsies," he sounded like he was calling up confidence from wherever he could get it. "If sailors know anything, it is knots."

Standing carefully to one side, I grappled the tongs in and caught the hairy end of the cow's filthy tail, tugging the whole thing snug against the nearest rear leg. That brought out a fresh green splurt of manure as expected, but I was out of range. Herman moved in and swiftly tied the tail tight and firm to the joint of the leg. Waltzing Matilda did not know what to make of this and kicked. Which yanked her tail hard enough to make her bawl at top volume.

"Quick!" I cried, but Herman already was sliding the milking stool into place and in no time milk was streaming into the bucket like hail hitting. There is the old braggart joke about milking a cow so fast she would faint away, and while Waltzing Matilda showed no sign of swooning, Herman was working those teats at incredible speed, his hands flying up and down as the level of milk in the bucket rose perceptibly. The angriest Guernsey on the planet attempted a few more tugs of leg and tail, only to bawl in frustration. Either out of confusion or an inkling of sense, she did not crap like Niagara anymore.

When Herman had stripped the teats to the last drops and set the frothing and nearly full milk pail safely away, our defeated adversary started to try a kick and thought better of it. Herman gingerly reached in from the side and undid the pigging string. Eyeing him as best she could from the stanchion, Waltzing Matilda now switched her tail, but neither kicked nor unloosed manure. I swear the cow got the idea.

And Jones surely did.

"ONE EYE, I want to see you after you get that milk up to the house," the determined foreman headed us off as we were leaving the barn and everyone else had dispersed. Me, he provided, "You're on your own for the day, laddie buck, find something to do to keep yourself out of trouble."

At loose ends, I drifted across the ranch yard, habit directing me to the bunkhouse while my mind sped to every here and there. In contrast, the hoboes had an enviable talent for taking time off, and the crew was a hundred percent at leisure. Sunning themselves in chairs propped against the bunkhouse, Shakespeare was working a crossword puzzle and Harv was deep in a *Police Gazette.* At the horseshoe pit, the others were trying to solve Midnight Frankie's evident ability to win at any game of chance ever invented, without success according to the clangs of his ringers and their echoes of frustration. I went and sat on the steps, waiting.

It did not take long. Herman emerged from the boss house and headed straight for me, the shift of his eyes as he neared telling me he wanted to talk in private.

That meant conferring in the crapper again. With our reflections registering us in the silvered mirror, Herman horse-laughed as he described Mrs. Costello nearly fainting away at receiving a milk bucket without Waltzing Matilda's splatter on it.

Then his words slowed, half proud, half cautious. "I am choreboy for good, Jones telled me. More wages, a little." He held his thumb and first finger apart just barely.

"I was hoping," was as much as I could say.

"Is what we wanted, hah? I hole up in Big Hole."

"I'll come see you sometimes," I blurted.

He drew a breath through his teeth as if the next words hurt, and they did. "Not a good eye-dea, Donny. There is trouble in that for us both. Your Gram might get too much curious about how I am here. And I can not have the Kate know my whereabouts." He paused before making himself say the rest. "So, Fritz Schneider of the Diamond Buckle and Wisdom town I am from now, someone you met on your travelings but must only remember, not come see. Savvy?"

I nodded, not trusting my voice.

"Many times have I said you are some good boy. Never more than now." His eyes damp, matching mine, he looked off past me. "I must make sorry to Highpockets about not going with them."

"Yeah, you'd better go do that." Still neither of us moved, and to break the awkward silence, I asked, "Where'd you learn to milk like that?"

He managed to smile. "Telled you the cows lived downstairs in Emden."

I laughed, a little. With neither of us finding anything more to say, Herman stirred himself. "Now I must see to chickens and hogs, big new responsibilities."

"I'll feed the horses for you," I volunteered, wanting something to do besides letting our separation eat my guts out.

THE BARN was as quiet as it ever got, the workhorses standing idle in their stalls, straw on the floor absorbing the shifting of their hooves except for a whispery rustle. I was welcomed with some snorts and a neigh or two as I picked up the pitchfork, shiny as new from Herman's sharpening of everything that would hold an edge, and climbed to the haymow to fork alfalfa into the manger in front of each horse. That chore done, I shinnied down and played favorites as I felt entitled with Queen and Brandy, after the distances we had covered together, stacker path upon stacker path, and treated them to a half pan of oats apiece. As they munched there in the stall, I stroked the gray expanse of Queen's neck and shoulder, reluctant to start yet another good-bye. Smartly the big mare flicked an ear. Laying my head against her in full confusion of emotions, I clung there with my cheek to the warm smooth hide, unable to do more than sob, "Queen, what am I gonna do?"

"I'm curious to hear how she answers that."

I jerked away from Queen's side, startled out of my wits by the tall figure shadowed in the doorway from the horse corral. At first I thought it must be Harv, at that size, but no. The unmistakable saunter and lanky presence told me even before the easygoing drawl. "Anything wrong we can fix with something besides spit and iodine?"

"Rags!" As he materialized out of the shadowed end of the barn, I saw he was in regular ranch wear except for the conspicuous belt buckle. In everyday getup or not, he carried himself like a champion, and I had to gulp hard to speak up adequately as he moseyed toward me. "Sorry, I—I didn't know you were here, didn't see your car."

"Aw, that weather last night will teach me about having a convertible," he said ruefully while he came and joined me in the stall. "It was raining like a cow taking a whiz on a flat rock when I pulled in from the Billings fair, so I stuck the Caddy in the equipment shed." He patted his way along Queen's side, softly chanting, "Steady, hoss, stand still, old girl," until he was alongside me and could reach up and fondly tug at her mane. "A horse and a half, isn't she. Seems like she just naturally lives up to her name. Pretty good listener, too, I gather." He looked down at me with a long-jawed grin, but his eyes a lot more serious than that. "Maybe I ought to lend an ear, too—Snag, do I remember you go by?"

"Uh-huh, when I'm not Scotty," I broke out of being tongue-tied. "You know how the ho—the crew—does with names."

"A little of that got on me ever since I dressed up to ride." Rodeo's leading fashion plate acknowledged the way of such things with an amused nod. He murmured something as he scratched behind the mare's ear that made her nicker and try to nudge him gently with her nose, an intelligent blue eye seeing into us, I swear. Casual but to the point, Rags glanced down at me standing at his side as if I were glued there. "Better let it out. What's got you talking to the Queen here?"

HOW MANY CHANCES in a lifetime does a person have to bare his soul to a Rags Rasmussen? If confession was good for the soul, mine was being reformed with every word that tumbled out of me. "I'm sort of caught between things. See, I'm supposed to go back to my grandmother, she's better after her operation and can be a cook again like she's always been, except it'd be in dumb Glasgow, and we'd live together with Letty, she's a waitress but a lady, too, and you'd really like her, everybody does, Harv especially, and I thought that's what I wanted most in the world. But I'm a handful for her, Gram I mean, she'd be the first to tell you, and I haven't exactly done what she thinks I was doing, all summer. She'll think I got too redheaded, as she calls it."

I faltered, but had to put the next part together to my intent listener.

"What happened was, I met up with, uh, Gramps I call him, although he's a sort of uncle." I sent a despairing look out the line of barn windows to where Herman could be seen joining the horseshoe players, still receiving slaps on the back for his triumph over Waltzing Matilda. "And now I don't want to leave him, he needs me too much."

"The new choreboy, while Smiley follows other pursuits." Rags made sure he was tracking the dramas of the ranch correctly. "What makes you think this gramps of yours needs you more than your granny does?"

There was a whole list of that all the way back to *Fingerspitzengehfühl*, but I made myself stick to the simple sum. "Bad stuff happens to him when he's on his own. And to me when I am, too. But when it's both of us, we sort of think our way out of things."

Not in a wiseguy way but just prodding me a little, he pursued that with "That's a pretty good trick. The two of you together amount to more than one and one, you figure? Like Queen and Brandy here?"

"Yeah, that's it! Something like that."

"And you need to stay on here for that to keep happening."

"Right." My hopes rose to the rafters of the barn.

Only to be dashed again as he contemplated Herman out there jawing happily with the horseshoe players, and then me dippily telling my troubles to a horse. "Nothing against being redheaded, understand," he began. "But we're running a ranch, not a charitable institution, and Jones is a bearcat about everyone on the place pulling his own weight. I don't see—"

The thunderous *whump* of a car on the livestock crossing took care of whatever he was going to say. Even Queen sharpened her ears at the telltale sound. Rags and I watched wordlessly as the Wisdom deputy sheriff's car, the star on the door a blaze of white, pulled into the yard.

My mouth went dry and Rags whistled silently through his teeth as the arriving car drew us out of the barn toward what could amount to trouble. "You happen to know anything about why we're being honored by this visit?"

Reluctantly I enlightened him that the crew had been in a little bit of a fight at the Watering Hole with the Tumbling T outfit. He frowned, saying that was simply Saturday night behavior and for as long as he had known her, Babs always wrote off fights as the cost of doing business. "This must be some other can of worms."

"Excuse me," I threw over my shoulder, already on the run, "I have to get over there to Gramps."

By the time I dashed across the yard to where Herman stood, caught motionless beside the horseshoe players, the deputy sheriff from Wisdom was climbing out of the patrol car and giving a sickly smile all around.

"Sorry to disturb you, gents." Which every one of us there knew meant disturbance of some sort was about to reach into our number. But I in particular should have seen what was coming when, on the passenger side, a big crow-black hat barely appeared above the top of the car.

HIS FIRST STEP out of the patrol car, the mean little sheriff from the first dog bus of all, back at the start of summer, spotted Harv taking life easy in the shade of the bunkhouse.

"Well, if it isn't the object of my affection." Sheriff Kinnick made a mock simper. "Harv the Houdini of the stony lonesome. Took me a while to run you down, but here we both are, just like old times."

"Howdy, Carl. You out seeing the country?" Casual as anything, Harv unfolded out of his chair and sauntered toward the lawmen, although not too close. Veterans at knowing trouble when they saw it, the rest of the crew guardedly drifted near enough to follow what was happening, with me doing all I could to steer Herman—looking guilty as sin, the way he did in the Butte depot—to the rear of them in the hope we wouldn't stand out. In the meantime, Skeeter set the tone for hobo attitude toward visits from the constabulary by piping up. "Shouldn't ye be tracking down horse thiefs or somethin' instead of botherin' honest citizens?" He was more or less backed in that by Jones arriving at a high trot and caterwauling, "What the hell's this about?"

"If you have to know, I been on the track of this character"—the sheriff from Glasgow pointed an accusing finger at Harv, standing quietly there looking like the least troublesome man on earth—"every chance I got all summer. Talked to bus drivers until they was running out my ears, but I lost his trail in Butte. Then I got smart and asked myself who else makes regular runs to burgs off the beaten path. Beer truck drivers." He let out his mean little laugh. "You make sort of a conspicuous hitchhiker, Harv."

"You're barking up the wrong gum tree, big hat," Highpockets took that on, bringing no small challenge with his height as he stepped forward and confronted the much shorter wearer of the badge. "Got the wrong man. I'll testify Harv's been with us following the harvests, California fruit to this here hay."

Hand it to Sheriff Kinnick, he didn't give ground, only chuckled that chilly way. "Nice try," he said up into Highpockets's face, "but no hearing judge in his right mind is gonna take the testimony of a hobo over the Wolf Point jailers who had Harv for company days on end, when the fool wasn't busting out. Besides"—he looked over the rest of the crew scornfully, with me half tucking out of sight behind Herman, standing so still he barely breathed—"you get in court, and there might be some natural curiosity about this crowd's propensity for law-abiding or not."

Harv followed that with a warning hand to the angry circle of men. "It's my tough luck, Pockets, Skeets, the whole bunch of you, thanks anyway."

Jones still was stomping mad at the intrusion, arguing to the deputy sheriff from town, "Goddamn it, Mallory, can't this wait until we're done haying in a few weeks? Harv's the best stack man I'll ever have." Looking sheepish, the local lawman replied that his colleague from up north seemed to be in more of a hurry than that.

By then Rags had strolled up. Mild as the day is long, he drawled, "What seems to be the difficulty?"

Mallory looked like he wanted to go someplace and hide rather than get into the difficulty, but he did his duty, introducing Rags to the strutty little visitor who barely came up to the shoulder of anyone in the gathering except me.

"Thanks for nothing, Mallory," the Glasgow sheriff huffed out. "You didn't tell me this is his spread." He rocked back on his pointy heels, impressed in spite of himself as he took in the most famous cowboy conceivable. "Saw you ride at the Calgary Stampede," he told Rags, as if that amounted to a private audience. "You do know how to stick on a horse."

"It's an honest living," Rags replied, glancing at the tin star on Kinnick's narrow chest as if comparing not that favorably. He turned to the other lawman. "What is this, a badge toters' convention? Should I be charging rent?"

"Sheriff Kinnick says your man here broke out of jail, more than once," came the reluctant answer.

"We could have told you he's a hard worker," Rags said. "Harv, what were you in for?"

"Fighting in a bar."

Harv aside, every man there gave Sheriff Kinnick a sideways look. Rags scratched his head and spoke the common thought. "Something like that means you could arrest just about everybody on the place, starting with me."

"That's as may be," the little sheriff muttered, glancing around the hostile ring of faces, "but none of you acted up any in my jurisdiction. I'm only interested in this knothead. Or am I."

It happened then. He peeked past the men in front, spotting me as I tried to fade behind Herman without appearing to. Parting the onlookers, the sheriff headed straight for me, prissing out, "Who's this I see over here?" with all too much recognition registering in the apple-doll face. "Huh, I thought you was going to visit relatives, punkin. Back east someplace. Doesn't look like that proved out, does it." He stopped short as Herman put a protective arm around me. "And just where do you fit into this, Horseface?" he asked suspiciously.

I KNEW IT. The arrest-happy little meanie was out to get us, was going to get us. Our life together, our lives separately, was going to fizzle into separation and incarceration, nightmare coming true.

Herman did his best to face down the challenge, looking squarely at the sheriff with his good eye. "Fritz, is the right name. Scotty's grandpa, I am."

"You sure sound like it, Scotch as all get out," the sheriff said cynically.

"Rasmussen, I'd bet my boots you're harboring a runaway," he crowed to Rags, who took that in mutely. "And maybe worse. Seems to me I've laid eyes on this mug before—how about you, Mallory?" the preening lawman spoke over his shoulder to the local deputy.

Herman's clasp of me held firmer than ever as Harv started forward to our aid, but Highpockets stopped him.

"You better think twice about this, Johnny Law," he warned, stepping in beside Herman and me. The scar at the corner of his mouth was white with anger. "These fellas are with us, they're not causing you any trouble. You can't breeze in here from bare-ass nowhere and start picking us off just because you feel like it. Take a look around you. This isn't some goddamn freight yard and you're the yard bull." Behind him, Skeeter and Peerless and Fingy and Midnight Frankie and Shakespeare and Pooch ranged around us in support.

"Oh, can't I breeze in here, like you say, and make an arrest?" The sheriff smirked and fingered his star as a pointed reminder. "Who's wearing the badge around here?"

That was the wrong thing to do. Something like a spell came over the hoboes, if a general sense of fury can be called that. I could see it in their eyes, the pent-up rage and hate from years of railyard bulls and Palookaville hick dicks beating them and throwing them into jail and kicking them out of town, the badge of authority the mark of adversity in their lives, Pooch a living reminder among them of the billy clubs of the law.

As the sheriff turned and strutted toward Harv, after warning Herman and me not to move, Highpockets murmured without moving his lips, "Skeeter, pass the toothpicks." Discreetly the old hobo drifted off to the shop where Herman sharpened things.

"C'mon, Harv, let's arrange some free board and room in lovely Wolf Point for you," the sheriff busied up. "Get in the patrol car. Front seat. Leave room in the back for other customers." He glanced back to check on Herman and me. I kept looking to Rags, still standing easy to one side, keeping Jones under control. If things were a matter of timing like he said, wasn't it about time to rein in this busybody lawman who was ready to cart Herman and me off to our doom along with Harv?

Meanwhile Harv folded his arms on his chest. "No."

"What's that supposed to mean?" The sheriff cocked a look up at the much taller man.

"Just what it sounds like. No."

"If you do the crime," the sheriff erupted, "you're supposed to do the time! That's practically in the Bible! Now get in the patrol car!"

"Still no," Harv declared, not budging. "Not until we work this out. That jurisdiction you talk about so much—it maybe's slipped your mind I busted out of jail in Wolf Point, and that's not in your county, the way I see it."

The Glasgow sheriff scowled. "You're turning into a regular jail-house lawyer, are you, all the experience you're building up behind bars." He poked his hat higher on his head to try to look taller as he faced Harv. "All right, let's get down to the pussy purr here. I'm taking you in for violating my custody, not once but twice when I packed you over there to the Wolf Point stony lonesome. Like I'm gonna do again, damn it."

Listening hard, the deputy sheriff from Wisdom appeared uneasy but didn't say anything. Harv did, though.

"Carl, I'll go with you, on a couple of conditions. First one is, you leave these other two fellows alone. You don't have to play bloodhound where you don't belong." The sheriff started to shake his head, but Harv lifted a warning hand. "Hear me out on the rest of this. I serve my sentence, how much was that again—?"

"Forty-five days," the sheriff answered peevishly.

"That's way to hell and gone too much for fightin' in a bar," Peerless objected, while others in the hobo circle whistled in disbelief.

"And they're brothers!" I could not hold that in any longer. "I heard them both say so, and I've got their names in my autograph book to prove it!"

"*Step*-brothers, damn it. Don't make it worse than it is," Sheriff Kinnick snapped, glowering at me. "But that don't matter," he plodded on, glaring around at his restive audience as Highpockets coldly mocked, "Of course not. You just didn't have anything better to do than track your own kin down across half the state."

"Like I was saying," Harv put the rest of his proposition, "I serve my sentence, but in your jail there in Glasgow. That way," he said, as if it made all the sense in the world, and to me it did, "Letty can visit me when she gets off work at the supper club and I won't need to bust out all the time."

"Nothing doing," the sheriff turned the proposition down flat, still a stickler or worse. "The foreign geezer and the loose kid ought to be hauled in for investigation, they're suspicious characters if I ever saw any, and that's that." He brushed his hands together as if we did not count for much, his real ire directed at Harv's other stipulation. "Wolf Point is where you broke jail, that's where you're going back in, period and end of sentence."

Harv shook his head that minimal way of his, enough and no more. "Carl, I'm sick of you yanking me around just to prove you can, and you shouldn't be arresting these other two for no good cause, either." He looked unflinchingly at the smaller man, the doll-like face turning red under his gaze. "As to packing me back to Wolf Point, they'd be happy not to have me back in that two-bit slammer of theirs, it'd save them a lot of trouble. Jugging me in Glasgow instead of booting me to the far end of the state isn't that much to ask, and you know it."

In my eyes and Herman's, fully as stalwart as any hero who ever faced a six-shooter, Harv stayed set as stone in front of his stepbrother. "If you won't do that for me, Carl, you'll have to shoot me to take me."

"You stubborn fool," the sheriff raged against being defied, dropping his hand to his holster. "That can be arranged, too, according to this pistol."

THE MOMENT SEARED into me, I can feel it yet. Was this how shootouts happened in the Old West? Some dumb pistoleer goes for his gun and, next thing, there is bloodshed everywhere? Both of us tense as sentinels, Herman and I could see it happening, clear as a bang-bang page out of Karl May. Except that Herman in a swift move rewrote that ending, thrusting me aside to safety and crying out, "No need for shooting! I will go with sheriff!"

"No, you won't," Highpockets's voice cut into the scene, the other hoboes fanning out around him and us as he spoke. "Harv has his reason to be hauled off with this little jaybird, but you don't need to." His words were backed up by the pitchforks Skeeter had distributed upon his return from the blacksmith shop, tines gleaming fresh from the grindstone.

The sheriff stared in disbelief at the cordon of grim men, weapons at the ready. "If that's the way you want it," he unsteadily tried to bluster, "getting a helping of lead for obstructing justice—"

"Whoa."

The word soft as a coax in a horse's ear came from Rags. "Let's sort the situation out a little bit." He ambled around to the far side of the confrontation. "Mallory, if I was you, I'd be looking the other direction during this."

"I was thinking that myself," the deputy sheriff said, moving off with his back turned to the situation created by the furious Glasgow sheriff.

"Jonesie, keep an eye on this with me," Rags resumed, still softly conversational. "Somebody's got to be witnesses if this buck-fever sheriff cuts loose on innocent men on their way to pitch some hay, don't you think?"

"I'm seeing the same thing ahead you are," the foreman agreed, sending the sheriff a look that meant it. "Manslaughter, if not murder, way beyond the performance of duty."

"Doesn't look good, does it," Rags suggested at large. Then said to the sheriff, as if calming him, "Maybe you ought to consider Harv's offer a little more. Sounds like a fair deal to me."

Scanning around furiously at man after man armed with a shiny pitchfork, the sheriff held his pose, his hand twitching over his gun butt.

"Carl, none of us are any use to you dead," Harv put in on him with surprising gentleness. The frustrated lawman cast one last look around at the united bunch of us, then slowly let his gun hand fall to his side.

Breathing hard, he faced Harv, who still was standing there waiting him out. "All right, you win. Glasgow and Letty it is, loverboy. I've got to put up with you under the same roof just like when we was kids, do I," he complained, as if he'd been sentenced to his own jail. Trying to fluff himself up, he turned to the waiting deputy and made another swipe of the hand at Herman and me. "On second thought, these other two yayhoos aren't my worry. Harv, grab your stuff and we'll head for Glasgow," he said, as if it had been his own idea all along.

First shaking hands all around with the crew, Harv went to fetch his bedroll from the bunkhouse while Skeeter collected the pitchforks and Highpockets kept an eye on things, and in a daze I realized Herman and I were free again.

Almost. Behind us, Rags proved that he had a boss voice when he wanted to. "Now, let's sort you two out. Find out what kind of desperadoes I've let on the place. Come on up to the house."

LEADING US into his office, Rags seated himself at a desk big as a dining room table and motioned us to sit down across from him. Perched there, I couldn't help but sneak peeks around the room, as I'd bet Herman was doing, too. On all the walls were framed photographs of Rags riding twisty broncs, and championship awards, the kind of marks of fame I had hoped to see on Aunt Kate's walls when I was under the impression she was Kate Smith. This was worlds better, leaving me open-mouthed as I gazed around the collection. Also, from right there at the heart of Rags Rasmussen's ranch empire, I could see the daybooks arranged as neatly as you would expect from the most scrupulous bronc rider in the world, and fine old furniture which put the Double W's to shame. One item I recognized from having read about the Pilgrims was a sinner's bench, a straight-backed hardwood church pew that must have been a rare antique. On it sat one of those hand-carved signs sold at the craft booths outside rodeo arenas, with the wording WHY IS TEMPTATION ALWAYS THE TASTIEST THING ON THE MENU? Well, nobody said Rags lacked a sense of humor.

Pretty quick, though, I snapped to, into full realization that big desks like the one separating us from Rags Rasmussen was where ranch bosses wrote out checks when they fired someone. Herman had that same awareness, I could tell from his spooked expression.

Looking as if he'd rather be in a saddle somewhere, Rags turned first to Herman. "Fritz, as I guess I better get used to calling you until further notice," he said, as if grading his behavior in the presence of a pistoleer, "you could have got your cozies shot off, you know, making that move when that peewee sheriff was itching for his gun."

"I did not think of myself," Herman answered simply. "I taked a leap of fate."

Rags digested that, long enough that our seats were growing as hard as that sinner's bench. Then he sat up a bit and sighed. "Better to be lucky than smart, I suppose. All right, tell me the rest of it, why fate had to plunk the two of you down on my ranch out of all the places in the Big Hole."

Between us, Herman and I owned up to everything, with Rags listening hard.

When we finally ran out of confessions, he rubbed his jaw longer than usual before saying that sneaking into America to get away from Hitler probably was the kind of infraction that would die away with time, and any choreboy who made Jones happy was worth keeping. That took care of Herman but left the matter of me, quivering inside as I waited.

"A kid kicking around on a ranch is a tricky proposition," Rags came right to the point, looking at me the frank, open way he'd done when it was the two of us in the stall with Queen, the crucial listener this time Herman. "I know firsthand—I was one, and I could be a champion nuisance sometimes." That description gripped me so squarely I couldn't even swallow.

"But that comes with ranch life, I suppose"—Rags looked around the office as if reminding himself he was sitting in the owner's seat of the Diamond Buckle—"sorting out which nuisances to put up with or not." He straightened up while I slumped to my fate. "What I started to tell you back there in the barn, before all the commotion," I heard him say, as if we were taking this ride into the unknown together, "is I don't see why it wouldn't work for you to stay on here with Gramps, if he'll be responsible for you. If he can stand the nuisance, I suppose I can," he said half humorously, then studied me soberly. "That's if you make up your mind to stay on here."

Fate or not, my mind leaped, in one direction and then the other. My choice was wide open now, Herman or Gram, heart against conscience, if it is ever that evenly divided. I heard my decision the same instant the two of them did.

"I—I want to stay."

I shall see the two of them forever in that moment, Herman looking like he was trying to catch his breath, Rags awarding himself a little grin before turning serious again.

"Since you're gonna stick around with us," he started, as if just making talk with me, "that opens up something else." He grimaced toward the kitchen, where Mrs. Costello had the radio blaring away and was making a racket with pots and pans as she clattered together the semblance of a meal. "A cook, did you say your sainted granny is?"

ACKNOWLEDGMENTS

As ever, through sixteen books and fifty years of marriage, Carol Doig has been my incomparable companion, cheerleader, and keen-eyed first reader. As I say every time a book is born in this household, I couldn't have done it without you, darling.

This novel and I have had the great good fortune to enlist the skills and enthusiastic backing of our longtime Montana friend, Marcella Sherfy Walter. Marcella worked research magic in reconstituting 1951 Manitowoc, Greyhound bus travel of the era, historic features of Crow Fair, and many other details that enrich a work of the imagination such as this. She's also served as a first-rate commentator on the manuscript-in-progress, saving me from errors large and small many a time.

Katharina Maloof wonderfully fulfilled the big job of keeping me straight, insofar as an author intent on lingual mischief can be steered, on the capricious lingo of Herman the German. John Maloof was a terrific bonus as an early reader, encouraging me with his own boyhood experience of being put on a bus to he knew not what.

Once again, Ann McCartney, trusted friend and eagle-eyed reader, lent her savvy to the manuscript. The further priceless loan was from her treasure trove of *National Geographic*s, so Donny could peruse faraway places where people wore surprisingly little.

The marvelous poet and friend Linda Bierds kept a straight face and helpful mien as I tried out some of the verses for Donny's autograph book—I am still sky-high that my line about memory, "Roses in the snow of long ago," met with her approval.

Ann and Marshall Nelson, fresh from the Pendleton Roundup, lavished rodeo material on me, which went a long way toward Rags Rasmussen's immortal ride of Buzzard Head.

I'm indebted to my college classmate and friend ever since, Kay Pride, for telling me about her joyous childhood adventure of turning breakfast toast into outlines of countries under the fond tutelage of her geography teacher grandfather. It sounded to me like one of the talents Herman the German had to have.

My fellow enthusiast for lingo and sayings, John W. Grubbs, provided the slang gem "I slipped on a banana peeling and hit the ceiling," which cried out to be part of a comedic inscription in Donny's autograph book.

How fortunate to have as a friend Tony Angell, an expert on all things avian through his art, to teach me the eagle screech.

And what a bonus of luck to have a tried-and-true wordmaster, my writing buddy David Laskin, as an enthusiastic early reader.

Once again, a manuscript does not become a finished tome without the skills and wiles of my blessed team of makers of books: Becky Saletan, Liz Darhansoff, and Michelle Koufopoulos.

A few words and confessions about the settings of this novel:

While I have striven to evoke the city of Manitowoc and the town of Wisdom as they might have appeared to a youngster more than sixty years ago, I have taken liberties whenever needed for plot purposes. Similarly, my version of Crow Fair is largely imaginary, and I apologize for the story's necessity that the great gathering coincide with the Fourth of July, when in actuality Crow Fair takes place the third weekend in August. I can't resist adding that my own experience at such a gathering dates back to the mid-1950s, when my family and I, residents of the Blackfeet Reservation in season sheep-herding for three years, never missed attending "North American Indian Days" in Browning. Some memories take deep root.

At the time of this story, 1951, the small Blackfeet Reservation community of Heart Butte had no high school and hence no Heart Butte Warriors team of famous basketball proficiency as I portrayed. But since then, Heart Butte has attained a high school and the Warriors have twice been Class C state basketball champions, an example of life copying art that can only make an author grin.

While Highpockets, the Jersey Mosquito, and the other haymaking hoboes are creations of my imagination, their tradition of following the crops derives from the magisterial study of transient harvest workers in American society, *Hoboes: Bindlestiffs, Fruit Tramps, and the Harvesting of the West* by Mark Wyman.

Donny's on-the-bus session with Jack Kerouac is of course of my own making, with the exception of the first paragraph in his inscription for Donny ("You think about what actually happened" et al.), which can be found on page 36 of *Writers on Writing*, edited by Jon Winokur.

Ivan Doig is an American treasure.

His novels are love songs to the West, paeans to vanished ways of life. A master storyteller, he transports us to clattering newsrooms and venerable saloons; one-room schoolhouses and sprawling boomtowns; the cusp of the Roaring Twenties and the first glimmering of the psychedelic sixties. His characters, beloved and unforgettable, reflect and amplify our country's diverse and colorful heritage. His stories are spirited and inventive romps and family sagas, full of humor and pathos. He has a gift for lively, loving observations of people and places that ring as vivid as the panoramic Montana countryside he's made indelibly his own.

by Carol Doig

T365-1213

THE BARTENDER'S TALE

An evocative saga about a boy and a community inching toward the future

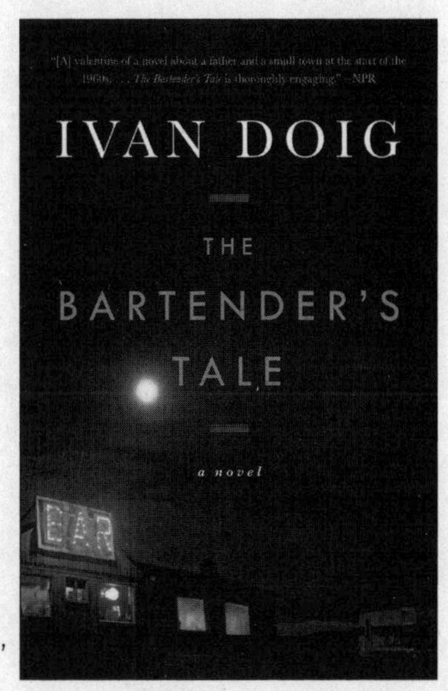

Tom Harry has a streak of frost in his black pompadour and a venerable bar called the Medicine Lodge, the chief watering hole and "holy oasis" in Gros Ventre, a small town in northern Montana. Tom also has a son named Rusty, "an accident between the sheets," whose mother deserted them both years ago. Yet the two manage just fine—until the summer of 1960, when change arrives with unsettling force, in the person of Proxy, a taxi dancer Tom knew back when, and her beatnik daughter, Francine.

The Bartender's Tale wonderfully captures how the world becomes bigger, and the past more complex, in the last moments of childhood.

"The rewards of *The Bartender's Tale*...remain very great and extremely rare." ***—The Washington Post***

"The perfect book for your bedside table." **—The Associated Press**

T368-1213